PENGUIN BOOKS

# THE WOMAN WHO WENT TO BED FOR A YEAR

**Praise for *The Woman who Went to Bed for a Year*:**

'Townsend's never lost the ability to make her readers laugh, cry and think, often in quick succession. A funny, poignant . . . look at modern family life' *Daily Express*

'Townsend will crack you up with this brilliantly funny novel' *Star*

'Townsend at her comic best' *Good Housekeeping*

'Full of Townsend's trademark observation, acerbic wit and kitchen-sink realism' *Independent on Sunday*

'Lovely and very funny. The questions Eva poses and the opinions she expresses offer an intelligent criticism of contemporary life' *Scotsman*

'Perfectly pitched sense of the pathos and absurdity of suburban life. Townsend's fiction has always hinted at a darkness beneath the humour, but this novel gives it freer rein than previously' *Guardian*

'Proves that Townsend's acerbic wit has lost none of its potency and there is so much to admire about this perfectly pitched comic novel. Wonderfully thoughtful, provoking and laugh-out-loud funny' *Independent* (Ireland)

'Unflinching comedy . . . Townsend remains a perceptive critic of contemporary foibles' *The Times*

'I love her comedy and ruthless exposure of absurdity' *Saga*

'Hilarious . . . tinged with some very real truths' *Woman*

'Under Townsend's double-edged pen, what starts out as a sometimes hysterical bedroom farce ends up as a haunting social commentary about how easy it is in twenty-first-century Britain for anyone, no matter how apparently strong their support network, to slip under the radar and simply disappear' *Herald*

'Brilliantly witty' *Stella*

'A LOL story' *Company*

'This joyous satire confirms Townsend as the absolute monarch of comic fiction' *Daily Mail*

'One of the great fictional creations of our time . . . a joy' *Scotsman*

**Praise for *The Secret Diary of Adrian Mole Aged 13¾*:**

'I not only wept, I howled and hooted and had to get up and walk around the room and wipe my eyes so that I could go on reading' Tom Sharpe

**Praise for *The Growing Pains of Adrian Mole*:**

'The funniest, most bittersweet book you're likely to read this year' *Daily Mirror*

**Praise for *The True Confessions of Adrian Albert Mole*:**

'Wonderfully funny and sharp as knives' *Sunday Times*

**Praise for *Adrian Mole: The Wilderness Years*:**

'A very, very funny book' *Sunday Times*

**Praise for *Adrian Mole: The Cappuccino Years*:**

'I can't remember a more relentlessly funny book' *Daily Mirror*

**Praise for *The Lost Diaries of Adrian Mole*:**

'Very funny indeed. A satire of our times' *Sunday Times*

**Praise for *Adrian Mole and the Weapons of Mass Destruction*:**

'The funniest book of the year. I can think of no more comical read' Jeremy Paxman, *Sunday Telegraph*

**Praise for *Adrian Mole: The Prostrate Years*:**

'Brilliant, sharp, honest, moving, an exquisite social comedy' *Daily Telegraph*

# The Woman who Went to Bed for a Year

SUE TOWNSEND

PENGUIN BOOKS

## PENGUIN BOOKS

Published by the Penguin Group

Penguin Books Ltd, 80 Strand, London WC2R 0RL, England

Penguin Group (USA) Inc., 375 Hudson Street, New York, New York 10014, USA

Penguin Group (Canada), 90 Eglinton Avenue East, Suite 700, Toronto, Ontario, Canada M4P 2Y3
(a division of Pearson Penguin Canada Inc.)

Penguin Ireland, 25 St Stephen's Green, Dublin 2, Ireland
(a division of Penguin Books Ltd)

Penguin Group (Australia), 250 Camberwell Road, Camberwell, Victoria 3124, Australia
(a division of Pearson Australia Group Pty Ltd)

Penguin Books India Pvt Ltd, 11 Community Centre, Panchsheel Park, New Delhi – 110 017, India

Penguin Group (NZ), 67 Apollo Drive, Rosedale, Auckland 0632, New Zealand
(a division of Pearson New Zealand Ltd)

Penguin Books (South Africa) (Pty) Ltd, Block D, Rosebank Office Park,
181 Jan Smuts Avenue, Parktown North, Gauteng 2193, South Africa

Penguin Books Ltd, Registered Offices: 80 Strand, London WC2R 0RL, England

www.penguin.com

First published by Michael Joseph 2012
First published in Penguin Books 2012

023

Copyright © Lily Broadway Productions Ltd, 2012

The moral right of the author has been asserted

Typeset by Jouve (UK), Milton Keynes
Printed in Great Britain by Clays Ltd, St Ives plc

A CIP catalogue record for this book is available from the British Library

B-FORMAT ISBN: 978–0–141–39964–5
A-FORMAT ISBN: 978–0–718–19452–9

www.greenpenguin.co.uk

To my mother, Grace

'Be kind, for everybody you meet is fighting
a hard battle'

*attributed to Plato, and many others*

# I

After they'd gone Eva slid the bolt across the door and disconnected the telephone. She liked having the house to herself. She went from room to room tidying, straightening and collecting the cups and plates that her husband and children had left on various surfaces. Somebody had left a soup spoon on the arm of her special chair – the one she had upholstered at night school. She immediately went to the kitchen and examined the contents of her Kleeneze cleaning products box.

'What would remove a Heinz tomato soup stain from embroidered silk damask?'

As she searched, she remonstrated with herself. 'It's your own fault. You should have kept the chair in your bedroom. It was pure vanity on your part to have it on display in the sitting room. You wanted visitors to notice the chair and to tell you how beautiful it was, so that you could tell them that it had taken two years to complete the embroidery, and that you had been inspired by Claude Monet's "Water-Lily Pond and Weeping Willow".'

The trees alone had taken a year.

There was a small pool of tomato soup on the kitchen floor that she hadn't noticed until she stepped in it and left orange footprints. The little non-stick saucepan containing half a can of tomato soup was still simmering on the hob. 'Too lazy to take a pan off the stove,' she thought. Then she remembered that the twins were Leeds University's problem now.

She caught her reflection in the smoky glass of the wall-mounted oven. She looked away quickly. If she had taken a while to look she would have seen a woman of fifty with a lovely, fine-boned face, pale inquisitive eyes and a Clara Bow mouth that always looked as though she were about to speak. Nobody – not even Brian, her husband – had seen her without lipstick. Eva thought that red lips complemented the black clothes she habitually wore. Sometimes she allowed herself a little grey.

Once, Brian had come home from work to find Eva in the garden, in her black wellingtons, having just pulled up a bunch of turnips. He'd said to her, 'For Christ's sake, Eva! You look like post-war Poland.'

Her face was currently fashionable. 'Vintage' according to the girl on the Chanel counter where she bought her lipstick (always remembering to throw the receipt away – her husband would not understand the outrageous expense).

She picked up the saucepan, walked from the kitchen into the sitting room and threw the soup all over her precious chair. She then went upstairs, into her bedroom and, without removing her clothes or her shoes, got into bed and stayed there for a year.

She didn't know it would be a year. She climbed into bed thinking she would leave it again after half an hour, but the comfort of the bed was exquisite, the white sheets were fresh and smelled of new snow. She turned on her side towards the open window and watched the sycamore in the garden shed its blazing leaves.

She had always loved September.

She woke when it was getting dark, and she heard her husband shouting outside. Her mobile rang. The display showed that it was her daughter, Brianne. She ignored it. She pulled the duvet over her head and sang the words of Johnny Cash's 'I Walk The Line'.

When she next poked her head out from under the duvet, she heard her next-door neighbour Julie's excited voice saying, 'It's not right, Brian.'

They were in the front garden.

Her husband said, 'I mean, I've been to Leeds and back, I need a shower.'

'Of course you do.'

Eva thought about this exchange. Why would driving to Leeds and back necessitate having a shower? Was the northern air full of grit? Or had he been sweating on the M1? Cursing the lorries? Screaming at tailgaters? Angrily denouncing whatever the weather was doing?

She switched on the bedside lamp.

This provoked another episode of shouting outside, and demands that she, 'Stop playing silly buggers and unbolt the door!'

She realised that, although she wanted to go downstairs and let him in, she couldn't actually leave the bed. She felt as though she had fallen into a vat of warm quick-setting concrete, and that she was powerless to move. She felt an exquisite languor spread throughout her body, and thought, 'I would have to be *mad* to leave this bed.'

There was the sound of breaking glass. Soon after, she heard Brian on the stairs.

He shouted her name.

She didn't answer.

He opened the bedroom door. 'There you are,' he said.

'Yes, here I am.'

'Are you ill?'

'No.'

'Why are you in bed in your clothes and shoes? What are you playing at?'

'I don't know.'

'It's empty-nest syndrome. I heard it on *Woman's Hour*.' When she didn't speak, he said, 'Well, are you going to get up?'

'No, I'm not.'

He asked, 'What about dinner?'

'No thanks, I'm not hungry.'

'I meant what about *my* dinner? Is there anything?'

She said, 'I don't know, look in the fridge.'

He stomped downstairs. She heard his footsteps on the laminate floor he'd laid so ineptly the year before. She knew by the squeak of the floorboards that he'd gone into the sitting room. Soon he was stomping back up the stairs.

'What the bloody hell has happened to your chair?' he asked.

'Somebody left a soup spoon on the arm.'

'There's soup all over the bloody thing.'

'I know. I did it myself.'

'What — threw the soup?'

Eva nodded.

'You're having a nervous breakdown, Eva. I'm ringing your mum.'

'No!'

He flinched at the ferocity in her voice.

She saw from the stricken look in his eyes that after twenty-five years of marriage his familiar domestic world had come to an end. He went downstairs. She heard him cursing at the disconnected phone then, after a moment, stabbing at the keys. As she picked up the bedroom extension her mother was laboriously giving her phone number down the line, '0116 2 444 333, Mrs Ruby Brown-Bird speaking.'

Brian said, 'Ruby, it's Brian. I need you to come over straight away.'

'No can do, Brian. I'm in the middle of having a perm. What's up?'

'It's Eva —' he lowered his voice '— I think she must be ill.'

'Send for an ambulance then,' said Ruby irritably.

'There's nothing wrong with her physically.'

'Well, that's all right then.'

'I'll come and pick you up and bring you back so you can see for yourself.'

'Brian, I can't. I'm hosting a perm party and I've got to have my own personal solution rinsed off in half an hour. If I don't, I shall look like Harpo Marx. 'Ere, talk to Michelle.'

After a few muffled noises a young woman came on the line.

'Hello . . . Brian, is it? I'm Michelle. Can I talk you through what would happen if Mrs Bird abandoned the perm at this stage? I *am* insured, but it would be extremely inconvenient for me if I had to appear in court. I'm booked up until New Year's Eve.'

The phone was handed back to Ruby. 'Brian, are you still there?'

'Ruby, she's in bed wearing her clothes and shoes.'

'I *did* warn you, Brian. We were in the church porch about to go in, and I turned round and said to you, "Our Eva's a dark horse. She doesn't say much, and you'll never know what she's thinking . . ."' There was a long pause, then Ruby said, 'Phone your own mam.'

The phone was disconnected.

Eva was astounded that her mother had made a last-minute attempt to sabotage her wedding. She picked up her handbag from the side of the bed and rooted through the contents, looking for something to eat. She always kept food in her bag. It was a habit from when the twins were young and hungry, and would open their mouths like the beaks of fledgling birds. Eva found a squashed packet of crisps, a flattened Bounty bar and half a packet of Polos.

She heard Brian stabbing at the keys again.

Brian was always slightly apprehensive when he called his mother. His tongue couldn't form words properly.

She had a way of making him feel guilty, whatever the subject of the conversation.

His mother answered promptly with a snappy, 'Yes?'

Brian said, 'Is that you, Mummy?'

Eva picked up the extension again, being careful to muffle the mouthpiece with her hand.

'Who else would it be? Nobody else phones this house. I'm on my own seven days a week.'

Brian said, 'But ... er ... you ... er ... don't like visitors.'

'No, I don't like visitors but it would be nice to have to turn them away. Anyway, what is it? I'm halfway through *Emmerdale*.'

Brian said, 'Sorry, Mummy. Do you want to ring me back when the adverts come on?'

'No,' she said. 'Let's get it over with, whatever it is.'

'It's Eva.'

'Ha! Why am I not surprised? Has she left you? The first time I clapped eyes on that girl I knew she'd break your heart.'

Brian wondered if his heart had ever been broken. He had always had difficulty in recognising an emotion. When he had brought his First Class Bachelor of Science degree home to show his mother, her current boyfriend had said, 'You must be very happy, Brian.'

Brian had nodded his head and forced a smile, but the truth was that he didn't feel any happier than he had felt the day before, when nothing remarkable had happened.

His mother had taken the embossed certificate, examined it carefully and said, 'You'll struggle to find an astronomy job. There are men with more superior qualifications than you've got who can't find work.'

Now Brian said, mournfully, 'Eva's gone to bed in her clothes and shoes.'

His mother said, 'I can't say I'm surprised, Brian. She's always brought attention to herself. Do you remember when we all went to the caravan that Easter in 1986? She took a suitcase full of her ridiculous beatnik clothes. You don't wear beatnik clothes at Wells-Next-The-Sea. Everybody was staring at her.'

Eva screamed from upstairs, 'You shouldn't have thrown my lovely black clothes into the sea!'

Brian hadn't heard his wife scream before.

Yvonne Beaver asked, 'What's that screaming?'

Brian lied. 'It's the television. Somebody's just won a lot of money on *Eggheads*.'

His mother said, 'She looked very presentable in the holiday wear I bought her.'

As Eva listened, she remembered taking the hideous clothes out of the carrier bag. They had smelled as if they had been in a damp warehouse in the Far East for years, and the colours were lurid mauves, pinks and yellows. There had been a pair of what Eva thought looked like men's sandals and a beige, pensioner-style anorak. When she tried them on, she looked twenty years older.

Brian said to his mother, 'I don't know what to do, Mummy.'

Yvonne said, 'She's probably drunk. Leave her to sleep it off.'

Eva threw the phone across the room and screamed,

8

'They were men's sandals she bought me in Wells-Next-The-Sea! I saw *men* wearing them with white socks! You should have protected me from her, Brian! You should have said, "My wife would not be seen dead in these hideous sandals!"'

She had screamed so loudly that her throat hurt. She shouted downstairs and asked Brian to bring her a glass of water.

Brian said, 'Hang on, Mummy. Eva wants a glass of water.'

His mother hissed down the phone, 'Don't you dare fetch her that water, Brian! You'll be making a rod for your own back if you do. Tell her to get her own water!'

Brian didn't know what to do. While he dithered in the hallway his mother said, 'I could do without this trouble. My knee has been playing me up. I was on the verge of ringing my consultant and asking him to chop my leg off.'

He took the phone into the kitchen with him and ran the cold tap.

His mother asked, 'Is that water I can hear running?'

Brian lied again. 'Just topping up a vase of flowers.'

'Flowers! You're lucky you can afford flowers.'

'They're out of the garden, Mummy. Eva grew them from seed.'

'You're lucky to have the space for a garden.'

The phone went dead. His mother never said goodbye.

He went upstairs with the glass of cold water. When he handed it to Eva, she took a small sip, then put it on the crowded bedside table. Brian hovered at the end of the bed. There was nobody to tell him what to do.

She almost felt sorry for him, but not enough to get out of bed. Instead, she said, 'Why don't you go downstairs and watch your programmes?'

Brian was a devotee of property programmes. His heroes were Kirstie and Phil. Unbeknown to Eva he had written to Kirstie, saying that she always looked nice, and was she married to Phil or was their partnership purely a business arrangement? He had received a reply three months later, saying 'Thank you for your interest' and signed 'Yours, Kirstie'. Enclosed was a photograph of Kirstie. She was wearing a red dress and showing an alarming amount of bosom. Brian kept the photograph inside an old Bible. He knew it would be safe there. Nobody ever opened it.

Later that night, a full bladder forced Eva out of bed. She changed from her day clothes into a pair of pyjamas that she had been keeping for emergency hospital admittance. This was on her mother's advice. Her mother believed that if your dressing gown, pyjamas and sponge bag were good quality, the nurses and doctors treated you better than the scruffs who came into hospital with their shoddy things in a Tesco's carrier bag.

Eva got back into bed and wondered what her children were doing on their first night at university. She imagined them sitting in a room together, weeping and homesick, as they had done when they first went to nursery school.

# 2

Brianne was in the communal kitchen and lounge of the accommodation block. So far she had met a boy dressed like a girl, and a woman dressed like a man. They were both talking about clubs and musicians she'd never heard of.

Brianne had a short attention span and soon stopped listening, but she nodded her head and said 'Cool' when it seemed appropriate. She was a tall girl with broad shoulders, long legs and big feet. Her face was mostly hidden behind a long straggly black fringe which she pushed out of her eyes only when she actually wanted to see something.

A waiflike girl in a leopard-print maxi dress and tan Ugg boots came in with a bulging bag from Holland & Barrett which she stuffed into the fridge. Half her head had been shaved and a broken heart tattooed on to her scalp. The other half was a badly dyed lopsided green curtain.

Brianne said, 'Amazing hair. Did you do it yourself?'

'I got my brother to help me,' the girl said. 'He's a poofter.'

The girl's sentences had a rising inflection as though she were permanently questioning the validity of her own statements.

Brianne asked, 'Are you Australian?'

The girl shouted, 'God! No!'

Brianne said, 'I'm Brianne.'

The girl said, 'I'm Poppy. Brianne? I haven't heard that before.'

'My dad's called Brian,' said Brianne tonelessly. 'Is it hard to walk in a maxi?'

'No', said Poppy. 'Try it on if you like. It might stretch to fit you.'

She pulled the maxi dress over her head and stood revealed in a wispy bra and knickers. They both looked as though they had been made from scarlet cobwebs. She seemed to have no inhibitions whatsoever. Brianne had many inhibitions. She hated everything about herself: face, neck, hair, shoulders, arms, hands, fingernails, belly, breasts, nipples, waist, hips, thighs, knees, calves, ankles, feet, toenails and voice.

She said, 'I'll try it on in my room.'

'Your eyes are amazing,' said Poppy.

'Are they?'

'Are you wearing green contacts?' asked Poppy. She stared into Brianne's face and pushed the fringe away.

'No.'

'They're an amazing green.'

'Are they?'

'Awesome.'

'I need to lose some weight.'

'Yeah, you do. I'm a weight loss expert. I'll teach you how to be sick after every meal.'

'I don't want to be bulimic.'

'It was good enough for Lily Allen.'

'I hate being sick.'

'Isn't it worth it to be thin? Remember the saying: "You can't be too rich or too thin."'

'Who said that?'

'I think it was Winnie Mandela.'

Poppy followed Brianne to her room, still in her underwear. They met Brian Junior in the corridor as he was locking the door to his room. He stared at Poppy and she stared back. He was the most beautiful man she had ever seen. She threw her arms above her head and affected a glamour girl pose, hoping that Brian Junior would admire her C cup breasts.

He said under his breath, but loud enough to be heard, 'Gross.'

Poppy said, 'Gross? It would be really useful to me if you would elaborate. I need to know which bits of me are particularly repellent.'

Brian Junior shifted uncomfortably.

Poppy walked up and down past him, did a twirl and rested one hand on a bony hip. She then looked at him expectantly but he did not speak. Instead, he unlocked the door to his room and went back inside.

Poppy said, 'He's a baby. A rude, mindblowingly awe-some-looking baby.'

Brianne said, 'We're both seventeen. We took our A levels early.'

'I would have taken mine early but I had a personal tragedy . . .' Poppy paused, waiting for Brianne to ask about the nature of the tragedy. When Brianne remained silent, she said, 'I can't talk about it. I still managed to get four A*s. Oxbridge wanted me. I went for an interview, but quite honestly I couldn't live and study somewhere so old-fashioned.'

Brianne asked, 'Where was your interview – Oxford or Cambridge?'

Poppy said, 'Do you have auditory defects? I told you, I was interviewed in *Oxbridge*.'

'And you were offered a place to study at *Oxbridge* University?' Brianne checked, 'Remind me, where *is* Oxbridge?'

Poppy mumbled, 'It's in the middle of the country,' and went out.

Brianne and Brian Junior had been interviewed at Cambridge University, and both of them had been offered a place. The Beaver twins' small fame had gone before them. At Trinity College they were given what looked like an impossibly difficult maths problem to solve. Brian Junior went to a separate room with an invigilator. When they each put down their pencil after fifty-five minutes of frenzied workings-out on the A4 paper supplied, the chair of the interviewing panel read their workings as if they were a chapter of a racy novel. Brianne had meticulously, if unimaginatively, worked her way straight to the solution. Brian Junior had reached it by a more mysterious path. The panel declined to ask the twins about hobbies or pastimes. It was easy to tell that they did nothing outside of their chosen field.

After the twins had turned the offer down, Brianne explained that she and her brother would follow the famous professor of mathematics Lenya Nikitanova to Leeds.

'Ah, Leeds,' said the chairperson. 'It has a remarkable mathematical faculty, world class. We tried to tempt the lovely Nikitanova here by offering her disgracefully extravagant inducements, but she emailed that she preferred to teach the children of the workers – an expression I have not heard since Brezhnev was in office – and was taking up the post of lecturer at Leeds University! Typically quixotic of her!'

Now, in Sentinel Towers student residence, Brianne said, 'I'd sooner try the dress on in private. I'm shy about my body.'

Poppy said, 'No, I'm coming in with you. I can help you.'

Brianne felt suffocated by Poppy. She did not want to let her inside her room. She did not want her as a friend but, despite her feelings, she unlocked the door and let Poppy inside.

Brianne's suitcase was open on the narrow bed. Poppy immediately began to unpack and put Brianne's clothes and shoes away in the wardrobe. Brianne sat helplessly on the end of the bed, saying, 'No, Poppy. I can do it.' She thought that when Poppy had gone, she would arrange her clothes to her own satisfaction.

Poppy opened a jewellery box decorated in tiny pearlised shells and began to try on various pieces. She pulled out the silver bracelet with the three charms: a moon, a sun and a star.

The bracelet had been bought by Eva in late August

to celebrate Brianne's five A*s at A level. Brian Junior had already lost the cufflinks his mother had given him to commemorate his six A*s.

'I'll borrow this,' Poppy said.

'No!' Brianne shouted. 'Not that! It's precious to me.' She took it from Poppy and slipped it on to her own wrist.

Poppy said, 'Omigod, you're such a materialist. Chill out.'

Meanwhile, Brian Junior paced up and down in his shockingly tiny room. It took only three steps to move from the door to the window. He wondered why his mother had not rung as she had promised.

He had unpacked earlier and everything had been neatly put away. His pens and pencils were lined up in colour order, starting with yellow and finishing with black. It was important to Brian Junior that a red pen came exactly at the centre of the line.

Earlier that day, once the twins' belongings had been brought up from the car, their laptops were being charged, and the new Ikea kettles, toasters and lamps had been plugged in, Brian, Brianne and Brian Junior had sat in a line on Brianne's bed with nothing to say to each other.

Brian had said, 'So,' several times.

The twins were expecting him to go on to speak, but he had relapsed into silence.

Eventually, he cleared his throat and said, 'So, the day has come, eh? Daunting for me and Mum, and even more so for you two – standing on your own two feet, meeting new people.'

He stood up and faced them. 'Kids, make a bit of an effort to be friendly to the other students. Brianne, introduce yourself, try to smile. They won't be as clever as you and Brian Junior, but being clever isn't everything.'

Brian Junior said, in a flat tone, 'We're here to work, Dad. If we needed "friends" we'd be on Facebook.'

Brianne took her brother's hand and said, 'It might be good to have a friend, Bri. Y'know, like, somebody I could talk to about . . .' She hesitated.

Brian supplied, 'Clothes and boys and hairdos.'

Brianne thought, 'Ugh! Hairdos? No, I'd want to talk about the wonders of the world, the mysteries of the universe.'

Brian Junior said, 'We can make friends once we've obtained our doctorates.'

Brian laughed, 'Loosen up, BJ. Get drunk, get laid, hand an essay in late, for once. You're a student, steal a traffic cone!'

Brianne looked at her brother. She could no more imagine him roaring drunk with a traffic cone on his head than she could see him on that stupid programme *Strictly Come Dancing*, clad in lime-green Lycra, dancing the rumba.

Before Brian left, there were some badly executed hugs and backslaps. Noses were kissed instead of lips and cheeks. They trod on each other's toes in their haste to leave the cramped room and get to the lift. Once there, they waited an interminable time for the lift to travel up six floors. They could hear it wheezing and grinding its way towards them.

When the doors opened, Brian almost ran inside. He waved goodbye to the twins and they waved back. After a few seconds, Brian stabbed at the Ground Floor button, the doors closed and the twins did a high five.

Then the lift returned with Brian its captive.

The twins were horrified to see that their father was crying. They were about to step in when the doors crushed shut, and the lift jerked and groaned itself downstairs.

'Why is Dad *crying*?' asked Brian Junior.

Brianne said, 'I think it's because he's sad we've left home.'

Brian Junior was amazed. 'And is that a normal response?'

'I think so.'

'Mum didn't cry when we said goodbye.'

'No, Mum thinks tears should be reserved for nothing less than tragedy.'

They had waited by the lift for a few moments to see if it would return their father again. When it did not, they went to their rooms and tried, but failed, to contact their mother.

# 3

At ten o'clock Brian Senior came into the bedroom and started to get undressed.

Eva closed her eyes. She heard his pyjama drawer open and close. She gave him a minute to climb into his pyjamas and then, with her back turned to him, she said, 'Brian, I don't want you to sleep in this bed tonight. Why don't you sleep in Brian Junior's room? It's guaranteed to be clean, neat and unnaturally tidy.'

'Are you feeling poorly?' Brian asked. 'Physically?' he added.

'No,' she said, 'I'm fine.'

Brian lectured, 'Did you know, Eva, that in certain therapeutic communities, patients are banned from using the words, "I'm fine"? Because invariably, they are *not* fine. Admit it, you're distraught because the twins have left home.'

'No, I'm glad to see the back of them.'

Brian's voice trembled with anger. 'That's a very wicked thing for a mother to say.'

Eva turned over and looked at him. 'We made a pig's ear of bringing them up,' she said. 'Brianne lets people walk all over her, and Brian Junior panics if he has to talk to another human.'

Brian sat on the edge of the bed. 'They're sensitive children, I'll give you that.'

'Neurotic is the word,' Eva said. 'They spent their early years sitting inside a cardboard box for hours at a time.'

Brian said, 'I didn't know that! What were they doing?'

'Just sitting there in silence,' Eva replied. 'Occasionally they would turn and look at each other. If I tried to take them out of the box they would bite and scratch. They wanted to be together in their own box-world.'

'They're gifted children.'

'But are they happy, Brian? I can't tell, I love them too much.'

Brian went to the door and stood there for a while, as though he were about to say something more. Eva hoped that he wouldn't make any kind of dramatic statement. She was already worn out by the strong emotion of the day. Brian opened his mouth, then evidently changed his mind, because he went out and closed the door quietly.

Eva sat up in bed, peeled the duvet away and was shocked to see that she was still wearing her black high heels. She looked at her bedside table, which was crowded with almost identical pots and tubes of moisturising cream. 'I only need one,' she thought. She chose the Chanel and threw the others one by one into the waste-paper basket on the far side of the room. She was a good thrower. She had represented Leicester High School for Girls in the javelin at the County Games.

When her Classics teacher had congratulated her on setting the new school record, he had murmured, 'You're quite an Athena, Miss Brown-Bird. And by the way, you're a smashing-looking girl.'

Now she needed the lavatory. She was glad that she had persuaded Brian to knock through into the box room and create an en-suite bathroom and toilet. They were the last in their street of Edwardian houses to do so.

The Beavers' house had been built in 1908. It stated so under the eaves. The Edwardian numbers were surrounded by a stone frieze of stylised ivy and sweet woodbine. There are a few house buyers who choose their next property for purely romantic reasons, and Eva was such a person. Her father had smoked Woodbine cigarettes and the green packet, decorated with wild woodbine, was a fixture of her childhood. Luckily, the house had been lived in by a modern-day Ebenezer Scrooge who had resisted the 1960s hysteria to modernise. It was intact, with spacious rooms, high ceilings, mouldings, fireplaces and solid oak doors and floors.

Brian hated it. He wanted a 'machine for living'. He imagined himself in a sleek white kitchen waiting by the espresso machine for his morning coffee. He did not want to live a mile from the city centre. He wanted a Le Corbusier-style glass and steel box with rural views and a big sky. He had explained to the estate agent that he was an astronomer and that his telescopes would not cope with light pollution. The estate agent had looked at Brian and Eva and been mystified as to how two such extremes of personality and taste could have married in the first place.

Eventually, Eva had informed Brian that she could

not live in a minimalist modular system, far away from street lighting, and that she had to live in a house. Brian had countered that he did not want to live in an old pile in which people had died, with bedbugs, fleas, rats and mice. When he first viewed the Edwardian house, he'd complained that he could feel a 'century of dust clogging my lungs'.

Eva liked the fact that the house was opposite another road. Through the large, handsome windows she could see the tall buildings of the city centre and, beyond that, woodland and the open countryside, with hills in the far distance.

At last, due to the extreme shortage of modernist living quarters in rural Leicestershire, they had bought the detached Edwardian villa at 15 Bowling Green Road for £46,999. Brian and Eva took possession in April 1986 after three years of living with Yvonne, Brian's mother. Eva had never regretted standing up to Brian and Yvonne about the house. It had been worth enduring the three weeks of sulking that followed.

When she turned the light on in the bathroom, she was confronted by myriad images of herself. A thin, early-middle-aged woman with cropped blonde hair, high cheekbones and French-grey eyes. At her instruction – she thought it would make the room appear larger – the builder had installed large mirrors on three sides of the room. Almost immediately she had wanted to tell him to take most of them away, but hadn't had the courage. So, whenever she sat down on the lavatory she could see herself ad infinitum.

She removed her clothes and stepped into the shower, avoiding the mirrors.

Her mother had said to her recently, 'No wonder you've got no flesh on your bones, you never sit down. You even eat your dinner standing up.'

This was true. After she had served Brian, Brian Junior and Brianne, she would go back to the stove and pick at the meat and vegetables in their respective saucepans and roasting tins. Anxiety about cooking a meal, taking it to the table on time, keeping it hot and hoping that the conversation around the table would not be too contentious, seemed to produce a surge of stomach acid that made food dull and tasteless to her.

The wire shelf unit in the corner of the shower was a jumble of shampoos, conditioners and shower gels. Eva spent a few moments selecting her favourites and threw the rejects into the bin next to the sink. Then she dressed quickly and put on her high-heeled court shoes. They gave her an extra three and a half inches in height, and she needed to feel powerful tonight. She strode around the room, rehearsing what she was going to say to Brian if he came back and tried to get into their bed.

She would have to act quickly, before she lost her nerve.

She would bring up how he undermined her in public, the way he introduced her to his friends by saying, 'And this is the Klingon.' How he had bought her twenty-five pounds' worth of lottery tickets for her last birthday.

But then she thought about how quickly his bombast deflated, and how sad he had looked when she had asked him to sleep somewhere else. She stood near the bedroom door for a few moments, thinking through the consequences, then climbed back into bed, withdrawing from the potential battle.

She was startled awake at 3.15 a.m. by Brian screaming and fighting the duvet. His bedside light snapped on. When her eyes focused on her surroundings, she saw Brian stamping his foot on the carpet and holding his right calf.

'Cramp?' she said.

'Not cramp! Your fucking high heels! You've kicked a hole in my bloody leg!'

'You should have stayed in Brian Junior's room and not come sneaking back into mine.'

Brian said, 'Your room? It used to be *ours*.'

Brian was not good with pain or blood and here he was in the early hours of the morning, with both. He began to wail. When Eva had orientated herself, she could see that there actually was a hole in his leg.

'A lot of blood ... wash the wound clean,' he said. 'You'll have to bathe it with distilled water and iodine.'

Eva could not leave the bed. Instead, she reached over and plucked the bottle of Chanel No. 5 off her bedside table. She pointed the nozzle at Brian's wound and pressed, keeping her finger on the spray mechanism. Brian squealed, hopped across the beige carpet and out of the door.

She had done the right thing, Eva thought, as she drifted back off to sleep. Everybody knows that Chanel No. 5 is a good antiseptic in an emergency.

*

At about five thirty Eva was woken again.

Brian was limping around the bedroom, yelling, 'The pain! The pain!' at regular intervals. When Eva sat up, Brian said, 'I phoned NHS Direct. They employ morons! Idiots! Plonkers! Fools! Halfwits! Dingbats! Cretins! Hamburger flippers! Pond life! An African witch doctor would have been better informed!'

Eva said wearily, 'Brian, *please*. Don't you get tired of fighting the world?'

'No, I don't much like the world.'

Eva felt a terrible pity for her husband as he stood at the end of the bed, naked, with a white linen napkin tied around one leg and with toast crumbs in his beard. Eva turned away from him.

He was an intrusion in what was now her bedroom.

Brianne wondered how long Poppy would be crying. She could hear her sobbing through the party wall.

She looked at the alarm clock she had owned since she was a child. Barbie was pointing to the four and Ken was indicating the one. It wasn't what she had expected from her first night at university.

She thought, 'I've been dragged into the pages of an *EastEnders* script by that awful girl.'

At about half past five she was startled awake from a ragged sleep by somebody banging on her door. She could hear Poppy whimpering. She froze. There was no escape from her on the sixth floor of the accommodation block – and anyway, the window only opened a few inches.

'It's me – Poppy. Let me in!'

Brianne shouted, 'No! Go to sleep, Poppy!'

Poppy beseeched, 'Brianne, help me! I've been attacked by a man with one eye!'

Brianne opened her door and Poppy fell into the room. 'I've been attacked!'

Brianne took a look up and down the corridor. It was empty. The door to Poppy's room was open and the emo track that she played incessantly – A Fine Frenzy's 'Almost Lover' – was blaring out. She glanced into Poppy's room. There was no sign of a violent struggle. The bedcover was unwrinkled.

When she returned to her own room, she was disconcerted to find that Poppy was wearing her favourite fluffy acrylic dressing gown, had climbed under her duvet and was sobbing into her pillow. Brianne didn't know what to do, so she put the kettle on and asked, 'Shall I phone the police?'

'Don't you think I've been defiled enough?' shouted Poppy. 'I'll just sleep in your bed tonight, with you.'

Thirty minutes later, Brianne was clinging on to the edge of the bed. She vowed to go to the university library tomorrow and source a book on how to grow a backbone.

# 4

On the second day Eva woke and threw the duvet back and sat on the side of the bed.

Then she remembered that she didn't have to get up and make breakfast for anyone, yell at anyone else to get up, empty the dishwasher or fill the washing machine, iron a pile of laundry, drag a vacuum cleaner up the stairs or sort cupboards and drawers, clean the oven or wipe various surfaces, including the necks of the brown and the red sauce bottles, polish the wooden furniture, clean the windows or mop the floors, straighten rugs and cushions, shove a brush down various shitty toilets or pick up soiled clothing and place it in a laundry basket, replace light bulbs and toilet rolls, pick up things from downstairs that were upstairs and bring them down or pick up things from upstairs that were downstairs, fetch dry-cleaning, weed the borders, visit garden centres to buy bulbs and annuals, polish shoes or take them to the key cutter, return library books, sort recycling, pay paper bills, visit one mother and worry about not visiting one mother-in-law, feed the fish and clean out the filter, answer the phone for two teenagers and pass on messages, shave legs or pluck eyebrows, give self manicure, change the sheets and pillow cases on three beds (if it was Saturday), hand wash woollen jumpers and dry flat on a bath towel, pay bills, shop for food she wouldn't eat herself, wheel it to the car, unload it into the boot, drive home, put the food away in the fridge and the cupboards and, on tiptoe, place tins and dried goods on a shelf that exceeded her reach but was perfectly comfortable for Brian.

She would not be chopping vegetables and browning meat for a casserole. She would not be baking bread and cakes because Brian preferred the home-made to the shop bought. She would not be cutting grass, weeding, planting and sweeping paths or collecting leaves in the garden. She would not be painting the new fence with creosote. She would not be chopping wood to light the real log fire that Brian sat next to after he came home from work in the winter months. She would not be brushing her hair, showering or hurriedly applying make-up.

Today she would not be doing any of those things.

She would not be worrying that her clothes were uncoordinated, because she could not see the time when she would be wearing clothes again. She would only be wearing pyjamas and a dressing gown for the foreseeable future.

She would rely on other people to feed her, wash her and buy her food. She didn't know who these people were but she believed that most people were longing to demonstrate their innate goodness.

She knew she wouldn't be bored – she had a great deal to think about.

She hurried to the lavatory, washed her face and under her arms, but it felt wrong to be out of bed. She thought that with her feet on the floor she would easily be lured downstairs by her own sense of duty. Perhaps in future she would ask her mother for a bucket. She remembered the porcelain potty under her grandmother's sagging bed – as a child, it had been Ruby's job to empty the contents early every morning.

Eva lay back on the pillows and quickly fell asleep, only to be woken by Brian asking, 'What have you done with my clean shirts?'

Eva said, 'I gave them to a passing washerwoman. She's going to take them to a babbling brook she knows and pummel them on the stones. She'll have them back by Friday.'

Brian, who had not been listening, shouted, 'Friday! That's no good to me! I need one now!'

Eva turned over to face the window. A few golden leaves were spiralling down from the sycamore outside. She said, 'You don't have to wear a shirt. It's not a condition of your employment. Professor Brady dresses as if he was in The Rolling Stones.'

'It's bloody embarrassing,' said Brian. 'We had a delegation from NASA last week. Every last one of them was in a blazer, collar and tie, and they were shown round by Brady in his creaking leather trousers, Yoda T-shirt and down-at-heel cowboy boots! On *his* salary! All the bloody cosmologists are the same. And when they're together in the one room, it looks like a meeting in a drug rehabilitation unit! I'm telling you, Eva, if it wasn't for we astronomers they'd be dead in the water!'

Eva turned back to him and said, 'Wear your navy

polo shirt, your chinos and your brown brogues.' She wanted him out of her room. She would ask her uneducated mother to show Dr Brian Beaver BSc, MSc, D Phil (Oxon) how to manipulate the simple dials on the washing machine.

Before Brian left the room she asked him, 'Do you think there *is* a God, Brian?'

He was sitting on the bed, tying his shoelaces. 'Don't tell me you've got religion, Eva. It always ends in tears. According to Steve Hawking's *latest* book, God's not fit for purpose. He's a character in a fairy tale.'

'Then why do so many millions of people believe in him?'

'Look, Eva, the stats are against it. Something *can* actually come from nothing. Heisenbergian uncertainty allows a bubble of space–time to inflate out of nowhere . . .' He paused. 'But I admit the particle side is . . . difficult. The string theory supersymmetry boys *really* need to find the Higgs boson. And the wave function collapse is always a problem.'

Eva nodded, and said, 'I see. Thank you.'

He groomed his beard with Eva's comb and said, 'So, how long do you intend to stay in bed?'

'Where does the universe end?' asked Eva.

Brian fiddled with his beard, twirling the scraggy end between his fingers. 'Can you tell me why you want to retreat from the world, Eva?'

'I don't know how to live in it,' she said. 'I can't even work the remote. I preferred it when there were three channels and all you had to do was go duh, duh, duh.'

She stabbed at the imaginary knobs on the imaginary television.

'So, you're going to loll about in bed because you can't work the remote?'

Eva muttered, 'I can't work the new oven stroke grill stroke microwave either. And I can't work out how much we're paying E.ON per quarter on our electricity bill. Do we owe them money, Brian, or do they owe us?'

'I don't know,' he admitted. He took her hand and said, 'I'll see you tonight. By the way, is sex off the menu?'

# 5

'I don't sleep with Steve no more,' said Julie. 'He's in the box room with his PlayStation and *The Best of Guns and Roses.*'

'Don't you miss him? Physically?' asked Eva.

'No, we still have sex! Downstairs, after the kids have gone to bed. We used to have to fit it in during the adverts – you know how much I love my soaps – but now we can just Sky Plus. Something had to be done, after I missed the bit where Phil Mitchell took heroin for the first time. So, why are you still in bed?'

'I like it here,' said Eva. She liked Julie but she already wanted her to go.

Julie said, 'My hair's falling out.'

'It's not cancer?'

Julie laughed. 'It's the stress of work. There's a new manager, a woman called Mrs Damson. God knows where she's from. She's one of them managers what expect you to work the full eight hours. When Bernard was the manager, we hardly did no work. We'd go in at eight o'clock, I'd put the kettle on, then me and the other girls would sit around in the staffroom having a laugh until the customers started banging on the door to be let in. Sometimes, for a laugh, we'd pretend not to hear them and we wouldn't open the door until half past nine. Yeah, Bernard were lovely to work for. Shame he's gone. It weren't his fault our branch never made a profit. The customers just stopped coming.'

Eva closed her eyes, feigning sleep, but Julie continued.

'Mrs Damson had only been there three days when I broke out in one of my rashes.' She pushed the sleeve of her jumper up past her elbow and shoved her bare arm in front of Eva. 'Look, I'm covered in it.'

Eva said, 'I can't see anything.'

Julie pushed her sleeve down. 'It's fading now.' She got up and walked about the bedroom. She picked up the bottle of Olay Regenerist, which promised to rejuvenate the skin, gave a little laugh and replaced it on the dressing table.

'You're having a breakdown,' she said.

'Am I?'

'It's the first symptom – when I went doolally after Scott was born, I stayed in bed for five days. Steve had to fly back to his rig. I was worried about him in the helicopter, they're always crashing, Eva. I wouldn't eat, wouldn't drink, didn't wash my face. I just cried and cried. I wanted a girl so bad. I'd already got four boys.'

'So, you'd got a reason for feeling depressed.'

Julie continued, ignoring Eva, 'I was so *sure*. I'd only got pink clothes. When I took him out in his pram, people would look in and say, "She's gorgeous, what's her name?" I'd say Amelia because that's the name I would have given my little girl. Do you think that's why our Scott is gay?'

'He's only five,' said Eva. 'He's far too young to be anything.'

'I bought him a little china tea service the other week. Teapot, milk jug, sugar bowl, two cups and saucers, little miniature spoons, very pretty, everything covered in pink roses. He played all day with it, as well – until Steve came home and kicked it over.' She gave a little laugh. 'Then he cried and cried.'

'Scott?' asked Eva.

'No, Steve! Keep up.'

'What did Scott do?' said Eva.

'Same as he always does when there's trouble in the house. He goes to my wardrobe and strokes my clothes.'

'Isn't that a bit –'

'A bit what?' said Julie.

'A bit weird?'

'Is it?'

Eva nodded.

Julie sat her large bulk on Eva's bed. 'To be honest, Eva, I've somehow lost my way with my boys. They're not bad lads but I don't know what to do with 'em all. They're so noisy and rough with each other. The *noise* they make when they're running up the stairs, the way they eat and argue over the remote, their horrible boys' clothes, the state of their fingernails. Me and Steve are thinking about trying for a girl again, next time he's got shore leave. What do you think?'

Eva said, 'No, I forbid it!'

Both women were surprised at Eva's vehement tone.

Eva looked out of the window and saw a boy climbing

the sycamore in her front garden. Nodding towards the window, she said casually, 'Isn't that one of your boys trying to climb our tree?'

Julie looked out of the window, then ran to open it. She yelled, '*Scott!* Get down, you'll break your bleddy neck!'

Eva said, 'He's a boy, Julie. Put his tea set away.'

'Yeah, I am going to try for a girl.'

As she was walking down the stairs, Julie thought, 'Wish it was me in that bed.'

# 6

Brianne glanced at her watch. It was 11.35 a.m. She had been awake since 5.30 a.m., thanks to Poppy's chronic need for attention.

Poppy had been on Brianne's phone for nearly an hour to somebody called Marcus.

Brianne thought, 'She's wearing *my* charm bracelet and using *my* phone and I haven't got the guts to ask – no, *demand* – them back.'

Poppy said, into the phone, 'So, you won't lend me a measly hundred quid? You're such a tight bastard.' She shook the phone, then threw it down on the narrow bed. 'The fucking credit's gone!' she said angrily, looking at Brianne as if it were her fault.

Brianne said, 'I was supposed to ring Mum.'

Poppy said, 'You're lucky to have a mum. I've got nobody.' She put on a 'funny' cockney accent. 'Oh, poor Poppy, she's all alone in the world. She ain't got nobody to love 'er.'

Brianne forced herself to smile.

Poppy declared, in her normal voice, 'I'm a good actress. It was a toss-up between coming here and going to RADA. To be honest, I don't like the look of the students here. They're so utterly provincial. And I'm dreading starting American Studies – you don't even get to visit America. I'm thinking of changing to what you're doing. What is it again?'

'Astrophysics,' said Brianne.

There was a gentle knocking on the door. Brianne opened it. Brian Junior stood in the doorway. 'Sultry' was the word to describe Brian's early morning appearance. His lids were heavy and his bedhair was seductively tousled.

Poppy shouted, 'Hi, Bri! What have you been doing in your room all this time, you dirty boy?'

Brian Junior blushed and said, 'I'll come back later . . . when . . .'

'No,' said Brianne, 'tell me now.'

Brian Junior said, 'It's nothing much, but Dad rang and said that after we'd gone Mum went to bed wearing all her clothes, even her shoes, and she's still there.'

Poppy said, 'I've often worn shoes in bed. There's not a man alive that doesn't like to see a woman in stilettos.' She elbowed her way past the twins, into the corridor and knocked on the next door along where Ho Lin – a Chinese boy studying medicine – lived. When he came to the door wearing his blue and white striped English pyjamas, Poppy said, 'An emergency, darling! Can I use your phone?' She pushed in and closed the door.

Brianne and Brian Junior looked at each other. Neither of them wanted to say what a monster Poppy was, and admit that she had singlehandedly made their first taste of freedom miserable. They had been brought up to think that if you didn't speak it aloud, it didn't exist. Their mother was a reticent woman who had passed her reticence on to them.

Brianne said, 'That's what happens to women when they get to be fifty. It's called the men-o-pause.'

'So, what do they do?' Brian Junior asked.

'Oh, they go mad, shoplift, stab their husbands, go to bed for three days . . . that kind of thing.'

Brian Junior said, 'Poor Mum. We'll phone her after the Freshers' Fair.'

When they got to the Students Union, they headed straight for the Mathematics Club. They pushed through the crowds of drunken students, and eventually stood in front of a trestle table covered in large laminated photocopied equations.

A youth wearing a tight knitted hat gasped and said, 'Jesus Christ, you're the Beaver twins! Huge respect. You two dudes are awesome! No, no, you're *legends*. A gold medal each at the IMO.' He looked at Brian Junior and said, 'And the Special Prize. Mega respect. "A solution of outstanding elegance." Can you talk me through it? It would be an honour.'

Brian Junior said, 'Well, yes, if you've got a spare two hours.'

The youth in the hat said, 'Listen, any time, anywhere. A tutorial from Brian Beaver Junior would look *sooperb* on my CV. Let me get a pen?'

A small crowd of onlookers had gathered around Brian Junior and Brianne. Word had spread that the

Beaver twins were in the hall. As Brian Junior recited from memory the proof he had conjured up from nowhere – the examining professors had never even imagined it as an answer – he heard Brianne say, 'Oh shit!'

Poppy had stolen up behind them. She shouted, 'Found you!' Then, playfully wagging a finger at them both, said, 'You really must get into the habit of letting me know where you're going. After all, you *are* my best friends.' She was wearing an old taffeta evening dress over a black polo neck. She turned to the youth in the hat and said, 'May I join, please? Although I'm a bear of very little brain, I might give your serious little group a bit of badly needed glam. And I wouldn't disturb you in your calculations. I would sit at the back and keep my pretty mouth shut until I'm up to speed!'

Brian Junior temporarily forgotten, the student handed Poppy an application form with an eager smile.

# 7

Eva regretted the day that Marks & Spencer had introduced elastane pyjamas for men. They did not flatter the middle-aged body. Brian's genitals looked like a small bag of spanners through the unforgiving material.

After three nights' troubled sleep, Brian had pleaded to be allowed to return to the marital bed, citing his bad back.

Eva reluctantly gave in.

Brian went through his pre-bed routine, as he always had: gargling and spitting in the bathroom, winding the alarm clock, turning the shipping forecast on, hunting in each corner of the room and under the bed for spiders with a child's fishing net he kept inside the wardrobe, switching what he called 'the big light' off, opening the small window, then sitting on the side of the bed and removing his slippers, always the left one first.

Eva couldn't remember when Brian had turned into a middle-aged man. Perhaps it was when he had started to make a noise as he got up from a chair.

Normally he would talk about his day in monotonous detail, about people she had never met, but tonight he was silent. When he got into bed, he lay so close to the edge that Eva was reminded of a man teetering on the edge of a snake pit.

She said, 'Goodnight, Brian,' in her normal voice.

He said, out of the darkness, 'I don't know what to say when people ask me why you've taken to your bed. It's embarrassing for me. I can't concentrate at work. And I've got my mother and your mother asking questions I can't answer. And I'm used to knowing the answers – I'm a Doctor of Astronomy, for fuck's sake. And Planetary Science.'

Eva said, 'You've never once answered me properly when I ask you if God exists.'

Brian threw his head back and shouted, 'For God's sake! Use your own bloody brain!'

Eva said, 'I haven't used my brain for so long, the poor thing is huddled in a corner, waiting to be fed.'

'You're constantly mixing up the concept of heaven with the bloody cosmos! And if your mother asks me one more time to read her stars . . . I have explained the difference between an astronomer and an astrologer a million fucking times!' He jumped out of bed, stubbed his toe on the bedside cabinet, screamed and limped out of the room. She heard the door to Brian Junior's room slam.

Eva fumbled in the cupboard of her bedside table, where she kept her most precious things, and pulled out her school exercise books. She had kept them clean and safe for over thirty years. As she leafed through them the moonlight shone on the golden stars she had won for her excellent work.

She had been a very clever girl whose essays were always read aloud in class, and she was told by her teachers that with hard study and a grant she might even get to university. But she had been needed to go to work and bring in a wage. And how could Ruby afford to buy a grammar school uniform from a specialist shop on a widow's pension?

In 1977 Eva left the Leicester High School for Girls and trained as a telephonist at the GPO. Ruby took two-thirds of her wages for bed and board.

When Eva was sacked for constantly connecting the wrong line to the wrong customer, she was too afraid to tell her mother, so she went and sat in the little Arts and Crafts-designed library and read her way through a selection of the English classics. Then, a fortnight after her sacking, the Head Librarian – a cerebral man who had no managerial skills – put up a notice advertising a vacancy for a library assistant: 'Qualifications Essential.'

She had no suitable qualifications. But at the informal interview the Head Librarian told Eva that in his opinion she was supremely qualified since he had seen her reading *The Mill on the Floss*, *Lucky Jim*, *Bleak House* and even *Sons and Lovers*.

Eva told her mother that she had changed her job and would in future be earning less, at the library.

Ruby said she was a fool and that books were over-rated and very unhygienic. 'You never know who's been messing about with the pages.'

But Eva loved her job.

To unlock the heavy outer door and to walk into the hushed interior, with the morning light spilling from the high windows on to the waiting books, gave her such pleasure that she would have worked for nothing.

# 8

It was in the afternoon of the fifth day that Peter, the window cleaner, called. Eva had slept on and off for twelve hours. She had promised herself this indulgence ever since the twins had been lifted out of her womb, and placed into her arms over seventeen years ago.

Brianne had been a sickly child, pasty and irritable with a scribble of black hair and a permanent scowl. She slept fitfully and woke at the slightest noise. Eva would hear her baby daughter's thin wail and dash to pick her up before it turned into relentless screaming. Brian Junior slept through the night, and when he woke in the morning he played with his toes and smiled at the Scooby-Doo mobile above his head. Ruby would say, 'This child has come straight from heaven.'

When Brianne was screaming in Eva's arms, Ruby's advice was, 'Put an inch or two of brandy in her bottle. My mam used to. It didn't do me any harm.'

Eva would look at Ruby's raddled face and shudder.

She had spoken to her window cleaner once a month for the past ten years, yet she knew nothing about him – apart from the fact that his name was Peter Rose and he was married, with a disabled daughter called Abigail. She heard his ladder scraping up the side of the house before coming to a rest on the window sill. Had she wanted to hide, she could have run into the bathroom but she decided to 'style it out' – an expression which Brianne frequently used and which Eva interpreted as smiling in the face of awkward social situations.

So, Eva smiled and waved awkwardly when she saw Peter's head appear above the sill. His cheeks reddened with embarrassment. He poked his head round the open window and said, 'Do you want me to come back later?'

'No,' she said. 'You can do them now.'

He smeared soapy water all over the window and asked, 'Are you poorly?'

'I just wanted to stay in bed,' she said.

'That's what I wanna do on my day off,' he agreed. 'Curl up and 'ibernate. But I can't. Not with Abigail . . .'

'How is she?' asked Eva.

'Same as always,' said Peter, 'but heavier. She don't talk, she can't walk, she don't do nothing for herself . . .' He paused while he rubbed furiously at the window. 'She's in nappies and she's fourteen. She ain't even pretty. Her mum dresses her beautiful. She's always colour coordinated and her hair is always done immaculate. Abigail is lucky, I reckon. She's got the finest mum in the world.'

Eva said, 'I couldn't do it.'

Peter was using a hand-held device that looked like a truncated windscreen wiper to clear the window of excess water.

'Why couldn't you do it?' he asked, as if he genuinely wanted to know.

Eva said, 'All that work. Humping a fourteen-year-old about and getting nothing back. I couldn't do it.'

Peter said, 'That's how I feel. She never smiles, never even acknowledges you when you've done something nice for her. Sometimes I think she's taking the piss. Simone tells me I'm wicked for thinking that. She says I'm stacking up bad karma. She says Abigail is the way she is because of me. She could be right. I done a lot of bad things when I was a kid.'

Eva said, 'I'm sure it's nothing you did. Abigail is here for a reason.'

Peter asked, 'What is the reason?'

Eva said, 'Perhaps it's to bring out your good side, Pete.'

As he gathered his equipment together to climb down the ladder, he said, 'Abigail sleeps in our bed now. I'm in a single bed in the spare room. I'm living like an old man and I'm only thirty-four. I'll be growing hairs in my ears next and singing "It's A Long Fucking Way To Tipperary".'

He disappeared from view and, moments later, the ladder was removed.

Eva was overwhelmed by Peter's sad story. She imagined him passing the bedroom where his wife and daughter lay together, before going into the spare room and lying down on the single bed. She started to cry and found that she couldn't stop.

She eventually slept and dreamed of being stuck on the top of a ladder.

*

The cordless phone in its flimsy holder startled her with its high-pitched electronic chirp. Eva looked at it with loathing. She hated this phone. She could never remember the combination of beige buttons she had to press to connect her to whoever was phoning. Sometimes a clipped voice informed the caller: 'Eva and Brian are not available to take your call. Leave a message after the beep.' Eva would run out of the room and close the door. Later, she would listen to the caller's message in an agony of embarrassment.

Eva tried to answer the phone but activated a message from the answering machine that she had not heard before. She wanted to run but, trapped in bed, all she could do was barricade her ears with pillows. Even so, her mother's voice came through.

'Eva! Eva? Oh, I hate these bleddy answerwhatsits! I'm ringing to tell you that Mrs Whatsit, the one who kept the wool shop, you know the one – tall, thin, big Adam's apple, always knitting, knit, knit, knit, had a little mongol boy what she put in a home, called him Simon, which is quite cruel when you think about it – her name's gone right out of my . . . it begins with a "B". That's it! Pamela Oakfield! Well, she's dead! Found her in the shop. She fell on one of her own knitting needles! Went straight through her heart. The question is who's going to run the shop? Simon can't do it in his condition. Anyway, funeral's a week on Thursday. I shall wear black. I know it's the trend to dress like clowns nowadays, but I'm too old to change now. So, anyway . . . Oh, I hate these answering whatsits. I never know what to say!'

46

Eva imagined a Down's Syndrome boy running a wool shop. And then wondered why the boy and his friends had an *extra* chromosome? Did we normal people *lack* a chromosome? Had nature miscalculated her ratios? Were the narrow-eyed kindly souls with their short tongues and ability to fall in and out of love in a day meant to rule the world?

Ruby's old message played for two minutes, but when it finally ended the phone continued to ring. Eva reached down and pulled the cord from its wall socket. Then she thought about the children. How else would they reach her in an emergency? Her mobile had run out of battery and she had no intention of charging it. She reconnected the phone. It was still ringing. She picked up the receiver and waited for someone to speak.

Eventually, an educated voice said, 'Hello, I'm Nicola Forester. Is this Mrs Eva Beaver breathing down the phone or is it a household pet?'

Eva said, 'It's me, Eva.'

The voice said, 'Oh dear, and you sound so nice. I'm going to throw a bucket of cold water over your marriage, I'm afraid.'

Eva thought, 'Why do posh people always bring bad news?'

The voice continued, 'Your husband has been having an affair with my sister for the last eight years.'

A few seconds of time stretched into an eternity. Eva's brain could not quite compute the words she had just heard. Her first reaction was to laugh aloud at the thought of Brian cavorting with another woman in a

47

house she did not know, with a person she had never met. It was impossible to think that Brian had a life outside of his work and their home.

She said to the woman, 'Forgive me, but could you possibly ring back in ten minutes?'

Nicola said, 'I realise that this must be a dreadful shock.'

Eva put the phone back into its cradle. She swung her legs out of bed and waited until she felt able to walk safely to the en suite, where she stayed upright by hanging on to the side of the washbasin. Then she started to transform her face, taking cosmetics from the grubby interior of her Mac make-up bag. She needed something to do with her hands. When she was finished, she went back to bed and waited.

When the phone rang again, Nicola said, 'I'm dreadfully sorry for the way I blurted it out like that. It's because I hate unpleasantness, so I have to get myself psyched up and it comes out rather brutally. I'm phoning you now because he's led my sister on by promising her a happy family life and he's blaming you for the fact that he's not leaving.'

Eva said, 'Me?'

'Yes, apparently now you've taken to your bed, he feels obliged to stay and care for you. My sister is distraught.'

Eva said, 'What's your sister's name?'

'Titania. I'm awfully cross with her. It's been one excuse after another. First it was he couldn't leave because of the twins' GCSEs, then it was A levels, then it was helping them to find a university. Titania thought that the day they left for Leeds was the day she and Brian would finally set up their own love nest, but once again the bastard let her down.'

Eva said, 'Are you sure that it's *my* husband, Dr Brian Beaver, she's carrying on with? Only, he's not the type.'

'He's a man, isn't he?' said Nicola.

'Have you met him?'

'Oh yes,' replied Nicola, 'I've met him many times. He's not exactly girl bait . . . but my sister has always liked a clever chap and she's a sucker for facial hair.'

Eva's pulses were racing. She felt quite exhilarated. She realised she had been waiting for something like this to happen. She asked, 'Do they work together? How often does he see her? Are they in love? Is he planning to leave us and live with her?'

Nicola said, 'He's been planning to leave you since they met. He sees her at least five times a week and the occasional weekend. She works with him at the National Space Centre. She calls herself a physicist, although she only completed her doctorate last year.'

Eva said, 'Jesus Christ! How old is she?'

Nicola replied, 'She's no Lolita. She's thirty-seven.'

'He's fifty-five,' said Eva. 'He's got varicose veins. And two children! And he loves *me*.'

Nicola said, 'Actually, he doesn't love you. And he told my sister that he knows you don't love him. Do you?'

Eva said, 'I did once,' and crashed the phone down into its nasty plastic holder.

*

49

Eva and Brian had met at the university library in Leicester, where Eva was a library assistant. Because she loved books, she forgot that a large part of her job would be sending stern letters to students and academics whose books were overdue or defaced – she had once found a large rubber condom being used as a bookmark in an early edition of *On the Origin of Species*.

Brian had received one of her letters and come in to complain. 'My name is Dr Brian Beaver,' he said, 'and you wrote to me recently in very officious terms, claiming that I had not returned Dr Brady's *simplistic* book *The Universe Explained*.'

Eva nodded.

He certainly sounded angry, but his face and neck were almost entirely hidden by a full black beard, a mass of wild hair, heavy horn-rimmed spectacles and a black polo-neck sweater.

He looked intellectual and French. She could imagine Brian lobbing cobbles at the despised gendarmerie as he and his fellow revolutionaries fought to overthrow social order.

'I won't be returning Brady's book,' he continued, 'because it was so full of theoretical errors and textual buffoonery that I threw it into the River Soar. I cannot take the risk of it falling into the hands of my students.'

He looked at Eva intently as he waited for her reaction. He told her later, on their second date, that he thought she was OK in the looks department. A bit heavy around the haunches, perhaps, but he would soon get the weight off her.

'Do you have a degree?' he had asked.

'No,' she said. Then added, 'Sorry.'

'Do you smoke?'

'Yes.'

'How many a day?'

'Fifteen,' she lied.

'You'll have to stop that,' he said. 'My father burned to death because of a cigarette.'

'One single cigarette?' she asked.

'Our house was unheated apart from the paraffin heater, which Dad would light when the temperature dropped below freezing. He'd been filling it with paraffin and had slopped some on to his trousers and shoes. Then he lit a cigarette, dropped the match and . . .' Brian's voice constricted. Alarmingly, tears brimmed in his eyes.

Eva said, 'You don't have to –'

'The house smelled of Sunday roast for years,' said Brian. 'It was most disconcerting. I buried myself in books . . .'

Eva said, 'My dad died at work. Nobody noticed until the chicken pies started coming down the conveyor without the mushrooms.'

Brian asked, 'Was he a mushroom operative at Pukka Pies? I did a few shifts there myself when I was a student. I put the onions into the beef and onion.'

'Yes,' said Eva. 'He was clever but left school at fourteen. He had a library card,' she said in her dead father's defence.

Brian said, 'We were lucky. We baby boomers benefited

from the welfare state. Free milk, orange juice, penicillin, free health care, free education.'

'Free university,' said Eva. She continued in a bad Brooklyn accent, 'I coulda' been a contender.'

Brian was puzzled. He hadn't seen many films.

Eva delayed marrying Brian for the three years of their interminable courtship because she kept hoping that he would light her sexual spark and make her desire him, but the kindling was damp and the matches spent. And anyway, she couldn't face abandoning her maiden name, Eva Brown-Bird, for Eva Beaver. She had admired him and enjoyed the status afforded to her at university functions, but the moment she saw him standing at the altar, with his hair shorn and his beard gone, he was a stranger to her.

As she reached his side, somebody – a female voice – said in a loud whisper, 'She'll not be an eager beaver tonight.'

A ripple of barely suppressed laughter ran around the cold church.

Eva shivered in her white lace wedding dress, transfixed by the awfulness of Brian's hair. Wanting to save money, he had cut it himself using a shearing device attached to a back-of-the-head mirror, sent for from a catalogue.

The Beaver family had occupied the right-hand pews. They were not an attractive brood. It would be a grave exaggeration to say that they were beaver-like, but there was something about their front teeth and their sleek brown hair . . . it would not be difficult to imagine them slinking through water and gnawing at the base of a young pine tree.

In the left-hand pews were the Brown-Birds. There was a lot of cleavage on view, both male and female. They were sequinned, feathered, frilled and bejewelled. They were animated, they laughed and fidgeted. Some picked up the Bible from the shelf in front of them. It was a book they were unfamiliar with. The smokers rummaged through pockets and handbags for chewing gum.

As Brian signed the register Eva saw his hair from another angle, then she noticed his extraordinary neck, which was surely the thinnest neck ever seen outside the Padaung tribe of Thailand. As they walked down the aisle as man and wife she noticed his tiny feet and, when he opened his jacket, saw his silk waistcoat decorated with rockets, sputniks and planets. She liked horses, but she didn't want images of them galloping across her wedding dress, did she?

Before they reached the church porch where the photographer had his tripod, Eva had fallen completely out of any kind of love she had ever felt for Brian.

They had been husband and wife for eleven minutes.

After Brian's speech at the sit-down wedding breakfast, when he did not compliment his wife or the bridesmaids, but instead urged the baffled wedding guests to give their full support to Britain's emerging space programme, Eva did not even like him.

Nobody is surprised by a bride's tears – some women

cry with happiness, some with relief – but when the bride sobs for over an hour, her new husband is bound to be a little irritated. And if he enquires of his wife the reason for her tears and receives the answer, 'You. Sorry.' What does a man do then?

# 9

After Brian came back from work that evening, he appeared in Eva's bedroom doorway with a side plate on which stood a mug of milky tea and two digestive biscuits. He sighed as he placed the plate on the bedside table. The tea slopped over on to the biscuits, but he didn't appear to notice that they were quickly turning to mush.

Eva looked at him with new eyes, trying to imagine him making love to the stranger called Titania. Would he use the same technique he employed once a week with Eva – a bit of back stroking, nipple twirling – would he mistake Titania's inner labia for her clitoris, as he did Eva's? Would he shout 'Come to Big Daddy!' seconds before he ejaculated, as he always did with her?

Eva thought, 'Thank you, Titania. I'm truly grateful. I'll never have to go through that weekly ordeal again.'

'Why are you walking backwards, Brian?' she laughed. 'You look as if you've just laid a wreath at the Cenotaph.'

The answer to Eva's question was that Brian no longer felt safe to turn his back on her. She was no longer the compliant woman he had married, and he feared her mockery – her two fingers gesturing behind his back. He couldn't allow that, especially not after his recent humiliation at work when Mrs Hordern, the cleaner, had discovered Titania and himself engaged in a sex act involving a model of the Large Hadron Collider.

Brian said, 'I'm glad you find it amusing. Haven't you noticed that my health is suffering? And, unbearably, my paper on Olympus Mons has been discredited by Professor Lichtenstein. I'm on the edge, Eva.'

'You look all right to me. Energetic, *virile* . . . positively brimming with testosterone.'

Brian looked at his wife. 'Virile? I'm exhausted. Why does housework take up so much time?'

Eva said, 'It's not the housework that's exhausting you.'

They stared at each other.

Eventually, Brian dropped his gaze and said, 'I've hardly been in the sheds.' He carried on aggressively, 'But I'm going now. The ironing can wait.' He stamped down the stairs and went out of the back door.

The house had an unusually large garden. The original owner, a Mr Tobias Harold Eddison, had taken advantage of his immediate neighbours' post-World War One financial difficulties and, over time, had induced them to sell small parcels of land – until he had enough to plant a small orchard, build a large ornamental fish pond and, unusual for the times, a children's tree house.

Brian's sheds were at the very bottom of the garden, shielded by a row of holly trees which bore a heavy crop of red berries in the winter months.

Over the years Brian had built a model of the solar system in his original shed, using reinforced drinking straws, ping-pong balls and further assorted spherical objects, such as the fruit he had bought from Leicester market and which had been given many coats of varnish until they were rock hard. Jupiter had been a problem – but then, Jupiter's huge dimensions were always a problem. He had tried using a modified Space Hopper, cutting off the horns, applying increasingly stronger patches, but Jupiter continued losing atmospheric pressure – or, as the ordinary bloke in the street called it, air.

Brian's three-dimensional interpretation had been slowly superseded by a network of computers and projection screens that attempted to model the visible universe, but he often looked back fondly to those nights when he had painted his planets to the accompaniment of Radio 4.

At the Space Centre he was one of the masters of the banks of mainframe computers and the encrypted information they held. But the sheds were where his heart was. As the known universe expanded, so did Brian's mother shed, which was now connected to three slightly smaller sheds. Brian had built doorways and corridors and laid an electricity cable from the house. And four years ago, after complaints from Titania that she had hurt her back after making love on a computer desk, Brian had bought two massive floor cushions – pink for her, blue for him. These had also been superseded by a standard double bed, smuggled into the shed complex when Eva was at work.

The original shed had a retractable roof, which allowed his home-built telescope to scan the night skies. There had been complaints from the neighbours – the ratcheting noise that the roof made when it was opening or closing 'could be annoying', Brian had conceded, as could the grinding of the gears as the instrument slewed across the sky. But didn't 'those intellectual pygmies' understand? They were rubbing shoulders with Brian Beaver, a true space explorer. There was nothing on the earth left to find – not when remote South American primitives were smoking Marlboro Lights.

Brian wanted something named after him, and any old star wouldn't do. After all, you could name one for £50 and give the certificate to your wife for Christmas. Brian had given Eva such a certificate on her fortieth birthday. She hadn't looked as thrilled as he had hoped – especially when he told her that Eva Beaver, the star, more usually known as SAO 101276, had died 380 million years ago and that it was only the ghostly light that could be seen from the earth.

No, Brian wanted something truly remarkable to bear his name, something that would bring him respect from the worldwide astronomical community. When he was a little boy of ten, he had watched some of the Nobel Prize awards ceremony on television with his mother.

She had said, 'If you work hard at your science, Brian, you could win the Nobel Prize. That would make Mummy very happy.'

Brian had taught himself to say, in Swedish, 'I could not have discovered [blank] without the backing of my mother, Yvonne Beaver.'

Swedish was a very difficult language. He wasn't sure about his pronunciation, and was unable to check. Real

Swedish people were thin on the ground in Leicester in those days.

Brian had worked so hard at school that he had alienated his fellow pupils, but he soared academically. Now, in late middle age, he had hit the ground and come to the cruel realisation that he was no longer especially gifted, was one of many clever scientists whose name the public would never know, and that he had been a fool to imagine that he could ever win the Nobel Prize.

He went to his sheds every night at eight thirty and every weekend afternoon.

Brianne had once said to Eva, 'For years I thought Dad was going to a place called Inished.'

Only recently – without Eva's knowledge – Brian had knocked two of the smaller sheds through and installed a new, supremely comfortable king-sized bed, two armchairs, a fridge and a small dining table, making a compact but stylish garden flat.

Titania often joined him, unlocking the garden gate that led on to the jitty at the back of the house, and tiptoeing through the open door of one of the sheds. The twins and Eva knew never to disturb him when the red light went on above the mother-shed doors and he was 'working'.

Now Eva lay awake in the dark.

'Working,' she said to herself. 'All those hours, all those years, and he chose to spend them with a stranger called Titania.'

# 10

Brian Junior was waiting outside the seminar room where Professor Nikitanova was due to meet her new students.

Brianne had just said, 'Butch up, our kid. Promise me you won't run away when I've gone.'

Brian Junior said, 'Our kid? Why are you talking like a *Coronation Street* actor?'

Brianne said, lowering her voice and turning away from the other students, 'Bri, we've got to *normalise*. Use a few more colloquialisms. You know? Like "cool", "random", "chill out", "dude", "you guys", "devastated", "amazing", "sick" . . .'

Brian Junior nodded.

When Brianne tried to leave for her own tutor meeting, he grabbed the leather sleeve of her jacket and said, 'Brianne, stay with me, my hands and feet have gone numb. I think I may have compromised my nervous system and suffered permanent neurological damage.'

Brianne was used to this manifestation of Brian Junior's anxiety when faced with a new experience. She said, 'Do your primes, Bri, and try to relax.'

There was a confusion of noise and people at the end of the corridor. Professor Nikitanova strode towards her students on peacock-blue five-inch heels, followed by the Vice Chancellor and her team of teaching assistants.

Brianne took in the bouncy blonde hair, the black jumpsuit, the scarlet mouth from which hung a forbidden lighted cigarette, and marvelled. She had met the rest of the Astrophysics faculty. It was headed by Professor Partridge, a man in a cardigan his wife had knitted with hair belonging to various family pets.

Nikitanova gave Brian Junior the keys and, while he fumbled at the lock, she said, 'Darling, slow down! Two years we have together, unless I tire of you.'

She laughed, and Brian Junior remembered the internet rumour – that Nikitanova's husband was a cultured oligarch who had ex-KGB Special Forces operatives guarding his brilliant, beautiful and good-natured wife. The operatives knew that should anything – *anything* – untoward happen to her, then they would die screaming (but grateful that their ordeal would soon be over).

Later that night, Brian was lying on his bed trying to find a solution to a problem Nikitanova had given her group – 'To give exercise to the brains' – when somebody rapped on the door.

It was Poppy.

She started talking before she was even in the room. 'I can't sleep, so I've come to dialogue with you . . . sweet Jesus, it's hot in here!'

She was wearing a winceyette nightgown, similar to the one traditionally worn by the wolf in *Little Red Riding Hood*. To Brian Junior's alarm she dipped down, took hold of the hem in both hands, peeled the nightgown off and threw it into a corner.

The only naked women Brian Junior had seen before were in pornographic magazines and internet videos, and the bodies in these were the colour of lightly roasted chicken and devoid of body hair, so it was a shock to see the wild black thatch of hair between her sinewy white thighs and the tufts under her arms.

Brian Junior sat on the side of his bed and began to run through the potentially infinite list of prime numbers in his head:

2, 3, 5, 7, 11, 13, 17, 19, 23, 29, 31, 37, 41, 43, 47, 53, 59, 61, 67, 71, 73, 79, 83, 89, 97, 101, 103, 107, 109, 113, 127, 131, 137 . . .

Poppy's breasts were thin and pendulous as she roamed around the tiny room, moving his toiletries and the equipment on his desk.

Brian Junior could not think of a single word to say. He wanted to climb back into bed and go to sleep. He felt that something very terrible lay ahead.

She came and sat cross-legged on the floor at his feet. 'You're a virgin, aren't you, my darling?'

Brian Junior scooted to the end of the bed and began to straighten the desk, lining up pens, pencils and highlighters. Alongside his laptop and notebooks his hand moved over a transparent box of paper clips, wondering where to place them satisfactorily. He tipped them out of their box and started to group the paper clips together in lines of ten.

Poppy crawled up to him, wrapped her arms around his legs and began to cry. 'I loved you the moment I saw your face.'

Brian Junior was left with a single paper clip. This was bad. One paper clip could not be allowed to exist. It did not fit in with the groups. It grabbed all the attention – it was selfish, thinking only of itself. Brian Junior looked at his face in the mirror above the desk. He knew he was unusually handsome. It was very annoying. He also knew that Poppy had stolen and misquoted her declaration of love from a song by Roberta Flack. It was one of his mother's favourites. She had sung it to him and Brianne when they were little kids.

He looked down at her and said, 'Ewan MacColl composed it in 1957. Roberta Flack recorded it in 1972. Coldcut used the Joanna Law a cappella in *70 Minutes of Madness*. Mixed with Luke Slater and Harold Budd.'

Poppy wondered when he would stop going on and on about the stupid record.

He looked down at her again and said, with some animation, 'It's the greatest mix tape ever made.'

Eventually, she lifted her head, took his hand and placed it over her left breast. She looked into his face and said, 'My love, it's like the beating throat of a cag-ed bird.'

Brian Junior was repulsed and quickly removed his hand. Some of her hair was stuck to the snot above her top lip. He could not bear to look at it. He took the strands and tucked them behind her left ear.

She said, 'I think our joy will fill the earth and last till the end of time.'

Brian Junior said, 'I know it won't.'

Poppy asked, 'What won't?'

Brian Junior said, 'Our joy. We have no joy to fill the earth and last till the end of time. In addition, both of these things are impossibilities. Joy cannot fill the earth. And neither can joy last till the end of time. Since time can never end.'

Poppy mimed an extravagant yawn.

He wanted to ask her to leave but didn't know how. He did not want to hurt or offend her, but he was desperate for escape and sleep. He got up, extricated himself from her and picked up her nightgown. It was cold and damp.

He handed it to her and said, 'I want to show you something.'

Poppy stopped crying.

He held out a hand, pulled her to her feet and indicated the rows of paper clips, then picked up the single one and said, 'Where would you place this?'

She stared down at the paper clips, then back up at his face. And then, in a voice he had not heard before, she said, 'I'd stick it up your fucking arse!'

She let herself out into the corridor, still naked.

Brian heard her banging on the door of the next room where Ho, the Chinese boy, lived. Brian had exchanged a nervous smile with Ho that first afternoon, when they were unpacking their food into the large fridge and their allocated cupboards. Now he heard him open the door, then he heard Poppy sobbing.

He went back to bed but couldn't sleep. He had the single paper clip in his hand and he twisted it into a tiny spear. He knew that, unless he placed it somewhere, he would be awake until daybreak.

He opened the window as far as it would go and flicked the twisted paper clip into the cold night. Before he closed the window he looked up at the clear sky, where hundreds of stars were shining down on him. He looked away quickly – before he had time to start identifying them, or could think too deeply about the billions that remained invisible.

Brian Junior woke at dawn, feeling agitated. He got out of bed and went outside to look for the paper clip. It didn't take long to find it. When he came to the main door, he couldn't get back inside. He had forgotten his key, as he had done at least twice a week since he was thirteen.

He sat on the cold concrete doorstep, and waited.

It was Ho who let him in and volunteered the information that he had been sent down by Poppy to buy breakfast for her. 'A double latte and an Early Bird Breakfast. Then, from the newsagent, twenty Silk Cut, *Hello!* and *The Sun*. I make joke with Poppy. I say to her, "Cannot buy Sun." She say, "Why not?" Then – this is my joke – I say, "Nobody can buy Sun, it too far away and too hot!"'

Ho's round face beamed.

He was delighted with his joke, until they heard Poppy

shouting through the crack in Ho's window, 'Yo! Ho! Get a fucking move on!'

Ho let Brian Junior into the building, then broke into a run as he headed for the shops.

# I I

After Eva had been in bed for a week, Ruby sent for Dr Bridges.

Eva could hear her mother talking to the doctor as they ascended the stairs.

'She's very highly strung. Her dad used to say that you could play a violin concerto on her nerve endings. My legs are very bad, Doctor. The veins on my inner thighs look like a bunch of purple grapes. Perhaps you could have a quick gander at them before you go?'

Eva didn't know whether to lie down or sit up. She was anxious that Dr Bridges would think she was wasting his time.

'Here's the doctor. You walked through the snow when she was ten and had meningitis, didn't you, Dr Bridges?'

Eva could see that Dr Bridges had tired of Ruby's imagined intimacy years ago. She sat up and hugged a pillow in front of her chest.

Dr Bridges loomed over her. With his tweed cap and Barbour jacket, he looked more like a gentleman farmer than a GP. He said, in his booming voice, 'Good morning. Your mother tells me that you have been in bed for a week, is that right?'

Eva said, 'Yes.'

Ruby sat on the side of the bed and held Eva's hand. 'She's always been a healthy girl, Doctor. I breastfed her for two and a half years. She ruined my poor boobies. They look like them balloons what have lost most of their air.'

Dr Bridges examined Ruby with a professional eye. 'An overactive thyroid,' he thought, 'and a red face – probably a drinker. And that black hair! Who does she think she's fooling?' He said to Eva, 'I'd like to take a look at you.' Then he turned to Ruby. 'Would you mind leaving the room?'

Ruby was hurt and disappointed. She was looking forward to giving the doctor the details of Eva's medical history. She reluctantly went out on to the landing. 'There'll be a cup of tea waiting for you when you're done, Doctor.'

Dr Bridges turned his attention back to Eva. 'Your mother tells me there is nothing wrong with you . . .' He paused and added, 'Physically.' Then he continued, 'I looked at your notes just now and I see that you haven't consulted me for fifteen years. Can you explain to me why you've been in bed for a week?'

'No, I can't explain,' Eva said. 'I'm tired – but everybody I know is tired.'

'How long have you felt like this?' the doctor asked.

'For seventeen years. Ever since the twins were born.'

'Ah yes,' he said, 'the twins. They're both gifted children, aren't they?'

Ruby said from the landing, 'You should see my front room, it's full of the lovely maths trophies they've won.'

This came as no surprise to the doctor, who had always thought that the Beaver twins belonged somewhere on the autistic spectrum. However, Dr Bridges was a firm non-interventionist. If his patients were uncomplaining, he left them alone.

Ruby, who was now pretending to dust the banisters while looking through the gap in the door, said, 'My blood pressure's terrible. The last time I had it took the black doctor at the hospital said he'd never seen anything like it – it's lower than a centipede's arse. He took a photo of the result with his phone.' She pushed the door open and continued, 'Sorry, but I've got to sit down.' She swayed towards the bed. 'It's a miracle I'm still here. I've died two or three times.'

Eva said irritably, 'So, how many times *is* it you've died? *Two* or *three*? You shouldn't be so casual about your own death, Mum.'

'Death's not as bad as they make out,' Ruby said. 'You just go down a tunnel towards the golden light, isn't that right, Doctor?' She turned to Dr Bridges, who was preparing to take blood from Eva's outstretched arm.

He said, as he began to draw up blood with a syringe, 'The tunnel is an illusion caused by cerebral anoxia. Your brain's subsequent expectational processing supplies the white light and feeling of peace.' He looked at Ruby's uncomprehending facial expression and said, 'The brain doesn't want to die. It is thought that the bright light is part of the brain's alarm system.'

Ruby asked, 'So, while I was in the tunnel I didn't hear James Blunt singing "You're Beautiful"?'

Dr Bridges muttered, 'A vestigial memory, perhaps.' He decanted Eva's blood from the syringe into three little vials. He labelled each one and placed them in his bag. He asked Eva, 'Have you have felt any pain anywhere in the last week?'

Eva shook her head. 'Not my own physical pain, no. But, and I know this is going to sound mad, I seem to pick up on other people's pain and sadness. It's exhausting.'

Dr Bridges was mildly irritated. His surgery was very near to the university. Consequently, he had more than his fair share of new age patients, who believed that a piece of moon rock or crystals could cure them of their genital warts, glandular fever and other maladies.

Ruby said, 'There's nothing much wrong with her, Doctor. It's that syndrome. Empty nest.'

Eva threw the pillow down and shouted, 'I've been counting the days until they left home from the moment they were born! It felt as though I'd been taken over by two aliens. All I wanted to do was to go to bed alone and to stay there for as long as I liked.'

Dr Bridges said, 'Well, it's not against the law.'

Eva asked, 'Doctor, is it possible to have post-natal depression for seventeen years?'

Dr Bridges suddenly had an overwhelming desire to be gone. 'No, Mrs Beaver, it's not. I'll leave you a prescription for something to minimise your anxiety, and you'd better wear surgical stockings for the duration of your –' he cast around for the right words and came up with '– holiday.'

Ruby said, 'It's all right for some, eh, Doctor? I wish it was me in that bed.'

Eva muttered, 'I wish it was you in your own bed.'

Dr Bridges clipped his bag shut, said, 'Good day to you, Mrs Beaver,' and, with Ruby slowly leading the way, went downstairs.

Eva heard Ruby saying, 'Her dad was given to melo-drama. He'd burst into the kitchen every night after work with some dramatic story. I used to say to him, "Why are you telling me stories about people I don't know, Roger? I'm not interested."'

After the doctor had driven away in his four-by-four, Ruby climbed the stairs again. She said, 'I'll go to the chemist for your prescription.'

'It's all right, I've taken care of it.' Eva had ripped up the prescription and placed the scraps on her bedside table.

Ruby said, 'You could get done for that.' She turned the television on, dragged the chair away from the dress-ing table next to the bed and sat down. 'I can come every day and keep you company.' She took the remote and Noel Edmonds appeared on the screen. He was doing something with hysterical contestants that involved opening boxes. The screaming of the studio audience and the contestants hurt Eva's ears.

Ruby watched with her mouth slightly open.

At six o'clock the news came on. Eight- and ten-year-old sisters had been taken from outside their house in Slough by a man in a white van. A woman in Derbyshire had jumped into a swollen river to rescue her dog and drowned, the dog turning up at her house four hours later, unharmed. There had been an earthquake in Chile, thousands were trapped under the rubble. Orphaned children wandered through what used to be streets. A toddler was shouting, 'Mamma! Mamma!' In Iraq a suicide bomber (a teenage girl) had detonated a nail bomb, killing herself and fifteen trainee policemen. In South Korea 400 young people had been killed in a stampede when fire broke out in a nightclub. A woman in Cardiff was suing an unlicensed tattoo parlour after her fifteen-year-old son had come home with 'HAT' tattooed on his forehead.

Eva said, 'What a catalogue of human misery. I hope that bloody dog is grateful.'

'They must have done something wrong.'

'Do you think that God is punishing them?'

Ruby said defensively, 'I know *you* don't believe in God, Eva. But *I* do, and I think that those people must have offended him in some way.'

Eva asked, 'Is it the old-fashioned God you believe in, Mum? Does he have a long white beard and live above the clouds? Is he all-knowing, all-seeing? Is he looking down on you right now, Mum?'

Ruby said, 'Look, I'm not getting into another argument about God. All I know is that he looks after me – and if I step out of line, he'll punish me in some way.'

Eva said gently, 'But he didn't save you from losing your purse, tickets and passport when you were at East Midlands Airport last year, did he?'

Ruby said, 'He can't be everywhere, and he's bound to be busy at peak holiday time.'

'And he didn't stop you from getting a cancerous melanoma?'

Ruby said heatedly, 'No, but it didn't *kill* me, did it? And you can hardly see the scar.'

Eva asked, 'Can you imagine a world without God, Mum?'

Ruby thought for a moment. 'We'd all be at each other's throats, wouldn't we? As it is, we tick along nicely.'

Eva said, 'You're only thinking about England. What about the rest of the world?'

'Well, they're mostly heathens, aren't they? They have their own way of carrying on.'

'So, why did your God save a dog and drown a woman? Perhaps he's a dog lover?' Eva grabbed the opportunity to amuse herself. She asked her mother what breed of dog God would choose to keep in his celestial kingdom.

Ruby said, 'I can't see God with one of them snappy dogs what the Queen has. And I can't see him with a daft little dog that you can put in your handbag. I think God would choose a proper dog, like a golden Labrador.'

Eva laughed. 'Yes, I can see God with a golden Labrador, sitting next to his throne tugging at his white robes, nagging for a walk.'

Ruby said, wistfully, 'Do you know, Eva, sometimes I can't wait to get to heaven. I'm tired of living down here since everything went complicated.'

Eva said, 'But the woman who drowned, I bet she wasn't tired of living. I'll bet when the water closed over her head she fought to live. So, why did your God choose the dog over her?'

'I don't know. The woman must have done something to incur his wrath.'

Eva laughed, 'Wrath?'

Ruby said, 'Yes, he's very wrathful, and that's how I like it. It keeps the riff-raff out of heaven.'

Eva said, 'Riff-raff like lepers, prostitutes, the poor?'

'That was Jesus,' said Ruby. 'He's another kettle of fish.'

Eva turned away from her mother and said, 'And God watched his only son die in agony on a cross and did nothing to help him when he shouted, "Father, Father, why hast thou forsaken me?"' Eva didn't want to cry, but she couldn't stop herself.

When she was eight, she had fainted in assembly during the headmistress's graphic description of the crucifixion.

Ruby collected her things, put her coat and hat on, wrapped her bright-pink scarf around her neck and said, 'Jesus must have done something wrong. And if you don't believe in God, Eva, why are you getting into one of your states?'

Eva calmed herself down enough to say, 'It's the cruelty. When he cried out, "I thirst!" they gave him vinegar.'

Ruby said, 'I'm going home to *my* bed.'

Ruby's home was a thin end-of-terrace. The front door opened on to the quiet street. It was only three-quarters of a mile away from Eva's, but to Ruby it felt like an epic

74

journey. She had to stop several times with the pain in her hip and lean against anything that would support her.

Bobby, her svelte black cat, was waiting for her. As Ruby unlocked the door, he insinuated himself around her legs and purred with what Ruby thought was pleasure to see her.

When they were both inside the immaculate front room, Ruby said to Bobby, 'I wish I was you, Bobbikins. I don't know if I can cope with looking after our girl for much longer.'

Ruby put three Tramadol on the back of her tongue and washed them down with a glug of syrup of figs. She went into the kitchen and took two willow-patterned mugs down from the shelf, then remembered and put one back. While the kettle boiled she looked through her wall calendar with the picture of the Angel of the North on the front. Next to it was a scaled-down year planner with the Christian festivals written in black marker pen:

Advent Season, Christmas, Epiphany, Shrove Tuesday, Lent, Holy Week, Maundy Thursday, Good Friday, Easter, Pentecost, Harvest Festival, All Hallows

Ruby spoke them aloud, like a litany. They were the scaffolding of her life. She felt sorry for Eva.

Without them, Ruby would not know how to live.

# I2

Later that night, when Eva had watched two television comedies without laughing, she got up and reluctantly went into the bathroom. It felt wrong when she put her feet on the floor, as though the carpet were a lagoon with piranha fish waiting to nibble at her toes.

When Brian found her coming out wrapped in a white towel, he said, 'Ah, Eva, glad to see you on your feet. I can't get the door of the washing machine open.'

She sat on the side of the bed and said, 'You have to hit it hard, twice, with the side of your hand, as though you were trained to kill.'

Brian was disappointed when his wife changed into a pair of pink gingham pyjamas and climbed back into bed.

He said, 'The washing machine.'

She said, 'The jugular,' and made a chopping movement with her right hand.

He said, 'There's no food left.'

'You'll find some in Sainsbury's,' she said. 'And when you go —'

He interrupted. 'When I go?'

'Yes,' she said, 'when *you* go to Sainsbury's. Will you buy a large funnel, a two-litre plastic bottle and a box of giant freezer bags? And from now on collect the plastic carrier bags for me? Will you do that? I'll be needing all those things to get rid of the waste.'

'What waste?'

'My body waste.'

He said, incredulously, 'There's a fucking en suite next door!'

She turned on her side and faced her husband. 'I can't walk those few steps to the en suite, Bri. I was hoping you'd help me out.'

'You're disgusting,' he said. 'I'm not messing about decanting your piss and dumping your shit!'

'But I can't leave this bed again, Brian. I can't make that little walk to the bathroom. So, what can I do?'

When Brian had gone, she listened for a while to him cursing and thumping the washing machine. She thought about all the problems caused by bowels and bladders, and wondered why evolution had not constructed something better for disposing of the body's waste products.

She thought for a long time and finally came up with the most efficient system.

The body would have to be redesigned to absorb the entirety of its own waste. Eva thought this might be possible if somewhere in the digestive system there was a spare organ. Apparently, the appendix was lying around doing nothing. It had no function since humans had stopped eating twigs and roots. Brian had told her that astronauts routinely had the appendix removed before their first launch into space. Perhaps it could be commandeered to help the body absorb every last drop of urine and every piece of faeces?

She was a little vague about the nature of the adaptation, but the adapted organ would be required to burn the waste products internally until the body had absorbed all food and liquid. There would probably be a little smoke, but this could be routed to the anus and absorbed by a charcoal filter held in the pants using Velcro. There were one or two details that would need finessing, but weren't British scientists leading the way in biotechnology? How marvellous it would be if the human race was spared the burden of excretion.

Meanwhile, thought Eva, she would have to dispose of her waste products in a very unsophisticated manner. How would she manage to squat over a funnel without putting her feet on the floor? There would be an inevitable spillage in the bed, and even more complicated gymnastics would be required to defecate into a freezer bag. She would have to get used to coming face to face with her bodily waste, but she would still need another person to remove the bottle and bags from her room.

Who loved her enough?

Eva and Ruby were reconciled the next day, when Ruby brought round a home-made ploughman's lunch covered in cling film.

After Eva had eaten every morsel she said, 'Mum, I've got something to ask you.'

When she explained her vision for the funnel, bottle and freezer bags, Ruby was horrified. She started retching, and had to run into the en suite and stand over the lavatory bowl with a pad of tissues held to her mouth.

When she returned, pale and shaken, she said, 'Why would a sane person prefer to pee into a bottle and pooh in a plastic bag when they've got a beautiful Bathrooms Direct en suite next door?'

Eva couldn't answer.

Ruby shouted, 'Tell me why! Is it something *I've* done? Did I toilet-train you too early? Did I smack you too hard for wetting the bed? You were frightened of the noise the cistern made. Did it give you a complex or syndrome or whatever people have these days?'

Eva said, 'I've got to stay in bed – if I don't, I'm lost.'

'Lost?' queried Ruby. She touched her gold – earrings first, then the chain and locket around her neck, finishing with her rings – straightening and polishing. It was a genuflection, Ruby worshipped her gold. She had ten krugerrands sewn into a pair of corsets in her underwear drawer. If England were invaded by the French, or by aliens, she would be able to keep the whole family in food and firearms for at least a year.

To Ruby, invasion by aliens was a likely scenario. She had seen a spaceship one night as she'd been taking her washing off the line. It had hovered over her next-door neighbour's house before moving off in the direction of the Co-op. She'd told Brian, hoping he would be interested, but he said she must have been at the brandy she kept in the pantry for medical emergencies.

Now Eva said, 'Mum, if I put one foot on the floor I'll be expected to take another step, and then another, and the next thing I know I'll be walking down the stairs and into the front garden, and then I'll walk and walk and walk and walk, until I never see any of you again.'

Ruby said, 'But why should *you* get away with it? Why should I, seventy-nine next January, be expected to baby you again? To tell you the truth, Eva, I'm not a very maternal woman. That's why I didn't have another kid. So, don't look to me to cart your pee and pooh around.' She picked up the plate and the screwed-up ball of cling film and said, 'Is Brian the cause of this?'

Eva shook her head.

'I told you not to marry him. Your trouble is, you want to be happy all the time. You're fifty years old – haven't you realised yet that most of the time most of us just trudge through life? Happy days are few and far between. And if I have to start wiping a fifty-year-old's bum, I would make myself very unhappy indeed, so don't ask me again!'

When Eva paid a late-night visit to the lavatory, it felt as though she were walking on hot coals.

She slept badly.

Was she actually going mad?

Was she the last to know?

# 13

The sycamore outside the window was hurling its branches about in the wind. Yvonne was sitting on the dressing-table chair, which she had dragged to the side of the bed.

She had brought an advanced dot-to-dot book for Eva, 'To pass the time.'

Under duress, Eva had finished the first puzzle. After fifteen tedious minutes she had joined up 'The Flying Scotsman', complete with a village railway station, a luggage trolley, booking office and a station master with whistle and a raised flag.

Eva said, 'Don't think you have to stay.'

Yvonne sniffed. 'You can't be on your own when you're poorly.'

Eva raged inside. When would they accept that what she told them was true – she wasn't ill, she simply wanted to stay in bed?

Yvonne said, 'You know it's a symptom of being mental, don't you?'

'Yes,' said Eva, 'and so is an adult filling in a bloody dot-to-dot book. Madness is relative.'

Yvonne snapped, 'Well, none of my relatives are mad.'

Eva couldn't be bothered to respond, she was weary

and wanted to sleep. It was exhausting, listening and talking to Yvonne – who, it seemed to Eva, wilfully misinterpreted most conversations, and lived from one grudge to another. Yvonne was proud of her straight-talking, though other people had described her as 'obnoxious', 'unnecessarily rude' and 'a total pain in the arse'.

Eva said, 'You know how much you value straight-talking?'

Yvonne nodded.

'I've got something to ask you . . . it's difficult for me . . .'

Yvonne said, encouragingly, 'Come on then, cough it up.'

'I can't use the en suite any more. I can't put my feet on the floor. And I was wondering if you would help to get rid of my waste.'

Yvonne paused, computing the information, then gave a shark's smile and said, 'Are you asking *me*, Eva Beaver, to dispose of your wee-wee and poopy? Me? Who's fastidious about such things? Who gets through a giant bottle of Domestos *a week*?'

Eva said, 'OK. I asked, and you said no.'

Yvonne said, 'I warned Brian not to marry you. I foresaw all this. I saw at once that you were neurotic. I remember when you and Brian took me on holiday to Crete and you would sit on the beach wrapped in a big towel, because you had "issues" with your body.'

Eva flushed. She was tempted to tell Yvonne that her son had been sleeping with another woman for the last eight years, but she was too weary to manage the after-math. 'You were very cruel to me after the twins were born, Yvonne. You used to laugh at my stomach and say, "It looks like a Chivers jelly."'

Yvonne said, 'Do you know what your problem is, Eva? You can't take a joke.' She picked up the dot-to-dot book and the pen. 'I'm going downstairs to clean your kitchen. The salmonella must be rife in there. Rife! My son deserves better than you.'

When she'd gone, Eva felt as though the furniture were crowding in on her. She pulled the duvet over her head and was comforted.

She thought, 'No sense of humour? Why would I want to join in laughing when Brian and his mother find it hilarious that somebody has suffered an accident or mis-fortune? Should I have laughed when Brian introduced me by saying, "And this is the trouble and strife – she spends my money, but she's mine for life."'

She was glad that her mother-in-law had refused her request. The thought of Yvonne criticising the colour and texture of her stools was intolerable. Eva felt that she'd had a very narrow escape. She started to laugh until the duvet fell away from her and slid on to the floor.

That night, Eva dreamed that she saw Cinderella run-ning down a red carpet, hurrying back to the pumpkin coach. As she woke, she imagined that the carpet was white and led from her bed to the bathroom. Within a second the carpet had turned into Eva's pure-white bed sheet, folded and draped and transformed into a rippling pathway which led from her bed to the adjoining bathroom. If she kept her feet on the white pathway she could, she thought, with a leap of imagination, still be in bed.

She knelt on the bed and pulled the bottom sheet free, threw it on to the carpet and then brought the sides of the sheet together, tucking the ends under the mattress. She stepped out and, working carefully, brought the edges together with a series of narrow folds until the sheet was ridged, like an expensive crisp.

The cotton pathway was a foot or so short of the toilet. Eva pulled a white towel from the rail in the bathroom, folded it and laid it down as an extension.

She felt that if she stayed on the sheet she would be safe – though from what, she didn't know.

When she had finished on the toilet, she leaned across to the washbasin and washed her body down with warm water. After cleaning her teeth she emptied then refilled the basin and washed her hair. She then crept back along the white pathway and on to the safety of her bed.

# 14

On Saturday, Eva woke late and the first thing she saw was Brian placing a cup of tea on the bedside table.

The second thing she saw was the huge freestanding wardrobe. It seemed to loom over the bed like a dark, sinister cliff face sucking air and light out of the room. Sometimes, when a heavy lorry drove by the house, the wardrobe trembled. Eva felt that it was only a matter of time before it crashed down on to the bed, squashing her to death.

She had mentioned her fears to Brian and suggested that they buy two white louvred replacements, but he had looked at her with incredulity.

'It's a family heirloom,' he'd said. 'My mother gave us that when she updated her hanging space. My father bought that wardrobe in 1947, and it served my parents well.'

'So, why did your mother palm it off on us,' Eva had muttered.

Now the phone rang. It was for Brian.

He said, 'Alex, my man! How's it hanging, bro?' He mouthed to Eva, 'It's Alexander, the man with the van.'

Eva wondered why Brian had affected such a strange accent. She could not tell from the following conversation what Brian's relationship with Alexander was. She gathered that Alexander was going to call round later that day and remove something for Brian from one of his sheds. Eva wondered if Alexander would be strong enough to dismantle and remove a heavy wardrobe without assistance.

She asked Brian to show Alexander upstairs when he had finished with him, saying, 'There's something I would like to move.'

She heard the van pull up outside the house later that morning. She had heard it approaching for at least a minute. It sounded like a cartoon vehicle – as if the exhaust pipe were scraping on the floor – and there was obviously something wrong with the engine. It took four slams before the driver's door would close. She knelt on the bed and looked out of the window.

A tall, slim man with scruffy greying dreadlocks reaching halfway down his back, wearing well-fitting clothes in muted colours, was reaching for a tool bag from the rear of the van. When he turned round, she saw that he was very handsome. She thought that he looked like African nobility. He could have modelled for the sculptures in the front window of the ethnic shop in the town centre.

He rang the bell.

She heard Brian's voice, loud and jovial, asking Alexander to come round the side entrance and, 'Ignore the mess, man, the missus is pulling a sickie!'

When Alexander disappeared, Eva raked her hair with her fingers and pushed it about, trying to give it extra height. She got up quickly, spread the sheet on the floor again and walked into the bathroom, where she applied her make-up and sprayed herself with Chanel No. 5.

Then, after reaching her bed, she pulled up the sheet, remade the bed and waited.

When Eva heard Alexander's voice in the hall, she shouted, 'Upstairs, second on the right.'

He smiled a greeting when he saw her. 'Am I in the right place?'

'Yes,' she said, and indicated the wardrobe.

He looked at it and laughed. 'Yeah, I can see why you'd want to get rid of that. It's like a wooden Stonehenge.' He opened the doors and looked inside.

The wardrobe was still jammed with Brian and Eva's clothes and shoes.

'Are you going to empty it?'

'No,' she said. 'I have to stay in or on the bed.'

'Sorry, I didn't realise you were ill.'

She said, 'I'm not ill. I'm just retreating from the world . . . I think.'

'Yeah? Well, we all have our own way of doing that. So, will you be staying in bed?'

She said, 'I have to.'

'And where do you want me to put the clothes and the shoes?'

It took hours to empty her side of the wardrobe.

They developed a system. Alexander got four large bin liners from the kitchen. One was for recycling, another for charity shops, a third for selling on eBay, and the last was to take to the vintage clothing shop that Alexander's sister ran in newly fashionable Deptford. There was a separate bag for shoes.

It took a long time because each garment evoked a memory of time and place. There was her last school uniform – a grey pleated skirt, white shirt and green blazer trimmed with purple braid, which she had worn until she left school. The sight of it shocked Eva. She was sixteen again, with the heavy hand of failure on one shoulder and a weighty bag of textbooks and folders on the other.

It went into the eBay pile.

Alexander pulled out an evening dress. It was off the shoulder, black chiffon scattered with non-precious gemstones.

'Now this I like,' he said as he took it over to her.

'My first Summer Ball with Brian at the university.' She sniffed the bodice and smelled patchouli oil, sweat and cigarettes. She couldn't make a decision as to where the dress should go.

Alexander did it for her. He folded it into the vintage bag. From then on, it was he who sorted the clothes.

There were the sundresses with halter necks that she'd worn at the seaside. There were many pairs of jeans: boot cut, straight leg, flared, white denim, blue, black. He refused to bag a cream chiffon evening gown she had worn at a dinner held in honour of Sir Patrick Moore, until she pointed out the large red stain on the bodice, caused by Brian's clumsiness with his late-night cheese and beetroot sandwich.

Alexander said, 'You're too hasty, Mrs Beaver, my sister's a genius with dye and a sewing machine. That girl can create magic.'

Eva shrugged and said, 'Do what you like with it.'

There were the Christian Dior evening shoes Brian had bought for Eva with a tax rebate when they were visiting Paris for the first time.

'These are too good to throw away,' said Alexander. 'Look at the stitching! Who made them? A gang of elves?'

Eva shuddered at the memory of having to wear a basque and stockings and parade up and down in that filthy, freezing garret on the Rive Gauche in her beautiful new shoes.

'Perhaps I didn't explain properly,' she said. 'All of my possessions have got to go. I'm starting again.'

He said, 'eBay, I think,' and continued sorting.

'No, give them to your sister.'

'That's too generous, Mrs Beaver. I'm not here to take advantage of you.'

'I want them to go to somebody who will appreciate them.'

'You don't want a cut of the money?'

Eva said, 'I don't need money any more.'

After Alexander had bagged up Brian's mostly sludge-coloured clothes and taken them on to the landing, the wardrobe was empty. He used an electric screwdriver to take off the doors and the internal fittings.

They didn't speak at first, because of the noise.

When it was quiet enough, she said, 'I'm sorry I can't make you a cup of tea.'

'Don't worry. I only drink herbal tea. I've got a flask.'

She said, 'How did Brian get hold of you?'

'Me and my kids walked the streets, posting flyers through doors. You're my first customer. I'm a painter – but nobody wants to buy my pictures.'

Eva asked, 'What kind of pictures do you paint?'

'Landscapes. The Fens. Leicestershire. I love the English countryside.'

She said, 'I lived in the country when I was a girl. Are there figures in your landscapes?'

'I paint in the early morning,' he said, 'when there is nobody about.'

'To capture the light at dawn?' Eva asked.

'No,' Alexander said, 'people get worried when they see a black man in a field. I got to be well acquainted with the Leicestershire police. Apparently, Jews don't ski and black men don't paint.'

Eva said, 'What other skills have you got?'

'Carpentry. The usual van-man skills – painting and decorating, garden clearance, lugging stuff about. I speak fluent Italian and I was a bad boy for ten years, a wanker banker.'

'What happened?'

He laughed. 'It was good for the first five years. We lived in a big house in Islington, and I bought my mother a little house with a garden back home in Leicester. She likes to grub around in the dirt. But don't ask me about the next five – I shoved too much stuff up my nose, my Smeg was full of stupidly expensive fizz. I wasted it and wasted myself. I missed the first five years of my kids growing up. I suppose I was dying – but nobody noticed, because we all were. I worked for Goldman Sachs. My wife didn't like me any more.

'We were going home in a car I'd only had for two days. It was too big for me, too powerful. She started to nag that I hadn't seen the kids for over a week and that nobody worked sixteen hours a day.' He looked Eva in the face and said, 'I did work sixteen hours a day. It was crazy. I started to shout, she was screaming about my coke bill, I lost control, we ran off the road and hit a tree – a not particularly tall, weedy-looking tree. You wouldn't have known she was dead. I ran home to Leicester with my kids.'

There was a long silence.

Then Eva said, 'Please don't tell me any more unhappy stories.'

'I don't make a habit of it,' Alexander said. 'If you draw up a list of all the jobs you'd like me to do, I'll price them up and give you a quote. The only problem might be that I have to pick my kids up from school . . .' He paused. 'Mrs Beaver, do you mind if I make an observation? There's no coherence in your clothes.'

Eva was indignant. 'How can there be coherence when I don't know who I am? I sometimes wish we had to wear a uniform, like the Chinese did during the Cultural Revolution. They didn't have to worry and dither over what to wear in the morning. They had a uniform – baggy trousers and a tunic. That's what I want.'

'Mrs Beaver, I know we've only just met,' said Alexander, 'but when you feel better, I'll gladly go shopping with you, to warn you off culottes and harem trousers and anything sleeveless.'

Eva laughed. 'Thanks. But I'm staying here, in this bed, for a year.'

'A year?'

'Yes.'

'Why?'

'I've got things to do. To sort out.'

Alexander sat down on the edge of the bed. Eva moved along to give him more room. She studied his face with great pleasure. It gleamed with health and the joy of living. 'He would make the world endurable for some lucky woman,' she thought. 'But not for me.' One of his dreadlocks needed retwisting. Eva took it automatically and was reminded of how she had plaited Brianne's hair every junior school morning. She had sent her off with plaits and ribbons. And every afternoon Brianne had slouched out of school, the ribbons lost, the plaits unravelled.

Alexander put a hand on Eva's wrist to gently restrain her. He said, 'Mrs Beaver, you'd better not start something you can't finish.'

Eva let the dreadlock fall.

'It takes more time than you think,' he said, softly. 'I have to pick my kids up at four o'clock. They're at a birthday party.'

'I still have that "time to pick up the kids" alarm in my head,' she said.

Later, when the component parts of the wardrobe had been taken outside, Eva asked Alexander how much she owed him.

He said, 'Oh, give me fifty pounds, on top of what your husband has already paid me for shifting that double bed.'

'Double bed?' checked Eva. 'From where?'

'From his shed.'

Eva said nothing, but raised her eyebrows.

He asked, 'Do you want me to take the wood away? It's solid mahogany. I could make something out of it.'

'Do what you like with it – set fire to it, anything.'

Before he left he asked, 'Is there anything I can do to make you more comfortable?'

For some reason, both he and Eva blushed. It was a moment. She was fifty, but she was better-looking than she knew.

She said, 'You could take the rest of the furniture away for me.'

He said, 'Everything?'

'Everything.'

'Well . . . *arrivederci, Signora.*'

She laughed when she heard the van starting up. She had been to a circus once and the clown's car had sounded very similar. She lay back on her pillows and strained her ears until there was nothing else to hear.

The bedroom was huge now the wardrobe was gone. She looked forward to seeing him again. She would ask him to bring some of his paintings.

She was curious to know whether they were any good or not.

## 15

Poppy was sprawled on Brianne's bed, applying black mascara to her stubby lashes. Brianne was sitting at her desk, trying to complete an essay before the 2 p.m. deadline. It was 1.47 p.m.

Poppy dropped the mascara brush and it rolled across her white T-shirt. She growled, 'Fucking fuckety fuck! Why don't you buy a decent fucking mascara?' She gave a little laugh – she knew she couldn't go too far. She had very few friends left on her corridor. There had been incidents concerning the theft of food and cigarettes.

Brianne was staring out of the window, trying to find the final paragraph and equations to complete an essay her lecturers had entitled 'Infinity: An Endless Conversation?' Her view from the window was of identical accommodation blocks, young trees and rain clouds the colour of gunmetal. She had been there for two weeks, and she still missed her mother. She didn't know how to make herself comfortable without all the small things Eva had done for her for as long as she could remember.

Brianne said, 'My mother bought me these cosmetics, but I've never used them.'

'You should,' said Poppy. 'You're a proper minger. It must piss you off big time that your brother is actually *beautiful*. How cruel is *that*? Did nobody ever mention plastic surgery?'

Brianne's hands froze on the keys of her laptop. She knew she wasn't pretty, but she hadn't thought that she was an actual minger.

'No,' she said, 'nobody has ever mentioned that I need plastic surgery.' Her eyes welled with tears.

'Don't go all emo on me. I believe in being cruel to be kind.' Poppy laid an arm across Brianne's shoulders. 'I'll tell you what you need.'

The essay deadline came and went while Poppy listed the defects that were going to ruin Brianne's future, unless she 'went under the knife'.

Poppy said, 'No man gives a toss how *clever* a woman is. Well, no man worth having. All they care about is what we look like. How many guys have I slept with since the first day of uni?'

'Loads,' said Brianne. 'Too many.'

'Don't be so fucking judgemental!' shouted Poppy. 'You know I can't sleep on my own – not since my body was violated by that monster.'

Brianne was not curious about the 'monster'. She knew he didn't exist.

Poppy flung herself down on the bed and began to wail like a Middle Eastern grandmother at a freshly dug grave.

Brianne had thought that she was only mildly fond of her mother, but she desperately wanted to speak to her now. She went outside into the corridor and phoned

Eva's mobile, but all she got was the dead tone. She let herself into Brian Junior's room.

He was sitting at his desk with his hands over his ears and his eyes closed.

She said, 'Mum's phone is dead! I need to speak to her about Poppy.'

Brian Junior opened his eyes and said, 'I need Mum, Bri. Poppy is pregnant, and she says I'm the father.'

The twins looked at each other, then leaned forward and embraced.

They tried the house phone. It rang and rang and rang and rang.

Brianne said, 'Mum always answers the phone! We'll have to phone Dad, at work. Anyway, she can't know if she's pregnant, you only met her a fortnight ago.'

'I don't think I impregnated her, either,' said Brian Junior. 'She got into my bed. She was upset about something.'

They were both aware of the hysterical crying coming from Brianne's room. Concerned voices could be heard in the corridor.

Their father's mobile rang eight times before the voicemail message clicked on: 'Dr Beaver is not available to take your call. Please leave a message after the beep. Alternatively, email me on doctorbrian dot beaver at leic dot ac dot uk. If I think that your communication is sufficiently important, I will be in touch.'

When Brianne went back to her own room, she found a small crowd of students. Ho was sitting on the bed, cradling Poppy in his arms.

He said, 'Brianne, I think you are not a good person! You are saying to Poppy she is slut and whore! And this day her mother and father crash their small plane and are taken to intensive care!'

The little crowd exclaimed sympathetically, then looked disapprovingly at Brianne.

Brianne said, 'She hasn't got parents. She's an orphan.'

Poppy sobbed louder. 'How can you say that? They've been better to me than any birth parents could ever have been. They *chose* me.'

Ho said, 'Please go from this room, now!'

Brianne said weakly, 'This is *my* room, and she's wearing my bracelet and my mascara.'

A Korean student with a severe fringe and an American accent rounded on Brianne, saying, 'Poppy has had so much tragedy in her life, and her adoptive parents are fighting for their lives and you insult her . . .'

Poppy struggled to be free of Ho's arms and said, in a little girl's voice, 'I forgive you, Brianne. I know you lack emotional intelligence. I can help you with that, if you'll let me.'

# 16

Brian was angrily showing a group of disabled children around the Space Centre. He was sure that some of them were deliberately crashing their wheelchairs into the back of his legs. Each child had a teacher with them. Before the tour, he had addressed the children and their helpers.

'I am Dr Brian Beaver and I work here as an astronomer and mathematician. I compile all the statistics to do with space, such as the distance of one star from another, and I protect you against fiery death from the impact of Near-Earth Objects. Now, I'm not going to patronise you. I expect there are several of you who are quite intelligent and are able to process information. The others who can't will just have to try and keep up as best you can. It would be a great help to me if you could desist from waving your arms about. And *please* try to keep your heads still. And those issuing the strange noises, could you please stop – it's extremely distracting.'

The teachers looked from one to the other. Should they say something to this man, who seemed not to understand that a new vocabulary was in use today?

Ms Payne, a teacher whose outfit included the grey version of the ubiquitous Ugg boots and a Palestinian scarf, could not remain silent. She said, 'The children's movements and noises are involuntary. Most of them have cerebral palsy. I'm afraid that your language is completely unacceptable!'

Brian said, defensively, 'At the beginning, I said I wouldn't patronise these unfortunate children, and I won't. But it does them no good, madam, if you swaddle them with acceptable words. Now, shall we get on? I have extremely important work to do after you've gone.'

Ms Payne said, 'You should rewrite the brochure, Dr Beaver. It says school parties are *welcome.*'

One of the lifts was out of order. It took over half an hour before everybody was on the next floor.

When Brian came home from work, he found two black children – a boy and a girl – wearing primary school uniform, sitting at the kitchen table eating toast and doing homework.

Brian's first instinct was to turn round and run to the front door – he was obviously in the wrong house. Then he saw his country-walk coat and one of Eva's jackets hanging on the coat hooks in the hall. But who were these children? Was the boy a burglar and the girl his accomplice?

Then he saw Alexander coming down the stairs. 'Thomas, Venus, say hello.'

The children turned round and said in unison, 'Hello.'

Brian thundered upstairs and into Eva's bedroom. It looked bigger and seemed to have more light. The dressing table, chair and chest of drawers were gone, as were the curtains.

Brian said, 'That furniture was a family heirloom. I wanted to hand some of it down to the twins.'

'Alexander took it away for me. He's going to paint the walls, floor and ceiling white.'

Brian opened his mouth like a goldfish. Then closed it.

Downstairs, Ruby let herself into the house and screamed when she saw Alexander buttering toast.

'Don't hurt me,' she pleaded. 'I'm a pensioner with angina and bad legs.'

'I'm sorry to hear that,' said Alexander. 'Would you like a cup of tea?'

'Well, yes.'

Ruby was staring at the children. Alexander introduced them and she sat down heavily at the table.

'I'm Mrs Brown-Bird. I'm Eva's mother. Are you a "friend" of Eva's?' she asked.

'A new friend,' he said. 'I'm her man with a van.'

'Oh, *you're* him,' said Ruby. 'She told me about you. She didn't say you were a coloured chap.'

Alexander cut two slices of toast diagonally and arranged the triangles on a geometrically patterned plate. He found a white napkin and a small tray. He poured the tea into a china cup with a matching saucer.

Ruby said, 'It's a bit of a kerfuffle for a cup of tea and a bit of toast, in't it?'

'You gotta look after the small things in life, Mrs Brown-Bird. There's nothing we can do about the big stuff.'

'That's very true,' Ruby said. 'We're all in the hands of fate. Look at Eva. I see her one week and she's as happy as a sandboy. Look at her now! Lolling about in bed like the Queen of Sheba . . . and she says she doesn't know when she's getting up! I didn't bring her up to be a lazy cow. My girl had to be up and dressed by half past seven on a school day and eight sharp at the weekend.'

Alexander said, 'It would be a boring world if we were all the same.'

Ruby said, 'It would suit me fine if we were all the same.' She sucked her teeth in, not realising that Alexander's mother used exactly the same non-verbal gesture to show her disapproval.

When Alexander took the tray up to Eva, he walked into a strained silence. It was as if Brian and Eva were fencing with invisible swords.

Brian was perched on the window sill, pretending to look out of the window. There was nothing much to see apart from a few straggling school kids and the occasional car obeying the 30 mph sign. There were trees, but Brian had never been much of a fan of trees. He had signed a petition to have the trees cut down, which would have made more parking available. He'd said to Eva, 'Those trees are two hundred years old. They've had a good run for their money.'

Now rain and low cloud were forecast, which meant that Brian wouldn't be stargazing tonight. This was not an unusual occurrence in England – Brian had often bemoaned the fact that Eva would not agree to move to an Australian desert where the skies were huge and clear, and there was no incessant English cloud.

Alexander asked Brian if he could get him anything. 'Tea? Coffee?'

'No!' Brian snapped. 'All I want, chap, is to see you and your offspring leave my premises.'

Eva said to Alexander, 'I'm so sorry, but he has had an awful lot to take on in the past couple of weeks.'

Alexander said, 'I'm working for Eva,' and got back to work, prising staples out of the carpet.

All that could be heard was Eva crunching on toast. Brian wanted to knock the toast out of Eva's mouth. She picked up her cup and unintentionally made an inelegant slurping noise. Brian could not control himself any longer. He walked up and down the bedroom floor, swerving past Alexander, who was still on his hands and knees.

'What is this bloody obsession with beverages? Do you know how many units of heat energy are squandered on making a single cup of tea? Well, you wouldn't understand, but I'll tell you, it's a lot! Multiply that by sixty-four million, which is the population of Great Britain, and it's even more! And don't even talk to me about the time wasted waiting for kettles to boil, the drink to cool down and the sipping time. Meanwhile, in the workplace, machines are turned off, there's nobody to fill the supermarket shelves, lorries are parked up on their bays. And what about our trade union brothers? Their tea breaks are enshrined in law! Who knows how many objects we've missed at the Space Centre because some bloody telescope operative has turned his back on the screen just as an important piece of space junk goes by! And all because somebody wanted to drink an infusion of leaves or beans during working hours! It's a national disgrace!'

Alexander said to Brian, 'So, I take it you *don't* want a hot drink?'

Eva said, 'There's more to a cup of tea than hot water and leaves. You're such a reductionist, Brian. I remember the night you said, "I don't know why people get so hot and bothered about sex. It's only the insertion of a penis into a nearby vagina."'

Alexander was gathering his tools together and laughed. 'Nice to know romance ain't dead. Shall I still come tomorrow, Eva?'

'Please.'


Eva waited until she could hear Alexander's laughter in the kitchen, then said, 'Brian, do you still love me?'

'Yes, of course I do.'

'Would you do anything for me?'

'Well, I wouldn't wrestle a crocodile.'

'No, but I've been wondering if you would sleep in your shed for a while.'

'How long is "a while"?' asked Brian aggressively.

'I don't know,' said Eva. 'It could be a week, a month, a year?'

'A year? I'm not sleeping in the bloody shed for a year!'

'I can't think with you in the house.'

He said, 'Look, can we stop fart-arsing around? What have *you* got to think about?'

'Everything. Do elephants sweat? Is the moon a construct of songwriters? Were we ever happy together?'

Brian said, softly, 'I'm the Mensa member. I can do your thinking for you.'

'Brian, I can hear you breathing through the wall.'

He said, coldly, 'So, if you won't get out of bed, how will you feed yourself? Because I'm not feeding you. Are you hoping that a fluffy mummy bird will keep you supplied with worms, if you cheep loudly enough?'

She didn't know who would feed her, so she said nothing.

He combed his beard and then left the room, banging the door so loudly that the frame shook. When he reached the bottom of the stairs, he could no longer hold on to his temper, and shouted, 'You're bloody mad! You need medication! I'm ringing the surgery for an appointment! It's time they heard my point of view.'

A few minutes later, the smell of frying bacon stole up the stairs.

Eva's mouth watered. Brian knew her weakness for bacon, it was the reason she was a lapsed vegetarian. She had gone as far as buying bacon by post from a prestigious pig farm in Scotland. There was a little speech she gave whenever somebody found out that Eva paid for bacon by direct debit. She would say, 'I don't drink or smoke [a lie] and I spend nothing on myself [untrue], so I think I'm entitled to a few rashers of bacon.'

She lay in bed, watching the light fade, and noticed one dying leaf still attached to a branch of the sycamore. She came to the conclusion that she wouldn't make the bacon speech again. It was banal and boring – and it wasn't true, anyway.

Downstairs in the kitchen Brian confronted Alexander. 'Will you please stop feeding my wife? You're encouraging her to stay in bed. And I can tell you now, it'll end in tears.'

Venus and Thomas looked up from their homework. Ruby, who was at the sink, turned, alerted by the confrontational tone in Brian's voice.

Alexander held his arms open and said, quietly, 'I can't leave her hungry and thirsty, can I?'

'Yes! Yes, you can!' shouted Brian. 'Perhaps then she would drag her lazy arse downstairs and into the kitchen!'

Alexander said, 'Hush, keep your voice down, man, my kids are here.' He continued, 'Eva's on a sabbatical. She needs to think.'

'Well, she's not thinking about me, is she? I don't know what's happened to her. I think she's going mad.'

Alexander shrugged and said, 'I'm no psychiatrist. I drive a van, and I'm taking your wife's carpet up tomorrow.'

'You're bloody well not! If you try to come back to this house, I'll call the police!' said Brian.

Ruby said, 'Steady on, Brian. We've never had a policeman cross this threshold, and we're not starting now.' She said to the children, 'If I were you, duckies, I'd put your coats on. I think your daddy's ready to go.'

Alexander nodded, and passed his children their coats. As they struggled into them, he went to the bottom of the stairs and shouted, 'Bye, Eva! See you tomorrow!' He waited for a reply.

When none came, he shepherded his children to the front door.

Brian followed. With Alexander and the children on the doorstep, he said, 'You bloody well won't see her tomorrow. So, goodbye! And have a nice life!'

# 17

Growing up in Leicester, Brian had been a clever little boy. As soon as he was able to manipulate his twenty-six alphabet blocks he began to arrange them into patterns. Two, four, six, eight were his favourites. He then proceeded to build – at first, a trembling brick tower which he never once knocked over. Then, one day, just before his third birthday, to the amazement of everyone who saw it, he spelled out the sentence 'I am bored'.

His father, Leonard, began to teach little Brian simple sums. The infant was soon adding, multiplying and dividing. Always in silence. His father worked long hours in a hosiery factory and got home long after Brian had been put to bed. Unfortunately, Yvonne did not speak to her little son. She moved around the house with grim determination, a duster in one hand, a damp cloth in the other. An Embassy Filter cigarette was permanently stuck in the corner of her mouth. She was not a demonstrative woman, but occasionally she shot Brian a look of such malevolence that he fell briefly into a trance-like state.

On his first day of nursery school he clung to Yvonne's legs. When she bent down to peel his hands away, a large piece of burning ash fell from her cigarette and on to his head. Yvonne tried to knock it off but succeeded only in scattering the ash on to his face and neck. A piece smouldered in his hair, so Brian's first morning was taken up with first aid and an enforced rest on a camp bed in the corner of the classroom. His teacher was a pretty girl with golden hair who told Brian to call her Miss Nightingale.

It wasn't until the afternoon, when the other children were colouring with wax crayons on sugar paper and Brian was filling his piece of paper with geometric shapes, using a freshly sharpened pencil, that Miss Nightingale and the school discovered they had a prodigy on their hands.

Now, after a great deal of manipulation of the automated appointment system, Brian had managed to secure a face-to-face appointment with Dr Lumbogo. Brian had made the appointment using his professional title, Dr Beaver. He found that it often paid to flag his status pre-consultation. It put the bloody generalists in their place.

He sat in the waiting room reading a tattered copy of *The Lancet*. He was engrossed in a paper on the relative sizes of the male and female brain. There was reasonable evidence that men's brains were ever so slightly larger. A female hand had written in the margin, 'So, why can't the big-brained bastards use a toilet brush?'

'Twisted feminist,' Brian muttered to himself.

An elderly Sikh tapped him on the shoulder and said, 'Doctor? Your turn, it has come.'

For a split second Brian thought that the wise-looking

Sikh was predicting his imminent death. Then he saw that the electronic sign on the wall above the reception area was flashing 'Dr Bee' in red.

He said to the man, 'I don't suppose you have this flashing-light nonsense in Pakistan?'

'I don't know,' replied the turbaned one. 'I have never been to Pakistan.'

Dr Lumbogo looked up briefly as Brian hurried through the door. 'Dr Bee, please take a seat.'

'I'm Dr Beaver,' said Brian. 'Your system has been –'

'So, how can I help you?'

'It's my wife. She's taken to her bed and says she intends to stay there for a year.'

'Yes,' said the doctor. 'My colleague Dr Bridges has already seen your wife. The tests say she is in excellent health.'

'I know nothing of this,' said Brian. 'Are we talking about the same woman?'

'Oh yes,' said Dr Lumbogo. 'He found her to be of robust health and –'

Brian said, 'But she's not of sound *mind*, Doctor! She started to cook our evening meal with a bath towel wrapped around her! I bought her an apron every Christmas, so why . . . ?'

Dr Lumbogo said, 'Let us stop there, and examine this bath towel business more closely. Tell me, Dr Bee, when did this start?'

'I first noticed it about a year ago.'

'And do you remember, Dr Bee, what she was cooking?'

Brian thought. 'I don't know, it was something brown, bubbling in a pot.'

'And the subsequent wearing of the bath towel? Do you remember the meals she was preparing?'

'I'm almost sure they were some kind of Italian or Indian thing.'

Dr Lumbogo lurched across the desk towards Brian with his index finger extended, as though he were pointing a gun, and exclaimed, 'Ha! Never salad.'

Brian said, 'No, never salad.'

Dr Lumbogo laughed and said, 'Your wife is afraid of the splashing, Dr Bee. Your aprons are inadequate for her needs.' He lowered his voice dramatically. 'I should not breach the laws of confidentiality, but my own mother makes our flat bread wearing an old flour sack. Women are mysterious creatures, Dr Bee.'

'There are other things,' said Brian. 'She cries at the television news: earthquakes, floods, starving children, pensioners who've been beaten for their life savings. I came home from work one evening to find her sobbing over a house fire in Nottingham!'

'There were fatalities?' asked Dr Lumbogo.

'Two,' said Brian. 'Kiddies. But the mother – single parent, of course – still had three left!' Brian fought to control his tears. 'She needs something chemical. Her emotions are up hill and down dale. The whole household is upside down. There's nothing in the fridge, the laundry basket is chock-a-block, and she's even been asking me to dispose of her body waste.'

Dr Lumbogo said, 'You're very agitated, Dr Bee.'

Brian began to cry. 'She was always there, in the kitchen. Her food was so delicious. My mouth would water as soon as I got out of the car. The smell must have seeped out of the gaps in the front door.' He took a tissue from the box that the doctor pushed towards him and mopped his eyes and nose.

The doctor waited for Brian to compose himself.

When he was calm again, he began to apologise. 'I'm sorry I blubbed . . . I'm under a lot of strain at work. One of my colleagues has written a paper questioning the statistical validity of my work on Olympus Mons.'

Dr Lumbogo asked, 'Dr Bee, have you taken Cipralex before?' and reached for his prescription pad.

# 18

The district nurse, 42-year-old Jeanette Spears, had been very disapproving when Dr Lumbogo asked her to visit a healthy woman who wouldn't get out of bed.

As she drove her little Fiat car towards the respectable district where Mrs Eva Beaver lived, small tears of self-pity misted her spectacles, which looked as though they had been dispensed by an optician sympathetic to the Nazi aesthetic. Nurse Spears did not allow herself feminine embellishment – there was nothing to soften the hard life she had chosen for herself. The thought of a healthy woman wallowing in bed made her sick, it really did.

Jeanette was up, showered, uniform on, bed made, lavatory Harpic'd, and downstairs by 7 a.m. Any later and she began to panic – but, sensibly, she kept brown paper bags in strategic places, and after a few inhalations and exhalations she was soon tickety-boo again.

Mrs Beaver was her last patient. It had been a difficult morning: Mr Kelly with the severely ulcerated legs had begged her for some stronger pain relief but, as she had told him time and time again, she could not give him morphine. There was a clear and present danger that he could become addicted.

Mr Kelly's daughter had shouted, 'Dad's ninety-two!

Do you think he's going to end up in a squat, injecting heroin into his fucking eyeballs?'

Jeanette had snapped her nursing bag shut and left the Kelly household without dressing his legs. She would not be sworn at, nor would she listen to a patient's relatives telling her how to do her job.

She used fewer palliative care drugs than any other district nurse in the county. It was official. Written down. She was very proud of that fact. But she couldn't help thinking that there ought to have been a ceremony with a plaque or cup handed to her by a VIP from the Regional Health Authority – after all, she must have saved them tens of thousands of pounds over the years.

She drew up outside Eva's house and sat for a moment. She could tell a lot from the exterior of a patient's home. It was always encouraging to see a flourishing hanging basket.

There was no hanging basket in Eva's porch. However, there was a bird feeder with splodges of bird droppings underneath on the black and white tiled floor. There were unrinsed milk bottles on the step. Leaflets for pizza, curry and Chinese takeaways had been blown into the corners together with dead sycamore leaves. The coconut-fibre mat had not been shaken for some time. A terracotta plant saucer had been used as an ashtray.

To Nurse Spears' disgust the front door was slightly open. She rubbed the brass doorknob with one of the antibacterial wipes she always carried in her pocket. She could hear male and female laughter coming from upstairs. She pushed the door open and went in. She climbed the stairs and headed towards the laughter. Nurse Spears could not remember the last time she had laughed aloud. The bedroom door was ajar, so she knocked and went straight in.

There was a glamorous woman in the bed, wearing a grey silk camisole and pale-pink lipstick. She was holding a bag of Thorntons Special Toffee. A younger man was sitting on the bed, chewing.

Jeanette announced, 'I'm Jeanette Spears, I'm the community nurse. Dr Lumbogo asked me to call. You *are* Mrs Beaver?'

Eva nodded. She was trying to free a lump of toffee from a wisdom tooth with her tongue.

The man on the bed got to his feet. 'I'm the window cleaner,' he said.

Jeanette frowned. 'I see no ladder, no bucket, no chamois leather.'

'I'm not on duty,' he said, with difficulty – due to the toffee. 'I've come to see Eva.'

'And bring her a gift of toffee, I see,' said Nurse Spears.

Eva said, 'Thank you for coming, but I'm not ill.'

'Have you undergone medical training?' asked Nurse Spears.

'No,' said Eva, who could see where this exchange was leading. 'But I'm fully qualified to have an opinion about my own body, I've been studying it for fifty years.'

Nurse Spears had known that she would not get on with anybody in this household. Whoever put those unrinsed milk bottles on the step was clearly a monster.

'Your notes tell me you intend to stay in your bed for at least a year.'

Eva could not take her eyes off Nurse Spears, who was buttoned up, belted, shiny clean and looked like a wizened child in school uniform.

'I'll get out of your way. Thanks for listening, Eva. I'll see you tomorrow. I know you'll be in,' Peter said, laughing.

When he'd gone, Nurse Spears unbuttoned her navy gaberdine coat. 'I'd like to examine you for pressure sores.'

Eva said, 'There are no sores. I apply cream to the pressure points twice a day.'

'What do you use?'

'Chanel body lotion.'

Nurse Spears could hardly conceal her contempt. 'Well, if you want to throw your money away on such an extravagance, go ahead.'

'I will,' said Eva. 'Thank you.'

There was something about Nurse Spears that disturbed Eva. She sat up straight in bed and tried to look cheerful.

'I'm not ill,' she said again.

'Not physically ill, perhaps, but there must be something wrong with you. It's certainly not *normal* to want to stay in bed for a year, chewing toffees, is it?'

Eva had a couple of chews on her toffee and said, 'Forgive my bad manners, would you like some?' She proffered the bag of Thorntons.

Nurse Spears hesitated, then said, 'Perhaps a small piece.'

After a thorough physical examination – during which the nurse ate two more quite large lumps of toffee (it was unprofessional of her, but she had always been comforted by confectionery) – she carried out a mental health evaluation.

She asked, 'What is today's date?'

Eva thought for a moment, then admitted that she didn't know.

'Do you know what month we're in?'

'Are we still in September, or is it October?'

Nurse Spears said, 'We're in the third week of October.' Then she asked if Eva knew the name of the current Prime Minister.

Again, Eva hesitated. 'Is it Cameron . . . ? Or is it Cameron and Clegg?'

Nurse Spears said, 'So, you're not certain who the British Prime Minister is?'

Eva said, 'I'll go for Cameron.'

'You have hesitated twice, Mrs Beaver. Are you aware of day-to-day events?'

Eva told Nurse Spears that she used to be very interested in politics and would often watch the parliamentary channel in the afternoon when she was ironing. It enraged her when apathetic non-voters maintained that all politicians were 'in it for what they could get'. She would lecture them in her head on the importance of the democratic process, and would stress the long and tragic history of the fight for universal suffrage – telling them, erroneously, that a racehorse had died for the vote.

But since Iraq, Eva had been vociferous in her condemnation of the political class. Her language on the subject was not measured. Politicians were 'lying, cheating, warmongering bastards'.

Nurse Spears said, 'Mrs Beaver, I'm afraid I'm one of your despised apolitical non-voters. Now, I'd like to take some blood, for Dr Lumbogo.'

She wrapped a tourniquet around Eva's upper arm, and took the cap off a large syringe. Eva looked at the needle. The last time she'd seen one that size had been on a documentary about hippopotamuses in Botswana, and the hippo had been sedated.

Nurse Spears said, 'Sharp scratch,' then the small mobile phone she wore on her belted uniform dress vibrated. When she saw Mr Kelly's number, she was incensed. While still drawing blood from Eva she used one hand to put the call on speaker.

The first sound that Eva heard was a man screaming as though he were being burned alive.

Then a woman came on the line and yelled, 'Spears? If you are not back here in five minutes with sufficient morphine to control Dad's pain, I'll put a pillow over his face! And I'll *kill* him!'

Nurse Spears said, quite calmly, 'Your father has had the correct quota of Tramadol for his age and condition. Any more opiates could result in over-sedation, coma and death.'

'That's what we want!' shouted the woman. 'We want him out of it. We want him dead!'

'And that would be patricide and you would go to prison. And I have a witness here with me.'

Nurse Spears looked at Eva and waited for her to nod.

Eva leaned towards the phone and shouted, 'Send for an ambulance! Take him to Accident and Emergency. They'll control his pain and ask Nurse Spears why she's left a patient in such agony.'

Mr Kelly's screams down the phone were unbearable.

Eva's heart was beating as fast as a clockwork drummer.

Nurse Spears pushed the needle further into Eva's arm, jerked it free and simultaneously terminated the call.

Eva gave a shout of pain. 'You could be in a lot of trouble. Why won't you give him what he needs?'

Nurse Spears said, 'Blame Harold Shipman. He killed over two hundred patients with morphine. We professionals have to be cautious now.'

Eva said, 'I can't bear it.'

Nurse Spears said, 'I'm paid to bear it.'

# 19

Over the following days, Alexander managed to see Eva on many occasions. In between other jobs he moved the radio, the television, the bedside tables, the phone, the seascape pictures, the model of the solar system with Jupiter missing and, last of all, Eva's Billy bookcase which she had bought from Ikea.

He had an identical one at home, though the books could not have been more different.

Alexander's books were immaculate heavy volumes, the size of small tea trays, on art, architecture, design and photography. Such was their combined weight that the bookcase had been attached to the wall with long masonry screws. Eva's books were English, Irish, American, Russian and French fiction classics. Some were tattered paperbacks, some were Folio first editions. *Madame Bovary* was in close proximity to *Tom Jones*, and *Rabbit Redux* had been placed next to *The Idiot*. Poor, plain Jane Eyre was flanked by David Copperfield and Lucky Jim. *The Little Prince* rubbed shoulders with *A Clergyman's Daughter*.

She said, 'I've had many of them since I was a teenager. I bought most of the Penguins at the Leicester market.'

Alexander asked, 'You're keeping them, of course?'

'No,' said Eva.

'You can't let these go,' he said.

'Will you take them in?' she asked, making the books sound as though they were orphans searching for a home.

'I'll gladly take the books, but I can't house another bookcase. I live in a *thimble*,' he said. 'But what about Brian and the children – won't they want them?'

'No, they're numbers people, they distrust words. So, you'll take the books to your house?'

'Yeah, I'll do that.'

Eva said, 'Will you lie to me and promise to read them? Books need to be read. The pages need to be turned.'

'Man, you're in love with those books. Why are you giving them away?'

'Since I learned to read I've used them as a kind of anaesthetic. I can remember nothing about the twins being born, apart from the book I was reading.'

'And what was it?'

'It was *The Sea, The Sea*. I was thrilled to have two babies in my arms, but – and you'll think this is awful – after twenty minutes or so I wanted to get back to my book.'

They laughed at this flouting of the maternal instinct.

Eva asked Alexander if he would take the bookcase to Leeds for Brianne. She sorted her jewellery and put aside all the valuable pieces – a diamond ring, bought by Brian and presented to her on their tenth wedding anniversary, several eighteen-carat gold chains, three slim silver bracelets, a necklace made of Mallorcan pearls, and platinum earrings in the shape of a fan with black onyx drops hanging from them, which she had bought for herself. Then she scribbled a note on a page torn from Alexander's notebook.

*My darling girl,*

*As you can see, I have sent you the family jewellery. I have no use for it any more. All the gold is eighteen carat, and the stuff that looks like silver is platinum. It may not be to your taste, but I beg you to hold on to it. I know you have sworn never to marry or have a child, but you may change your mind. You might have a daughter one day who will enjoy wearing some of it. Tell Brian Junior I will send him something of equal value. It would be lovely to hear from you.*

*All my love,*
   *Mum*

*PS: The pearls are genuine and the diamonds were cut in Antwerp (they are D grade – the best – and have no inclusions). So, please, however poor you may be, do not be tempted to sell or pawn any of this jewellery without consulting me about the value.*

*PPS: I suggest you keep it in a security box in a bank. I enclose a cheque to cover your expenses.*

She was still left with a huge amount of stuff. There were four drawers under the bed, in which were:

    a Chanel handbag with gold chain handle
    a pair of binoculars
    three watches

a gold-plated powder compact
three evening bags
a silver cigarette case
a Dunhill lighter
a lump of plaster into which twin hands and feet
    had been pressed
a stopwatch
a certificate to prove that Eva had once attended
    an advanced First Aid course
a tennis racquet
five torches
a small but heavy model of Lenin
an ashtray from Blackpool (complete with tower)
a pile of Valentine's Day cards from Brian.

One card said:

*I will love you until the world ends,*
    *Brian*

*PS: World predicted to end in five billion years (Red Giant*
*expansion during end of Solar Main Sequence).*

There was also:

a Swiss Army knife with forty-seven tools (only
    tweezers used)
a Hermès silk scarf with a white horse design on a
    blue background
five pairs of designer sunglasses, each in a case
three travel clocks

diaries
scrapbooks
photograph albums
two baby books.

Tomorrow, Alexander said, he would take the carpet up, ready to start painting. Before he left the room he asked, 'Eva, have you eaten today?'

She shook her head.

'How can he go to work and leave you hungry?'

'It's not Brian's fault. We keep different hours.' Eva was very critical of Brian's behaviour sometimes to herself, but she did not like him being criticised by others.

Alexander foraged downstairs and found a banana, half a packet of cream crackers and five small triangles of Laughing Cow. He also found a flask and filled it with drinking chocolate.

When Brian came home from work, Alexander was washing up the cups that he and Eva had used throughout the day. Alexander watched him picking his way through the black bags and boxes on the hall floor.

Brian said, 'I'm thinking of asking you for rent soon. You're getting to be a permanent fixture. I shall be buying you a birthday card next.'

'I'm working for Eva, Brian.'

'Oh, it's work, is it? So, how does she pay you?'

'Cheque.'

'Cheque! Nobody uses cheques any more,' scoffed

Brian. 'I hope you're not going to leave this crap lying around.'

'I'm taking most of it to Oxfam.'

Brian laughed. 'Well, if Eva thinks she'll be helping the poor by donating her old knickers, let her. The rest of us know that the so-called "charity" bosses drive around Mogadishu in Lamborghinis, chucking a few handfuls of rice at the destitute and starving.'

Alexander said, 'I would hate to be you, man. Your heart must look like them ugly pickled walnuts they sell at Christmas. *Naasty* tings!'

'I'm one of the most compassionate men I know,' said Brian. 'Every month the sum of ten pounds is taken out of my bank account by direct debit, which enables an African family to feed and care for two water buffalo. It shouldn't be too long before they're exporting Fair Trade mozzarella. And if you think that by affecting a West Indian patois I will be intimidated by you, you're wrong. I've got a pal called Azizi – he's African, but he's a good chap.'

Alexander queried, '"But" he's a good chap? Think about it. And I'm trilingual. I spoke like dis until I was adopted, man. Then I slowly learned to speak like this,' he said, affecting an exaggerated form of received pronunciation.

Brian eyed Alexander's muscled torso and bulging triceps, and wished that he too could wear a tight white T-shirt. He was anxious to reduce the increasing heat of their confrontation. He cast about for something innocuous to say. 'I don't need to think about it, Azizi *is* a good chap.'

Alexander changed the subject. 'While we're talking about mozzarella, who's in charge of feeding Eva?'

'Eva thinks the people will provide – very biblical, isn't it? But until that miracle happens it's down to my mother, her mother and muggins here.'

He put a lump of lard in a frying pan and watched it melt. Before it got hot, he threw two slices of white bread in.

Alexander burst out, 'No, man! Let the fat get hot first!'

Brian quickly turned the bread over and cracked an egg in the gap between the slices. Before the white of the egg had set, he slid the eggy mess on to a cold white plate. He ate standing up at the counter.

Alexander watched him in disgust. Each one of Alexander's meals was an occasion. Those eating must be seated, there must be a tablecloth and proper cutlery, children under ten were not allowed free access to the sauce bottles, and hands must be washed. Children were required to ask permission to leave the table. It was Alexander's contention that food cooked without love was bad food.

Brian had fallen on the slimy mess like a starving dog. When it was gone, he wiped his mouth and put the plate and the fork he'd used into the dishwasher.

Alexander sighed. 'Sit down, man. I'm gonna cook that again. Watch and learn.'

Brian, who was still hungry, sat down.

# 20

Ruby came the next morning with Eva and Brian's washing. It was ironed and folded so immaculately in a raffia laundry basket that Alexander, who had arrived ten minutes earlier to remove the carpet in Eva's bedroom, was touched almost to tears at the trouble she'd taken.

When Ruby asked, 'Kids at school?' he could hardly answer.

He had spent the first ten years of his life in dirt and chaos, getting up early enough to sift through the piles of clothes on the bedroom floor so that he could wear the least dirty items to school.

When Ruby hobbled upstairs, Alexander laid his face on the laundry and breathed in.

After manoeuvring Eva's bed around the room with her in it, Alexander almost lost his patience, but all he said to her was, 'It would be so much easier if you got out of bed.'

She said, 'If you can't do it alone, shall I ask Brian to help when he comes home from work?'

'No,' said Alexander. 'I'll do it myself.'

Eventually, after a lot of encouragement from Eva, he managed to roll the carpet up, tie it securely and throw it out of the window. He went downstairs and stuck a Post-it note under the string holding it together. It said: 'PLEASE HELP YOURSELF.'

By the time he'd made tea and toast and gone to the doorstep with an empty milk bottle, the carpet was gone. On the reverse of the note was written in biro: 'THANK YOU SO MUCH. YOU'VE NO IDEA WHAT THIS MEANS TO ME.'

While Alexander sanded down the old floorboards, Eva knelt on the bed and looked out over the open sash window. She was wearing an industrial respirator, which soon led to a rumour in the area – spread by Mrs Barthi, the newsagent's wife – that Brian had contaminated his wife with some kind of moon bacteria, and that she had been confined to her room by the authorities.

Later that afternoon, Brian was mystified when the queue in the newsagent's melted away as he joined it.

Mr Barthi covered his nose with a handkerchief and said, 'Sir, you should not be out in our community spreading your unearthly moon germs.'

Brian spent so long explaining the situation at home to Mr Barthi that the newsagent grew bored and longed for the bearded customer to leave the shop. But then, to his dismay, Dr Beaver gave a lengthy dissertation about the lack of germs on the moon, which somehow led to a monologue on the moon's lack of atmosphere.

Eventually, after many hints, which included yawning in Brian's face, Mr Barthi closed the shop early. 'It was the only thing I could do to make him go away,' he told his wife.

She turned the OPEN sign to face the street again and

said, 'So, why do you have tears on your face, you big fat booby?'

Mr Barthi said, 'I know you will mock me, Sita, but I was actually bored to tears. The next time he comes into the shop *you* can serve him.'

Later, Brian came out of the butcher's, where he had been buying a piece of rump steak for himself and eight chipolata sausages for Eva. He saw the lights in the newsagent's flicker back on. He crossed the road and headed towards the shop. Mr Barthi saw Brian approaching, and had just enough time to turn the sign over and slide the bolt.

Brian banged on the door and shouted, 'Mr Barthi! Are you there? I forgot my *New Scientist*.'

Mr Barthi was crouching behind the counter.

Brian shouted through the letter box, 'Barthi, open the door, I know you're there!'

When there was no response, Brian aimed one kick at the door, then turned away and walked back without his magazine to face the chaos at home.

Mr Barthi only raised his head when five minutes had passed.

Brian told Eva later that night that, in future, he would have his scientific journals posted directly to the house. He said, 'Barthi is cracking up. He yawned in my face and then started to cry. He doesn't deserve our patronage.'

Eva nodded, though she wasn't really listening. She was thinking about Brian Junior and Brianne.

They knew she didn't answer the phone any more, but there were other forms of communication.

*

Ho was in his room, writing to his parents using note-paper and a pen. He could not email them such news, they must be slightly prepared – when they saw the letter in his handwriting, they would know that he had something serious to tell them. He wrote:

*My Dearest Mother and Father,*

*You have been excellent parents. I honour and love you. It hurts me to tell you that I have not been a good son.*

*I have fallen in love with an English girl called Poppy. I have given her my love, my body and everything I possess, including the money you both worked so hard for in the Croc Factory to send me to an English university.*

*Poppy's parents are both in intensive care in a place called Dundee. She has spent all of her money, so I gave her my money until I had none left. Yesterday I asked her when she could pay the money back to me and she wept and said, 'Never.'*

*Mother and Father, I don't know what to do. I cannot live without her. Please don't judge her too harshly. Poppy's parents are rich important people who crashed their light aircraft into the side of the White Cliffs of Dover. They are both in a coma. Poppy says that doctors in England are corrupt, as they are at home. And they will only keep her parents alive if they are paid enough. If not, they will switch off the machines.*

*Will you please send me more money? Are you still thinking about selling the apartment? Or cashing in your pensions?*

*Poppy says an international money order made out to Poppy Roberts would be best. Please help me, my parents – if I lose her love, I will kill myself.*

*I hope you are both well and happy.*

*Greetings from your son,*
   *Ho*

Ho went downstairs and posted the letter in one of those red cylindrical structures that the English call a 'box'. He was on his way back to the accommodation block when he bumped into Brian Junior who was, as usual, walking along the pavement while simultaneously reading a book of equations and listening to an MP3 player through over-ear headphones. A snatch of music could be heard faintly – it sounded to Ho like Bach.

Brian Junior acknowledged Ho's presence by blinking his eyes rapidly and grunting an approximation of, 'Hello.'

Ho looked up at Brian Junior and wished he was as tall as him and had such a handsome face. He would also like that thick blond hair, and those teeth! And how was it possible that Brian Junior's cheap shabby clothes looked so good on him?

If Ho had been English, he would have worn the clothes of a gentleman. Burberry tweeds and shirts from Savile Row. Shoes from Church's. His parents had bought him clothes to wear at his English university, but the clothing they'd chosen was that of the proletariat. It was most difficult wearing a Manchester United football shirt in Leeds. Strangers accosted him and called him names. It was good that he had Poppy to love him.

He said, 'Brian Junior. Could I speak to you about money?'

'Money?' repeated Brian Junior, as though he had never heard the word before. Brian Junior had never spent a day worrying about money, and he assumed – was absolutely certain – that he would be independently wealthy one day.

Ho said, 'I think you have money. And I do not. So, if you give me some of the money you have, we will both be happy, yes?'

Brian Junior mumbled, 'Cool.' Then he turned round and walked back in the direction he'd just come from, his face blazing with embarrassment. He couldn't bear Ho's humiliation.

Later that night, there was a knock on Ho's door.

It was Brian Junior, clutching a handful of banknotes. He shoved them at Ho and ran back to his room.

Ho counted the notes on his bed. There was £70. It was nothing, nothing!

It would buy rice and vegetables for him, but what about Poppy?

How could he tell her that he had no money for the corrupt English doctors?

## 21

Eva was entranced by her all-white room. Alexander had worked all day and into the evening, painting the ceiling, the walls, the woodwork around the window and the floorboards eggshell white. Eva had asked him to leave her bed up against the window. From there she could see along the road and beyond, to the faint shadow of hills, the smudge of evergreens and the bare branches of deciduous trees.

The smell of fresh paint was overpowering when Brian eventually came home from work. He walked around the house, opening windows. He opened the door to what he was now trying to call 'Eva's room'. He was temporarily blinded by the dazzling whiteness of the space.

Eva said, 'Don't come in! The floor's still wet!'

Brian's right foot hovered over the sticky floor, but he managed to regain his balance.

Eva apologised. 'Sorry!'

'What are you sorry for?' asked Brian.

'I didn't mean to be sharp with you.'

'Do you think a few sharp words from you are going to hurt me, when you have already destroyed my life and our marriage?' Brian was choking on his words.

A vision of orphaned Bambi came to him, and he almost lost control of his emotions.

Eva said, 'I've got one word to say to you . . .' She mouthed the 'T', but then bit it back. She knew that she was partly to blame for the situation they found themselves in.

She had known Brian intimately for nearly thirty years. He was part of her DNA.

Eventually, Brian said, 'I'm dying for a pee.'

He looked longingly at the en suite, but the wet paint lay between them, like half-frozen water between two icebergs. Eva pulled the cord to turn the ceiling light off, and he left to use the family bathroom.

She turned towards the window.

The was almost a full moon, shining through the skeleton of the late autumn sycamore.

Brian sat downstairs in the sitting room. What had happened to the lovely comfortable home he had once enjoyed? He looked around the room. The plants were dead, as were the flowers still standing in slimy stinking water. The lamps which had once given the room a golden glow were also dead. He couldn't be bothered to turn them on. There was no fire in the grate, and the colourful jewelled cushions that had once eased his comfort when he watched *Newsnight* at the end of the day were stacked on either side of the fireplace.

He looked up at the framed family photograph on the mantelpiece. It had been taken at Disney World. They had called in at Orlando after two weeks in Houston and he had bought Single Day Tickets. He'd been disappointed at Eva and the twins' lacklustre response when he had revealed them, and had mimed playing and singing a trumpet fanfare.

Inside the theme park, when a giant Mickey Mouse had asked in a squeaky voice if they'd like a photographic memento of their visit, Brian had agreed and handed over twenty dollars.

They had struck a pose while Brian told Eva and the twins, 'Give bigger smiles!'

The twins had bared their teeth like frightened chimpanzees, but Eva had looked steadily ahead, wondering how Mickey Mouse could manipulate the camera with his large, gloved pseudo-hands.

After the last shot, Goofy had approached, dragging his feet on the hot asphalt. Speaking through a gap between his flying-buttress teeth, he'd said to Mickey, 'Man, I just fuckin' quit.'

Mickey had answered, 'Jeez, dude! What the fuck happened?'

'That fuckin' bitch, Cinderella, just kicked me in the fuckin' balls again.'

Brian had said, 'Do you mind? I've got my children with me!'

'Children?' scoffed Goofy. 'You gotta be fuckin' kidding me! They look old, British man. They got teeth like broken rocks!'

Brian had said to Goofy, 'You can bloody talk – look at your bloody teeth! They'll be on the fucking floor if you carry on insulting my children!'

Mickey had placed himself between Brian and Goofy, saying, 'Whoah! Whoah! Come on, this is Disney World!'

Brian got up and looked closely at Eva's face in the photograph. Why hadn't he noticed before that she looked so unhappy? He took his handkerchief out of his pocket and dusted the glass and the frame, then put it back where it had stood for six years.

The house was dead now that Eva had gone.

# 22

Brianne was sitting on her narrow bed, staring at the wall opposite. Alexander had left half an hour earlier, leaving the bookcase and the jewellery, but unwittingly taking Brianne's previously unused heart with him. She was filled with the most amazing joy.

She said out loud, 'I love him.'

She wished now that she had bothered to make some friends. She wanted to ring somebody and tell them her good news. Brian Junior would not be interested, Poppy would turn news to her advantage and her mother had gone mad. There was only *him* she could tell.

She picked up his business card and reached for her mobile. He answered immediately and illegally – he was doing 75 mph and was in the middle lane of the M1, going South.

'White Van Man.'

'Alexander?'

'Brianne?'

'Yes, I forgot to thank you for bringing Mum's stuff up. It was very kind of you.'

'It wasn't kindness. It was work, Brianne. I'll get paid for it.'

'Where are you?'

'I've just turned on to the motorway. I'm trapped

between two lorries. If the front one brakes, I'm mince-meat.'

Brianne exclaimed, 'Alexander, you must turn the phone off at once!'

She could imagine his mangled body on the motor-way, surrounded by emergency vehicles. She could clearly see a helicopter hovering above him, waiting to take him to a specialist unit somewhere.

She said, 'You will take care of yourself, won't you? Your life is precious.'

He did as she had asked and switched his phone off. He didn't know the girl had such strong feelings – she had shown very little emotion when he had handed over her mother's jewellery.

Brianne went outside and walked briskly up and down in front of the accommodation block. It was a cold night and she was not dressed for the outdoors, but she didn't care. The possibility of love had softened her face and straightened her back.

How could she have lived so long without knowing of his existence?

All that love stuff that she had once despised: the hearts, the songs, moon/June, the flowers. She *wanted* him to give her a white teddy bear clutching a plastic rose. Before today she could take men or leave them, most of them were spoilt man-boys. But he – he was worthy of worship.

He looked like a black prince.

She had never allowed a man to touch her breasts, or

what she called her private bits. But as she paced in the cold she could feel her body melting, dissolving. She yearned for him. She was incomplete without him.

Poppy looked out of her window and was astonished to see Brianne walking up and down in her pyjamas, her breath visible, like ectoplasm. She rapped on the window and saw Brianne look up, wave and smile. Poppy wondered which drug she had been taking. She threw on the red silk kimono she had shoplifted from Debenhams, and hurried downstairs.

# 23

It was the day before Guy Fawkes Night, but some pre-mature fireworks were being let off as Brian and Titania joined a hastily convened staff meeting at the National Space Centre.

Titania's husband, Guy Noble, known as 'Gorilla' to his friends, had written to Professor Brady complaining that his wife was having 'a torrid sexual affair at work with that buffoon Dr Brian Beaver'. Titania had confessed to having sex in the Clean Room, which housed the next generation of moon probe. It was called *Walkers on the Moon*, after their main sponsor, a local crisp manufacturer.

All the staff were in the meeting, including the cleaners, the maintenance crew and the groundsman. It was part of Professor Brady's (aka Leather Trousers) management philosophy that his team be 'inclusive'. They were seated in the planetarium, which added an epic universal edge to their discussion.

Leather Trousers said, 'I don't care who you shag, Dr Beaver. The issue is that you chose to do it in the Clean Room. You could have polluted the atmosphere, corrupted the instrumentation and jeopardised the whole project. And ultimately defiled the surface of the moon.'

Brian asked defiantly, 'Well, *have* we?'

Leather Trousers admitted, 'No, the readings are clean. But it has taken thirty-six man and woman hours to verify – time we do not have. We are already behind schedule.'

Titania, who was hiding behind a long fringe of red hair, put her hand up and said, 'Can I just say, in my own defence, that the sex was indeed "torrid"? But the danger was minimised – we were both wearing steriles, and it was all over in ninety seconds.'

Their colleagues laughed and looked at Brian.

Various veins throbbed in his head and neck.

He was quick to retaliate. 'It was nothing but a quick leg-over.' He looked around, hoping the company would find this amusing.

There was a sharp intake of breath, and one of the cleaners squeezed Titania's hand.

Brian continued, not realising that he had volunteered to dig his own grave, '"Turgid" would better describe our affair these days.'

One of the clerical staff rushed towards the door with a handkerchief pressed to her face.

Leather Trousers said, 'C'mon, guys, let's cool it, we're all professionals, yeah? Even the cleaners, right?' He smiled at the group of cleaners to show that he valued them and their work.

Titania sobbed. 'Sex with the Gorilla went on a bit, but once he'd stumbled over my clitoris we both had good times.'

There was an appalled silence, and the cleaner withdrew her hand from Titania's.

A technician whispered to his neighbour, 'I like to experiment, but I draw the line at bestiality. That sounds bloody dangerous to me.'

Titania was surprised by Brian's obvious and public contempt for her. She arranged her fringe so that it hid the lines on her forehead, and rummaged through her handbag for the lipstick she thought took ten years off her face.

She said, in a voice that threatened to crack, 'Anyway, Brian, our lovemaking is quite often torrid.' Turning to the assembled staff, she confessed, 'Only last week he was tickling my nipples with his wife's hairbrush, and shouting that I was a dirty whore, and he was going to punish me by tying me to the large telescope and have Professor Brady take me from the rear.'

Brian jumped up and shouted, 'Not from the rear! I did not say the rear!'

Wayne Tonkin, the groundsman, laughed out loud.

Professor Brady said angrily, 'Listen, Beaver, do not include me in your sicko fantasies!'

Titania looked around the meeting and said, 'He's used you all at some time.'

Some of Brian's colleagues were repulsed by this revelation, but most were secretly pleased.

Professor Brady was in a dilemma. Could he suspend or otherwise discipline Dr Beaver for using his colleagues as sexual stimulants? Did sexual fantasies come under the heading of 'sexual harassment in the workplace'? Was there anything in their contracts that implied they had been abused by Beaver's thoughts?

Mrs Hordern straightened her overall and said, 'It's his poor wife I feel sorry for. I'll bet she's looking everywhere for that hairbrush.'

Titania said, 'Don't waste your time feeling sorry for Eva Beaver, Mrs Hordern, she's a mere lump in the bed. She never gets up! Brian has to cook his own dinner every night.'

Leather Trousers intervened. 'Look, guys, this is not helping us to move forward. Our minds should be focused on the upcoming launch of *Walkers on the Moon*.'

Wayne Tonkin said, 'And 'ow many billions of fuckin' pounds are you spendin' on another cack-'anded attempt to 'it the fuckin' moon, eh? Ain't you 'eard? The Yanks already done it in 1969. And in the meantime I 'ave to try and cut the bleedin' grass with a lawnmower what don't mow!'

Leather Trousers sometimes regretted his inclusive policy. This was one such time.

The flight operations engineers – a bolshie, troublesome group – took the opportunity to continue an earlier technical discussion about velocity. Phrases like 'regressive elliptical orbit' and 'delta-v budget' were hurled across the room.

Leather Trousers tried to shout over them, saying, 'C'mon guys!'

But no voice was louder or more vociferous than that of Wayne Tonkin, who was a Barry White tribute singer in his local pub, the Dog and Compass. His voice rattled the artificial heavens above their heads.

''Ands up who wants a new, state-of-the-art, sit-on lawnmower?'

The resolution was carried almost unanimously.

Titania was the first to leave, together with an escort of sympathetic female staff. Brian was left on his own in the room.

He was afraid he would lose his job. It had been rumoured that there were to be involuntary redundancies, and he was fifty-five, a dangerous age in a young man's game. Holes were beginning to show in Brian's knowledge. He felt that the bandwagon was rolling away from him and that, however fast he ran now, he would never be able to catch up.

# 24

Eva was lying in bed watching the night sky, which was filled with small explosions of glorious colours and shapes. She could hear a fire engine in the distance and smell the smoke of countless bonfires. She pitied all the women out there who were, at this very moment, catering for their families and guests at their bonfire parties. She thought back to bonfire night 2010, otherwise known as The Great Disaster. Brian had put up a poster at work which said:

> CALLING ALL BRIGHT SPARKS!
> Join Brian and Eva and celebrate Guy Fawkes' death!
> Catholics Beware!

Eva had shopped on the morning of the fifth. Brian had told her to prepare enough food for thirty people, so she had driven to Morrisons and bought:

60 pork sausages
2 kilos of onions
60 torpedo rolls
35 baking potatoes
a huge lump of Cheddar cheese
a slab of Heinz baked beans
30 novelty Guy Fawkes biscuits

a large bottle of Heinz tomato sauce
3 packs of butter
toffee-apple ingredients for 30
1 Guy Fawkes mask and hat
10 livestock-friendly Chinese lanterns
6 bottles of rosé wine
6 bottles of white wine
6 bottles of red wine
1 barrel of Kronenbourg
2 crates of John Smith's.

She had hurt her back hefting the Kronenbourg from the trolley into the boot of the car.

On the way home she had spent almost £200 on two boxes of assorted fireworks, and sparklers for the children.

The afternoon was taken up dragging a damp mattress from the garage down the garden and manoeuvring it on to the small bonfire, constructing an effigy of Guy Fawkes, making toffee apples (including chopping kindling for toffee-apple sticks), cleaning the downstairs lavatory, vacuuming the sitting room, deep-cleaning the kitchen, selecting listener-friendly CDs and jet-washing the patio.

Brian had asked his guests to turn up at six, so Eva filled the oven with a first sitting of potatoes at five thirty, set out the cold food and the drinks, rinsed and dried the glassware, placed candles into windproof lanterns, and waited.

*

At seven ten the doorbell finally rang and Eva heard Brian's voice saying, 'Mrs Hordern, lovely to see you. Is this Mr Hordern?' As he was taking their coats, he asked, 'Have you come in a crowd? Are the others parking?'

She said, 'No, we've come on us own.'

When they'd finally gone, Eva declared, 'That was the most excruciating night of my life – and I include in that giving birth to the twins. What happened, Brian? Do your colleagues hate you that much?'

'I can't understand it,' he replied. 'Perhaps my notice fell off the board. I only used one drawing pin.'

'Yes,' she said, 'that's what must have happened. It was the drawing pin.'

Later, as they were sharing a second bottle of burgundy, Brian asked, 'Did you notice, when I let off my Beaver Special rockets? Neither of them gave so much as an "ohhh" or an "ahhh". They just sat there, filling their stupid faces with carbohydrates and grease! I spent seven days building those. At great risk to myself. I mean, I was working with unstable materials. At any moment I could have blown myself and the sheds to smithereens.'

Eva said, 'They were very beautiful rockets, Brian.' She felt genuinely sorry for him.

She had watched his face each time he launched a rocket. He was as excited as a child, and had followed each projectile's trajectory and height with the look of a proud father watching his baby walk for the first time.

Now, Eva looked around her white room and thought, 'But that was then and this is now. I have absolutely nothing to do but to watch light move across the sky.'

# 25

Eva had been in bed for seven weeks and had lost a stone in weight. Her skin was flaky and it seemed to her that she was losing too much hair.

Sometimes Brian would bring her tea and toast. He would hand it to her with a self-pitying sigh. On many occasions the tea was cold and the toast was underdone, but she would always thank him effusively.

She needed him.

On the mornings he forgot about her, or was too rushed to think about breakfast, she went hungry. By now it was against Eva's own rules to keep food in the room. And the only drink she allowed herself was water.

One day, Ruby made an attempt to persuade Eva to drink a glass of sparking Lucozade, saying, 'This'll get you up and about. When I had pneumonia and were hovering between life and death – I were just at the mouth of the tunnel, I could see the light at the end – your dad came to visit me with a bottle of Lucozade. I took a sip and, well, I were like Frankenstein's monster after lightning struck him. I got up from my bed and walked!'

Eva said, 'So, it was nothing to do with the antibiotics they were pumping into you?'

'No!' Ruby snorted. 'My consultant, Mr Briars, admitted that he was at his wits' end. He'd tried everything, even prayer, to keep me from going down that tunnel.'

Eva said, 'So, Mr Briars – who had trained for ten years, and given lectures and written numerous papers on pneumonia – had failed you? Whereas a few sips of a sparkling glucose drink brought you back to life?'

Ruby's eyes were shining. 'Yes! It were the Lucozade what done it!'

In the early days of Eva's self-incarceration her mother-in-law, Yvonne, had cooked every other day. She was a plain, good meat and two veg cook who believed that a liberal application of Oxo gravy made every meal a gourmet feast. She was never suspicious of Eva's clean plates, believing that Eva had, at last, given up her taste for silly foreign food and had happily reverted to the traditional English cooking that Yvonne excelled at.

Yvonne must never know that her food (cooked with bad grace and many martyred sighs, crashes of pottery and slammed-down saucepans) was given to a family of foxes who had taken up residence behind an overgrown laurel in Eva's front garden. These outrageously confident creatures, bored of feeding on leftover risotto, taramasalata and suchlike from the authentically middle-class residents who were the majority in Eva's road, fought over Yvonne's chops and mince. It seemed that they too preferred traditional English food.

At about 7 p.m. on every Yvonne evening, Eva would go to the end of the bed and scrape her plate out of the open window. She loved to see the foxes eating and licking their muzzles clean. Sometimes she even imagined that the vixen looked up at the house and saluted her in a gesture of female solidarity. But this was only Eva's imagination.

Once, Yvonne had been mystified when she found a piece of liver and bacon on the porch, and one of her home-made faggots on the pavement outside Eva's house.

One day, in mid-November, Alexander called in to see Eva on his way to a job.

He said, 'Do you know you're on your way to looking like a skeleton?'

'I'm not on a diet,' Eva said.

'You need some good food inside you, food that you like. Write a list and I'll sort it out with your husband.'

Eva enjoyed thinking about the food she truly liked. She had endless time in which to think, but eventually she came up with a surprisingly small and modest selection.

'She'd soon get out of that bed if her arse was on fire,' said Ruby to Brian. 'You're too soft with her.'

'She frightens me,' admitted Brian. 'I used to look up from a book or from cutting a chop and she'd be *looking* at me.'

They were walking around Morrisons with a trolley, selecting the ingredients for Brian's evening meals. Brian had Eva's list in his pocket.

'She's always had that look,' said Ruby, pausing at the stir-fry section. 'I've often fancied doing a stir-fry, but I haven't got a wonk.'

Brian couldn't be bothered to correct his mother-in-law. He wanted to concentrate on Eva and the reason why she wouldn't leave what used to be called 'their' bed.

He wasn't a bad husband, he thought. He'd never hit her, not hard. There had been a bit of pushing and shoving, and once – after he'd found a Valentine's Day card she'd received and hidden behind the boiler that said: 'Eva, leave him, come to me' – he had dangled her upside down from the landing. It had been a joke, of course. True, he'd had trouble pulling her back over the balustrade, and at one point it had looked like he might drop her on to the tiles below. But there had been absolutely no need for Eva to scream as loudly as she did. It was pure exhibitionism.

She had very little sense of humour, he thought – though he had often heard her laughing with other people in the next room.

He and Titania were always laughing. They shared a love of Benny Hill and The Goons. Titania could do a side-splitting impression of Benny singing 'Ernie (The Fastest Milkman In The West)'. She hadn't minded being thrown in the reservoir at Rutland Water either. She'd laughed it off.

Now Ruby was asking him how much wonks cost.

He guessed and told her, 'About forty pounds.'

She shuddered and said, 'No, I might not get the use out of it, I'm living on borrowed time as it is.'

Brian took out Eva's shopping list. He showed it to Ruby and they both laughed. Eva had written:

2 croissants
basil plant
large bag mixed nuts
hand of bananas
box of grapes (seedless if poss)
6 eggs laid by free roamers
2 tubes of Smarties for Alex's kids
Red Leicester cheese
1 bag mozzarella
2 firm beef tomatoes
small sea salt
1 black and red pepper pot
4 large bottles of San Pellegrino ($H_2O$)
2 cartons grapefruit juice
serrated-edge knife
bottle extra virgin olive oil
bottle balsamic vinegar
1 large bottle vodka (not Smirnoff)
2 large bottles diet tonic (only Schweppes)
*Vogue*
*Private Eye*
*The Spectator*
Dunhill Menthol cigarettes.

After crying with laughter, Ruby needed to mop her tears. Neither of them had a handkerchief but, as they were walking down the toilet roll aisle, Ruby opened a packet of Andrex and took out a roll. She failed to find the end of the tissue, so Brian took it from her and located the end, which was infuriatingly stuck to the other sheets underneath. After a few moments' struggle, he bellowed his frustration, then tore a wad of paper out of the roll and stuffed the rest back on to the shelf.

Ruby laughed for a long time when they found the San Pellegrino, and even longer when she saw the extra virgin olive oil. 'I used to pour olive oil in Eva's lugholes when she had the earache,' she said. 'And now she's pouring it on her salad.' She was scandalised in the news and magazine section, when she saw the price of *Vogue*. 'Four pounds ten? I can buy two bags of oven chips for that! She's havin' a laugh, Brian. If I were you, I'd starve her out of bed.' The croissants provoked another outburst. 'They're nothing but a few flakes of pastry and air!'

'She's always been a snob about food,' Brian said.

'It's since she went to Paris with the school,' said Ruby. 'She came back full of herself. It was all *merci* and *bonjour* and, "Oh the *bread*, Mum!" And she had that little woman with the voice that grates on you playing night and day.'

'Edith Piaf,' said Brian. 'A frog I'm very familiar with indeed.'

'She went back after she left school,' said Ruby. 'She worked in a chip shop doing double shifts for her ticket to Paris.'

Brian was amazed. 'She didn't tell me this. How long was she there?'

'It were exactly a year. She came back with a Louis Vuitton case full of the most beautiful clothes and shoes.

Handmade! And the perfume! Big bottles. She'd never talk about it. I think some rich French ponce broke her heart.'

They were blocking the aisle. A young woman with a toddler sitting in the trolley crashed into them. The toddler shouted, 'Again!'

'What did she do in France?' asked Brian. 'And why didn't she tell me about this Paris jaunt?'

Ruby said, 'She was a secretive girl, and she's turned into a secretive woman. Now, where's this bleedin' sea salt when it's at home?'

Eva gave Brian instruction on how to assemble a tomato and mozzarella salad.

She said, 'Please don't add or subtract any of the ingredients, and I beg you to keep to the quantities.'

She told him which plate to use and which napkin. This precision made Brian even more cack-handed than usual.

Had he overdone the extra virgin oil? Did she say to tear the basil, or cut? Should he add lemon and ice to her vodka and tonic? She hadn't said, so he left them out.

She could smell the basil and tomatoes before he pushed the bedroom door open with his foot.

He placed the tray on her lap and stood by the bed, waiting for her approval.

She saw at once that the tomatoes had been cut thickly with a blunt knife, that the stalks were still on the basil and that it obviously hadn't been washed. Despite her strict instruction not to add anything else, Brian had improvised a pattern around the edge of the plate with dried oregano.

She managed to contain herself, and when he asked, 'All right?' she answered, 'My mouth is watering.'

She was truly grateful to him. She knew how difficult it was to run a household and keep down a full-time job.

And she suspected he was missing Titania.

# 26

It was six thirty in the morning. Hoar frost had decorated the trees and shrubs overnight, giving an ethereal glow to the Space Centre car park as Mrs Hordern approached. It was obvious to her by the positions of the randomly parked cars that something big had happened. Normally, each member of staff parked strictly in their designated places. In the past, there had been fist fights over trivial infringements of the Conditions of Use (which were displayed behind glass in a slender cabinet on top of a wooden stake in a far corner of the car park).

Mrs Hordern met Wayne Tonkin coming out of the Research Block as she was going in.

'What's up?' she asked, nodding towards the car park.

Wayne said, 'I hope you've not booked yer 'olidays, Mrs Hordern, cos we're all being burned to a crisp next week.'

'What time?'

'High noon,' he said, making an effort to pronounce the aitch.

'So, I needn't bother buying a Christmas tree then?' She gave a little laugh, expecting Wayne to join in.

'No,' said Wayne.

When Mrs Hordern went inside, she saw that the staff had come straight from their beds.

Leather Trousers was in a pair of pale-blue silk pyjamas. For once, he did not give her his Hollywood smile.

'What's goin' on?' she asked.

'Nothing, nothing at all,' he replied. 'The earth is still turning.'

Mrs Hordern went into the staff cloakroom to hang her coat and change out of her boots into the Crocs she wore at work. She heard sobbing coming from a lavatory cubicle. She knew it was Titania because Dr Clever Clogs often went to the cloakroom to cry. Mrs Hordern knocked on the lavatory door and asked Titania if she could help in any way.

She was rebuffed when the door opened and Titania shouted, 'I think not! Do you understand the Standard Model of particle physics and its place in the space–time continuum, Mrs Hordern?'

The cleaner admitted that she did not.

'Well, butt out then! My problem is entirely related to my research, which I will now never complete. I've given my life to those particles!'

As Mrs Hordern walked the corridor, pushing the floor-washing machine in front of her, she thought, 'Things are not right.'

When she passed the door labelled 'Near-Earth Objects', Brian Beaver burst out and shouted, 'For Christ's sake, turn that fucking machine off! We're trying to think in here!'

Mrs Hordern said, 'That may be so, but this floor's

not going to clean itself, is it? No need to swear. I won't have it at home, and I'm not having it here!'

Brian retreated to his desk, where banks of computers were displaying rapidly scrolling numbers and a flashing red trajectory that intersected with a large spherical object. The room was crowded with people silently watching the screens. Several of his colleagues jostled closer and peered nervously over his shoulder as his fingers flew across the keyboard.

Leather Trousers said, 'It might be good if you checked your Australian data again, Dr Beaver, before the eyes of the world are upon us. It's kinda important that we get this right.'

Brian said, 'I'm almost certain. But the computer models don't all agree.'

'Almost!' bellowed Leather Trousers. 'Do we wake the Prime Minister, the Secretary General of the United Nations and the President of the United States and tell them that we're *almost* certain that the earth is fucked?'

Brian explained pedantically, 'You don't wake the President. The call will go to the NASA Political Liaison officer in Washington.' Then he continued weakly, 'It could be that the metadata from the star maps is corrupted. We've always known that our database integration was potentially suspect. And I trusted Dr Abbot's interpolation techniques –'

Leather Trousers shouted, 'And where is she when we need her? On fucking maternity leave up her precious Welsh mountain, suckling that moon-faced dribbler, with no landline, no mobile signal, and the most high-tech thing she's got in that mould-filled hovel she calls a cottage is a fucking Dualit toaster! Get hold of the leek-muncher!'

Several hours later, when Mrs Hordern passed the office again with the electric polishing machine, she looked in warily through the half-open door and saw a small crowd of people laughing and shaking hands. The scene reminded her of Skippy, the television kangaroo, when he and his human friends had overcome their difficulties at the end of each episode.

Brian was sitting apart, with his hands linked together, staring down at the floor.

As Mrs Hordern left work, she passed Wayne Tonkin. He was polishing his new sit-on lawnmower.

He stopped and said, 'So, the world ain't finishin' next week. Dickhead Beaver got his sums wrong. That aster-oid's gonna miss us by twenty-seven million miles.'

'I was sort of looking forward to there being no Christmas,' said Mrs Hordern. 'It's such hard work. No bugger lifts a finger in my house, 'part from me.'

Wayne rolled his eyes and turned the lawnmower engine on. He was longing to use it, but the bastard wea-ther wouldn't let him for a few months yet.

## 27

Brian Junior and Brianne were not quite sure how Poppy came to be in their dad's car when he drove them back from Leeds to Leicester for the Christmas holiday. Neither of them wanted her in the car, or in their house, and the prospect of spending four weeks with her appalled and horrified them both.

Poppy had been told that Brian was expected and she hung about in the lobby downstairs, waiting to introduce herself to him. She had overheard the twins laughing about their father's abysmal dress sense – and she had seen a photograph she knew to be Dr Beaver, in which his face was lurking behind a straggling black beard – so she knew what to look for. Several likely candidates walked through the lobby before Dr Beaver appeared.

When Brian pressed the button to summon the groaning lift, Poppy slipped in beside him and said, 'This lift's awfully slow. I sometimes think that I'm in a Samuel Beckett play.'

Brian laughed. He had played Lucky in a student production of *Waiting for Godot* and had won praise for his 'frenetic energy'.

While they slowly ascended to the sixth floor, Poppy told Brian that her parents were in a coma at Ninewells

Hospital in Dundee. It was the first time she would be alone at Christmas, she told him.

Brian thought she might cry. His heart went out to her.

Poppy had a quick flash of memory. It was the Ninewells Hospital Wikipedia page. She gave him a big brave smile and said, 'But Mum and Dad are lucky, in a way. They're in the first Frank Gehry building in Britain. Bob Geldof opened it. I can't wait to tell them . . . when they wake up.'

'Yeah, I like Gehry's work,' said Brian. 'Very space age. It's much like the module we intend to build, well, on the moon.' When she asked him what he did for a living, he said, 'I'm Dr Brian Beaver, I'm an astronomer.'

Poppy squealed and clapped her hands together. 'Wow!' she said. 'That's what I want to be! What an amazing coincidence!'

Brian agreed, and said, 'It is, indeed, amazing.'

Then she slapped her hand over her mouth and said, 'OMG! You must be Brianne's dad, he's an astronomer!'

'Guilty as charged,' said Brian. He thought Poppy was a sweetheart, enchanting, with her wild hair and pale skin. Her sinewy, exotic sexuality diverted him from asking any further questions about her unlikely astronomical aspirations.

'So, what will you do for Christmas?' he asked. 'Where will you go?'

'Oh, I'll just stay here and go out for walks. I've no

money. I've spent it all visiting Mum and Dad,' she explained, wistfully.

There was a companionable silence for a moment.

'So, you know Brianne?'

'Know her? We're the best of friends. I can't bear the thought of being apart from her for four whole weeks.'

She smiled bravely, but Brian could see that the poor kid was crying inside. He didn't take long to decide. When they got out of the lift, he told her to pack a bag and gave her his car keys.

'When you're ready, go and sit in the silver Peugeot Estate. It'll be a fantastic surprise for the twins.'

Poppy fell on his neck, uttering thanks and other appreciative sounds that were not quite words.

Brian held her tight, laughing at first, but as she continued her iron grip around his neck he began to take notice of her young, firm flesh and the musky perfume she wore. He instructed himself to think about the gristly meat he had been forced to swallow at school dinners – it usually did the trick.


The twins travelled down in the lift, leaving their father to use Brian Junior's en-suite lavatory in preparation for the hundred-mile journey back to Leicester.

Brianne said, 'Four weeks without that crazy cow.'

Brian Junior smiled one of his rare smiles. Before the lift door opened, they unsuccessfully executed a high five.

Brianne said, 'Brian Junior, you never get the *timing*

right! How many have we practised? You must be hopeless in bed. You have absolutely no sense of rhythm.'

'I had enough to impregnate Poppy.'

'You can't make a woman pregnant if you keep your underpants on and don't get an erection.'

'I know *that*! I also know that if you don't let the sperm out, your balls explode.'

They left the warmth of the building and emerged into a confluence of harsh winds and snow flurries. They approached their father's car and saw somebody sitting in the front passenger seat.

As they neared the car the front passenger door opened, and Poppy shouted, 'Surprise!'

The journey was horrible.

The boot was full of Poppy's suitcases and black bin liners bulging with her mad clothes and customised boots and shoes. Brianne and Brian Junior sat uncomfortably with their own luggage jammed in around them.

Poppy talked all the way from Leeds to Leicester. If he hadn't been driving, Brian would have sat at her feet – as if she were Homer and wise beyond her years.

He thought, 'She's the daughter I should have had, a girl whose shoe size is smaller than mine. Who takes forever in the bathroom, titivating herself – unlike Brianne, who sounds like a grunting pig when she washes her face and is out of the bathroom in two minutes.'

Brian Junior thought about the tadpole baby inside Poppy's womb. He couldn't remember what had happened on the night she came into his bed. The images he summoned up were a tangle of arms and legs and heat and a fish-finger smell, the clash of teeth, of rapid breathing, and an unimaginably wonderful feeling of falling away out of his mortal body and into an unexpected universe.

Brianne wanted to rid the world of Poppy, and spent the journey planning in detail how it could be done.

As they turned off the motorway at junction 21 Brian tried to prepare the twins for the 'changes in our domestic arrangements'.

He told them, 'Mum's been a bit off colour.'

'Is that why she hasn't phoned us for three months?' said Brianne bitterly.

Poppy turned her head and said, 'That's shocking – a mother not ringing her children.'

Brian said, 'You're right, Poppy.'

Brian Junior said to Brianne, 'We could have kept trying.'

## 28

Eva was longing to hold the twins in her arms, especially since she wouldn't have to clean their rooms or put clean sheets on their beds, and somebody else would be responsible for their meals and buying their Christmas presents. And perhaps it was Brian's turn to be irritated by their sloth and mess.

'Yes,' she thought. 'Yes, let somebody else grovel under their beds and retrieve the cereal bowls with the dried-on milk and sugar, and the mugs and plates. The brown apple cores, dried banana peel and the dirty socks.' She laughed out loud in her pure, white room.

Brianne and Brian Junior were shocked when they saw their mother sitting up in bed in the white box that used to be their parents' bedroom. Eva held her arms wide open, and the twins shuffled into them.

She could not speak. She was overcome with the pleasure of holding them, of feeling their bodies – which had perceptibly changed in the three months since she had last seen them.

Brianne needed her hair cutting. Eva thought, 'I'll give her sixty quid, so she can go somewhere decent.'

Brian Junior was agitated – Eva could feel the tightening of his muscles – and unusually he had allowed several days' worth of stubble to grow on his face, which she thought made him resemble a blond Orlando Bloom. However, Brianne's black facial hair cried out for a waxing appointment.

They pulled away from her and sat awkwardly on the edge of the bed.

Eva said, 'Well, tell me everything. Are you happy at Leeds?'

The twins looked at each other, and Brianne said, 'We are, apart from –'

Eva heard somebody downstairs exclaim, 'Wow, I already feel at home!'

The twins exchanged another look, and they got up and hurried out.

Brian shouted upstairs, 'Twins, help me with this luggage!'

There was a thundering of footsteps on the stairs and landing, and then a strange-looking girl in a tatty cocktail dress, which she wore with an old man's dressing gown, the cord of which she had wound around her head Gaddafi-style, threw herself into Eva's arms. Eva patted her back and shoulders and noticed that the girl's white bra straps were filthy.

'Bob Geldof has been keeping a twenty-four-hour vigil at the side of my parents' beds,' announced the extraordinary girl.

Eva asked, 'Why?'

'You don't know?' the girl said. 'I'm Poppy. I'm Brianne and Brian Junior's best friend.'

Eva could hear Brian Junior and Brianne grunting as

they staggered up the stairs with Poppy's luggage, and was startled when Poppy shouted, 'I hope that's not my luggage you're throwing about. There are precious objets d'art in those cases.' She got up from Eva's bed and went into the bathroom, where she left the door ajar.

A few seconds later, Eva heard Poppy's one-sided conversation.

'Hello, Peaches Ward, please.'

Silence.

'Hello, is that Sister Cooke?'

Silence.

'I'm very well. I'm staying with friends in the country.'

Silence.

'How are Mum and Dad?'

Silence.

'Oh no! Should I come up?'

Silence.

'Are you sure? I could easily –'

Silence.

'How long do you think they've got? Tell me, I need to know!'

Silence.

'No! No! Not six weeks! I wanted them to *be* there when I graduated.'

Silence.

'It breaks my heart when I think that this will be their last Christmas! [Pause] Thank you, Sister, but I only do what any loving daughter would do for her dying parents.'

Silence.

'Yes, I wish I had the money to visit them over the Christmas holiday, but I am penniless, Sister. I've spent my money on rail fares and, er . . . grapes.'

Silence.

'No, I am an only child and I have no living relations. My family were wiped out in the last Chicken Flu epidemic. But, hey ho.'

Silence.

'No, I'm not brave. If I were [sob] brave [sob], I wouldn't be crying now.'

Eva slid down the pillows and pretended to be asleep. She heard Poppy come back into the bedroom, give a tut of annoyance and stomp out in her workman's boots, which she wore without laces. The boots clumped down the stairs, out of the front door and into the street.

Brian, Brianne and Brian Junior were on the landing, discussing whose room they should take Poppy's luggage to.

Brian Junior sounded uncharacteristically vehement. 'Not mine, *please*, not mine.'

Brianne said, 'You invited her, Dad. She ought to sleep in *your* room.'

Brian said, 'Things are bad between me and Mum. I'm sleeping in the shed, at Mum's request.'

Brianne said, 'Oh God! Are you getting a divorce?'

Brian Junior asked, at exactly the same time, 'So, will we be buying two Christmas trees this year, Dad? One for us in the house, and one for you in the shed?'

Brian said, 'Why are you wittering on about divorce and bloody Christmas trees? My heart is breaking as we speak here. But never mind about silly old Dad! Why should he enjoy the warmth and light of the house he's still bloody paying for?'

He would have liked his children to give him a comforting hug. He remembered watching *The Waltons* on television, when he was young. His mother would be making up her face, preparing to go out with whoever was the latest 'uncle'. Brian remembered the smell of her powder and how deft she was with the little brushes. The last scene, when the whole family said goodnight to each other, had always brought a lump to his throat.

But instead, Brianne said angrily, 'So, where do we put the mad cow's luggage?'

Brian said, 'She's your best pal, Brianne. I naturally assumed that she would sleep in your room.'

'My best pal! I'd sooner have an incontinent tramp with mental health issues as my "best pal" than that . . .'

Brianne could not properly articulate her loathing. She had come home to find her mother permanently in bed, in a stark-white box, obviously mad, and now her father expected her to share a room with that bloodsucking vampire, Poppy, who had ruined her first term at university.

The luggage was still on the landing when Poppy rang Brian to say that 'an old man with a horribly scarred face' had followed her from the newsagent's where she'd been buying her Rizlas. She had called the police and was hiding from him in a park nearby.

Brian said into his mobile, 'That's almost certainly

Stanley Crossley, he's a lovely man, he lives at the end of our road.'

Brianne snatched the phone from her father. 'His face is scarred because he was almost burned alive in a Spitfire. Or have you never heard of the Second World War? Phone the police now and tell them you've made a mistake!'

But it was too late. They could hear the sirens wailing outside. Poppy disconnected the call.

Eva punched the pillows in her rage and frustration. Her peace had been shattered. She didn't want to hear raised voices outside her bedroom door, or sirens in the street. And she didn't want that mad girl to spend another five minutes in her house. The Stanley Crossley she knew was a reserved and polite man who never failed to lift his hat when he and Eva passed in the street.

Once, only last spring, he had joined her on the wooden bench he had bought as a memorial to his wife, Peggy. They had exchanged banal observations about the weather. Then, out of nowhere, he had talked about Sir Archie McIndoe, the surgeon who had reconstructed his face, giving him eyelids, a nose and ears.

'I was a boy,' he had said. 'Eighteen. I had been handsome. There were no mirrors in the Nissen huts where the other boys and I lived.'

Eva had thought that he might continue, but he had got up from the bench, tipped his hat and made his ungainly way to the local shops.

Now Eva lay back on the pillows. She could hear Brian Junior and Brianne bickering in the next room.

She had meant to visit Stanley, who only lived a hundred or so yards away. She had intended to invite him for tea. She imagined a white tablecloth, a cake stand, and cucumber sandwiches arranged in triangles on a china platter. But to her shame, despite passing his front door at least twice a day, she had issued no such invitation.

Eva was furious with Brian. Bringing Poppy into an already tense household was like introducing nitroglycerine into a bouncy castle. She said, 'Brian, go and find that malicious little cow. She is your responsibility.'

A couple of minutes later, she watched Brian hurrying in his carpet slippers towards the end of the road, where police cars, motorcycles and a dog van were trying to park.

Brian approached a thickset policewoman. He wondered who or what had given her such a very badly broken nose.

He said, 'I think I can clear up this stalking nonsense.'

'Are you the gentleman we are looking for, sir?' asked Sergeant Judith Cox.

'Certainly not! I am Dr Brian Beaver.'

'Are you here in a medical capacity, Dr Beaver?'

'No, I am an astronomer.'

'So, you are you not a medical doctor, sir?'

'I believe a medical doctor trains for only seven years, whereas we professional astronomers are still in training until the day we die. New stars and new theories are born every day, Sergeant –'

'Beaver, sir? As in "agile little dam-builder"?' Before

Brian could speak again, she added, 'There is one question I'd like you to answer, Dr Beaver.'

Brian put on his professional, listening face.

'I'm Aries. I've just been asked out by a constable of my acquaintance. My question is, he's Sagittarius, are we compatible?'

Brian retorted angrily, 'I said *astronomer*. Are you trying to provoke me, Sergeant?'

She laughed. 'Only joking, sir! I don't like being called a pig by the public either.'

Brian failed to see the comparison, but he went on, 'I can personally vouch for the character of Stanley Crossley. He is a scholar and a gentleman, and I only wish that England had more like him.'

Sergeant Cox said, 'That may be true, sir, but I believe Peter Sutcliffe's exquisite manners are legendary in Broadmoor.' She listened to the crackling of her lapel radio, said, 'No, mine's the beef chow mein with the oyster sauce,' into it, raised her hand to Brian and went into the park to interview Poppy, the stalkee.

Eva was kneeling on her bed, looking out of the window, when Stanley Crossley went by in a police car. She thought he might look at the house, so she waved, but he stared ahead. There was nothing she could do to help him, and there was nothing she could do to help herself. She was filled with a savage rage and understood, for the first time, how easy it would be to murder somebody.

Another police car passed the house. Poppy was sitting in the back, apparently weeping.

Eva watched Brian plodding up the road, his beard blowing in the wind, his head down against a flurry of snow. She dreaded him coming upstairs and reporting what had happened.

'In fact, at this moment,' she thought, 'I could happily murder *him*.'

Brian bustled into Eva's dark room, looking like an eager, hairy, Hermes anxious to impart his message. He switched the overhead light on and said, 'Poppy is distraught, suicidal and downstairs. I don't know what to do with her.'

Eva asked, 'How is Stanley?'

'You know what these old servicemen are like – stiff upper lip. Oh Christ!' Brian exclaimed. 'I shouldn't have said that, given that he actually *has* a stiff upper lip. What's the politically correct way of referring to somebody like Stanley, I wonder?'

Eva said, 'You simply call him Stanley.'

'I have a message from him. He'd like to call and see you, before Christmas.'

'Can you bring my chair up?' Eva asked.

'The soup chair?'

She nodded, and said, 'I need to talk to people face to face, and with Christmas coming . . .'

# 29

The next morning, when Brian and Brian Junior carried the lovely chair in and set it at the side of the bed, Eva asked, 'So, what's Ms Melodrama doing now?'

'She says she's got pains in her belly,' said Brianne, appearing in the doorway.

'The police were quite rough with her, apparently,' said Brian.

'That could mean a police officer raised their voice to her. She doesn't look like somebody who's been roughed up in the cells.' Brianne looked accusingly at Brian. 'Send her away, Dad! Now!'

'I can't send a penniless young girl out into the snow a fortnight before Christmas, can I?'

'She's hardly the Little Match Girl! She'll always land on her feet!'

Brian Junior agreed. 'Poppy will always win. She believes that she is superior to everybody else in the world. She thinks we are subhuman, here only to serve her.'

Poppy appeared in the doorway, clutching her belly. She said faintly, 'I've sent for an ambulance. I think I'm having a miscarriage.'

Brian moved forward and supported her to the soup chair.

She said, 'I can't lose this baby, Brian Junior. It's all I have . . . now that I've lost you.'

Eva remarked, 'The awful dilemma we have here, Brian, is that she might be telling the truth.'

Eva watched from her bed as Poppy was carried out to the ambulance. She was wrapped in a red blanket.

Snow was falling heavily now.

Poppy raised a hand and waved weakly to Eva.

Eva did not wave back. Her heart was as cold as the pavement outside. She wanted rid of the interloper.

At eleven o'clock that night, a hospital clerk rang to say that Poppy had been discharged, and could someone give her a lift home?

When Brian arrived at the Accident and Emergency waiting room, he found Poppy lying across three plastic chairs, with a cardboard bowl in her hands and a wad of tissues held to her mouth.

She said, 'Thank God you're here, Dr Beaver! I was hoping it would be you.'

Brian was touched by her pallor and the delicacy of her fingers holding the bowl. He put a hand beneath her shoulders and lifted her until she was upright. She was shivering. Brian took off his fleece jacket and made her put it on. He borrowed a wheelchair and asked her to sit in it, though she protested, 'I'm perfectly able to walk.'

The snow had coated the pavements and buildings, giving a gentle edge to the brutalist hospital blocks. When they got to Brian's car, he unlocked the doors, picked Poppy up in his arms, lowered her gently on to the back seat and covered her with a blanket. He abandoned the wheelchair on the edge of the car park. Normally, he would have taken it back to where he found it, but he did not want to be away from her for too long.

He drove home carefully. The main roads had been gritted, but the snow was falling so fast that the grit was soon covered in fresh snow.

Every now and then, Poppy whimpered.

Brian turned his head as far as it would go and said, 'Not long now, little one. We'll soon have you home and in bed.' He wanted to ask her if she had miscarried the baby, but he recognised that he knew very little about women and their emotions, and he was nervous about discussing gynaecological mechanics.

Soon he was driving through a blizzard. He opened his window but could not see the verge of the pavement. He carried on for a few minutes and then, only a hundred yards from the house, he stopped the car but kept the engine running.

Poppy sat up and said weakly, 'I love the snow, don't you, Dr Beaver?'

Brian said, 'Please, call me Brian. It's certainly a fascinating substance. Did you know, Poppy, that no two snowflakes are the same?'

Poppy gasped, though she had known this about snowflakes since she was at infants school. 'So, each is unique?' she said, with wonderment in her voice.

Brian recalled, 'The twins played snowflakes in their first nativity play. The imbecilic teacher had made them *identical* costumes. Nobody else in the audience noticed, but I did. It spoiled the whole thing for me.'

Poppy said, 'I was always Mary.'

Brian looked at her intently. 'Yes, I can see why you were chosen.'

'Do you mean you can tell that I'm the chosen one?'

'Oh yes,' said Brian.

Poppy reached forward, took Brian's hand off the steering wheel and kissed it. She manoeuvred herself into the front of the car, over the gearstick, and sat on his lap. She said in her little-girl voice, 'Are you my new daddy?'

Brian remembered the last time Titania had sat on his knee. She'd put on weight recently and the experience had been rather painful. Now he wanted to push Poppy into the passenger seat, before his todger came to life, but she had her arms around his neck and was stroking his beard and calling him 'Daddy'.

He found all of this to be irresistible. He did things that were, as everyone said these days, 'completely inappropriate'. And he was flattered to think that such a lovely young innocent girl could be attracted to a 55-year-old fool like himself.

He wondered if Titania would be waiting for him in the shed. Perhaps the snow had prevented her from making her usual journey – he hoped not, because he needed a woman tonight.


When the blizzard had abated, and it was a mere snow-storm, Brian and Poppy got out of the car and walked to the house.

Eva saw them arrive at the gate.

Brian was beaming, and Poppy was whispering something in his ear.

Eva knocked so fiercely on the window that one of the panes broke. Snow rushed in like water through a dyke, then melted slowly in the heat.

## 30

The next morning, Eva was sitting cross-legged on the bed as Alexander replaced the broken glass, squeezing putty around the pane like she used to squeeze pastry around the edge of a pie to make a fluted pattern.

She said, 'Is there anything you can't do?'

'I can't play the saxophone, I don't know the rules of croquet, I can't remember my wife's face. My navigation is crap. I can't pole-vault, and I'm hopeless at fist-fighting.'

Eva admitted, 'I can't tune a digital radio. I gave up after a day with my smartphone. On my computer the Microsoft wouldn't engage with the internet, and neither could I. I couldn't watch a film on an iPad – and why should I, when there's a cinema half a mile away? I should have been born a hundred years ago. I can't download on my MP3 machine. Why do people keep buying me these gadgets? I'd be happier with a simple radio, a television with knobs on the front, a Dansette record player and a phone like we had when I was a child. Something important that stood on the hall table. It rang so loudly that we could hear it all over the house and garden. And it only rang when there was something important to say. Somebody was ill. An arrangement had to be changed. Or the person who had been ill had died. People ring now to say that they've arrived in McDonald's and are about to order a cheeseburger and fries.'

Alexander laughed. 'You're a technophobe like me, Eva. We're happier with a simpler way of life. I should go back to Tobago.'

Eva said, vehemently, 'No! You can't!'

He laughed again. 'Take it easy, Eva. I'm going nowhere. It costs a lot of money to have a slower pace of life, and I had my one shot at that.'

She asked, 'Do you ever talk about your wife?'

'No. Never. If the kids ask, I lie and say she's gone to heaven. My children believe that she is up there in the arms of Jesus, and I ain't gonna disabuse them of that comforting picture.'

'Was your wife beautiful?' Eva said, quietly.

'No, not beautiful. Pretty, elegant – and she looked after herself. Her clothes were always good, she had her own style. Other women were a bit afraid of her. She never wore a tracksuit, didn't own a pair of trainers. She didn't do casual.'

Eva glanced at her ragged nails and slid them under the duvet.

The door opened abruptly, and Brianne said, 'Oh, Alex, I didn't know you were here. Would you like a cup of tea, or a drink perhaps? It is nearly Christmas, after all.'

'Thank you, but I have to work and drive.'

Eva said, 'I'd love a cup of tea.'

Brianne's expression changed when she looked at her mother. 'Well, I am busy, but I'll try to bring you one up.'

There were a few moments of awkwardness between the three of them.

Brianne said to Alexander, 'Bye then. See you downstairs?'

He said, 'Maybe,' and turned back to the window. 'I'll make you a cup of tea, Eva, when I've finished this.'

There was an uneasy atmosphere in the house over the next week.

There were silences and whisperings and slammed doors. The women circled around each other. Eva tried to interest them in decorating the house and stringing up the fairy lights, and they would agree with her that it should be done – however, nobody actually did anything.

Poppy had made her base in the sitting room. She had commandeered every item of furniture for her possessions and clothes, so the Beavers had taken to sitting in the kitchen. Whenever Brian and Poppy met accidentally in the house, they managed to touch each other briefly, and both enjoyed the conspiracy. Brian particularly relished the contact – especially on the nights when Titania was waiting for him in the shed.

## 31

On the evening of the 19th of December, Brian asked Eva, 'What are we doing for Christmas?'

Eva said, 'I'll be doing nothing at all.'

Brian was shocked. 'So, you're expecting *me* to do *Christmas*?' He rose from the soup chair and walked up and down the room, looking like a prisoner on Death Row waiting for the dawn.

Eva forced herself to stay silent as Brian faced the awful fact that he might have to be responsible for Christmas, the Becher's Brook of family festivals. Many good women, and a few men, have fallen due to the weight of expectation that rests on their shoulders.

'I don't even know where you *keep* Christmas,' he said, as though in previous years Eva had deposited Christmas inside a locked container at an out-of-town storage depot, and all she had to do was pick Christmas up and take it home before December the 25th.

'Do you want me to tell you how to do Christmas, Brian?'

'I suppose so.'

Eva advised him, 'You may want to take notes.'

Brian took out of his pocket the little black notebook with moleskin covers that Eva had bought for him as compensation for failing his motorcycle exam. (He had argued with the examiner over the precise meaning of the phrase 'full throttle'.) He unclipped his fountain pen (a school prize) and waited.

'OK,' said Eva. 'I'm going to talk you through. Stop me at any time.'

Brian sat back down in the soup chair with his pen poised above his notebook.

Eva took a breath and started.

'You'll find the Christmas card list in the bureau in the sitting room, together with stamps and unused cards. Write them tonight, before you go to bed. After work tomorrow, drive around garden centres and garage fore-courts looking at Christmas trees. In your mind's eye you are seeing a perfect tree, lushly green and aromatic, rounded at the bottom and rising in ever-decreasing cir-cles until topped with a single branch. However, there are no such trees. You drive around all week and fail to find one. At nine p.m. the day before Christmas Eve, just as Homebase is closing, you will panic and push through the doors and snatch at the nearest tree. Do not be too disappointed when you end up with a tree a social worker would describe as "failing to thrive".'

Brian said, 'For Christ's *sake*, Eva, stick to the bloody *list*!'

Eva closed her eyes and tried to discipline herself to keep to the bare facts of how she had prepared for Christmas 2010.

'Tree decorations in box marked "TD". Fairy lights for tree in box marked "FLFT". Fairy lights for sitting room, kitchen, dining room, hall stairs, outdoor porch in box named "FL General". *Do not* throw horrible papier-mâché bells or similar cack-handed ornaments away. Brian Junior and Brianne made them in infants school before they fully discovered maths. NB – box of extension leads and multiple plug sockets in box marked "Christmas Electricals". Note – spare bulbs for FLs in here. All boxes to be found in attic next to wooden giraffe. Stepladder in cellar. Buy firelighters, kindling and logs from Farm Shop in Charnwood Forest. Pick three bags of coal up from BP garage. Buy candles for candlesticks – open bracket, check widths, close bracket.

'Drive into countryside for mistletoe, ivy, pine cones, branches and seed heads. Dry out on radiators. Buy silver and gold spray paint. Spray dried-out foliage, et cetera. Clear out fridge – use disparate leftovers to make strange little meals, flavours disguised by chilli flakes and garlic. Go to local butcher, order a turkey. Watch him laugh in your face. Go to supermarket, try to order a turkey. Leave to the sound of laughter from the poultry department. Buy ten tins of Quality Street for fifty quid. Queue for an hour and ten minutes to pay for them. Decide how much to spend on distant or near relations, trawl round shops, ignore present list and make ludicrous impulse buys. Arrive home, unload presents, immediately suffer from buyer's remorse. Take everything back the following day and buy twenty-seven pairs of red fleece socks with reindeer motif. Go online, order latest technical must-have gadget for Brian and twins, find that there are none left in the country, go to Currys and get told by youth that a container ship has just docked at Harwich and lorry is due to deliver on 23rd December. Ask if you can order three of the latest must-haves. Currys youth advises you to join queue at five thirty a.m. as this will be your only chance.'

Brian said, 'Eva, that was last Christmas! I need to focus on this year! Half of your advice is redundant!'

But Eva was reliving the nightmare of Christmas 2010.

'Go late-night shopping for Christmas outfit for self, to prevent row like last year's when Brian said, "Eva, you can't wear jeans on Christmas day." Make impulse buy of red sequinned cardigan and black lace skirt. In Marks, buy twins pyjamas and dressing gowns, ditto Brian. In food hall, buy ingredients for Christmas dinner for six, plus cakes, biscuits, flans, mince pies, sliced bread for sandwiches, salmon, et cetera, et cetera, et cetera –'

Brian interjected, panicking now, 'How can one person possibly deal with all those different components?'

But Eva couldn't stop.

'Poultry supervisor says must queue from four a.m. to guarantee getting a turkey. Stagger outside with bags, cannot find car, ring police to report stolen car, then remember just before police arrive that came by taxi, ring taxi firm for return journey, harassed-sounding man says, "Not a chance, we're fully booked for office parties." Ring friends, they have all had a drink, ring relatives, Ruby says, "It's eleven thirty. How can I help? I haven't got a car." Phone runs out of battery, hurl it in temper into prickly car-park bush. Calm down and search for phone. Find phone but scratched and bleeding from search. Eventually husband reports you missing, police say they will keep an eye out, patrol car delivers you home at one thirty a.m. Snatch two hours' sleep before driving car to Marks & Spencer to join queue. At four a.m. nineteenth in queue. Dressed turkey's gone, no choice but to buy undressed turkey with head, neck and claws attached. Its eyes stare at you with unbearable sadness, you apologise to it – in your mind, you think. Actually, you have spoken aloud, and people around you think you are a madwoman because you said, "I'm so sorry, turkey, that you had to be murdered for the sake of tradition."'

Brian gave a deep sigh and said, 'Eva, Eva, Eva.'

'Are about to drive home when remember have to queue for latest device. Drive to Currys to find queue already snaking round car park. To join it or not – that is the question. While try to decide, fall asleep at wheel of car causing very slight damage to Renault in front of you. Renault driver reacts badly, as though you have injured his children and killed his dog. Swap insurance details then realise insurance out of date. Decide to join queue and suffer the unbearable tension of wondering if Currys will run out of devices before you reach the front door. Manage to get to counter before must-have gadgets sell out. Try to pay, card rejected by machine, given lecture by twelve-year-old cashier who says, "If you keep it loose in your bag, it's bound to get scratched. Why didn't you keep it in the cardholder compartment in your purse?" Tell child that I will be as disorganised as I want to be. She says, "Do you have another card?" Say, "Yes," and forage inside bra cups, searching for other card. Give it to cashier who says card is warm, won't work until is cold. We wait and wait. People in queue behind protest loudly at delay. Shout at queue, queue shouts back, supervisor brings tray of mini mince pies to placate cold and tired customers. Man chokes on raisin inside mince pie. Eventually, card is cool enough to insert into machine and is declined for purchase of must-have gadgets.'

Eva started to cry.

Brian took her hand and said, 'Eva, darling, I had no idea. Why didn't you say? I didn't want that bloody iPhone 4, it's been in a drawer since Boxing Day.'

But Eva was inconsolable. 'Beg cashier to try one more time. She does — but mutters under her breath — think she used the f-word, this against Currys policy. Tell her so, consider making formal complaint, but brain and mouth not working, so let it go. Machine accepts card, weep with relief. Drive home with turkey and must-have gadgets on passenger seat, held secure with seatbelt. Return home and, through fog of anxiety and sleep deprivation, unpack turkey, leave on kitchen table. Drag stepladder up cellar stairs, untangle fairy lights, drape along picture rails, start with artistic plan in head, end with fairy lights thrown over any ledge or surface. Bulbs go, search for replacements. Ask for help to decorate the tree. Twins and Brian traumatised by the sadness in turkey's eyes and claim to be incapable of movement, swear they will never touch any kind of meat again. Cross pork joint and gammon off Christmas food list. Go into kitchen, find next-door's cat mauling turkey's head, turkey's eyes expressing woes of world. For once don't hit cat with wooden spoon but usher cat and turkey head outside. There are seventeen carrier bags on kitchen table. Bite into a carrot, pour tiny amount of whisky into small glass, take bite out of mince pie, arrange on a festive plate, bring through to sitting-room fireplace. Will I still be doing this when twins are thirty-five?'

'Eva, I can see you're tired. I can google the rest . . . There must be a Delia's Christmas app –'

Eva said, 'No, let me finish doing Christmas Day. Cook full English breakfast. Drink toast with Buck's Fizz. Open presents. Pick up wrapping paper, fold and place in recycling bin. Ring and thank relatives for presents. Change from dressing gown into sequinned cardigan and lace skirt, Brian says look like madam of whorehouse, change into jeans.'

Brian said, 'Eva, that lace skirt barely covered your bum!'

'Cook Christmas dinner, almost collapse after assembling food on table. Drink too much, ask Brian to help wash up, he says, "Later." Twins gone somewhere, make Christmas tea, turkey sandwiches, trifle, Christmas cake. Twins come back, refuse to play games, play maths games with Brian. Refuse to watch Christmas TV, all three watch DVD lecture series on advanced topology from MIT. Eat half tin of Quality Street. Prepare supper. Drink self into stupor. Feel sick from Quality Street and vodka, go to bed.

'So, that was my Christmas last year. You may find it useful,' Eva concluded. 'And, Brian, I am. Never. Doing. Christmas. Again.'

## 32

It was teatime on Christmas Eve and snow was still falling. Eva liked the snow – the beauty of it, the interruption it made to daily life – and she enjoyed the chaos it caused. She was looking out of the window for Stanley Crossley, who had sent a message that he wanted to talk to her. It was a meeting she dreaded. To divert herself she concentrated on the outside window sill, where flakes were settling and intermingling, all the time forming an even, white ledge.

It reminded her of the time she had thrown the ten-year-old twins out into the snow when they carried on bickering after she had asked them to stop. They had knocked on the sitting-room window and pleaded to be let back in while Eva pretended to read *Vogue*. A few minutes later, Brian had arrived home from work to find his son and daughter shivering, coatless in their school uniforms, while his wife sat by a crackling log fire reading a magazine, apparently oblivious to her children's misery.

Brian had bellowed, 'Our children could end up in the care of the local authority! You know how many social workers live around here.'

It was true – there were a disproportionate number

of new-model Volkswagen Beetles parked in the surrounding streets.

Eva laughed aloud at the memory.

The twins had been forced to huddle together for
warmth before Brian let them back inside the house. She
told Brian that it had been a bonding exercise – and since
he had only just returned from a team-building trip to
the Brecon Beacons, where he had been forced to catch,
skin, cook and eat a rabbit, he had believed her.

She saw Stanley approaching the house and watched
as he hesitated at the gate. He was entirely coated in
snow, from his trilby hat to his black brogues. She came
away from the window and heard him stamping his
feet in the porch. The doorbell rang as Eva got into bed
and readied herself for whatever was coming. She had
asked Brian to make sure that Poppy was out of the
house.

Brian had said, 'The only way I can guarantee that is
to take her out somewhere myself. It will be a bloody
nuisance, but I suppose I'll have to do it.'

Even though Stanley had been released without
charge, Eva didn't want to risk him bumping into Poppy.
There was no guarantee that she would not make the
same accusations again. Eva would have to explain that
the false stalking was only one of many such painful
Poppy dramas. The hypochondria, the deep-black lies,
the hysteria if anybody touched 'her things', the household items that had gone missing . . .

Had Stanley come to burden her with an account of

his near-death experience inside a burning Spitfire? Would he sob as he recounted how his face had melted and fallen away? Would he try to describe his agony?

It was the details Eva feared.

Brianne led Stanley up the stairs. She was mute with embarrassment and horror. 'His face is gross,' she thought. 'Poor Mr Crossley. If I was him, I'd wear a sort of mask.' She wanted to tell him that she was not Poppy's friend, that she hated Poppy, didn't want her in the house and couldn't understand why her parents didn't throw her out. But, as usual, the words wouldn't come. When they got to the top of the landing, she called, 'Mum! Mr Crossley is here.'

Stanley stepped into a white space in which the only colour was a yellow embroidered armchair with an orange and red stain that reminded him of a dawn sky. He gave a slight bow and held his hand out. Eva took it and held on to it for a fraction longer than was usual.

Brianne said, 'Can I take your coat and hat?'

As Stanley struggled out of his coat and handed Brianne his hat, Eva saw from the light above his head that his scalp was a relief map of scars. 'Do sit down, Mr Crossley.'

He said, 'Had I known you were indisposed, Mrs Beaver, I would have waited until you were better.'

'I'm not indisposed,' said Eva. 'I'm giving myself a break from the usual routine.'

'Yes, it's rather good for one, it shakes one up and invigorates mind and body.'

She told him that Brianne could bring tea, coffee or

some of the mulled wine that Brian had simmered over-night.

He waved the suggestion away, saying, 'You're too kind. Thank you, but no.'

Eva said, 'I'm glad you came. I want to apologize to you for what happened the other day.'

'You mustn't apologise, Mrs Beaver.'

'That girl is a guest in my house. I feel responsible.'

'She's obviously troubled,' Stanley said.

Eva agreed. 'Troubled and dangerous.'

'It was very good of you to take her in.'

'Not good . . . I had no power to stop it. I've got nothing but contempt for her.'

Stanley said, 'We're all fragile, and that is why I'm here. It's important to me that you understand, I did nothing at all to frighten the girl. I did glance at her extraordinary clothes, but I did nothing more than that.'

Eva said, 'You don't have to tell me this. I know you are a man of honour, and I imagine you live by the strictest of principles.'

'I have not spoken to a living soul since I returned from the police station. This is a statement, I am not asking you to pity me. I have many friends I can call on, and I'm a member of many clubs and institutions, but as you can clearly see, my face is not my fortune.' He laughed. 'I confess to wallowing in self-pity during the early days, after my little accident with my plane – most of us did. There were a few who denied they were in pain – sang, whistled – at least, those with lips. They were the ones who tended to crack. The smell of rotting flesh was indescribable. They tried to disguise it with Izal disinfectant – made from coal, I believe – but . . . it was always there, in your mouth, on your uniform. But we laughed a lot. We called ourselves Guinea Pigs. Because Sir Archie McIndoe experimented on us, told us he was pushing the parameters of plastic surgery – which he was, of course. For six weeks I had a skin flap from my upper arm attached to where my nose used to be.

'Archie was very fond of us boys. Actually, I think he did love us like a father. He used to laugh and say, "Marry a girl with terrible eyesight." A lot of the boys married the nurses, but I followed his advice and married a lovely poor-sighted girl, Peggy. We helped each other. Both of us were normal in the dark.'

Eva said, 'I know you don't want to hear it, but I'm going to say it anyway. I think you're incredibly brave, and I hope we will be friends.'

Stanley looked out of the window and shook his head. 'The uncomfortable truth is, Mrs Beaver, that I took advantage of my wife's lack of sight and I . . .' He broke off and looked around the room, searching for something for his eyes to settle on. He found it impossible to look Eva in the face. 'During my marriage, starting when we returned from a fortnight's honeymoon, I visited a very respectable lady once a week and paid her rather a lot of money to have sex with me.'

Eva's eyes widened. After a few moments, she said, 'I have known for some time that my husband has been having an affair with a woman he works with called Dr Titania Noble-Forester.'

Stanley felt sufficiently emboldened by this confidence to tell Eva more. 'I have been in a rage since 1941. I was irritated beyond telling when my wife dropped something or spilled her tea or knocked over a glass of water. She was always blundering into the furniture and tripping over rugs, and she refused to use any of those gadgets that are designed to help. She knew Braille. God knows why she learned it – I sent for the books but she wouldn't touch them. But I loved her dearly, and when she died I couldn't see the point of carrying on. With her by my side in bed, the horrible dreams were almost tolerable. I would cry out and wake and my dear wife would hold my hand and talk to me about the things we had done together, the countries we had visited.' He gave a tight smile, which he seemed to use as a form of punctuation.

Eva asked, 'And your lady friend, is she still alive?'

'Oh yes, I still see her once a month. We do not have a sexual relationship now. She's quite frail. I pay her twenty-five pounds to talk and be held.'

'What's her name?'

'Celia. I've longed to say her name aloud to somebody who would understand. You do understand, don't you, Mrs Beaver?'

Eva patted the duvet next to her, and Stanley sat on the edge of the bed and took her hand. They both heard Brian and Poppy's voices as they came through the front door.

Brian was saying, 'Committing suicide would do you no good. We're not asking you for the ultimate sacrifice, Poppy.'

Poppy said, 'But he was looking at me in such a horrible way.'

Brian was on the stairs now, saying, 'He can't help but look at you in a horrible way. He's got a horrible face.'

Brian was disconcerted to see Crossley and his wife holding hands, but nothing would surprise him now. The world seemed to have gone mad.

He said, 'Poppy is asking for money. She wants to visit her parents over Christmas.'

Eva said, 'Give her what she's asking for. I want her out of this house. And Brian, Mr Crossley will be spending Christmas Day and Boxing Day with us.'

Brian thought, 'Well, I'm not sitting opposite the ugly bastard.'

Mr Crossley said, 'I'm afraid I'm terribly dull company, Dr Beaver. I wish I was more gregarious. I do not know any jokes, and most of my stories are rather sad. Are you sure you want me as a guest?'

Brian hesitated.

Eva *looked* at him.

Brian said quickly, 'No, of course you must come. And don't worry about the jokes – there will be jokes in the Christmas crackers, and paper hats and little trinkets we can talk about, so there won't be any of that English awkwardness. We'll be a jolly crowd. There'll be two sulky autistic teenagers, my mother – who is the most argumentative woman I know – and my mother-in-law,

Ruby, who thinks that Barack Obama is the head of Al Qaeda. And me, of course, who will no doubt be in a filthy temper, having never cooked Christmas dinner before. And then there's my wife, the issuer of your invitation, who has done bugger all to help this Christmas and who will be stinking in her pit above our heads as we eat.'

Brian's speech was greeted with silence. He had forgotten what he came in for, so he went out, closing the door with exaggerated care.

Eva swung round in the bed and lay down with her head flat on the mattress. She said, 'He exhausts me. Poor Titania.'

They both laughed.

As Mr Crossley turned away from the light, still laughing, Eva saw for herself the shadow of a handsome man.

He said, 'I must go now, Mrs Beaver.'

She pleaded, 'Please come and join us tomorrow. I plan to get drunk in the afternoon and smoke many cigarettes.'

He said, 'That sounds quite irresistible. Of course I'll come.'

When he opened the door to leave, Brian was skulking on the landing.

After Stanley had politely informed Brian that he would be coming for Christmas Day, Brian followed him downstairs, hissing, 'You hold my wife's hand again and I'll have it off at the wrist.'

Stanley said quietly, 'I know your sort. We had one or two in the squadron. Big mouths, braggarts. They were always the last in a scramble, always the first to come home. Hadn't engaged with the enemy, but did have a lot of bad luck with sudden and mysterious lack of visibility, radio malfunction and guns jamming. Cheated at cards, rough with their women and all-round total shits. Goodnight, Dr Beaver.'

Before Brian could think of a reply, Stanley had put his hat on and left.

The icy pavement shone in the lamplight. He held on to the walls and fences as he slowly made his way to the safety of his own house.

# 33

Early on Christmas Day morning Eva woke and looked out of the window to see snow falling from a navy-blue sky. The house was silent. But when she listened carefully, she heard the hot water circulating around pipes and radiators, and the faint creaking of the floorboards as they made the slightest of contractions and expansions. There was an intermittent bird noise emanating from the eaves. The bird was not singing but making an irritated squawk: 'Clack-ack-ack.'

Eva opened the sash window and craned her neck backwards, looking for the bird. Snow settled on her upturned face before melting instantaneously. She saw a blackbird with a yellow beak and one gimlet eye. The other eye had gone, revealing a bloody socket.

The blackbird flapped its wings and attempted to fly, crying, 'Clack-ack-ack.' One wing was distorted and would not retract.

Eva said, 'What's happened to you?'

Brian Junior came in, running his fingers through his hair. 'That blackbird has a very annoying alarm call.'

Eva said, 'It's lost an eye and has a damaged wing. What shall we do?'

Brian Junior said, '*You* do nothing and *I* do nothing. If it's badly injured, it will die.'

Eva objected, 'There must be something –'

'Close the window, snow is falling on your bed.'

She closed the window and said, 'Perhaps if I brought it inside?'

Brian Junior shouted, 'No! Life is hard! Nature is cruel! The strong overpower the weak! Everything dies! Even you, Mum, with your gigantic ego, even you can't escape death!'

Eva was too shocked to speak.

Brian Junior said, 'Happy Christmas!'

Eva said, 'Happy Christmas.'

When he'd gone, she pulled the duvet around her while the blackbird continued its mournful cry.

'Clack-ack-ack.'

Brian had prepared for cooking his first Christmas dinner by studying the various timings and advice in the cookery books he had bought Eva over the years. She always referred to them as 'Delia', 'Jamie', 'Rick', 'Nigel', 'Keith', 'Nigella' or 'Marguerite'.

After extensive reading he had designed a 'fail-safe' computer program, which he intended to follow with a stopwatch in one hand and various implements in the other – for beating, basting, paring, cutting, draining, stirring, peeling, mashing, opening, pouring and blending. He had told his guests to arrive at 12.45 p.m. for drinks and the exchange of pleasantries. He wanted them seated at the dining table no later than 1.10 p.m. for the starter of avocado and lavender soufflé.

He was sorry that Poppy had gone to Dundee to see

her dying parents. He had hoped to impress her even further with his culinary achievements over Christmas. She had left the night before, wearing Brian's fifty per cent cashmere overcoat, taking only a small bag and leaving the rest of her mess all over the sitting room. It had taken Brian an hour before the room was presentable enough to use over Christmas.

At mid-morning Brianne came into Eva's room wearing the silk pyjamas with a tea-rose print that Eva had paid for and Alexander had ordered online from his phone. The whole process had taken under five minutes.

Brianne had done something good with her hair, and her face looked less severe.

She said, 'These are the loveliest pyjamas! I don't want to take them off!'

'Alexander chose them,' said Eva.

'I know. Isn't he the nicest man?'

'You should thank him when you see him.'

'I already have. He's outside with his kids. I invited them for dinner. Aren't they the cutest kids ever, Mum?'

Eva was surprised but pleased that Alexander was here. She said, '*Cutest*?' That's not a word you use.'

'But they *are* cute, Mum. And they're so *clever*! They know *reams* of poetry and all the capital cities of the world. Alex is so proud of them. And I love his name – Alexander. He really is Alexander the Great, isn't he, Mum?'

Eva agreed. 'Yes – but Alexander is forty-nine years of age, Brianne.'

'Forty-nine? That's the new thirty!'

'You once ranted that nobody over twenty-five should be allowed to wear jeans, or dance in public.'

'But Alex looks so good in jeans, and he did A level maths, Mum! He understands nonhomogeneous equations!'

'I can tell you're *fond* of him,' said Eva.

'Fond?' said Brianne. 'I'm *fond* of Grandma Ruby, I'm fond of whiskers on kittens and bright copper kettles, but I'm passionately in fucking *love* with Alex Tate!'

Eva said, 'Please! Don't *swear.*'

'You're such a fucking hypocrite!' yelled Brianne. 'You swear! And you're trying to spoil my relationship with Alex!'

'There's nothing to spoil. You're not Juliet. This is not a Montague and Capulet situation. Does Alex even know you love him?'

Brianne said, defiantly, 'Yes, he does.'

'And?'

Brianne lowered her eyes. 'He doesn't love me, of course. He hasn't had time to get to know me. But when I saw him struggling with that bookcase in Leeds, I knew immediately that he was the person I've been waiting for since I was a kid. I always wondered who it would be. Then he knocked on my door.'

Eva tried to hold Brianne's hand, but she pulled it away and put it behind her back.

Eva asked, 'And he was kind to you?'

'I rang him three times on his mobile when he was on the motorway. He told me to go out more and meet people of my own age.'

Eva said, gently, 'He is right, Brianne. His hair is grey. He has more in common with me than with you. We've both got Morrissey's second solo album.'

Brianne said, 'I know that. I know everything there is to know about him. I know his wife died in a car crash and that he was driving. I know that Tate was his family's slave name. I know how much he earned in the noughties. And I know how much tax he paid. And which school his children go to, and what their grades are. I know his previous romantic history. I know he's overdrawn by £77.15 and that he doesn't have an agreed overdraft facility.'

'And he told you all this?'

'No, I've hardly spoken to him. I doxed him.'

'What's "doxed"?'

'It's like talking to Neanderthal woman! I've read every document about him. If there's info I want, I can find it on the net. I've mapped the story of his life, and one day I'll be part of it.'

'But, Brianne, don't forget his children. You don't *like* children, remember?'

Brianne screamed, 'I like *his* children!'

Eva had never seen her in such an emotional state. She heard Brian Junior's bedroom door open, and seconds later he crashed into her room.

'I can hear you slagging my sister off, Mum. Why don't you butt out and leave us alone?'

The twins drew together, as they must have done in her womb.

She was glad when they went out, but she had never

felt more alone. She heard them talking in Brian Junior's bedroom. Their voices were low and insistent, as though they were conspirators plotting a political outrage.

Brian's hand-held computer had fallen into the turkey gravy. He tried to pick it up with a pair of tongs but it fell back into the pan, splashing drops of boiling gravy on to his face. He screamed and splashed his face under the cold tap. He tried again with the tongs, and this time he managed to lift it out. He threw it into the already crowded sink. As he had expected, the screen had died.

Brian panicked.

What came next?

For how much longer should the turkey cook?

What time should he turn on the sprouts?

Should he take the Christmas pudding out of the steamer?

Was the bread sauce thick enough?

Where was the potato masher?

Ignoring the noises coming from the kitchen, including the faint screams and curses, Ruby and Yvonne lay back on comfortable armchairs in the sitting room, in front of a log fire, and reminisced about the many Christmas dinners they had cooked over the years.

'Without the benefit of a computer,' said Ruby.

'Or a husband who would cook,' said Yvonne.

Outside, Alexander was walking alongside his children in the middle of Bowling Green Road, watching out for cars. The pavements were still icy with flattened snow.

He was helping Venus to ride a new bicycle with stabilisers. Thomas was pushing a doll's pram with a stuffed giraffe propped up against a pink pillow. Alexander wondered if he had gone too far with the gender politics.

Stanley Crossley slammed his front door as they were passing his house. After congratulating the children on their Christmas presents, he said, 'I hope I'm not too early.'

Alexander laughed and said, 'We may be eating a little later than was planned.'

'It's of no matter to me,' said Stanley.

Outside the Beavers' house, Thomas told Stanley that the giraffe's name was Paul.

The old man remarked, 'That's an entirely suitable name for a giraffe.'

Venus stared at Stanley and asked, 'Does your face hurt?'

'Not now,' he said. 'But it looks horrible, doesn't it?'

'Yes,' said Venus. 'If I was you, I would cover it in a mask.'

Stanley laughed, but Alexander was embarrassed and tried to apologise.

Stanley said forcefully, 'That's the child's honest reaction. She'll soon get used to me.'

Hearing the voices outside, Eva pushed the sash up and poked her head out. 'Merry Christmas!' she shouted.

They all looked up at the window and shouted, 'Merry Christmas!' back.

Alexander thought, 'She looks beautiful – even with her mad hair on end.'

Stanley thought, 'If Tiny Tim came hobbling round the corner now, one would not be surprised.'

They eventually sat down to dinner at 5.15 p.m. Brianne managed to secure a chair opposite Alexander.

Parts of the meal were quite edible.

Ruby said, after clearing her plate, 'There were only a few things that let you down, Brian. Your roast potatoes were not crispy, they had no rustle to them, and the gravy had a funny taste.'

Yvonne said, 'Plasticky.'

Brian Junior corrected her, 'No, metallic.'

Stanley said, 'I thought the turkey itself was quite superb. Many congratulations, Dr Beaver.'

Brian was exhausted. He had never been through such a physical and intellectual ordeal. Behind the closed kitchen door he had, in turn, wept, cursed, screamed, fallen into despair, and laughed hysterically as he struggled to serve everything together at the same time and keep it all hot. But he had heroically managed to get the thirteen main components of the meal into serving dishes and on to the table. Crackers had been pulled, paper hats worn and jokes groaned over.

Ruby congratulated Alexander on the polite behaviour of his children.

Venus said, 'Daddy told us he would give us ten pounds if we were good.'

Alexander laughed and shook his head.

'Define goodness!' Brian Junior said to Venus.

Yvonne chided him, 'The child is only seven years old, Brian Junior!'

Venus put her hand up and looked urgently at Brian Junior, who nodded.

She said, 'Goodness means telling good lies, so that people won't get hurt by true words.'

Brian said, 'Venus, I would like to know your opinion on the meal that I cooked and you have just eaten.'

Venus asked, 'Daddy, do I have to be good?'

'No, just tell the truth, sweetheart.'

Venus placed her napkin on the table. She unrolled the white cotton square, revealing a burned stuffing ball, a charred chipolata, a fat-logged roast potato, three over-cooked Brussels sprouts and an undercooked Yorkshire pudding.

There was a shout of laughter, and Alexander hid his face in his hands. When he looked through his fingers, he saw Brianne mouthing, 'I love you.' He shook his head and quickly looked away.

Brian said, 'I see that you managed to eat the turkey, Venus.'

Thomas adjusted his nurse's cap and, speaking for the first time, said quietly, 'She threw the turkey under the table.'

There was another burst of laughter.

Alexander was surprised and horrified to realise that he had forgotten Eva. Lately, she seemed to be constantly on his mind. 'Did anybody feed Eva?' he asked.

There was scandalised laughter as each of them

realised they had forgotten her. There were only a few leftovers. Even the turkey had been well picked over. But Alexander managed to gather enough to make a decent plateful. He placed it in the microwave and turned the dial to three minutes. Then he made some fresh gravy, poured it into a little jug and went in search of another box of crackers that Brian said were in the house somewhere.

The other guests were reluctant to move from the table. More drinks were poured and conversation was easy. There were frequent outbursts of laughter. Even Stanley and Brian were talking.

Brian was just saying, 'Yes, Stanley, I think a five-tog duvet is all anyone needs for winter,' when the kitchen door burst open and Poppy almost fell into the room, announcing in the little-girl version of her voice, 'They're dead. Mummy and Daddy are dead!'

The laughter stopped.

Ruby said, 'Your mam and dad have died?'

Yvonne said, 'You poor kid! And on Christmas Day.'

Brianne sneered, 'Yeah, well, I'll believe it when I see the death certificate.'

Yvonne said, 'Brianne, what a thing to say! I'm ashamed of you.'

Poppy looked at Brianne defiantly and said, 'Well, it hasn't been issued yet.'

'Until I see an official death certificate, I'm not going to show you the slightest bit of sympathy, OK?' said Brianne. 'When did they die? Yesterday? Today?'

Poppy said, 'This morning.'

'And you were there?'

'Yes, I was with them until the end.'

'They died at precisely the same time, did they?'

'Yes,' said Poppy. 'I was holding both their hands.'

Brianne looked around the table at the fascinated audience and said, 'Now, that is the most amazing coincidence I've ever heard. That is spooky.'

Poppy declared, with the spasm of a triumphant smile, 'Their machines were switched off at the exact same time, at my request.'

Brianne ploughed on. 'At what time did they die?'

'At ten o'clock this morning,' said Poppy.

'In Dundee?' checked Brianne.

'Yes,' said Poppy.

'So, how did you manage to get from Dundee to Leicester by six thirty on Christmas Day? There's no public transport, is there?'

'No,' said Poppy. 'I caught a cab.'

Brianne, sounding increasingly like Inspector Morse, said, 'In deep snow? There are blizzards up there. White-outs.'

Poppy said, 'We must have been lucky with the weather.'

'Did you stop to eat?' Brianne hectored.

'No, I'm starving,' said Poppy. 'I feel quite faint.' She gave a little stagger and sat down on a vacant chair at the end of the table.

Brianne said, 'What did you really do with the money my parents gave you to fly to Dundee?'

Brian snapped, 'That's enough now, Brianne!'

The microwave pinged.

Alexander took Eva's plate of food out and put it at the end of the table, then turned to find a tray. Poppy pulled the plate in front of her, reached for a clean knife and fork and said, 'Thank you.'

Everyone watched in horrified silence for a moment, as she began to cram food into her mouth, then they all shouted at once that it was Eva's food. Poppy picked up the plate and hurried out of the kitchen.

Alexander shouted after her, 'I hope you're taking that up to Eva!'

Brian Junior said quietly, 'Why did she come back? She's going to spoil everything again.'

Alexander ran upstairs.

Eva was lying with her face to the wall. She turned to him and, seeing he was empty-handed, turned away again and said, 'I'm so hungry, Alexander. Have I been forgotten?'

Alexander sat on the edge of the bed and said, 'Not by me. I think about you all the time. Feel my heart.' He took her hand, placed it over his white shirt front and said, 'Hear the rhythm? It's saying "Eva".'

Eva said, trying to lessen his intensity, 'I could eat your heart right now – with ginger, garlic and chillies.' She thought, 'Oh no, now there's a *situation*, and I'll have to manage it.'

He turned her hand over and kissed the palm.

She examined his face, noting the age spots around his eyes and the grey stubble on his cheeks. She said, 'All I can think about is food.'

He got up abruptly. 'Turkey sandwich?'

When he got downstairs, he saw Poppy in the sitting room. She was cramming the last of the food into her mouth with her fingers.

# 34

At lunchtime on Boxing Day, Brian laid a big wooden tray on Eva's lap. On it was the Beavers' traditional Boxing Day meal.

He said, 'It's like fucking Groundhog Day down there. Same faces, only the food is different. They're all Billy No Mates with nowhere else to go.'

Brianne had invited Alexander and the children back, despite Brian's disapproval, and Alexander had accepted because he wanted to spend as much time with Eva as possible before he went to visit his ex-mother-in-law.

Stanley was there at Ruby's invitation. She said it made a change to have a gentleman in the house.

Only Poppy was missing. She had left early in the morning to 'feed the poor', she said, at a warehouse run by Crisis at Christmas in the city centre.

Brian said, 'That kid has got a heart of gold.'

The twins had simultaneously put their fingers down their throats.

Eva said, 'This salad looks lovely.'

'My mother pillaged Sainsbury's this morning,' said Brian. 'There was no flesh left on that turkey.'

Eva looked down at her plate, which was layered in cold meats. 'It all looks very pretty.'

'Your mother was fart-arsing about with it all morning,' said Brian, contemptuously.

There was a small bowl of salad arranged in concentric alternating circles of tomato, cucumber, beetroot, large radish and bumper spring onions. In another bowl was a huge steaming baked potato, cut with a cross, revealing in the centre a quickly melting slab of butter. A small oval dish held a tiny peaked mountain of grated orange cheese. Two slices of pork pie were flanked by carrot sticks and crooked half-moons of green pepper. An egg cup was full of HP sauce. Her napkin had been folded into a fan. Eva was pleased to see a large glass of rosé wine.

Brian said, 'Alexander's boy is wearing a pink tutu, but nobody has mentioned it yet.'

'Your mum told me that after you'd seen *The Wizard of Oz*, you wanted a pair of Dorothy's red shoes,' said Eva.

Brian said, in a resentful tone, 'But I didn't get them, did I?'

When Brian went downstairs to join the others, Alexander asked him, 'Eva all right?'

Brian said, 'Why shouldn't she be all right? She's waited on hand and foot. If she's not careful, she'll lose the use of her limbs.'

Yvonne put a wafer-thin roll of ham in her mouth and said, 'Now, I don't agree with most of what you have to say, Brian, but I'm in full agreement with you about Eva. It's sheer laziness. What would happen to her if we stopped feeding her? Would she starve to death, or would she come downstairs and feed herself?'

'We ought to try it,' said Ruby.

Alexander said, 'Don't try it for the next week, because I'm going away.'

Brianne was alarmed. 'Where are you going?'

Venus answered, 'We're going to see my mummy's mummy.'

Thomas said, 'And we're going to put some flowers at the place where our mummy's under the ground.'

Yvonne turned to Alexander and said, 'You're not dragging these little children around graveyards, are you?'

Alexander said, unsmilingly, 'No, only the one.'

Brian Junior was tweeting to the worldwide twitterati:

Worst xmas dinner evar. It was actually carbon, dudes. Now boxing day, bored – sitting with living dead, desire zombie apocalypse.

He said to the room, 'At the moment, mine and Brianne's priority is getting rid of Poppy.'

'The child is ill,' said Brian, in Poppy's defence. 'I spoke to her this morning. She offered to leave this afternoon, but I said she must stay until she feels able to cope on her own.'

Ruby said, 'It took me years to get over my mam's death. I used to think about her hanging out the washing on a windy day. Let's hope that poor little Poppy has a lovely memory of when her mam and dad were fit and well.'

Venus said to Stanley, 'Your face is getting better.'

'I'm very pleased to hear that,' said Stanley. Turning to the others, he asked, 'On the subject of Poppy, did anybody else notice that she has a swastika tattoo underneath that gaudy ring she wears? I wonder if she realises the significance of such an emblem.'

Brian said, 'Young people flirt with all kinds of shock imagery, it doesn't make her Eva Braun. She'll have a place in this house for as long as I'm living here.'

Stanley said, 'You surprise me, Dr Beaver. Are you not offended by fascist symbols? I wouldn't have marked you down as a Nazi sympathiser.'

'A Nazi sympathiser!' retorted Brian. 'She's eighteen years old, flirting with different philosophies.'

The doorbell rang. Thomas climbed down from his chair and went to answer it.

'Ahh, bless his little heart,' said Ruby, 'he won't be able to reach.'

Thomas stretched up and, with both hands, pulled down on the front-door handle.

Dr Titania Noble-Forester was surprised to see a small black boy wearing a pink tutu and ballet shoes.

Thomas said, 'Have you been crying?'

'Yes,' she said. 'Yes, I have.'

'I was crying in the car for ten minutes.'

'Why?'

'I had nothing else to do,' said Thomas. 'How long were you crying?'

'All night, and an hour or two this morning.' She added, 'Is that bastard Dr Beaver at home?'

Thomas said, 'Yes,' and remained standing in front of the door.

'I'd like to speak to him. Would you move away from the door, please?'

Titania could hear raised voices coming from the back of the house. One of them was Brian's. He was shouting something about Norse mythology, pagan symbolism and Odinism.

'Do you want to come in?' asked Thomas.

'Yes, please,' said Titania.

Thomas led Titania into the kitchen.

Brian almost choked on the skin of his baked potato.

Titania announced, 'He's thrown me out, Brian. I can't go to my mother's, it would kill her. And I can't go to my sister's. I wouldn't give that bitch the satisfaction. You said you would leave Eva after Christmas. Well, it's after Christmas now.'

There was a general gasp of surprise from everybody except Brian. He propelled his heavy bulk from his chair, as though he'd been shot from a cannon. He landed at Titania's side, the floor joists groaning suddenly under his weight. He tried frantically to push her out of the kitchen, but she stood her ground.

Stanley Crossley, who had risen to his feet when Titania first came in, said, 'Madam, you look distressed. May I offer you a drink?'

Brian roared, 'It's my bloody house! I'll decide who drinks in it!'

Titania crossed her arms and planted her feet. She

had not moved from the doorway. She said, 'I would like a double vodka, diet tonic, a slice of lemon and half a handful of crushed ice, with a pink drinking straw, if you have one. Thank you.'

Ruby enquired, 'So, who's she when she's at home?'

Titania said, 'Old lady, I have been Dr Brian Beaver's lover for many years.'

'Lover?' said Ruby. Brian was one of the people, together with the Queen, who Ruby could not equate with any kind of sexuality.

Brian looked around his kitchen.

What had happened to his world? He seemed to strongly dislike all the people in it. There was a man with a burned face mixing a drink for Titania – a woman he used to desire. There was a little boy in a ballet tutu and a seven-year-old girl who appeared to practise her own school of Utilitarian philosophy, two old women who belonged in the Middle Ages (or the mid-1950s), his twins who were cleverer than he was and had ostentatiously turned their chairs and their backs to his lover, and an annoyingly well-educated black man with hair that fell almost to his waist. And, to put a tin lid on it, upstairs there was a wife who needed to *think* and was taking her time over it.

Was he the only normal Homo sapiens left? Did the ignorant public really expect to find people like themselves living on a planet on the far side of the cosmos? It was highly unlikely that any of these aliens wrote notes to the milkman or paid pet insurance. Didn't these ignoramuses understand that human beings were the real aliens?

He thought back to his childhood, when breakfast had been at 7.30 a.m., lunch at 12.45 p.m. and their evening meal at 6 p.m. on the dot. Bedtime was 7.15 p.m. until he was twelve, and 8 p.m. until he was thirteen, when it increased by half an hour. There were no computers to distract him then – though he had read about them in the comic *Look and Learn*. For a treat his mother had taken him to see Leicester's first computer, which was housed in the offices of a hosiery factory and was twice as big as his bedroom. Yet again, he began to mourn the fact that he would be dead for certain in fifty years, and would not see the rise of nanotechnology, quantum computing or the subsequent planetary consciousness. With his high blood pressure he would be lucky to see the Mars landing.

Yvonne said sharply, 'Brian!'

'Yeah?'

'You're doing that thing again.'

'What thing?'

'That moaning thing you did when you were a boy, looking at the sky.'

Brian aggressively cleared his throat, as though there were some physical obstruction.

Ruby said, 'I know I'm a bit old-fashioned, but is it only me who thinks this whole situation is disgraceful?' She glared at Titania. 'In my day, Brian, you'd have been beaten up by the woman's husband. You would have been lucky to keep your kneecaps. You should be ashamed of yourself.'

Titania said, emphatically, 'Brian has been unhappily married for years.' Then, addressing him, she said, 'I'm going upstairs to talk to your wife, Brian.'

Thomas asked, 'Can I come?'

Titania gave one of her barking laughs and said, 'Why not, little boy? You are not too young to find out that your sex is inherently simple-minded and cruel.'

Alexander said, 'Thomas, sit down.'

Taking her vodka with her, Titania stalked out of the kitchen and shouted, 'Eva!'

'Up here!'

Eva's first thought on seeing Titania was that she looked like a funeral director, in her black skirt and white shirt. The skin around her eyes was so puffy that she had either developed a serious allergy, or the poor woman had been crying for a very long time.

Titania said, 'He didn't tell me you were beautiful. He told me you were a scrag-hag. Are you a natural blonde?'

'Yes,' said Eva. 'Are you a natural redhead, Titania?'

Titania sat on the soup chair and began to cry, again. 'He promised he would leave you after Christmas.'

'Perhaps he will,' said Eva. 'Boxing Day is still Christmas. Perhaps he'll leave me tomorrow.'

'My husband has thrown me out,' said Titania. 'I've got nowhere to go.'

Eva was rarely malicious – she had a heart as soft as

her goose-down pillows – but she resented the eight years she had been lied to. 'Come and live here,' she said. 'You can join Brian in his main shed. There's plenty of wardrobe space. As we both know, Brian has no clothes to speak of.'

Titania said, 'I don't sense that this is an altruistic gesture.'

Eva admitted, 'No, it's not. He likes his solitude. He will hate having somebody else living full-time in his precious shed.'

The two women laughed, though not companionably.

Titania said, 'I'll finish my drink, then I'll get my stuff out of the car.'

Eva said, 'Tell me something. Do you fake your orgasms?'

'There usually isn't time, he's finished in a couple of minutes. I sort myself out.'

Eva said, 'Poor Brian, in the football league of lovers, he's Accrington Stanley.'

'Why has nobody told him?' said Titania.

'It's because we pity him,' said Eva, 'and we're stronger than him.'

Titania confided, 'When I was invited to CERN to work on the collider, he said, "Really? They *must* be in trouble."'

Eva said, 'When I first showed him the embroidered chair that I'd worked on for two years, he said, "*I* could learn to embroider, if I put my mind to it. It's only cloth, needle and thread, isn't it?"'

Titania ran her hands over the arms of the chair, and said, 'It's exquisite.'

When she'd gone, Eva knelt at the window and watched Titania struggle to bring in what looked like the contents of a small household.

# 35

In the kitchen, Titania and Brian started to row over his reluctance to carry her belongings down to the shed. The others drifted away from the kitchen table and sat on the stairs, not knowing where to go or what to do.

Eva heard their subdued voices echoing in the hallway, and invited them into her room.

Ruby lowered herself into the soup chair, Stanley perched on the end of the bed, using his walking stick as a support, and the others sat cross-legged on the floor, with their backs against the walls.

Alexander caught Eva's gaze, and held it for a moment.

Thomas and Venus began to play Cruel Russian Ballet Teacher, a game they had perfected over Christmas. When Venus ranted at Thomas that his arabesque was 'rubbish', and threatened to beat him with an imaginary stick, Alexander sent them downstairs to play.

Brian Junior's mobile rang.

It was Ho.

Brian Junior said, 'Yes?' into the phone.

'Where do I go to collect government money?' asked Ho.

Brian Junior was momentarily confused. 'I'm not with you. Explain.'

Ho said, 'I have no money left for food. And I am

hungry. I have phoned Poppy, but she does not answer. So, do you know the location of the government money office in Leeds?'

Brian Junior explained, 'It won't be open today. And they won't give you any when they do open – you're a full-time student.'

Ho asked again, 'Where will I get money?'

Brian Junior said, 'Ho, I can't help you. I haven't got room in my head for somebody else's problems.'

'If I go to one of your churches, and ask one of the priests for money, will they give me some?'

'Probably not.'

'But if I tell them I am very hungry, and have not eaten for two days and two nights?'

Brian Junior squirmed and said, 'Please, this is making me feel ill.'

'But I am like your Jesus in the desert. Sometimes he had no food.'

Brian Junior passed the phone to Brianne, who had been listening closely.

Brianne said angrily to Ho, 'Now you've made three of us miserable.'

Ho said, 'The phone is telling me that I have low credit power.'

Brianne said, 'This is what you do. You put on your coat and your red scarf, and you go to the Sikh temple. It's on the main road at the rear of our building. There are orange flags flying outside. They will give you food. I know, because a boy in my seminar group blew his loan on a second-hand motorbike and a drum kit in the first week of term, and the Sikhs had to feed him for a month. Now, repeat back the instructions I have just given to you,' she said, sternly. She listened for a moment, then said, 'Right – coat, scarf, keys. Go now,' and switched the phone off.

Alexander murmured, 'Another Nazi in the house.'

Eva said, 'Why is the poor boy in such a state?'

Brianne said, 'He gave Poppy most of his money.'

Stanley observed, 'All roads lead to Poppy. What's to be done with her?'

Brianne said, 'I would happily see her walking away from our house, barefoot and dying in the snow.'

Eva held her head in her hands and said, 'Brianne, please don't talk like that. It makes you sound so callous.'

Brianne shouted, 'You know nothing about her or the damage she's caused! Why do you allow her to stay in our house? You know that me and Bri hate her guts!'

Ruby said, 'Well, I for one feel sorry for the poor kid. Her mam and dad have just died! I had a long talk with her yesterday. They're bringing the bodies back to Leicester, and I told her to use the Co-op funeral service. They did a lovely job for your granddad. It wasn't their fault they went to the wrong house to pick the body up. Fairtree Avenue does sound like Fir Tree Avenue.'

Brianne knelt at the side of the soup chair and said, very slowly and deliberately, looking into her grandmother's face, 'Gran, why would the Dundee authorities bring her parents' bodies back to Leicester? When, according to Poppy, they lived in a house in Hampstead, surrounded by their rich relations and celebrity friends. Hugh Grant was her next-door neighbour.'

Ruby said, impatiently, 'I know that! Poppy told me that they used to give him rides in their plane. He took over the controls once, when Poppy's dad fell ill at the wheel. He had to make an emergency landing on Hampstead Heath. A policeman was slightly hurt.'

Brianne shouted, 'You stupid old woman! Everything she's told you has been a complete lie!'

Ruby's face crumpled. 'I'm surprised at you, Brianne. Talking to your elders in such a way. You used to be such a nice quiet girl. You've changed since you went to that university.'

Brianne leapt up. 'There are no bodies coming back to the Co-op! Her parents are alive and living in Maidenhead! Her mother was on Facebook this morning, telling her "friends" that she'd had an electric blanket for Christmas!'

Eva said, 'How can you possibly know that?'

Brianne and Brian Junior exchanged a look, and Brian Junior said, 'We're good with computers.'

Brianne put her arm around Brian Junior's shoulder and said, 'She isn't Poppy Roberts. Her name is Paula Gibb. Her parents live in a council house. They don't own a private plane. They don't even have a car, or central heating.'

Alexander said, 'At least they've got an electric blanket.' He looked around the group.

Nobody but Eva was laughing.

Stanley asked, 'How long have you known?'

Brianne said, 'A couple of days. We saved it. There's never anything to do on Boxing Day, is there?'

Yvonne remarked, 'I think it's disgusting personally, myself. The two of your big brains against that little grieving girl.'

Brianne said, calmly, 'Bri, time to fetch the Poppy files.'

Brian Junior got up, stretching his arms in an attempt to relax his rigid muscles, as if imploring Brianne to show him more respect. Heaving a deep sigh, he went into his bedroom.

When he returned with a large green box file, Brianne said, 'Hand the papers round.'

'What, like, at random?'

She nodded.

He dispersed the official-looking papers, some stapled, all printouts.

There was silence for a few moments, as people read the opening paragraphs of the documents they had been handed.

Ruby said, 'Well, I've read this first bit of mine twice and I still don't understand it.'

Yvonne asked, 'Are we to be tested by the Big Brains?'

Brianne said, 'You've got the birth certificate, Yvonne. Read it to us.'

'Stop talking to me as if I'm a dog, a mongrel dog. When I was a girl –'

Brianne interrupted, 'Yeah, when you were a girl, you were writing on a slate with a piece of chalk.'

Eva ordered her daughter, 'Apologise to Granny.'

Brianne muttered ungraciously, 'Soz.'

'Well, it says here, this is the birth certificate of a child called Paula Gibb, born on the 31st of July 1993, her dad was Dean Arthur Gibb, car park attendant, and her mum was Claire Theresa Maria Gibb, bowling alley assistant.'

Brian Junior laughed out loud and said in a bad American accent, 'Fuck it, dude, let's go bowling.'

His family had never heard Brian Junior swear before. Eva was pleased at this proof that Brian Junior could be a normal foul-mouthed teenager.

Brianne turned to her brother. 'Bri, no Lebowski, please. This is serious business.'

Alexander said, 'I've got a social worker's report here. When she was three and a half, Paula was temporarily taken into care and fostered.'

A stillness settled over the room.

Eva looked up from her printouts. 'I've got an admission report for University Hospital, on the 11th of June 1995, and a six-month review written by her social worker, Delfina Ladzinski.' Eva scanned the papers. 'Where do I start?' She cleared her throat and read out what she thought were the most important details, as though she were reading the shipping forecast.

'Medical assessment on being taken into care: cigarette burns on the backs of her hands and forearms, head lice, infected fleabites, impetigo. She was malnourished, unable to speak. Afraid to use the toilet. It's hardly Rebecca of Sunnybrook Farm, is it?'

Yvonne got up. 'Well, I don't know about anyone else, but I've had enough of this. It's Boxing Day. I want some turkey sandwiches and a game of Mr Potato Head, not all this wallowing in the gutter.'

Ruby said, 'Sit down, Yvonne! There are some things that have to be faced full on. I've got a report here from Thames Valley Police, about an arson attack on a children's home in Reading. Paula Gibb was questioned but said she'd only been trying to light a cigarette using a Zip firelighter. She'd panicked and thrown the firelighter into the Activities Room, where it landed in the middle of the pool table –'

Yvonne interrupted. 'All this is making me poorly.'

Eva said, 'It explains everything.'

Stanley insisted, 'But none of that excuses her current behaviour.'

Alexander nodded. 'My mum used to leave me locked in my room in the dark. I don't know where she went. She ordered me to keep clear of the window and told me that if I cried she would send me away, so I did as I was told. But *I've* done OK.'

He looked up to find Eva gazing back at him with a fierce look in her eyes, as if she were seeing him for the first time.

Yvonne said, miserably, 'If I'd known there was a deranged person staying here – well, another deranged person – I would never have come.'

Eva countered, 'I'm not deranged, Yvonne. Can I remind you that your son, my husband, is downstairs arguing with his mistress?'

Yvonne looked down and straightened the rings on her arthritic fingers.

Brian Junior said, 'I've got her GCSE and A level certificates here. She got twelve GCSEs, nothing below a C grade, but only two A levels – an A in English, and an A* in Religious Studies.'

'So, she's not just a psychopath,' Alexander said, 'she's *quite* a clever psychopath. Now that is frightening.'

They all jumped and stared at the bedroom door as they heard the front door slam, followed by the familiar clump of Poppy's boots in the hall.

Eva said, 'I want to talk to her. Brian Junior, will you ask her to come up here, please?'

'Why me, why do I have to go? I don't want to speak to her. I don't want to look at her. I don't want to breathe the same air as her.'

Everybody looked at everybody else, but nobody moved.

Alexander said, 'I'll go.'

He went downstairs and eventually found her pretending to be asleep on the sofa in the sitting room, covered in a red blanket. She didn't open her eyes, but Alexander could see by the flickering of her eyelids that she wasn't really asleep.

He said, loudly, 'Eva wants to see you,' then watched her impersonating someone waking up. He felt a mixture of pity and contempt for her.

Poppy/Paula exclaimed, 'I must have fallen asleep! It was an exhausting morning. Everybody at the shelter wanted a little bit of Poppy time.'

Alexander said, 'Well, now Eva wants a little bit of Poppy time.'

When they walked into Eva's bedroom, Poppy was met by a room full of accusatory faces. But she'd been in similar situations many times before. 'Style it out, girl,' she said to herself.

Eva patted the side of the bed and said, 'Sit here, Paula. You don't have to lie any more. We know who you are. We know your parents are alive.' She held up a piece of paper. 'It says here that your mother went to the Department of Work and Pensions on the 22nd of December, and asked for a crisis loan, claiming that she had no money for Christmas. Your mother *is* Claire Theresa Maria Gibb, isn't she? Incidentally, are you Poppy or Paula?'

'Poppy,' the girl said, with a crooked nervous smile. 'Please, don't call me Paula. Please. Don't call me Paula. I gave myself a new name. Don't call me Paula.'

Eva took her hand and said, 'OK. You're Poppy. Why don't you try to be yourself?'

Poppy's first instinct was to pretend to cry, and sob, 'But I don't *know* who I am!' Then she became curious: who *was* she? She would try to drop the little-girl voice, she thought. When she looked at the fraying 1950s evening dress she was wearing, it suddenly didn't seem as charmingly eccentric as vintage clothes did on Helena Bonham Carter. And her big boots, with the carefully loosened laces, no longer gave her 'character'. She shifted the gears in her brain into neutral and waited a few seconds to see where this would take her. She said, testing her new voice, 'Can I stay until uni starts, please?'

Brianne and Brian Junior said, in unison, 'No!'

Eva said, 'Yes, you can stay until term starts. But these are the house rules. One, no more lies.'

Poppy repeated, 'No more lies.'

'Two, no more lounging on the sofa in your underwear. And three, no more stealing.'

Brianne said, 'I found our egg timer in her bag last night.'

Poppy sat down next to Alexander, who said, 'You've been given a great chance. Don't fuck it up.'

Brianne said, 'So, that's it, is it? She's forgiven, is she?'

'Yes,' said Eva. 'Just like I've forgiven Dad.'

Stanley raised his hand and asked, 'May *I* say something?' He looked at Poppy. 'I'm not a very forgiving person, and I cannot tell you how angry and distressed I am about your swastika tattoo. It has been preying on my mind. I know you are young, but you must have studied modern history and be fully aware that the swastika symbolises a great evil. And please don't tell me that your fascist tattoo represents a Hindu god, or some such nonsense. You and I know that you chose a swastika either because you're a Nazi, or because you wanted to boast about your alienation from our mostly decent society in order to shock. You could have chosen a snake, a flower, a bluebird, but you chose the swastika. I have in my house a collection of videos which chart the progress of the Second World War. One of those videos shows the liberation of Belsen, the concentration camp. Have you heard of Belsen?'

'It's where Anne Frank died. I did her for GCSE.'

Stanley continued, 'When the Allied troops arrived to free the prisoners, they found skeletal creatures barely alive, pleading for food and water. A large pit was discovered, full of dead bodies. Horrifically, some poor wretches were still alive. A bulldozer –'

Ruby shouted, 'No more, Stanley!'

'I apologise, I didn't want to upset . . .' He turned back to Poppy. 'If you would like to see the video, you are welcome to come and sit with me, and we will watch it together.'

Poppy shook her head.

There was silence.

Eventually, Poppy said, 'I'll have it removed, lasered off. I adore Anne Frank. I forgot she was a Jew. I cried when the Nazis found her in the attic. I only had a swastika tattoo when I was fourteen because I was infatuated with a boy who loved Hitler. He had a suitcase under his bed, full of daggers and medals and stuff. He told me that Hitler was an animal lover and a vegetarian, and he only wanted to bring peace to the world. When we were in his bedroom, his rule was that we called each other Adolf and Eva.'

Everybody looked at Eva, who said, 'Blame my mother.'

Ruby said indignantly, 'You're named after the film star. Eva Marie Saint.'

'He went off me after two months,' said Poppy, 'but the tattoo stayed.'

Stanley nodded. 'I shan't speak of it again.' He gave a little cough, which acted as a punctuation mark, then turned to Ruby and said, 'Ah, Eva Marie Saint. The scene with Marlon Brando. The swing, the glove, her lovely face.'

The conversation had turned.

Alexander was the last to leave Eva's room.

'If you need me, ring,' he said, 'and I'll come running.'

When he had gone, Eva could not get the words of the song out of her head. She started to sing it quietly, to herself. 'Winter, spring, summer or fall . . .'

In the middle of the night, when the rest of the household were asleep, Poppy crept into Eva's room. The walls were illuminated by the full moon, and it was by this light that Poppy climbed into the bed.

Eva stirred but did not wake.

Poppy laid her face against Eva's shoulder, and put her arm around Eva's waist.

In the morning, Eva felt the presence of another person. But when she turned to look, she saw only a depression in the pillow.

## 36

Mr Lin was excited when he saw Ho's handwriting on a letter he had picked up from his district post office in the Beijing suburbs. Perhaps Ho was writing to express holiday greetings. Mr Lin knew that in England people celebrated the birth of Jesus Christ – who, he had been told, was not only the son of their God, but had also been a revolutionary communist who was tortured and executed by the authorities.

He thought he would wait until he got home to open the letter. Or perhaps he would hand it to his wife and see the pleasure on her face. They both missed their child. It had been a difficult decision to send Ho to England, but they did not want him to be a factory worker like themselves. They wanted Ho to be a plastic surgeon and make a great deal of money. Young Chinese women across the world were growing ashamed of their oval eyes and small breasts.

Mr Lin stopped at a stall to buy a live chicken. He selected one that would provide meat for several days, paid for it and then carried it upside down to the vegetable and fruit market, where he bought a gift pack of holy apples as a present for his wife. The apples cost five times as much as ordinary apples, but Mr Lin liked his wife very much indeed. She hardly ever quarrelled with him, her hair was still black and her face had few lines. The only time she was sad was when she spoke about the daughter they could never have.

He reached the playground, which lay at the foot of the tower block where he and his wife lived on the twenty-seventh floor. He looked up and located their window. He hoped the lift was still working.

When he arrived home, panting and breathless, his wife rose from her chair and came to greet him.

He said, 'See who is writing to us,' and handed her Ho's letter.

She smiled with delight and touched the colourful red, green and gold nativity stamp as though it were a precious artefact. 'It is the birth of their Jesus,' she said.

The chicken squawked and struggled to be free. Mr Ho took it into the tiny kitchen and threw it into the sink. Then he and his wife sat down together, facing each other at the small table. Mrs Ho lay the letter down between them.

Mr Ho took the holy apples out of the plastic bag and placed them next to Ho's letter.

His wife smiled with delight.

He said, 'They are for you.'

She cried, 'But I have not bought you anything!'

'No need, you gave me Ho. You open the letter.'

She opened it slowly and carefully, and scanned the first few lines. Then she paused and her face became stone. She pushed it across the table and said, 'You must be strong, husband.'

Mr Lin gave several cries as he read through the document. When he came to the end, he said, 'I have never liked the Poppy flower. It is vulgar and it spreads its seeds too easily.'

The chicken squawked.

Mr Lin got up, took a sharp knife and a wooden block, and quickly severed the chicken's neck. He threw it back into the sink and watched the bright blood gush down the plughole.

# 37

On New Year's Eve a stranger, a woman, called at the door and asked to speak to Eva.

Titania, whose turn it was to answer the door, asked, 'Who may I say is calling?'

The woman said, 'I live at the end of Redwood Road. I'd rather not give my name.'

Titania invited the woman to wait in the hall while she went upstairs.

When Eva saw her, she said, 'You're wearing the awful apron Brian bought me for Christmas. What else have you commandeered?'

Titania laughed and said, 'Only your husband.'

Eva observed, 'That drab olive green suits you, though. You should wear more of it.' Then she said, 'Fetch her up.'

When Titania had gone downstairs, Eva combed her hair with her fingers and straightened the pillows.

The woman was in youthful middle age and had made the decision to let her hair grow au naturel. It was grey and wiry. She was wearing a grey tracksuit and grey Hi-Tec trainers. She looked like a pencil scribble on a white page.

Eva invited her to sit on the soup chair.

The woman announced, in well-spoken tones, 'My name is Bella Harper. I walk past your window at least four times a day.'

Eva said, 'Yes, I've seen you taking your kids to school.'

Bella pulled a handful of tissues out of her tracksuit pocket.

Eva braced herself for what was to come. She had developed a revulsion for tears. People cried too easily these days.

Bella said, 'I need some advice about the best and kindest way to leave my husband. This Christmas has been torture. We've all been tormented by him. I feel as though my exposed nerves have been agitated by a cold wind. I'm not sure that I can cope with any more.'

Eva asked, 'Why have you come to me?'

'You're always here. Sometimes I walk around the area in the small hours, and I often see you at the window, smoking.'

'I'm a fool,' said Eva. 'You don't want to take advice from me.'

'I've got to share my story with somebody who I don't know and doesn't know me.'

Eva stifled a yawn and tried to look interested. In her experience, nothing good came from giving advice.

Bella twisted a tissue around her fingers.

Eva prompted, 'OK, once upon a time . . . would that help?'

Bella said, 'Yes, once upon a time there was a boy and a girl who lived in the same village. When they were both

238

fifteen, they became engaged. Both of their families were very happy. One day, the boy lost his temper because the girl could not keep up with him when he went running. He shouted at the girl and frightened her. Then, just before the wedding, the boy and girl were in his car. She pulled the cigarette lighter from the dashboard, and accidentally dropped it on the carpet. The boy punched her on the right side of her face. Then he pulled her round to face him and punched her on the left. She lost two teeth and went to an emergency dentist. It took six weeks for the bruises to fade. But the wedding went ahead. It wasn't long before the boy was hitting the girl whenever he lost his temper. Afterwards, he would beg me to forgive him. I should have left him before the children were born.'

Eva asked, 'How many children?'

'Two boys,' replied Bella. 'I became so frightened of him that I couldn't relax when he was in the house. When he came home from work, the boys would go to their rooms and close the door.' Bella was wringing her hands. 'That's the end of the story.'

Eva said, 'You want to know what to do? How many strong men do you know?'

Bella said, 'Oh no, I don't condone violence.'

Eva repeated, 'How many strong men do you know?'

Bella counted in her head. 'Seven.'

'You must phone these men, and ask them to come to your rescue. You'll know when it's time.'

Bella nodded.

'What's your husband's name?'

239

'Kenneth Harper.'

'And for how much longer are you going to live with Kenneth Harper?'

Bella lowered her eyes and said, 'I want to start the New Year without him.' She looked at her watch and said, in a panic, 'No! He's in the pub, but he's coming home for dinner at nine. It's eight now and I haven't peeled a potato! I'll have to go. He won't like it if his dinner's late.'

Eva shouted over Bella's panic, 'Where are your children?'

'At my mother's,' said Bella, who had jumped up and was pacing from the bed to the door.

'Gather some men together, phone them now. Tell them to meet here.'

'I don't approve of vigilantism,' said Bella.

'It isn't vigilantism, it's your family and friends protecting you and your children. Imagine living in the house without him. Go on, close your eyes and imagine.'

Bella closed her eyes for so long that Eva thought she might be asleep.

Then Bella took out her phone and started to speed-dial.

When Brian came back from the off-licence with six bottles of cava, a slab of Carling Black Label, a box of rosé and two giant bags of mixed crisps for seeing in the New Year, he was astonished to find a group of men sitting on the stairs and leaning against the walls in the hallway.

He nodded and said, 'I'm afraid you're too early for our Open House, the house isn't open yet.'

Their spokesman, a man in a padded plaid shirt and slurry-covered wellingtons, said, 'My sister has asked us to help chuck her husband out of the house.'

Brian said, 'On New Year's Eve? Poor chap. Isn't that a bit off?'

A younger man, whose fists were clenching and unclenching, said, 'That bastard's had it coming. I wanted to tear his head off at the altar.'

A man with a weather-beaten face and DIY haircut said, 'The kids are terrified of him. But she would never leave him 'cause he threatened to top himself. I wish.'

An older man with tired eyes, who was sitting on the stairs, said, 'When he asked if he could marry my daughter, I should have kicked him into the bloody silage pit.' He looked at Brian, a man he assumed to be of a similar age to himself, and asked, 'Have you got a daughter?'

Brian said, 'I have, indeed. She's seventeen.'

'What would you do if you knew your daughter was being beaten up on a regular basis?'

Brian put the box of wine down on the floor, tugged his beard and thought.

Eventually, he said, 'I would gag and bind him, put him in the boot of my car, drive him to a quarry of my acquaintance and attach him by means of nylon rope, using mariner's knots, to a loose rock. I would then roll him and the rock over the edge of the quarry, and wait for the splash. Problem solved.'

A nervous-looking man said, 'You can't do that.

Where would we be if we went round murdering everybody we didn't like? We'd end up living in a cooler version of Mogadishu.'

Brian retorted, 'This chap asked me what I'd do, and I told him. Anyway, I've got the Open House to organise. But if you need the sat nav coordinates for that quarry . . .'

The older man said, 'Thank you, but I don't think it'll come to that. But if it does, we've got a silage pit round the back of the house, and pigs that are always hungry.'

'Well, I wish you all the best. Have a happy New Year,' said Brian. He barged past with the alcohol, went into the kitchen and began to unpack it on to the table. Titania was already polishing the glasses.

Brian said, 'Every time I open my own front door, I'm presented with other people's dramas.'

Upstairs, Bella was talking to her husband on the phone. He was shouting so loudly that Eva half expected the phone to explode. Bella's voice was trembling. She was saying, 'Kenneth, I'm with my family. We're only up the road. We're leaving for home now.' She switched off the phone and said to Eva, 'I can't do it to him.'

Eva said, 'They get away with it because they know we pity them. They play on their weakness. If you go now, he could be out of the house by ten.'

'But where will he go?' wailed Bella.

'Is his mother alive?' asked Eva.

Bella nodded and said, 'She only lives five miles away, but he never goes to see her.'

'Well, it will be a lovely New Year's Eve surprise for her then, won't it?'

Later, Eva watched from the window as the seven men and Bella talked on the pavement.

They walked purposefully down the road towards Bella's house.

# 38

Eva knew it was midnight by the sound of church bells ringing and rockets exploding. She heard corks popping downstairs and Brian's voice booming, 'Happy New Year!'

She thought about all her previous New Years. She had always expected more from the night. Had waited in vain for something extraordinary and magical to happen once the long hand of the clock moved away from the twelve.

But everything had always been the same.

She had never been able to join in with 'Auld Lang Syne'. She liked the words 'We'll raise a cup of kindness' and she envied those celebrating, but she could not link arms and dance in a circle with the others. People would break the circle and invite her in to fill the space, but she invariably refused.

'I like watching,' she always said.

Brian would say, as he flung himself about, 'Eva doesn't know how to have fun.'

And it was true. She even disliked the word. 'Fun' suggested enforced gaiety, clowns, slapstick. North Korean parades where ranks of synchronised children danced with a fixed smile.

Now she was hungry and thirsty. She had obviously been forgotten again.

Earlier that morning, Brian had gone up and down the street delivering leaflets inviting the neighbours to an Open House party. The leaflet had said (she had shuddered at the word 'pop'):

Please pop in, and have some fun.

Let's get to know each other.

Bring a bottle.

Nibbles supplied, but I suggest you eat before coming.

Well-behaved children tolerated.

Our door will be open to you from 9.30 p.m.

PS: Dr Brian Beaver will conduct a short tour of his observatory and, depending on the seeing (or, as you non-astronomers define it, atmospheric conditions/cloud cover), it may be possible to view Saturn, Jupiter, Mars and perhaps the more minor planets.

Yvonne had bought Eva a charming brass temple bell from Bali via Homebase, as a means of communicating with others in the house, but Eva had yet to ring it. There was something distasteful about summoning others to attend to her needs. She would wait until somebody remembered her and brought her something to eat. Through the wall she could hear the twins muttering and tapping on their laptops. The speed of the keys was uncanny. Every now and again there was harsh laughter, and cries of, 'High five!'

She heard her mother and Yvonne making their way up the stairs.

Ruby said, 'I don't know whether to go to the doctor's with it or not. It could be a harmless cyst.'

Yvonne said, 'As you know, Ruby, I was a doctor's receptionist for thirty years. I can tell a cyst from something nasty.'

She heard them go into the bathroom together.

Ruby sounded uncertain of herself, for once. 'Should I take my corset, vest and bra off?'

Yvonne replied, 'Well, I can't tell anything through layers of cloth, can I? Don't be shy, I've seen thousands of titties in my time.'

There was silence, which was broken by Ruby gabbling nervously, 'Do you think Eva is having a nervous breakdown?'

Yvonne instructed her, 'Put your arm above your head, and keep still . . . Yes, she's had a breakdown. I said it from the first day.'

There was silence again.

Then Eva heard Yvonne say, 'Put your clothes back on.'

Ruby asked, 'Well? What do you think?'

'I think you ought to have an X-ray. There's a lump the size of a walnut. How long have you known about it?'

'I'm too busy to hang about at the hospital.' Ruby lowered her voice. 'I have to look after *her*.'

Eva wondered if she *was* having a breakdown.

A few years ago, Jill – a colleague of hers at the library – had suddenly started to talk to herself, muttering that she was unhappily married to Bernie Ecclestone. She then started to throw all the books with red covers on to the floor, saying that they were spying on her and relaying messages to MI5. When anyone approached her, she had screamed at them that they were agents of The System. Some fool had called security and tried to drag her out of an emergency exit. She had fought them off like a wild animal, all teeth, fingernails and snarls, and had run towards the public park that bordered the university grounds.

Eva and the security men had followed her. The overweight security men were soon out of breath. It was Eva who caught up with her. Jill had thrown herself face down on the grass and was holding on to the tufts, saying, 'Help me! If I let go of the grass, I'll float away.'

Eva thought the kindest thing would be to sit on Jill's back and pin her to the ground. When the panting security men approached, Jill had started to scream and struggle again. A police car had driven across the park at high speed, with its siren screaming. Eva could do nothing more to help her friend. The policemen and the security men finally managed to restrain her, and the car had taken Jill away.

When Eva was finally allowed to visit Jill in the psychiatric unit, she did not at first recognise her. She was in a featureless room, sitting on a plastic chair, rocking slightly. The other patients scared Eva. The noise of the television was intolerable.

'This is bedlam,' she thought. 'It is actually Bedlam.' As she walked through the hospital grounds, she thought, 'I would rather be dead than be sent to a place like this.'

Years later, she had seen an amateur production of

*Marat/Sade* performed by The Faculty Players. Brian had been a very convincing lunatic. For some weeks afterwards, she had been haunted by the thought that madness could be lurking just around the corner, waiting to sneak inside your head while you were sleeping and engulf you.

Eva did sleep for a while. When she awoke, she was startled to see Julie, her neighbour, sitting in the soup chair.

Julie said, 'I've been watching you sleep, you were snoring. I came to wish you a happy New Year, and to get out of that madhouse I call home. I'm at breaking point, Eva. They don't listen to me now. They've lost all respect for me. We spent a fortune on their Christmas presents. Steve bought the eldest boys a PlayStation each, and a television for Scott so he can watch his cartoons as he goes to sleep. They all had a big sack from Santa, full of toys, and half of them are already broken. Steve can't wait to get back to work, and neither can I.'

Eva, who was feeling irritable due to lack of food, said, 'For Christ's sake, Julie, if they play you up, you confiscate their bloody PlayStations! Lock them away until they learn some respect. And remind Steve that he's an adult male. That cajoling tone he uses with them isn't working. Can he actually raise his voice?'

'Only at the football on the telly.'

Eva said, 'You and Steve are scared to discipline them because you think they won't love you any more.' Then she roared, 'You're wrong!'

Julie jumped and started fanning her fingers in front of her eyes.

Eva regretted shouting so loudly, but neither of them knew what to say next.

Julie looked critically at Eva's hair. 'Want me to give you a trim, and do your roots?'

'When the boys are back at school, eh? I'm sorry I shouted, Julie, but I'm so hungry. Will you fetch me some food, please? They keep forgetting I'm here.'

'Either that, or they're trying to starve you out!' said Julie.

When Julie had gone back to her anarchic household, Eva felt a surge of self-pity, and almost wished she was downstairs grazing the buffet. She heard Brian shout, '"Brown Sugar"! C'mon, Titania.'

When the music started, she imagined them strutting in the kitchen and singing along with The Rolling Stones.

## 39

It was New Year's Day. Brian and Titania had been making love for most of the afternoon. Brian had ingested Viagra at 2.15 p.m. and was still going strong.

Every now and again, Titania moaned, 'OMG!' But the truth was that she'd had enough. Brian had explored most of her orifices and she was glad he appeared to be having a good time, but she had things to do, people to see. She drummed her fingers on his back, absent-mindedly. But this only served to spur him on and before she knew it he had turned her upside down so that she was almost suffocated by the duck-feather pillows gathering around her face. She had to fight for air. 'OMG!' she shouted. 'Are you trying to kill me?'

Brian stopped to get his breath back for a few moments, and said, 'Look, Titania, can you go back to shouting "Oh my God!"? OMG does nothing for me.'

Titania, who was still upside down with her legs leaning against the wall, said, 'We're like two water buffalo yoked together, endlessly turning a bloody wheel. How many Viagra did you take?'

'Two,' said Brian.

'One would have been sufficient,' complained Titania. 'I could have finished your ironing by now.'

Brian made a superhuman effort, summoning up

images that had served him well over the years: the cleavage of Miss Fox, who had taught him physics at Cardinal Wolsey Grammar; French women lying topless on a beach near St Malo; the woman eating a cream horn in the back of the bakery, the cream on the end of her tongue.

Nothing worked. They battled on and on.

Titania kept looking at her watch. Her head and torso were now hanging over the end of the bed. She saw a rolled-up pair of her socks she had thought were lost under the chest of drawers. 'OMGIH!' she shouted. 'How much longer?'

Brian whispered, 'Let's have angry sex.'

Titania said, 'I'm already having angry sex, I'm totally pissed off! If you don't get off me soon, I'm going to –'

She didn't need to finish her sentence. Brian ejaculated so violently and noisily that Ruby, who was in the garden standing over a drain and rinsing the fetid head of an old-fashioned mop with a garden hose, thought that he had started keeping wild animals in his shed.

Nothing could surprise her any more. She'd once thought that paying £1.70 for a bottle of water from Iceland was about as daft as you could get – especially when there was nice cold water in the tap. But she'd been wrong.

Somehow, while her attention had been elsewhere, everybody in the world had gone mad.

Alexander let himself into Eva's house – the door was usually on the latch these days – and shouted, 'Hello!'

Nobody apart from Eva answered.

He walked upstairs, rehearsing what he was going to say. It was a long time since he had declared his love for a woman.

Eva said, 'Happy New Year. You look cold.'

He said, 'I am . . . and Happy New Year too. I've been on Beacon Hill, painting. I've never tried a snowscape before. I didn't know how many shades of white there are in snow. I made a dog's dinner of it. I passed Ruby on the main road and gave her a lift. She said that Brian and Titania were doing very noisy animal impressions in his shed.'

'I can hear the neighbours sharpening their pencils for the petition.'

They both laughed.

Eva said, 'I'm mystified by their relationship.'

'At least they've got a relationship.'

'But they don't seem to like each other.'

Alexander said, 'I like you, Eva.'

Eva said, holding his gaze, 'I like you, Alex.'

There was a fragility to the space between them, as though their breath had frozen and could easily shatter if the wrong word were said.

Eva knelt at the window to check on the snow. 'Fresh drifts . . . good for snowmen, sledging. I'd love to –'

She stopped herself, but he was quick to jump in and say, 'You could, Eva! You could speed down a hill with your arms around my waist, I've got a sledge in the back of the van.'

Eva said, 'Don't you start trying to get me out of bed!'

Alexander said, 'A few years ago, I was working hard to get a woman into bed.'

She smiled. 'I think my first New Year resolution is to avoid having a new man in my life.'

'I'm sorry to hear that. I've come here to tell you that I love you.'

Eva moved from the middle of the bed to the edge, pressing herself against the wall.

Alexander asked, 'Have I got it wrong?'

She said carefully, not wanting to hurt his feelings, 'Perhaps I gave out the wrong signals. As the sacked railwayman said.'

'Perhaps we both gave out the wrong signals. Shall I just say what I feel?'

She nodded.

'I love you,' he said. 'I want to live with you for the rest of my life. You wouldn't have to get out of bed. I'd push you round Sainsbury's in it, take you to Glastonbury.'

She shook her head. 'No, I don't want to hear this. I will not be responsible for another person's happiness. I'm no good at it.'

Alexander said, 'I'll look after you. We can still be together. I'll sit in bed with you. I'll be Yoko to your John, if you like.'

'You have children, and I have children,' she said. 'And you must know that Brianne is in love with you. I wouldn't want *her* as a love rival.'

'She's a kid, it's just a crush. The love of her life is Brian Junior.'

'I've finished the daily routine of looking after small children.'

He said in amazement, his voice going up an octave, 'You don't like my kids?'

'They're lovely, funny kids,' Eva said. 'But I'm finished with child-rearing. I can't bear to watch their disillusionment when they find out what sort of world they live in.'

Alexander said, 'Shit happens, but it's still a fantastic world. If you'd seen the sun shining on the snow this morning . . . and the trees, with the ice falling off them like silver rain . . .'

Eva said, 'I'm sorry.'

'Can I lie down next to you?'

'On top of the duvet.'

He took his wet boots off, and put them on top of the radiator. Then he lay down next to her.

There were no lights on, and the sun had gone down, but the luminous snow outside made it possible to see the outline of the room. They held hands and looked at the ceiling. They talked about their previous lovers, about his dead wife and her present husband. The room was warm, and the light was low, and soon they were asleep, side by side like marble effigies.

When Brianne returned from spending her John Lewis gift tokens on a bound watercolour artist's notebook for Alexander, she pushed open Eva's door and saw that her mother was asleep on top of the duvet.

There was a note on the pillow. She took it on to the landing to read. It was from Alexander. It said:

*Dearest Eva,*

*I had one of the best days of my life today. The snow was magical, and lying next to you this afternoon was the happiest I've been for many years.*

*We do love each other, I know this for certain. But I will stay away.*

*Why is everything connected with love so painful?*
*Alex*

Brianne took the note into her own room, ripped it into tiny pieces and hid the fragments inside an empty crisp packet she retrieved from the bin.

# 40

Brian and Titania were eating a late-night supper after a long session of stargazing. The conditions were perfect, and they had seen wonders and marvels in the cold cloudless sky. They never failed to be moved by the reality of what they saw through an actual telescope. The computer screens at work could not convey the true beauty of the universe.

As Brian chewed on a cold lamb cutlet he said, 'You were rather wonderful tonight, Tit. You kept your mouth shut for most of the time, and you spotted that variable star, which I'm pretty sure hasn't been logged yet.'

Titania forked a stuffed olive out of the jar. She couldn't remember a time when she'd been as happy as this. She wanted Brian to go forward and do great things. His dedication to his work was total. Titania felt that, in the past, Eva had held him back by expecting him to take on his share of the child-rearing. Poor Brian had not been able to finish his book, *Near-Earth Objects*, because of Eva's demands on his time. Did Mrs Churchill insist that her husband set the table before attending to the war?

She reached a hand out.

Brian said, 'What?'

Titania whispered, 'Hold my hand.'

Brian cautioned, 'I should warn you, Tit, that I'm still half in love with my wife.'

Titania withdrew her hand. 'Does that mean you're half in love with me?'

Brian said, 'For over twenty years, my synapses have been attuned to living with Eva Beaver. You'll have to give them a chance to adapt to you, Tit.'

Titania thought, 'I'll make him love me. I'll be the perfect lover, colleague and friend. I will actually iron his fucking shirts.'

Later, when they were in bed, talking about their childhoods and their first conscious sight of the stars, Brian said, 'It was when I was seven, lying on my back in my grandmother's garden in Derbyshire. It was dusk and the stars started to appear, almost one by one. Then the sky slowly turned from deep blue to black, until the stars seemed to be blazing. The next day at school, I asked Mrs Perkins what kept them up. Why didn't they fall down? She told me they were all suns and that they were held up by something called gravity. I went into my first reverie. At going-home time she gave me a book, *The Ladybird Book of The Night Sky*. I've still got it. And I want to be buried with it – in Death Valley, Nevada.'

'For the seeing?' asked Titania. She was rewarded when Brian put his arm around her fleshy shoulder and held her right breast. She continued, 'I used to take a Milky Way wrapper out into the garden and try to match the illustration with something in the night sky. I loved those chocolate bars, because they were advertised as being something one could eat between meals.'

Brian laughed. 'On the rare occasions when the sky was clear in Leicester, I saw the Milky Way, and I was overwhelmed. I felt very small indeed.' He went on, pedantically, 'Although I wasn't overwhelmed at first. That only came when I actually understood that the Milky Way is one of the spiral arms of our own galaxy.'

'Galaxy!' said Titania, who was emboldened by Brian's chumminess. 'Another delish space-nomenclature chocolate bar! But the Milky Way had the moral high ground. Our parents approved of it. The name "Milky Way" would be a good replacement for your wife's White Pathway.'

Brian was not listening to what he called 'Tit's burble'. He was thinking about the Mars Bar. The war horse of chocolate bars.

Titania said, 'Do you think she's clinically mad, Bri? There's the sheet to get to the loo, and she's started talking to herself now. Because, if so, we should think about getting her diagnosed. And possibly hospitalised – for her own sake.'

Brian didn't like Titania's use of 'we'. He said, irritably, 'It's hard to tell with Eva.' He was loath to criticise his wife in front of his lover. He thought of Eva's lovely face, then looked at Titania. There was no comparison in the looks department. He said, 'She's not talking to herself, she's reciting all the poems she learned by heart at school.'

Brian switched the bedside light off and they settled down, ready for sleep.

Half an hour later, they were still awake.

Titania was mentally organising her marriage to Brian. She thought they would have a traditional wedding. She planned to wear ivory silk.

Brian was wondering if he could stand to live with Titania, a woman who got through a large bag of Maltesers *every* night. He didn't begrudge her buying them for herself, but he hated the way she rolled several of them around in her mouth.

He could hear the tiny collisions with her teeth.

# 41

On the 6th of January, before their return to Leeds, the twins were sitting in the Percy Gee Building sipping Diet Coke.

'You don't know what it's like,' said Brianne. 'You've never been in love.'

She and Brian Junior were waiting to take part in the out-of-term maths competition held at the University of Leicester. The Norman Lamont Cup attracted very few British entrants. The majority of the other competitors did not have English as their first language.

Brian Junior said, 'I may not have experienced romantic love myself, but I've read books about it. And to be honest, I don't think it's up to much.'

'It's a physical pain,' said Brianne.

'But only if it's unrequited, like yours for Alexander.'

Brianne banged her head on the plastic table. 'Why can't he love me back?'

Brian Junior thought for a long time. Brianne waited patiently. They both respected the process of turning precise thought into clear expression.

Eventually, Brian Junior said, 'One, he's in love with Mum. Two, you're not loveable, Brianne. And three, you're not pretty either.'

Brianne said, 'It really is annoying that you're the one with Mum's physical-beauty genes.'

Brian Junior nodded. 'And you've been given Dad's intimidating masculinity. I'd quite like that.'

'Why don't you just, like, *say* I'm big and butch?' said Brianne.

There was a loudspeaker announcement: 'The participants of Level One are asked to make their way to the David Attenborough room.'

The twins remained seated. They watched as the majority of competitors shuffled towards the examination room, much as First Class passengers watch disdainfully as Economy Class passengers traipse towards the boarding desk with their cheap suitcases and grizzling children.

It was a moment the twins always savoured. They said, 'Sick!' and slapped a high five.

Their remaining opponents looked up nervously from their laptops. The Beaver twins were a formidable team.

Brianne asked her brother, 'Do you think we'll ever find some randoms to love us, Bri?'

'Does it matter? We both know we'll be together for life, like swans.'

# 42

It was three o'clock in the morning. A time when frail people die. Eva was keeping watch on her territory. She saw the foxes casually crossing the road, as though they were shoppers in a village high street. Other small mammals that she couldn't identify were out and about.

She watched as a black cab turned into the road opposite and then turned again to park outside her house. She watched the driver get out; he was a big man. He rang the doorbell.

Eva thought, 'Who in this house has rung for a cab at this time of the morning?'

After a moment, the bell rang again.

She heard Poppy running along the hallway to open the door, shouting, 'OK, OK, I'm coming!'

There was an altercation on the doorstep – Poppy's high voice and a man's deep rumble.

Poppy shouted, 'No, you can't come in, she's asleep!'

The man insisted, 'No, she isn't. I've just seen her at the window. I've gotta talk to her.'

Poppy said, 'Come back tomorrow.'

'I can't wait until tomorrow,' the man said. 'I need to see her now.'

Poppy screamed, 'You can't come in! Go away!'

'Please,' the man begged. 'We're talking life and death here. So, if you wun't mind, get out of my way.'

'Don't touch me, don't touch me! Take your hands off me!'

Eva was rigid with fear and guilt. She must go downstairs and confront the man herself but, although she swung her legs out of the bed, she could not lower her feet on to the floor. Not even to save Poppy. She wondered if she could have run downstairs if the twins were exposed to a similar danger.

'Sorry, sorry, but I've got to see her.'

Eva heard a heavy tread on the stairs. She swung her legs back into the bed and pulled the duvet around her neck, like a child might after a nightmare. She braced herself for the man's entrance.

Suddenly he was there, in her room, blinking in the bright light. He had a night-shift worker's exhausted face. He needed a shave and his hair was lank as he pushed a few locks out of his eyes and behind his ears. His clothes looked rumpled and neglected. He was breathing heavily.

Eva thought to herself, 'I mustn't antagonise him. I must try to keep calm. He's obviously in a state.' She looked to see if he was carrying anything that could be construed as a weapon. His hands were empty.

'You're Eva Beaver, aren't you?'

Eva lowered the duvet a little and asked, 'What do you want?'

'The other drivers were talking about you. They don't

know who you are, but they see you sometimes in the window through the night. Some of them think you're a prostitute. I never thought that. But then one of Bella's brothers told me that you'd helped 'em out.'

'Bella Harper?' said Eva.

'Yeah,' said the man. 'He said that you gave free advice twenty-four seven. He said you were a saint.'

Eva laughed. 'Your informant was wrong.'

Poppy had run into the twins' bedrooms and woken them up. They stumbled into Eva's room, Brian Junior holding his old cricket bat, wide-eyed with fear. Brianne stood behind him with a martyred screwed-up expression on her face, yawning and blinking.

Brian Junior said viciously, 'Get out of my mother's bedroom!'

'I'm not going to hurt her, son,' the taxi driver said. 'I just need to talk to her.'

'At three a.m.?' said Brianne, sarcastically. 'Why? Is it the end of the world? Or something more important?'

The man turned to Eva with such a forlorn look that she said, 'I don't know your name.'

'I'm Barry Wooton.'

'I'm Eva. Please, sit down.' Then, to the twins, 'It will be all right, go back to bed.'

Brian Junior said, 'We're not leaving.'

Barry sat down in the soup chair and closed his eyes. 'I can't believe I'm here.'

Poppy, who was desperately trying to ingratiate herself with Eva, asked, 'Can I get anybody a cup of tea?'

Brianne said, 'I sometimes think Dad's right about this bloody country and tea.'

'I'll have one,' said Eva.

'Yeah, me too,' said the driver. 'Not much milk, two sugars.'

Brian Junior said, 'Green tea, and I'll have it in here.' He leaned against the wall and swung the cricket bat into the palm of his right hand, making a smacking sound.

Brianne was wearing a pair of her father's pyjamas. They fitted her well. She sat down on the bed and put her arm protectively around her mother's waist.

Poppy said, 'Should I tell Brian and Titania?'

'Absolutely not,' said Eva.

Barry looked around at the four strangers and said, 'I don't usually carry on like this. I'm surprised at myself. I've been wanting to talk to you, Mrs Beaver. Every time I've passed your house, I've wanted to stop the cab and knock on your door.'

'Why tonight?'

'I suppose I wanted to talk to somebody before I do myself in.'

Brianne said, 'Oh, how lovely. You must surely know, Barry, that my mother, whose heart is as soggy as Romney Marsh, will try to talk you out of it.'

Brian Junior said in a monotone, 'You've no intention of killing yourself, Barry.'

Brianne asked, 'Have you posted it online?'

'What?' said Barry.

'It's almost obligatory now, Barry. You have to go on

the net and join the queue with the rest of the attention whores.'

Eva looked at her children. What had happened to them? Why were they so heartless?

Barry shifted in the chair. He felt that he could easily die of embarrassment. His tongue was huge in his mouth. He thought that he would not be able to speak again. Water started to drip from his eyes. He was glad when the weird-looking girl came in with three mugs of tea and handed one to him. He had never seen anybody dressed in such extravagant bits of cloth before. He slurped on his tea and burned his mouth, but he said nothing about the pain.

The silence was oppressive.

Eventually, Eva said, 'Why do you want to kill yourself?'

Barry opened his mouth to speak, but Brianne interrupted him. 'I think I'll take myself off to bed now. I cannot bear the thought of all the clichés that are presently stirring inside Barry's head, and their imminent arrival at, and escape from, Barry's voice box.'

Brian Junior said, 'You're out of your element, Barry.'

Brianne drew her dressing gown tightly around her and went haughtily back to bed.

Eva said, 'Poppy, you go to bed now.'

Poppy sulked out of the room.

Barry couldn't work out whether he had been insulted or not by the tall, chunky black-haired girl. He hadn't expected other people to be there when he talked to the woman, Eva. He had made things worse for himself, he thought. He had almost certainly been disrespected, he had burned his mouth, he'd lost fares, and he'd forgotten until now that the first high-speed train that he was planning to throw himself under didn't leave Sheffield until 5 a.m. So he had three hours to kill.

'As usual,' he thought, 'I've mucked everything up. I've done it all my life: lost stuff, broken stuff, stolen stuff, been caught with stuff.' He felt that he had never learned the rules of life, whereas every other man, woman, kid and animal knew them. He was always lagging behind – sometimes literally – shouting, 'Wait for me!' He'd only ever been able to court the dregs of women that his mates had discarded.

A girl had once said to him, 'I'm not being funny, Barry, but you don't half stink.'

Since then, he had bathed twice a day. But it took up a lot of time without a shower, and his hot-water bill had doubled. He was earning less these days – people weren't going out at night, or giving many tips. Sometimes he didn't even cover his petrol costs. He had no family. After he had fought with his new brother-in-law at the wedding reception, his mother had said to him dramatically, 'You are no longer my son. You are dead to me.' But, to be honest, he had enjoyed knocking that tosser on to the dance floor. Nobody called his sister a slag. But even she had turned against him. In the day, while he was trying to sleep, the fight went round and round in his head. He was so tired, but he could never sleep properly . . .

Eva said, 'You look exhausted.'

Barry nodded. 'I am. And I've got worries.'

'What's at the top of the list?'

'How much will it hurt when the train goes over me neck? That's my main worry. It's bound to hurt before I die.'

Eva said, 'There are easier ways, Barry. And think about the train driver, he'll have it on his mind for ever. All you'd be to the passengers is an hour's delay, while they search the track for your head and limbs. Think of a stranger swinging your decapitated head in a Tesco's carrier bag.'

Brian Junior said, 'Is that what they do?'

'I saw a documentary,' said Eva.

Barry said, 'So, you don't think the train?'

'No,' said Eva. 'Definitely not the train.'

Barry said, 'I thought about hanging. I've got a beam . . .'

'No,' said Eva, firmly. 'You could hang there for minutes. Fighting for breath. It doesn't always break the neck, Barry.'

'Right, strike that off the list then. Have you got any thoughts about drowning?'

'No. I've got a friend called Virginia Woolf,' lied Eva, 'who filled her pockets with stones and walked into the sea.'

Barry asked, 'Did it work?'

'No,' she lied again. 'It didn't work. She's glad it didn't work now.'

'What about Paracetamol?' said Barry.

'Not bad,' said Eva, 'but if you don't die, you could

poison your liver and suffer an agonising death a fort-night later. Or have your kidneys fail and end up on dialysis. Four hours a day, five times a week, with your own blood going round in plastic tubes in front of you.'

Barry said, 'Sounds easier to live.' He gave a humour-less laugh.

Brian Junior said, morosely, 'I could cave your head in with this cricket bat.'

Barry laughed again. 'No, I think I'll leave it, thank you.'

Eva said, 'You might as well live, Barry. What's the second worry on your list?'

'How to make some real friends,' said Barry.

Eva asked, 'Do you smoke?'

He shook his head. 'No, it's a disgusting habit.'

'You should take it up, and then you could join all the little groups standing outside their pubs and clubs. You'd be part of a despised minority, with a great sense of soli-darity. You'd soon make friends. And you wouldn't actually have to smoke the fags, just light them and hold them between your fingers.'

Barry looked dubious.

Eva said, 'Don't like that idea?'

'Not really.'

Eva snapped, 'OK, so buy a dog.'

Brian Junior said, 'Have you got a computer, dude?'

Barry was thrilled to be called 'dude'. It had never happened to him before. 'Yeah, I gotta laptop, but I only use it for DVDs.'

Brian Junior was scandalised. 'Don't tell me that! It's

like only putting a toe in the water instead of swimming. There's another world, Barry. And I'm not talking about the deep web. Even a beginner can access amazing things, things that will change your life. There are millions of dudes like you online, you could connect with them. A couple of days and you'd have an entirely different perspective on your life. There are people out there who want to be your friend.'

'I wouldn't know where to start,' Barry said. 'I've got the book that came with the computer, but it's all a load of gobbledegook to me.'

Brian Junior encouraged him, 'It's easy! You just press a few keys, and there it is – the internet, the world, laid out in front of you.'

'Which keys?'

Brian Junior was growing tired of Barry's obduracy. 'I can give you some guidance, a few sites, but don't ask me to get involved with any of that emo suicide crap. I'd help you, man, but I'm so bored with hearing the same story. Fat, bad teeth, no friends, no girl at the prom. The end.'

Barry ran his tongue over his derelict teeth.

Eva said to Barry, 'Ignore Brian Junior and his sister, they live in a very small world called the internet, where cynicism is the norm and cruelty has taken the place of humour.'

Brian Junior agreed, 'It's undeniably true.'

Eva said, 'I can give you some practical advice, if you want it.'

Barry nodded. 'I'll take anything that's going.'

'When you're in the bath,' said Eva, 'wash and rinse your hair properly and use a conditioner. And go to a barber's and ask for a modern cut. And your clothes . . . don't wear such childish colours. You're not a presenter on kids' TV.'

Barry was leaning forward with his mouth slightly open, listening carefully.

Eva continued, 'Find a good NHS dentist and get those teeth fixed. And when you talk to women, remember that conversation is like ping pong. You say something, she says something. Then you respond to something she's just said, then she bats it back. You ask her a question. She replies. Do you get the idea?'

Barry nodded.

'Get a good twenty-four-hour deodorant. And smile, Barry, show her those new teeth.'

Barry said, 'I should be writing this down.'

Brian Junior was enjoying his role as an IT guru. 'No need. There are websites for shut-ins. There's a sort of guidebook for losers. Lots of useful information. For instance, it tells you how to walk down the street without scaring people: no direct eye contact with approaching women, and never walk behind a woman at night. Food: don't choose spaghetti on a first date. Clothes: what colour socks to wear with brown shoes. *Never* wear grey shoes at any time. And stuff about sex, and so on.'

Barry half smiled. 'I'd better go home and chuck all my grey shoes out then.'

Eva checked, 'So, you're not going to the railway line?'

'No, I'm knackered. I'm gonna go home and get some sleep.'

Brian Junior said, 'The best website is basementdwellers dot org. It's got an American bias, but ignore all the stuff about how to behave at a baseball game.'

Barry admitted, 'I'm not much good at reading, but I'll give it a go. Thank you.' He got to his feet and said to Eva, 'I'm sorry for turning up like that. Can I come back at a proper time?'

'Yes, we want to know how you get on, don't we, Brian Junior?'

Brian Junior said, 'I have very little human curiosity, Barry, so I'm not especially bothered, but I know my mother would appreciate another fleeting visit. Perhaps when your teeth are fixed? I'll show you downstairs, give you some internet basics and the web address.'

At the door, Barry turned and flashed a smile at Eva. His mouth looked like the Colosseum without the cats.

For a few minutes, there was a low mumbling from the hallway. When she heard the door slam, Eva moved to the window and waved Barry off.

He started the engine, then did a three-point turn . . . and another . . . and another.

She realised eventually that Barry was doing the taxi drivers' equivalent of a victory roll.

# 43

The snow had disrupted the country. Transport and services, including postal deliveries, were erratic.

At six thirty in the evening, a week later, a postcard from Alexander was pushed through the letter box, together with junk mail and bills. Brian took the post and sorted through it at the kitchen table. On one side of the postcard was a hand-painted watercolour snow scene of the Thames, with Westminster Bridge and the Houses of Parliament.

Brian turned the card over and read:

> *Dear Eva,*
>
> *I am going crazy in my mother-in-law's house, she insists we all start the day at 7 a.m., and that we are in bed by 9 p.m. 'to save on the electric'.*
>
> *I have sold four pictures since I've been here. Although my mother-in-law thinks that 'daubing a bit of paint on paper is no way for a man to make a living'.*
>
> *We're back in Leicester next week. I think about you every day.*

Brian looked at the small painting on the postcard and made a camel-like noise. It didn't look much like the Houses of Parliament to him. And since when had the

Thames been blue and spilled over on to the Embankment like that? He considered Impressionism to be cheating, in any case.

He threw the postcard into the 'miscellaneous' drawer of the kitchen dresser, then turned back to the tray he was preparing for Eva. It held a plate of cheese sandwiches, an apple, an orange and half a packet of digestive biscuits.

He filled a flask with hot tea, then took the tray upstairs to Eva, and said, 'That will keep you going until I get back. Why the fuck did they have to go to Leeds? We've got two fine universities on our bloody doorstep. I can see them when I'm shaving!'

There was silence in the car. Poppy was playing the penitent.

Brian said to her, after a few miles, 'You're not your usual chatterbox self, Poppy.'

Poppy said, quietly, 'No, I've been meditating. I'm trying to find out who I am, Brian. I have individuation issues.'

The twins sniggered.

Brianne said, from the back seat, 'I know exactly who you are, Poppy. Would you like me to tell you?'

Poppy said, meekly, 'No, but thank you, Brianne.'

Brianne sat back in her seat, enjoying the moment.

Brian Junior said, 'I can't take any more of this tension. It's not only that you're a dangerous driver, Dad, it's the knowledge that we all have this bitter internal monologue running inside our heads. Can we put some music on, please?'

Brian said, 'I'll take criticism of my driving when you've been behind the wheel a good few years, son. And I'm still hopeful that we can forget Christmas and move forward. Why don't we have an interesting conversation? I've chosen a few topics – would you like to hear them?'

Poppy said, 'Yes,' while the twins said, 'No,' at the same time.

Brian said, 'OK, how about youth unemployment?'

Nobody responded.

'The euro?'

Again, nobody responded.

'All right, something for you young people. Which would kill you faster – a shark or a lion?'

Brian Junior said, 'A shark. By a fifteen-second leeway.'

Brianne said, 'How about, how long have you been shagging Titania? Let's talk about that.'

Brian said, 'You're not a man, Brianne. You wouldn't understand.'

Brian Junior stated blankly, 'I'm a man, and I don't understand.'

'You're a boy,' said Brian. 'And, Brian Junior, I suspect you'll be a boy for the rest of your life.'

'That's an incredibly hurtful thing to say,' observed Brian Junior, 'especially coming from a man who sometimes wears a baseball cap backwards.'

Brianne added, 'Who listens to Rice Krispies after the milk has been poured, and sings a little song, "Snap Crackle and Pop".'

Poppy said, in her breathy voice, 'I never met a more mature man in my life. I wish that I'd had you for a father, Brian.' She placed her hand on top of Brian's, which was resting on the gearstick.

Brian made no move to free himself from her little hand. When he changed gear, he took Poppy's with him.

Brianne asked, 'How can you prefer Titania to Mum? Mum is still beautiful. And she's kind, and interested in people. Titania looks like the contents of a specimen jar, and she's not kind, Dad. She calls Alexander "Magnum Man" behind his back. She says he's dark brown and chocolatey on the outside, white ice cream in the middle.'

Brian laughed and said, 'You must admit, Brianne, that he does sound and behave like minor royalty by way of Scarborough, Tobago.'

Brianne shouted, 'He was adopted by an English couple who sent him to Charterhouse. He can't help the way he speaks!'

Brian was trying to move a juggernaut into the middle lane by the use of his lights and tailgating. He shouted over the crashing of gears, 'Methinks she doth protest too much. You sound as though you've got quite a crush on him.'

'It's more than a crush. I love him.'

Brian lost concentration on the road, and had to jerk

on the steering wheel to bring the car back into line. He said, 'He's thirty-two years older than you, Brianne!'

She said, 'I don't care.'

'You'll care when you're wiping his ancient arse, and his teeth are in a glass by the side of your bed. Does he return your love, Brianne?'

Brianne looked out of the window through the snow at the halo of tail lights ahead. 'No,' she said.

'No,' repeated Brian, 'because you're an infatuated stupid teenager. You're just a kid.'

Brian Junior leaned forward until his mouth was very near to Brian's ear and said, quietly, 'And you're a hypocrite. You're eighteen years older than Titania.'

Brian gesticulated despairingly as he roared, 'Do you think I don't know that? For years I was terrified that she'd leave me for a younger man.'

The car swayed from side to side.

Poppy removed her hand from Brian's and squealed, 'Please, put both hands back on the steering wheel!'

Brian Junior said, 'I want to know when exactly you fell out of love with Mum. I want to know how long you've been lying to our family.'

'I haven't fallen of out of love with your mum. Adults' lives are complicated.' After a long silence, Brian continued, 'We should have stuck to "The Euro – Fight or Flight?" It does nobody any good to pick at old scabs.'

Brianne said, 'I love picking at scabs. It's so satisfying when they come away and you see the fresh skin beneath.'

Brian exploded, 'All right! You're both so fucking

mature! I'll tell you exactly how it was with me and Titania! Ask me anything you like!'

The twins were silent.

Poppy said, 'Was it wonderfully romantic? Did you fall for her at first sight?'

'It was more of a slow burn. I was impressed with her intelligence, and her brilliant research. She was like a terrier, clinging on to what she knew to be right. She made herself unpopular, but not with me.'

The twins exchanged a mocking glance.

Poppy said, 'How did you first get together?'

Brian smiled in the dark. 'One night in the University Library, amongst the Philosophy stacks . . .'

'In the library?' Brianne was horrified. 'That's where Mum worked! That is gross!'

Brian said, 'Couldn't do it now, bloody CCTV cameras everywhere.'

Brian Junior asked, 'When *was* this?'

'It was around about the time of the Columbia disaster.'

'So, you've been having an affair with Titania since 2003?'

'The disaster hit me hard, son. I was in a very vulnerable state. Your mother didn't seem to understand my distress. But Titania was there, equally upset. It was Columbia that brought us together. We found solace in each other.'

Brian Junior said, 'Yeah, but it didn't take you eight years to get over a failed shuttle re-entry, did it?'

Brian turned to look at his son. 'OK,' he said, 'I

admit it. There was passion there, and physics. I was the unstoppable force, and Titania was the immovable object.'

The driver of a dangerously close Scandinavian articulated lorry sounded his klaxon. Brian braked so hard that Poppy immediately thought of whiplash and a possible claim for damages.

When they were calm again, Brian Junior said, 'So, first we discover that you're an adulterer, and now we realise that you are intellectually bankrupt. The analogy you used, your supposed gravitational force, could only have issued from the mouth of an intellectual pygmy. Your pop-science analogy is misapplied and your faulty logic is as dangerous as your driving. Millions have died because of so-called scientists like you.'

'Go, Bri,' said Brianne.

The ensuing argument developed quickly and raged back and forth, reaching towering peaks of misunderstanding, until eventually father and son found themselves on a scientific plateau, discussing six-dimensional space.

Poppy was bored. To pass the interminable time (they were only at the junction for East Midlands Airport, for God's sake) she allowed herself a fantasy, imagining herself as Brian's child bride. Standing at the altar, she would look spectacular in her white lace next to his bulky, bearded self. She would make him sell the house, with Eva in it, finish with prune-face Titania and buy a loft apartment in the middle of town. She would charm his faculty into realising his ambition of a full professorship.

She would insist that he fork out £350 to have his hair and beard trimmed by Nicky Clarke. After fitting him out with a casual academic uniform (corduroy trousers, suede brogues, soft tweed jacket, horn-rimmed spectacles), she would act as his agent, get him television work, and they would eventually move in celebrity circles. She had always wanted to meet Katie Price and the Dalai Lama. She would insist on Brian having a vasectomy. She would charge him for sex, and later – when he was frail, or starting to lose his marbles – she would put him into a home. Although there was always the possibility of a mercy killing. She would wear deep black at the trial, and a modest little hat. She would clutch a white linen handkerchief and occasionally dab her eyes. When the foreman of the jury pronounced, 'Not Guilty,' she would faint very prettily in the dock. By the time they reached the Ikea turn-off, she had married, reconstructed and buried Brian.

He drove on, oblivious to his fate.

Poppy came out of her reverie to interrupt Brian Junior, who was droning on about something she could not and did not want to understand.

'It's obvious to me that your father was deeply in love with Titania. She must have been beautiful then. Was she, Brian?'

Brian hesitated. 'Not beautiful, not even pretty. And I wouldn't have called her handsome either. But she understood my passion for my subject. If I arrived home late, Eva showed no curiosity in what I'd been doing. She would barely look up from her sodding embroidery.

Yes, if the world was about to end, there she'd be . . . stitch, stitch, stitch.'

Brianne said, sadly, 'All those lies, Dad, for all those years.'

Poppy shifted round in her seat to face Brian. Her Shantung silk skirt fell away. Brian caught a glimpse of her pale-green French knickers.

They travelled a mile in silence.

Brian said, 'Time for music.'

He pushed a button on the CD player and the Nelson Riddle Orchestra filled the car. This was torture for his children, but it became worse when Brian and Poppy started to sing along with Sinatra to 'Strangers In The Night'. Brian sang with a pseudo-American accent, and Poppy's falsetto was painfully out of tune.

The twins put their fingers down their throats and clapped their noise-cancelling headphones firmly on to their ears. By the time the car passed the sign for the Leeds turn-off, Brian and Poppy were serenading each other with 'I've Got You Under My Skin'.

As soon as Brian had dropped them outside Sentinel Towers, the twins headed towards the lift, to put their Christmas presents from their family on eBay – the secondhand iPad 1s were laughably out of date and irrelevant to their needs. The iPads lay at the bottom of a black plastic bag together with the scarf Ruby had knitted for Brian Junior and the Tony Blair autobiography, inscribed on the title page: 'To Brianne, Happy Christmas from Grandma Yvonne'.

But Poppy lingered and tried to convey by the use of her eyes that Brian was the most fascinating man she'd ever known and that she could not bear to drag herself away from him.

At 3.30 a.m. Brian Junior heard Poppy's door open and her shower start.

She was singing, 'I've got me under my skin.'

It enraged Brian Junior. He thumped on the wall with his fist and frightened himself by thinking, 'I could actually kill her.'

He knew from his research on the deep web that it was possible to 'disappear' someone and never be caught.

# 44

Nurse Spears ordered Eva to remove her nightgown. She wanted to examine her body for bedsores.

Eva covered her nakedness as much as she could with the duvet.

Nurse Spears said, 'I've known people die from bedsores, Mrs Beaver. If unattended, they can lead to infection, ulceration – and, eventually, amputation.' She lifted Eva's ankles and stared at her heels critically. She then moved to Eva's buttocks, and finished by checking her elbows. She seemed almost disappointed to find no angry sores. 'You've obviously been using a good barrier cream.'

'No,' said Eva, 'but I know about bedsores, I just keep moving and changing position.'

When Eva was dressed, the nurse took her blood pressure and frowned at the result, even though it was in the normal range. She stuck a thermometer in Eva's ear and, again, frowned at what she saw. She put the thermometer away and asked, 'How are your bowels?'

Eva said politely, 'Mine are fine, how are yours?'

'I'm delighted that you are able to be so light-hearted, Mrs Beaver, considering your circumstances. I understand, from your mother downstairs, that your husband is living with another woman in the garden extension.'

'It's a shed.'

'Your mother also tells me that when you need to use the bathroom facilities, you construct what you call a "White Pathway", which you seem to think is an extension of your bed. Is this true?'

'Yes, it's true. It *is* an extension of the bed. If I fired a bullet at your skull and it blew it apart, Nurse Spears, would the bullet that did so be a property of itself or the gun?' She half remembered this from overhearing a conversation one morning at breakfast, between Brian and Brian Junior about quantum physics, which had only ended when the marmalade jar had slipped through Brian's hands and fallen on to the floor.

Nurse Spears was writing on Eva's notes.

Eva said, 'I'd like to see what you've written.'

The nurse said, moving the notes out of Eva's reach, 'I'm afraid your notes are confidential.'

Eva said, 'You're mistaken, Nurse Spears. The law allows patients to read their notes.'

'I have made a judgement that you are not mentally strong enough to read your own notes. It could set off another psychotic episode.'

'I am physically and mentally well.'

'It is quite common for psychotic patients to think themselves well.'

Eva began to laugh. 'So, you win both ways?'

Nurse Spears said, 'There's a touch of paranoia in that question.'

Eva asked, 'Are you trained in mental health diagnostics?'

'Trained, no, but it is a special interest of mine. There

was mental ill health in my own family, it's nothing to be ashamed of, Mrs Beaver.'

Eva felt a chill, a physical sensation of fear. 'Of course, you're implying that I have a mental illness?'

Nurse Spears said, 'I will go back to the surgery and inform your doctors that, in my opinion, you are having a breakdown of some kind. Again, Mrs Beaver, you need not be frightened. Some of our most notable men and women have suffered, like you. Think of Churchill, Alastair Campbell, Les Dennis.'

Eva insisted, 'But I'm not mentally ill!'

'We have moved on since poor Mr Churchill suffered from his "black dog". We have some miraculous drugs now, and within a few weeks you will be feeling your old self again. You will be able to get out of bed and rejoin the rest of us.'

'I don't want to join the rest of you.'

Nurse Spears put on her navy-blue mac and carefully threaded the belt through the brown leather buckle. 'I'll call again, of course. Goodbye, Mrs Beaver.'

When she heard her mother's voice in the hall five minutes later, and then the sound of the front door slamming, Eva shouted, 'Mum!'

It took longer than usual for Ruby to climb the stairs, and she was breathless when she arrived at the side of Eva's bed.

Eva did not want to upset her mother, but she needed to talk frankly with her. She asked, 'So, you had a good talk with the nurse?'

'Yes,' said Ruby. 'She was telling me about Dr Bridges. He's been off work for three days. He did some bad damage to his nose with a pair of animated nose clippers.'

Eva corrected irritably, 'Automatic. And she shouldn't be gossiping about the doctors.'

'She doesn't like that dark doctor, Lumbago, she says he's lazy. Well, they are, aren't they?'

Eva said, 'No, *they* are not.'

'I wouldn't have her job for the world. The things she has to do. She told me about some of her worst cases. It's disgusting what that poor woman has to work with.'

'You told her about Brian and Titania. You said they were living in a garden extension.'

'Well, I could hardly call it a shed, could I?'

'And I wish you hadn't told her about the White Pathway.'

Ruby said, 'But everybody *knows* about the White Pathway.'

'Everybody?'

'Well, everybody *I* know. And I'll tell you the truth, Eva. Everybody thinks it's barmy. And I'll tell you another thing, Nurse Spears thinks it's barmy, an' all.'

'And you, Mum? What do you think? Do you think it's barmy?'

Ruby shook her head sadly and said, 'I feel like I've never known you, and now I never will. None of us know you, any more. We all want the old Eva back.'

'I didn't like the old Eva. She was a miserable coward.'

'All you need is a change of scenery. You've had a

lovely four months' rest. Why don't you get up, have a shower, wash your hair with some of your lovely vegetable stuff –'

'*Herb*,' said Eva.

'– put some warm clothes on and we could go to the shops. And there's snowdrops in the park. I could borrow Stanley's wheelchair. You weigh nowt, I could easily push you. I want to look after you, Eva.'

'You don't understand, do you, Mum? Think of me as a giant grub. I'm here, in this room, pupating.'

Ruby began to feel uneasy. 'You're talking daft, stop it!'

Eva said, 'But one day, I'll shed my skin. I'm looking forward to that. I wonder what I'll be?'

'On your own, if you carry on talking like that.'

Ruby went downstairs and found Titania unloading the washing machine. Hers and Brian's clothes were tangled together. One of his shirts was enveloping one of her nightgowns.

Ruby said, 'So, you're not at work?'

Titania, who thought that Ruby was one of the thickest people she had ever met, said, 'Obviously not, I'm here, in the kitchen, in three dimensions. Four, including time.'

Ruby said, with a nod towards Eva's bedroom, 'She's getting worse, she's just told me that she's a giant grub.'

Titania's eyes widened. 'Are you sure she didn't say "I need some grub", or "Bring me some grub", or something similar?'

'I know I'm getting on a bit, but I definitely heard her say that she *was* a giant grub.'

'As in insect?'

'Yes.'

Titania muttered, '*Très* Kafkaesque.'

Ruby said, 'Will you tell Brian, when he comes home from work, that Eva now thinks she's a giant grub?'

Titania said, 'Oh yes, I'll be delighted to pass on that message.'

'I'm going home now,' said Ruby. 'I'm feeling a bit poorly.' When she had put her hat and coat on, she said, 'Titania, what would happen to Eva if I passed away?'

Titania said, 'We'd cope.'

Ruby checked, 'You'd feed her?'

'Obviously.'

'Do her washing, change her sheets?'

'Of course.'

'Keep her clean?'

'Yes.'

'But you wouldn't love her, you and Brian, would you?'

'There are plenty of people who love her.'

Ruby's voice cracked. 'But she needs her mam, and if I went to the arms of Jesus, she wouldn't be looked after *properly*, would she?'

Titania said, 'I sense Alexander loves her.'

Ruby picked up her empty shopping bag and said, 'That's sex, I'm talking about love.'

Titania watched her walking down the hall, and thought that she had visibly aged in the last week. She looked unsteady on her feet, and her shoulders were stooped. She might suggest that Ruby swap her mid-heeled court shoes for a pair of Merrell body-shaping trainers.

When Brian opened the front door, he could smell curry, his favourite food. Titania was at the stove, cooking chapattis over a gas flame. Every surface that could be burnished, shone. There was a faint smell of bleach. All the surfaces had been washed down. There was a small pot of snowdrops on the table, which had been set for two, and a bottle of Burgundy was breathing. Glasses had been polished, and reflected the lights.

He lifted the lid off a saucepan and asked, 'What is it – chicken?'

'No, goat,' said Titania. 'And before I forget, your wife now thinks she's a giant grub. A "monstrous vermin".'

Brian had a delicate stomach. He replaced the lid. His appetite waned a little. 'A giant grub?' he said. 'Couldn't you have waited until after dinner?'

# 45

The next morning, Barry Wooton turned up on the doorstep with a woman he described to Yvonne as 'a new friend'.

Yvonne, who was on the morning shift, led them upstairs to Eva's bedroom, talking as she went. Like a parlour maid in a costume drama, she announced, 'Mr Barry Wooton and Miss Angelica Hedge.'

Eva sat up in bed and said to Barry, 'You're still here then?'

Barry laughed and said, 'Yeah, thanks for that.'

Eva looked at Ms Hedge, waiting to be properly introduced.

Barry said, 'She likes to be called Angel. She was waiting in line for a cab at the station. She said, "You look cheerful for a February morning," and I said, "Well, it's all down to the amazing Eva Beaver." She wanted to meet you.'

Angelica was a small, slight girl, with a no-style haircut. Heavy make-up could not conceal her owl-like features. She held out an unmanicured hand to Eva. Her voice was light and devoid of accent. She said, 'It's an honour to meet you, Mrs Beaver. I think it's wonderful that you saved Barry's life.'

Barry said, 'She's a saint.'

Angelica continued, 'But beware, I think it was Confucius, or it might have been Plato, who said, "If you save a man's life, he is yours for ever."'

Barry said, 'Well, I wun't mind that, but I don't know about Eva.'

Eva gave a weak smile, and allowed her hand to be shaken for slightly too long. She made general demurring sounds.

Angelica asked, 'Was it your mother-in-law who showed us in?'

'Yvonne,' said Eva.

'And how old is Yvonne?' asked Angelica.

Eva said, 'How old? I don't know. Seventy-five, seventy-six?'

'And does she live here?'

'No, she calls in three or four times a week.'

'And your children?'

'They're seventeen,' said Eva. Then she asked herself, 'Why does she want to know how old everybody is? Perhaps the girl is autistic.'

'And you, how old are you?'

Eva thought, 'Yes, she's autistic.' She asked Angelica, 'How old do you think I am?'

'I can never tell with older people. You could be a young-looking sixty or an old-looking forty. Who knows now we've got Botox?'

Eva said, 'Well, I'm a fifty-looking fifty.'

'And how long have you lived here?'

'Twenty-six years,' said Eva. She thought, 'This is going to be tiresome.'

Angelica said, 'Barry tells me that you are bedridden. That's tragic.'

'No, I'm not bedridden and it's not tragic.'

'You're so *brave*. Is your husband's name Brian?'

'Yes.'

'And how old is he?'

'He's fifty-five.'

Yvonne came into the room and asked, 'Would your guests like some refreshments, Eva? We have tea, we have coffee, we have hot chocolate and, of course, we have various cold drinks. And I think I could rustle up a few light snacks.'

Eva could almost have leapt out of her bed, strangled Yvonne and thrown her down the stairs, such was her rage. She thought, 'Yvonne has never really liked me, and now here's the proof.'

Barry and the girl turned to Yvonne gratefully and said, 'Hot chocolate,' in unison. This made them laugh, and Barry invited Angelica to sit in the soup chair. He perched on the arm and they both stared at Eva. Eva threw herself back on the pillows. Yvonne took her time on the stairs, unaware that Eva was counting every second before her unwanted quests were on the street side of the front door.

An agonising thirty-five minutes followed, during which Yvonne handed scalding-hot mugs of milky drinking chocolate to Barry and Angelica, who promptly dropped them when their knuckles came into contact with the fearsome heat.

The boiling brown liquid splashed over Barry's legs and

ran along the white floorboards. His nylon socks retained the heat and he screamed in pain. There was a lot of ker-fuffle as Yvonne tried to stem the flow with a meagre handful of toilet tissue she'd taken from the lavatory.

Eva was shouting, 'Cold water! Put your feet in cold water!'

But nobody was listening.

Above Barry's cries of pain, and Angelica's little squeals, Yvonne raged at Eva, shouting, 'Don't blame me, there's nowhere in this room to put anything down! Why did you have to get rid of your furniture?'

Eva tried to lower the metaphorical heat, saying with a smile, 'A tip, Yvonne, when handing out mugs of boiling liquid try supplying asbestos gloves beforehand.'

Yvonne shouted, 'A *tip*, Eva? Here's one for you! People lolling in their beds, admiring their navels, should not try to ridicule people who are walking about actually *doing* things! I should be at home. This is not even my day for looking after you, *Ruby* should be here! But, guess what? She's having one of her convenient "heads". And I'm expecting a parcel from Amazon! It's Alan Titchmarsh's *When I Was a Nipper*, and they've been kind enough to track down a signed first edition for me. It will make a complete set. I've left a note on the front door, asking the courier to put it in the coal bunker – but that's supposing he can read English!'

Angelica said, 'What is a coal bunker?'

Yvonne snapped, 'It's a bunker for putting coal in.'

Eva said, 'Don't you want to know the age of the coal bunker?'

'Well, how old *is* it?'

'It will be sixty next birthday.'

There followed a great palaver as the floor was mopped, clothes were removed and scalded skin was cooled with unguents that Yvonne brought out of her large handbag. While Yvonne found a dressing gown big enough for Barry, and was washing his socks and trousers, Angelica engaged him in conversation.

She started with, 'How old are you, Barry?'

'I'm thirty-six,' said Barry. 'Don't tell me I look older, I know I do. It's the nights. I can't sleep in the day. I've got Massive Attack on one side of me and summat classical on the other. I've asked them to turn it down but they're both bastards. I've got high heels above me and a bloody barking dog below. Never move to a modern flat. It's no wonder I was desperate. If I hadn't knocked on Eva's door, I would've had my head in a Tesco's carrier bag, i'n't that right, Eva?'

Eva said, faintly, 'Possibly.'

'I'm telling you, this woman is a saint. Who else do you know who'd open their door to a desperate man like I were?'

Eva muttered, 'The Samaritans?'

Barry carried on. 'It's just knowing that there's somebody in this world who'll give up their sleep to talk to a stranger in the night.'

Eva said quietly to Angelica, 'I had no choice. He forced his way in.'

Angelica said, 'Exactly what time was this?

Barry said, 'It was three twenty-seven a.m.'

'And how did you feel when this stranger forced his way into your bedroom? Alarmed, shocked, terrified?'

Eva said, 'Well, I was certainly surprised.'

Barry said, 'She should get a medal or something.'

'So, would you say that you were a compassionate woman?'

Eva thought for a moment. 'Not particularly.'

Every nerve in her body was taut with irritation. She felt her temper stirring, like a bear waking from hibernation. She tried to disassociate herself from the present and attempted to think of other things. She began to walk on the beach of a Greek island. The sparkling Aegean Sea was to her left, and her rented villa was a few steps to her right. But after a few moments, she lost the struggle and was back in the bedroom with her tormentors.

Barry was droning on. 'I've made some friends on the computer. They're people like me what want to kill themselves. They're a lovely bunch, we had a right laugh.'

Angelica said, 'I've often felt that life is not worth living. Have you got the web address?'

Barry rummaged in his jacket pocket, and brought out a little red diary. He spelled out the address laboriously. 'It's topurselfuk dot org.' Then he turned to Eva and asked, 'Is Brian Junior in? I'd like to thank him for his help, an' all. Would you mind if I gave my new friends your address?'

Eva wailed, 'Barry, no!'

He said, 'You're too modest, Eva, people should know what a great woman you are. You shouldn't hide your light under a whatsit.'

Eva shouted 'Yvonne!'

She heard her mother-in-law's snail-paced progress upstairs before she eventually came into the bedroom.

'Yvonne, Barry and his friend are leaving now. Will you please fetch his clothes?'

Yvonne said, 'They won't be ready yet, I've only just popped them into the dryer. If he puts them on now, he'll get pneumonia.'

Eva said, struggling to keep her voice even, 'That is a myth perpetuated by old-age pensioners. You cannot catch pneumonia from wearing damp socks and trousers. If that were the case, my whole school would have contracted pneumonia after a wet playtime.' Her temper began to struggle out of her throat. 'I spent half of my childhood wet or damp. A gaberdine mac is not impervious to snowstorms or torrential rain. I slept in a room with a bucket in the corner because the fucking roof leaked. So, Barry, go downstairs with Yvonne and Angelica, put on your damp clothes, and leave!'

Barry was near to tears, he'd thought that Eva was his friend. This was a big blow.

Angelica switched off the little Sony machine that had been recording in the top pocket of her cowboy shirt.

Yvonne said to her daughter-in-law, 'We haven't seen Mr Temper for a long time, have we, Eva? No, and Mr Temper hasn't got a leg to stand on. I've lost count of my relatives, friends and acquaintances who've contracted pneumonia because they didn't sufficiently air their washing!'

Eva yelled back, 'And that myth is why we had to put up with bloody washing hanging around the house until Saturday! It would be washing on Monday, drying in front of the coal fire on Tuesday, folding on Wednesday, ironing on Thursday, and airing on Friday and Saturday. Put the clothes away on Sunday, and start all over again on Monday! And, on each of those bloody days, my mother was a martyr. It was like living in a Chinese laundry!'

Angelica said, 'Well, I've got to go back to work anyway.'

Barry said sadly, 'I'll give you a lift.'

Yvonne said, 'Goodbye, Eva, you may not see me for a while. I've been extremely hurt by your remarks. I've been badly done by.'

Eva said, 'Barry, you look fantastic, a different man. I'm sorry I've been such a cow. If you're driving and you see me at the window, give me a wave. I'd like to see your lights in the dark. It'll reassure me you're still around.'

Barry said, 'You are a lovely woman, Eva. I want to buy you a present. What do you like?'

'I like everything. Anything you choose, Barry, would be gratefully received.'

Eva watched Barry and Angelica drive away.

A few minutes later, Yvonne left the house.

Eva saw with dismay that she was limping heavily. She was wearing her knitted beret with the pompom back to front. Eva thought about opening the window and telling her so, but she did not want to risk Yvonne thinking that she was mocking her in any way.

After three days had passed and Yvonne had not returned, Brian went to find out why.

He came back, looking worried, saying, 'Mother seems to have developed an obsession with Alan Titchmarsh, and is threatening to make Mr Titchmarsh a beneficiary in her will.' He added, 'She wasn't wearing any make-up, I didn't recognise her at first.' Then, sadly, 'I think she might be losing her marbles.'

# 46

The next day, when Brian was at work, Mrs Hordern came into his office and said, 'Your wife's on the front of the *Mercury*.'

Brian grabbed the local paper, and saw that the front page was dominated by a blurry, wide-angle photograph of Eva sitting up in bed. The headline said: 'MAN SAVED BY "SAINT".'

Brian turned to page three, and read:

Local woman, Eva Beaver (50), of Bowling Green Road, Leicester, has, according to suicidal black cab driver, Barry Wooton (36), 'a special gift'.

'She saved my life,' said the burly cabby. (See above, top right.) 'She is a saint.'

There was a murky black and white photograph of Barry, looking like Fungus the Bogeyman. Brian read on, with mounting incredulity:

'On Friday night, I was desperate,' Barry told *Mercury* reporter Angelica Hedge, talking in the neat lounge of his flat at Arthur Court, Glenfield Estate. 'I was low, and thought that my life was not worth living.'

Barry's eyes filled with tears as he told of the calamities that had brought him to such a desperate state: 'I ran over my own dog, Sindy, gas and electric went up, my heating's broke, yobs slashed the leather seats in the back of the cab, and I've spent a fortune on lonely heart adverts and I've still not found a wife.' Barry explained that he was 'drawn' to Mrs Beaver's house. 'She is bedridden and I'd often seen her at her window in the small hours. I was on my way to the railway line to put my head on the rails, when I felt something pulling me towards her house. It was 3.27 a.m. but I rang her bell.'

Brian read on, and discovered that his wife was 'an angel', 'a saviour', 'a miracle worker' and 'a saint'. He, Brian Beaver (75), was 'a top nuclear scientist' and they had '18-year-old triplets, Poppy, Brianne and Brian Junior'.

He immediately sat down at his desk and typed an email to the editor.

Sir,

I wish to protest in the strongest possible manner about your front-page article concerning my wife, Eva Beaver. It contains many falsehoods and inaccuracies, e.g. I am not a nuclear scientist. I work in astronomy and I am 55 years of age. There is a compulsory retirement age at my place of work. I would certainly not be allowed to carry on at the age of 75 years.

I am not the father of triplets. The Poppy you refer to is a house guest and not one of my progeny.

Furthermore, my wife is certainly not 'an angel', 'a saviour', 'a miracle worker' or 'a saint', and neither is she 'bedridden'. She has chosen to take to her bed for reasons of her own.

You will be hearing from my lawyers in due course.

Yours faithfully,
Dr Brian Beaver, BSc, MSc, D Phil (Oxon)

When he had pressed 'send', Brian hurried along the corridor to show Titania the front page. She laughed all the way through the article, and had a mild form of hysterics when she read that Brian was seventy-five.

When Brian told her that he had emailed a letter to the editor of the paper, she said, 'You fool! That will keep the whole bloody thing going.'

One of Titania's young interns, Jack Box, said, 'It's already on Twitter. The hashtag's "womaninbed". Do you want me to bring it up?'

Brian and Titania had never sent a tweet before, and neither had they read one.

Jack Box's fingers flew over the keyboard. He said, 'There have been three posted over the last hour.'

Brian read, in descending order:

Eva Beaver a saint? I don't think so, she's a slag.

I need your help Eva, I want to kill myself, where are you?

Die! Brine Beevar!!! y ru stil aliv 75 yr old man!! newcleer enege wil kill uz al! an diform are babis!!!!

Brian said, 'Hate mail now, Tit. And does Eva care? No, she is indifferent to my suffering.'

He read on:

> #WomanInBed, are you reading this? I wish I was in bed with you. You look fit.

As they watched the screen, it displayed: 'One more tweet available.'

Jack Box clicked the mouse and the Tweet popped up, from GreenMan2478:

> #WomanInBed. I understand your need for spiritual replenishment. Remember, we are all made from stars, but you are sprinkled with stardust. Go Well Sister.

Brian said, 'Stardust, my arse. If Eva were to be covered in residue from a supernova, she wouldn't last long.'

By 10 p.m. that night, there had been 157 tweets, and by 6 a.m. the next day, this figure had almost trebled.

One tweeter asked the simple question, 'Why is she in bed?'

Suggestions came from across the world.

# 47

The next day, a Friday, a regional television team of two turned up at the door, requesting an interview with Eva.

Ruby, who had answered the door, said, 'I'm her mother. I'm Ruby Brown-Bird.' She immediately recognised the presenter. 'You're Derek Plimsoll. I'm a big fan of yours, I watch you every night on the news.'

This was true. Ruby was a great admirer of his. He was so handsome and funny, and always made a little joke at the end of his six o'clock news round-up. Over the years, she had watched his black hair turn grey and his body spread, but he still wore lovely pastel suits and jazzy ties. When he interviewed politicians, he was very respectful. He was never irritated by them when they wouldn't answer a question – not like that Jeremy Paxman. He was like an old familiar pal. And sometimes, when he said, 'Goodnight, East Midlands, see you tomorrow,' she would speak to the screen, and say, 'Yes, see you tomorrow, Derek.'

The girl with him, who was carrying the camera on a tripod, said, 'And I'm Jo.'

Ruby didn't take to her. She was one of those women like Poppy, who wore bright-red lipstick and big boots. Ruby couldn't make head nor tail of young women today.

She asked them into the kitchen and apologised for the non-existent mess.

Derek wrinkled his suntanned nose and said, 'What *is* that delicious smell?'

Ruby said, 'I've got a cake in the oven.'

'A cake!' he said, sounding both amazed and delighted. He wagged a plump finger at Ruby and said, 'Are you sure you've not got a *bun* in the oven?'

Ruby screeched with laughter and put her hands over her face. 'Me, have a bun in the oven?' She shrieked again, 'I'm seventy-nine! I've had my womb took away!'

Derek said, 'I bet you were a proper minx, Ruby. Oh, just the thought of you, my dear, and I'm getting excited.'

Jo rolled her eyes and said to Ruby, 'D'you see what I have to put up with? He's an unreconstructed nuisance.'

Derek said, 'We're old school, aren't we, Ruby? We used to enjoy a bit of sexual banter without the Sex Police rounding us up.'

Ruby agreed. 'I'm scared to open my mouth, these days. Every time I do, I seem to offend somebody or other. I've no idea what to call black people any more.'

Jo said, flatly, 'Black. You call them black.'

Derek said, affecting a West Indian accent, 'No, we is persons of colour now, innit?'

When Ruby poured the tea, Derek rhapsodised over the teapot. He exclaimed, 'A teapot, a milk jug, a sugar bowl, china cups and saucers, and apostle spoons!'

Ruby was thrilled that here, at least, was a person who appreciated the niceties of life.

Jo stood the camera on its three legs and fiddled with

the lens. She mumbled to Derek, 'The light is good,' and switched on.

Derek said to Ruby, 'Can I ask you a few questions about your daughter?'

Ruby was flattered. 'Of course you can.' It had always been her ambition to appear on television.

Derek motioned towards Jo, and said, 'She'll need to thread a wire through your clothes, so watch out, Ruby, she bats for the other side.'

Ruby was baffled.

Jo said, 'He's trying to tell you that I'm a lesbian, and implying that I would like to sexually assault you.'

Ruby looked a little fearful.

Derek said, 'It's all right, Ruby, our Jo has got what they call a "same-sex life partner", she's not on the pull.'

After Ruby had applied her fuchsia-pink lipstick, and a small microphone had been clipped on to the neck of her blouse, the interview began.

Derek said, 'We need to check for sound level. Mrs Brown-Bird, what did you have for breakfast?'

Ruby recited, 'Two cups of tea, cornflakes, egg, bacon, sausages, black pudding, grilled tomato, fried bread, beans, mushrooms and toast.'

Upstairs, Eva woke from an uneasy dream. She had been running away from Michael Parkinson.

When she was fully awake, she went into her normal routine. She shook her duvet, straightened the pillows and looked out of the window. She saw a Mercedes van with *East Midlands Tonight* written on the side, parked opposite. She could hear voices coming from the kitchen, including her mother's.

She shouted, 'Mum!'

After a moment, she heard the kitchen door open, and footsteps in the hall.

Her mother's voice reached her, complaining about the stairs. 'These bleddy things will be the death of me.' She staggered into Eva's room and sat down heavily on the soup chair. 'Why don't you get a stair lift?' she panted. 'I can't go on doing this five or six times a day.'

Eva asked, 'Who's downstairs?'

'Derek Plimsoll and a lesbian.'

Eva looked blank.

'*Derek Plimsoll*. You know the one. He's on the telly. *East Midlands Tonight*. He makes a joke and taps his papers together at the end.'

Eva nodded.

'Well, it's him, and a lesbian. I've just done an interview with them.' She touched the clip-on microphone.

Eva said, 'Have you won the accumulator on the Bingo?'

'No, it's about *you*.'

'Me!' said Eva.

'Yes, you,' said Ruby. 'Derek Plimsoll reads the *Mercury* like everybody else in the country. He wants to interview you for what Derek calls "an extended slot".'

Eva stood up in her bed and stamped up and down on the mattress. She shouted, 'Absolutely not! I'd rather eat my own vomit! Go downstairs and tell them I decline.'

Ruby said, 'And the magic word?'

Eva yelled, 'Please!'

Ruby was not used to Eva shouting at her. She said, tearfully, 'I thought you'd be happy. It's *television*, Eva. It means you're special. I can't go down there and tell him you won't do it. He'll be disappointed, heartbroken even.'

'He'll cope,' said Eva.

Ruby dragged herself out of the chair, muttering, and began her descent.

Once Ruby was back in the kitchen, she told Derek, in a loud whisper, 'She says no, she's in decline, and she'd sooner eat her own sick.' She said to Jo, 'We had a dog that did that . . . disgusting! I was glad when it died.'

Derek's smile slipped. 'Ruby, I can't leave this house without interviewing Eva. I am an extremely experienced and respected journalist. I have my professional pride. So, madam, would you please be so kind as to go back upstairs and stress to your daughter that I have interviewed every celebrity to set foot in the East Midlands. I have shadow-boxed with Muhammad Ali. I have asked Mr Nelson Mandela some penetrating questions about his terrorist past and, may God rest her soul, I have flirted with Princess Diana.' He bent down and whispered in Ruby's ear, 'And, by God, did she flirt back at me. I sensed that, had she been alone without her hangers-on, we could have had a few drinks and . . . well, who knows what might have happened? I was game for it, she was game for it . . .' His voice tailed off, and he gave Ruby a salacious wink.

Ruby was a thrilled co-conspirator. She nodded and turned.

Eva was waiting impatiently for the sounds of departure but could hear only her mother, talking to the staircase, saying, 'It's all right for you, staircase, all you have to do is stand there, it's me that has to climb you. Yes, I know you're creaking, but at least you're made of wood. When *I* creak, it's my poor bones you're hearing, and it's painful.'

Eva was not surprised by this.

Her mother had always talked to household objects. Eva had heard her only yesterday, saying, 'Come on now, iron, don't run out of steam, I've got three of Eva's nighties to do yet.'

Ruby leaned against the door jamb, trying to get her breath back.

Eva stood on the bed, glaring down at her mother. 'Well?' she said. 'Why haven't they gone?'

Ruby hissed, 'You can't say *no* to Derek Plimsoll. He interviewed Princess Diana, when she was alive.'

Jo was watching Ruby's interview on the camera screen. The fuchsia lipstick made her look as though she was haemorrhaging from the mouth.

Ruby was saying, 'Eva's always been a bit strange. We thought she was retarded for years, doolally. She used to make up plays in the back garden, using the rabbit in a non-speaking part. They'd practise all day, then I'd have to go out and watch. I'd take some knitting to pass the time. The rabbit was rubbish.'

Jo told Derek, 'We can't use any of Ruby's long shots. She had her legs open, you can see her big knickers.'

Jo was fed up. Her love of cinéma-vérité was the reason she'd studied film at Goldsmith's, but she'd hoped to work with Mike Leigh and improvising professional actors, not the general public. They were hopelessly inarticulate and usually fell back on familiar phrases, such as 'It was a nightmare', 'We were devastated', 'It hasn't sunk in yet' and – the old favourite – 'I'm over the moon'.

Five minutes later, when Eva still hadn't come down, Derek said, 'I've had enough of all this fart-arsing about, I'm going up. Follow me!'

He was slightly unnerved by the prospect of what was upstairs. He'd had a few nasty surprises in the past, like the 103-year-old man who, when Derek asked for the secret of his longevity, shouted, on a live interview, 'Wanking!' He whistled the theme from *The Exorcist* as he slowly climbed the stairs.

Jo said, 'We're skating on thin ice here, Derek,' as she followed him up, filming as she went.

When Derek reached the landing, he hissed at Ruby, 'Get out of the way, you're blocking the shot!' then pushed by her, making her stagger a little.

Jo said, 'A nice shot of you pushing an old lady aside there, Derek.'

*

Eva saw Derek Plimsoll and a woman with a camera on her shoulder coming through the door towards her. She shouted, 'Don't let them in, Mum! Close the door!'

Ruby didn't know what to do. Jo was also conflicted; she didn't like the way this was going. The lovely woman she saw through her lens was obviously terrified, but Jo was surprised by the starkness of the white room. The light was beautiful. She could not turn her camera off, so she adjusted the white balance, and carried on filming.

Eva scrambled under the duvet and shouted, 'Mum! Mum! Phone Alexander! His number's in the book!'

Jo managed to film a couple of seconds of the woman's face before she scrambled under the white duvet.

Derek walked into the shot. He announced, 'I'm in the bedroom of a woman called Eva Beaver – or, as tens of thousands of people are now calling her, "The Saint of Suburbia". I was invited into the house by a Mrs Brown-Bird, Eva's mother, but Eva is a shy, nervous woman who has requested that her face should not be filmed. *East Midlands Tonight* will honour that plea. She's there. She's the lump in the bed.'

Jo's viewfinder showed a hump under the white duvet.

Eva shouted from under the duvet, 'Are you still there, Mum?'

Ruby said, 'Yes, but I can't tackle them stairs for a bit.' She plumped herself down in the soup chair. 'I've been up and down like a bleddy pogo stick. I'm seventy-nine. I'm too old for this carry-on. I've got a cake downstairs I'm neglecting.'

Derek shouted, 'Mrs Brown-Bird, we're trying to film here! Please do not talk, whistle or sing.'

Ruby got out of the chair and said, 'I'm not staying here, if I'm not wanted.'

She staggered to the banisters on the landing and leaned heavily against them until she felt able to go downstairs to the kitchen, where she began to look for Eva's phone book. Alexander's name was the first number in it, in his own handwriting. Ruby sat down at the kitchen table and laboriously pressed buttons on the phone.

He answered immediately, saying, 'Eva?'

'No, Ruby. She wants you to come round. There's some television people here and she wants them gone.'

'What? She wants a bouncer?'

'Yes, she wants you to come and chuck them out of the house,' said Ruby, expanding on Eva's instructions.

'Why choose me? I'm not a street-fighting man.'

Ruby said, 'Yes, but people are more frightened of black men, aren't they?'

Alexander laughed down the phone. 'OK, I'll be there in five minutes. I'll bring my deadly paintbrushes, shall I?'

Ruby said, 'Good, because I'm fed up with all this argy-bargy. I'm going home.'

She placed the phone carefully in its charger, put on her hat and coat, took her shopping bag from the back of the kitchen door and went out into the cold afternoon.

*

Eva had persuaded Jo to switch the camera off and was sitting up in bed with her arms folded, looking – in Derek's eyes – like a modern Joan of Arc.

Derek said, 'Now, are you going to be sensible, and give me a face-to-face interview in your own words, or do I have to speak on your behalf? If so, you may not like what I have to say.'

'This is what I've got to say. Fuck off out of my house!'

'I'm not happy with this,' Jo said. 'You're bullying her, Derek, and I may have to inform Human Resources.'

Derek said, 'It's OK, we can lose anything you're not happy about in the edit.'

'But I'm not involved in the edit. All I'm allowed to do is point a camera.'

'You weren't so high-minded when we doorstepped that grieving widow last week.'

'Which one? There were two grieving widows last week.'

'The one whose idiot husband fell into the industrial bread mixer.'

'I wasn't happy.'

Derek grabbed Jo by the shoulders and said, 'But that was such an artistic end shot you took – the tears running down her face, that kind of rainbow effect you got.'

Jo said, 'I shot her tears through a crystal vase. I'm not proud of it. I'm ashamed.'

'We're all ashamed in television, deary, but it doesn't stop us doing it. Never forget, we give the public what they *want*.'

Derek dropped his voice and murmured to Eva, 'By the way, can I say how sorry I am that your husband's about to leave you? You're probably devastated, aren't you?'

Eva said, 'Do you know the meaning of the word "devastated"?' She didn't wait for him to answer. 'It means, "destroyed or ruined, shattered into a thousand pieces". But here I am, sitting up in bed, in one piece. Now, please close the door behind you.'

As he stamped down the stairs, Derek said, 'This is why I loathe working with women. They can't think further than their fanny.' In a falsetto voice that was meant to be female, he said, 'Oh dear me, I'm getting emotional and my hormones are taking over and everything must be ethical and from a woman's point of view!'

They heard a key turn in the lock, and Alexander walked in carrying a large framed painting covered in bubble wrap.

'Is it you who's bothering Eva?' he asked.

Derek said, 'Are you the Alexander Mrs Brown-Bird's been telling us about? Friend of the family, eh?'

Alexander said, firmly, 'Please leave immediately, nobody wants you here.'

'Look, sunshine, this is a big story in our neck of the woods. It's not every day we find a saint in suburbia. We've got close-up shots of her in the window, we've got an interview with the mother, and Barry Wooton has told us his very boring, but very tragic story. All we need is Eva. Just a few words.'

Alexander gave a broad smile, reminding Plimsoll of the pregnant crocodile they'd recently filmed in Twycross Zoo.

'You interviewed me at the opening of my first exhibition,' he said. 'I think I know your introduction by heart. "This is Alexander Tate, he's a painter, not of the ghetto, not portraits of gang members, not edgy depictions of urban decay. No, Alexander paints watercolours of the English countryside . . ." Then cue the harpsichord music.'

Derek said, 'I thought it was a nice little piece.'

Jo said, 'Derek, you were patronising Alexander, and implying that painting watercolours was an unusual activity for black people.'

Derek said, 'It is.'

Jo turned to Alexander. 'My life partner is black. Do you know her – Priscilla Robinson?'

Alexander said, 'No, funny that. I really ought to know the ten thousand black folk toiling in Leicester's cotton fields.'

'Don't lay that shit at *my* door, Uncle Tom!' Jo said, angrily.

Derek Plimsoll sat down heavily on the stairs and said, 'This is the last time I do house calls. In future, everybody comes to me in the studio.'

Alexander looked down at Derek's hairline. The white roots would need touching up soon, he thought. It was pitiful.

# 48

Eva watched Derek and Jo walk to the Mercedes van in silence. She kept watching until Jo had driven the van out of sight.

She quickly laid out the White Pathway. Every time she took a step on it, she imagined herself walking along the Milky Way, far beyond the earth and its complications. After peeing and washing her hands, she reached for her make-up. She wanted to look as good as she could. The expensive, shiny black pots and brushes she had accumulated over the years were talismans – the discreet gold logo protected her from harm. She knew she was being exploited, she could have bought the same contents for a sixth of the price, but she didn't care, the overpricing had made her feel edgy and reckless, as if she were a circus performer about to traverse the high wire without a safety net.

She sprayed herself with the perfume she had used since she was a young librarian, and could not afford it. She had been very taken by the story of Marilyn Monroe who, when asked, 'What do you wear in bed?' had replied, 'Chanel No. 5.'

'It probably wasn't true,' thought Eva now. Nothing was true for long. In time, everything was deconstructed. Black turned out to be white. The Crusaders were rapists, looters and torturers. Bing Crosby thrashed his children. Winston Churchill hired an actor to broadcast some of his most famous speeches. When Brian had told her all these things, she had said, 'But they *should* be true.' She wanted heroes and heroines in her life. If not heroes, people to admire and respect.

After making up her face, she returned to bed, pulled the white sheet up like a drawbridge, folded it carefully and put it under her pillows. She was proud that she had never once strayed from the White Pathway in nearly five months. Part of her knew it was a contrivance, but she felt that if she fell off the pathway and on to the wooden floor, she would spiral out of control, spinning, following the earth as it journeyed around the sun.


Halfway up the stairs, Alexander stopped. He shouted, 'Is it OK to come up?'

Eva shouted back, 'Yes.'

When he walked up two more steps, he could see Eva sitting on her bed. She looked very beautiful. There was flesh on her bones and the deep hollows in her cheeks had been filled.

He stood at her bedroom door and said, 'You look well.'

She said, 'What's that under your arm?'

'It's a painting, it's for you. A present. For the bare wall facing you.'

She said, softly, 'But I like the bare wall, I like to watch the light move across it.'

'I froze my bloody arse off painting this.'

Eva said, 'I don't want anything in here that interferes with my thinking.'

The truth was, she was very frightened that she might not like his work. She wondered if it were possible to love a man whose artistry she did not admire? Instead, she said, 'Did you know that we haven't said hello to each other yet?'

'I don't need you to say hello to me, you're always with me. You never leave.'

'I don't know you,' Eva said, 'but I think about you constantly. I can't take the painting, but I'd love the bubble wrap.'

This wasn't what Alexander had hoped for. He'd thought she would be wild about the painting, especially when he pointed to the tiny figure of Eva on the brow of a hill with her blob of yellow-blonde hair. He'd seen her flying into his arms. They would kiss, he would cup her breasts, she would gently stroke his belly. At some stage, they would climb under the duvet and explore each other's bodies.

He didn't expect to find himself sitting on the side of her bed, popping little transparent mounds in the bubble wrap. He said, between satisfying pops, 'You need a gatekeeper. Somebody to decide who's allowed in the house and who isn't.'

'Like Cerberus,' she said, 'the three-headed dog who guarded the entrance to the cave where somebody – I can't remember who – lived. There was something about a pomegranate and a seed, but no . . . I can't remember.'

There was a timid ringing of the doorbell.

Eva froze.

Alexander said, 'I'll go.'

After he had left, Eva thought hard about the first time she had heard of the dog Cerberus.

She was in a classroom, rain was battering the long windows. She was worried because she had forgotten her fountain pen again, and at any moment the class would be asked to write something down. Mrs Holmes, her English teacher, was telling thirty-six twelve-year-old girls a story.

Eva could smell the teacher's scent – it was a mixture of Evening in Paris and Vicks vapour rub.

Alexander reappeared. 'There's a woman downstairs who read about you on the internet and is desperate to see you.'

'Well, I'm not desperate to see *her*,' snapped Eva.

'Her daughter has been missing for three weeks.'

'But why would she come to me? A woman who can't get out of bed?'

'She's convinced you can help her,' said Alexander. 'She's driven from Sheffield. The kid is called Amber, she's thirteen years old –'

Eva cut in, 'You shouldn't have told me her name or her age, I've got the child inside my head now.' She picked up a pillow and screamed into it.

Alexander said, 'So that's a no, is it?'

# 49

Amber's mother, Jade, had not allowed herself to bathe, shower or wash her hair, and she had not changed her clothes since her daughter's disappearance. She was still wearing the baby-pink tracksuit, now grey with dirt, that she had been wearing on the day Amber went missing.

'Amber was a happy, bubbly girl. I would normally have driven her to school but we got up late, I wasn't dressed. We didn't have time to make her a packed lunch. I was going to make it up and take it to her later. She wouldn't have been abducted . . . she's not pretty enough. She's big-boned. She's got awful hair. She's got a brace on her top teeth. She wouldn't have been abducted . . . these perverts go for prettier girls on the whole, don't they?'

Eva nodded, then asked, 'When was the last time you slept?'

'Oh, I mustn't sleep or have a shower, and I can't wash my hair until Amber is back. I lie down on the settee at night with the Sky news on, in case there's word about her. My mother blames me. My husband blames me. I blame me. Do you know where Amber is, Eva?'

'No, I don't,' said Eva. 'Lie down next to me.'

*

When Alexander brought tea up for Eva and Jade, he found them fast asleep, side by side. He felt a painful stab of jealousy, Jade was in *his* place. He started to back out of the room but Eva heard a floorboard creak and opened her eyes.

She smiled when she saw him, and carefully slid from under the duvet to the end of the bed, where she sat with her legs dangling.

Alexander noticed that her toenails needed cutting and that the pink varnish on them had almost vanished. Without speaking, he took out the Swiss Army knife his wife had given him. It had many tools within it, and was a bulky weight, but Alexander kept it close to him at all times. He took Eva's right foot, put it on his lap, and whispered, 'Pretty feet, but the toenails of a slut.'

Eva smiled.

Jade was still sleeping. Eva hoped that she was dreaming of Amber, that they were together, in a place where they had been happy.

When Alexander had carefully trimmed all of Eva's toenails, he pressed the clippers back into the body of the knife and pulled out a small metal file.

Eva laughed quietly as he began to run it across her newly clipped toenails. 'Do you think Jesus was the first chiropodist?'

'The first famous one,' said Alexander.

'Is there a celebrity chiropodist today?' asked Eva.

'I dunno. I cut my toenails myself, over a page torn from the *London Review of Books*. Doesn't everybody?'

They were talking at normal volume now, conscious that Jade was sleeping the deep sleep that follows misery and exhaustion.

Alexander went out to his van and came back with a bottle of white spirit and a white rag.

Eva said, 'Are you going out to torch the neighbourhood?'

'You may have been in bed for months, but there's no excuse for letting yourself go.' He dipped the rag into the spirit and wiped the old nail varnish from her fingers and toes. When he'd finished, he said, 'And now I'm going to "jooge" your hair.' He produced a tiny pair of scissors from the Swiss Army knife.

Eva laughed. 'They're from *Grimms' Fairy Tales*! What did you do over the weekend, cut the long grass in a meadow?'

'Yeah,' said Alexander, 'for a wicked elf.'

'And what would happen to you, if you failed your task?'

'Seven swans would peck my big brown eyes out,' he said, and then laughed too.

It took less than fifteen minutes to transform Eva's hair from 'Safe Eva' to 'Hey Eva!'

'And finally,' said Alexander, the magical helper, 'eyebrows.' He picked up his knife and, with great concentration, teased out a pair of tweezers so small that they were almost lost between his long fingers. 'We want quizzical arches, not unusually hirsute caterpillars.'

Eva said, 'Hirsute?'

'It means –'

'I know what it means, I've been living with an unusually hirsute man for the last twenty-eight years.'

Eva felt a lightness in her body, a lack of gravity. She had experienced the sensation before when she was a child and a game of make-believe with other children had, for a few moments, soared and fused so that the world of their imagination was more real than the dull everyday world, which consisted mostly of unpleasant things. She felt the beginnings of a wild exhilaration and could hardly keep still enough for Alexander to pluck her brows.

She wanted to dance and sing but, instead, she talked. She felt as though a gag had been removed from her mouth.

Neither of them heard Brian and Titania come in, eat supper, or go to bed.

At half past five in the morning, Alexander said, 'I've gotta go home. My kids are early risers, and their grandma ain't.' He looked at Amber's mother and said, 'Should we let her sleep?'

'I don't want to wake her,' said Eva. 'Let her come to life in her own time.'

Alexander picked up the painting and, keeping the bare side of the canvas towards Eva, took it downstairs and left it in the hall.

Eva heard him drive away in the still morning. He had left his Swiss Army knife on the window sill. She picked it up, it was cold to the touch.

She held it in her hands until it was warm.

Eva was kneeling, looking at her reflection in the window, trying to check her Joan of Arc haircut, when Amber's mother stirred and woke. Eva watched her face and saw the precise moment when the sleepiness left and the stark reality that her child was missing hit her.

'You shouldn't have let me *sleep*!' she said, scrambling for her shoes and putting them on. She switched her phone on and said, angrily, 'Amber could have been trying to ring.' She checked her phone. 'Nothing,' she said. 'So, it's good news, isn't it?' she said, brightly. 'It means they haven't found her body, doesn't it?'

Eva said, 'I'm sure she's alive.'

'You're sure?'

Jade grabbed at this morsel of optimism as though Eva were the supreme keeper of all knowledge. 'They said on the internet that you've got special powers. Some people said that you're a witch and you do black magic.'

Eva smiled. 'I haven't even got a cat.'

'I believe that you're a good person. If we both sit quietly and concentrate, do you think you could find out where she is? Can you see her?'

Eva tried to backtrack, saying, 'No, I haven't got extra-sensory perception. I'm not a criminologist. I'm not qualified to give an opinion, and I don't know where Amber is. I'm sorry.'

'Then why did you say you're sure she's alive?'

Eva was disgusted with herself, what she had wanted to say was, 'Most runaways are found alive.'

'No, I think you're right,' said Amber's mother. 'I'd know if she was dead.'

Eva said, 'A lot of teenage girls run away to London.'

'She's been once before. We saw *Les Misérables*. She said she'd be on the side of the aristocrats. I couldn't get her into Poundstretcher.' She was shaking her head. 'What do I do next?'

'Have a shower, wash your hair, clean your teeth.'

When Jade emerged from the bathroom, Eva could tell that she was better equipped to face the misery that had threatened to engulf her.

Eva asked, 'Where are you going now?'

'I've got a cash card, I've got petrol. I'll drive to London and look for her.'

Eva confided, '*I* went to Paris when I was sixteen. My God! Every morning I woke up in a different place, but at least I knew I was *living*.'

Neither woman was used to outward shows of affection, but they clung to each other for a few moments before Eva let Amber's mother go.

When she'd left, Eva stared at the white wall opposite, until Amber and Jade had been pushed into a compartment in the very back of her mind. A place that Eva thought of as the hidden side of the moon.

# 50

As a journey begins with one step, so a crowd begins to collect with one person. Sandy Lake was an aggressively English 41-year-old who thought that if she wore eye-catching colours and a wacky hat, people would be deceived into thinking that she had a 'quirky, off-beat' personality. She had been one of the first to shout, 'Come on, Tim!' from her seat on Centre Court at Wimbledon – once, daringly, after the umpire had called for silence. She had been reprimanded by the Asian umpire, which she thought was a bit rich.

She had read about Eva on Twitter. Many tweeters said that Eva was a wise woman who had taken to her bed as a protest against how horrid the world was, what with wars and famine, and little babies dying and stuff (though it was partly their mothers' fault for having too many children and choosing to live miles from the nearest waterhole). She had also read on SingletonsNet that Eva could contact the dead and see into the future.

Sandy felt compelled to be near to Eva. So, the day before yesterday, she had travelled from Dulwich to the pavement opposite Eva's house, equipped with a pop-up tent, sleeping bag, a thermal mat, a folding chair, a tiny Primus stove and a box of army rations in case of emergency.

She had researched Eva's immediate environs and found a pleasant parade of shops. She needed to be within easy walking distance of a newsagent's. She laughed to others that she was slightly addicted to her celebrity magazines. Nothing gave her more pleasure than seeing a picture of Carol Vorderman with an arrow pointing to her cellulite.

Sandy had inherited the large detached house in Dulwich. It was full of dark heavy furniture, Wilton rugs and swagged curtains. When she was at home, she lived in the kitchen and rarely ventured into the rest of the house. She kept her few clothes on a rail in the former butler's pantry and slept inside her sleeping bag, on the battered sofa that Mum and Dad's dogs had slept on.

She had resisted taking 'silly money' for the house. She knew it was worth over a million pounds, and that it was a 'highly desirable residence', but she had heard that estate agents were untruthful and untrustworthy, and she did not have a best friend to give her advice about money and things.

But she'd got millions of online friends! It was they who told her where the best queue would be forming, or the whereabouts of the next demonstration to be taking place. She had walked to Trafalgar Square on numerous occasions for many disparate causes. She had no politics of her own. She marched with everybody, from the Palestine Liberation Organization to the Sons of Zion, and had a jolly good time with them all. They were all lovely people.

Her favourite queue of all was the line-up for Centre

Court tickets at Wimbledon, closely followed by the promenaders who waited alongside the Albert Hall for the few available standing tickets for the Last Night of the Proms. Sandy knew all the words to 'Land Of Hope And Glory'.

In 1999, she had become so excited by the orchestra's rendition of 'The Floral Dance' that she had agreed to have sexual intercourse round the back of the Albert Hall with Malcolm Ferret, a pale teacher with ginger lashes. She couldn't remember much about their tryst, only that she had not been able to remove the brick dust from her pale-green polar fleece. She had spotted Malcolm in the queue the following year, but he had ignored her little wave and pretended to be absorbed in the wrapper of the Snickers bar he was eating.

One of her highlights of the year had been the launch of the latest iPad. The orderly mob outside the Regent Street Apple Store had been semi-hysterical. They were a very much younger crowd, but Sandy told them she was young at heart and knew plenty of modern phrases, such as 'drag and drop'. She also knew very modern words such as 'dreg' and 'dro'. She knew she impressed the young men around her when she employed these terms.

It seemed to Sandy that she was constantly renewing her technological appliances. It was a good job for her that Mum and Dad had left money in the bank. But what would happen if the money ran out and she was left behind with obsolete technology, and the prospect of never catching up?

There was always somewhere to go. The post-

Christmas sales in Oxford Street were great fun because otherwise Sandy would not speak to anybody over the Christmas period. True, she had been caught up and knocked down in a stampede for the half-price cutlery in Selfridges, but she had picked herself up and managed to snatch a soup ladle before being knocked down again.

Sandy was never lonely, there was always a queue she could join. It didn't matter to her if she was thirty years older than those around her. Neither did she mind admitting that she had once pushed an unaccompanied child out of the way in the last Harry Potter queue. There had been a limited number of signed special editions – and those books were far too good for children, anyway. She had felt desolate when JKR had announced there were to be no more HP books. She consoled herself with fan fiction on MuggleNet.

And now she had her Eva, her beautiful Eva.

Sandy was not sure how long Eva would stay in bed – but whatever happened, she knew that 2012 was going to be a big year for her. There would be many returned-ticket queues she could join for the Olympics. There was the launch of the iPad 3, and the iPhone 5. And her trip to Disneyland in Florida was already booked. She had heard that the attractions were spectacular, and that the lines for these marvels sometimes moved so slowly that at peak times it could take two hours to reach the head of the queue. By then, she would have made many new friends from around the world.

*

After only an hour on the pavement opposite Eva's house, whilst Sandy was struggling in a cruel east wind to keep her tent from blowing away, she was joined by Penelope, who believed that angels lived amongst us and that Eva was undoubtedly 'a very senior angel' who had been caught between heaven and earth. And the reason she had gone to bed was that she needed to hide her wings.

When a white feather flew out of Eva's window, was caught in the wind and landed near Sandy's feet, Penelope said, 'See! I told you!' She added, in awed tones, 'It's a sign that your own personal angel is at your shoulder.'

Sandy was an instant believer.

When she thought about it, she realised that she had always liked angels, and her favourite carol was 'Hark The Herald Angels Sing'. Yes, it all made sense now: Daddy had called her 'my little angel', even though she was twice the size of him. Now she was fifteen stone eleven pounds, dangerously near the weight limit of her folding chair.

Eva first saw Sandy and Penelope when she woke from a deep, dreamless sleep.

She looked out of the window at two middle-aged women on the opposite pavement, one wearing a fun Noddy hat with a bell on the end, the other using binoculars that were trained on her window.

They both waved, and Eva automatically waved back – before dipping down out of sight.

\*

Two miles away, Abdul Anwar sat at the kitchen table yawning, watching his wife fill his tiffin tin with small aluminium containers with screw-on lids. He glanced down at the photographs of Eva and his fellow taxi-driver Barry Wooton on the torn-out front page of the *Leicester Mercury*.

Abdul's wife, Aisha, was cooking chapattis for the evening meal – though Abdul would not be there. He was about to go on night shift. She always made him a meal, which he ate from his collection of silvery aluminium pots. His children called it 'Dad's picnic'.

He said, 'Aisha, be sure to post a copy of the article to our family. I have spoken to them before about my friend Barry.'

She said, 'I won't send it by snail mail, I'll scan it in. You are still living in the past, Abdul.'

While both of her hands were occupied with a chapatti, Abdul got up and put his arms around her waist. He glanced down at the flat pan where his wife was pressing the uncooked side of a chapatti with a bunched-up tea towel. When she flipped it over with her fingers, he gasped and said, 'May Allah be blessed! It is the woman in bed, the saint!'

Aisha said, 'Praise be to God!' and turned the stove off.

They examined the chapatti together. It looked uncannily like Eva's face. The black and brown well-done pieces made up her eyes, eyebrows, lips and nostrils. Her hair was represented by the excess chapatti flour. Abdul brought the front page to the stove and compared the two. Neither man nor wife could quite believe what they were looking at.

Aisha said, 'We will wait for it to cool. It may change.'

She hoped it wouldn't change. She remembered when the Hindu baker had found Elvis Presley in a doughnut. The shop had been besieged. Then, after three days of exposure, Elvis had looked more like Keith Vaz, the local MP, who had subsequently increased his majority at the next general election.

When the chapatti was cold, Abdul took photographs and filmed Aisha at the stove, standing between Eva's picture and what Anwar was later to call 'the blessed chapatti' on Radio Leicester.

After Abdul had left for work, forgetting his tiffin tin in the excitement, Aisha sat at the computer desk in the space beneath the stairs. She created a Facebook page for 'The Woman in Bed' in ten minutes, then set up a link to her own page, calling it 'Eva – the saint appears in Aisha Anwar's chapatti'. It was a thrill for her to press the key that sent it to her 423 friends.

By next morning, Bowling Green Road was chock-a-block with cars. There was a cacophony of car horns, Bollywood music and excited and angry voices as people tried to park.

Ruby was flustered when she opened the door to three bearded men, who asked if they could see the 'Special One'. Ruby said, 'Not today, thank you,' and closed the door.

Meanwhile, queues had formed outside Aisha Anwar's

house, and she was obliged to take them through to see the resemblance between 'Wali Eva' and the face on the chapatti. Aisha was also obliged to offer her visitors food and drink, but after hearing one of them say, in a loud whisper, 'Her kitchen's a seventies *antique*. Those orange tiles!' she regretted her impulsiveness, and fantasized about eating the Eva chapatti with aloo gobi and dhal.

## 51

Over the next week, Eva remembered more of what she had learned at her junior and secondary schools. The world's longest river. The capital of Peru. Which countries constitute Scandinavia. The nine times table. How many pints there were in a gallon. How many inches in a yard. Britain's principal manufacturing industries. How many soldiers were killed on the first day of the First World War. How old was Juliet. The poetry she had learned by heart: 'I must go down to the seas again, to the lonely sea and the sky', 'Hail to thee, blithe Spirit!', 'Fools! For I also had my hour; / One far fierce hour and sweet'. And during this time, the crowd grew and became a constant background noise.

There were complaints from the neighbours about the inconvenience, and the parking problem escalated. But it wasn't until some of the residents were unable to park in their own road and were forced to leave their cars half a mile or more away that the police became involved.

Unfortunately, Constable Gregory Hawk found it impossible to park anywhere near Eva's house, and had to walk an uncomfortably long distance. When he finally reached the front door, he found Ruby sitting outside in the early spring sunshine, selling tea and slices of fruit cake from a trestle table in Eva's front garden. She had put a daffodil in a posy vase on the table to help attract customers, and was charging variable rates which were entirely dependent on whether or not she liked the look of them.

PC Hawk was about to ascertain whether Ruby had a trading licence and a food hygiene certificate, and had completed the paperwork for a risk assessment, when he was diverted by an outside broadcast truck that was backing down the road, only narrowly avoiding the cars parked on either side. After informing the driver that there was nowhere legal to park, he returned to the trestle table in time to hear Ruby shouting, 'Next for the toilets!' and to see a man in Druid's headgear and robes leave the house, while a woman with 'Eva' painted on her forehead entered.

PC Hawk tried to remember whether charging the public to visit a private lavatory was a civil or criminal offence.

When he approached Ruby, she said that the pounds she had in her anorak pockets were donations to the Brown Bird & Beaver Charity. PC Hawk asked if this charity was registered with the Charity Commission, and was told that the registration was 'in the post'.

He then moved to the crowd of what he thought of as 'weirdos', warning them that if they didn't stop singing, ululating, tinkling bells and chanting 'Eva! Eva! Eva!' he would charge them all with a breach of the peace.

An anarchist in an army greatcoat, camouflage trousers and a black polo-neck sweater had spent an hour writing 'HELP THE POLICE – BEAT YOURSELF UP' on his forehead. He shouted feebly, 'We're living in a Police State.'

PC Hawk's hand twitched towards his Taser, but he was reassured when a bulky woman in a Noddy hat said, 'England is the best country in the world, and our police are absolutely terrific!'

The anarchist gave a harsh laugh.

PC Hawk said, 'Thank you, madam, it's nice to be appreciated.'

He thought the whole set-up was a disgrace. There were Asian people everywhere he looked, some on their knees praying, some sitting on a blanket having what looked like breakfast, and a large gang of elderly Muslim, Christian and Hindu women had gathered under Eva's window, clapping and singing. There were no crowd barriers, no surveillance team, nobody directing the traffic. He rang for reinforcements, then walked over to the two old women standing in the doorway of number 15.

He demanded of Yvonne that he be taken to see the householder.

Yvonne said, 'My son, Dr Brian Beaver, is at work, saving the world from attack by meteorites. You'd better talk to Eva herself. She's upstairs, second on the left.'

PC Hawk could not help but be a little thrilled that he was about to meet the Eva woman who'd been on the front of the paper, and all over the internet, and who he'd seen on the television news refusing to talk to good old Derek Plimsoll. This proved to him that she had something to hide.

Who wouldn't want to be on television?

It was his ambition to be the police spokesman for a murder enquiry. He knew all the phrases and sometimes practised them inside his head when he was driving around, bored, on his way to caution a youth for riding a moped without lights.

He saw Eva before she saw him. He was startled by her beauty – she was supposed to be an old woman of fifty, wasn't she?

Eva was shocked to see a gangly baby-faced boy in a police uniform. She said, 'Hello, have you come to arrest me?'

He took out his notebook and said, 'Not at this stage, madam, but I'd like to ask you a few questions. For how long have you been in bed?

Eva tried to do the maths inside her head, then said, 'Since the nineteenth of September.'

The constable blinked a few times and said, 'Nearly five months?'

She shrugged her shoulders.

'And are you separated from your husband?'

'No.'

'Are you planning to leave your husband in the near future?' he asked, emboldened by her frank response.

Eva had watched her fair share of police dramas on television, and thought she knew about police procedures. But as the interview progressed, she began to realise that PC Hawk's questions were entirely centred on herself – and her willingness to be courted by a young policeman.

Their final exchange was particularly ludicrous.

'What is your attitude towards the police?'

'I think they're a necessary evil.'

'Would you ever consider dating a police officer?'

'No, I don't get out of bed.'

She was relieved when the blushing boy finally said, 'One last question. *Why* won't you get out bed?'

Eva answered, honestly, 'I don't know.'

When PC Hawk returned to the station, he asked his superior officer if he could act as a family liaison officer for The Woman in Bed.

'She's causing a lot of trouble, the residents are posh and there's talk of a petition. And one of 'em's a solicitor, sir.'

Sergeant Price was wary of the middle classes. He'd once been involved in a court case for slapping a youth about in the cells. How was he to know that the youth's father was a solicitor's clerk?

'Yeah, why not?' he said to PC Hawk. 'The family liaison officers are both off on maternity leave. And you're the nearest thing we've got to a woman.'

As PC Hawk walked towards his car, his soft cheeks blazed. He thought, 'Yeah, I'm definitely growing a moustache as soon as my beard comes through.'

\*

It was an off-duty policeman called Dave Strong who found Amber. She was begging at the base of the Gherkin with a seventeen-year-old youth called Timmo, known to his parents as Timothy.

PC Strong had acted on his intuition – he had thought it odd to see a young girl in a soiled school uniform with her hand out, beseeching indifferent office workers to, 'Spare some change!' accompanied by Timmo singing his desultory version of 'Wonderwall'.

However, when interviewed by the press, Amber's mother attributed her daughter's rescue to Eva, rather than to the policeman. 'She has special powers,' Jade told a sceptical journalist from the *Daily Telegraph*. 'She can see things that we can't.'

As a news item, it had everything – young love and possible underage sex in *The Sun* and (because Timmo had run away from his A levels) an article in the *Guardian*: 'Are we pushing our young too hard?'

The press eagerly pounced on this nugget of new Eva information. The *Daily Mail*, who were about to go with 'Eva is ex-librarian', scrapped their front page and replaced it with 'ESP Eva finds runaway'.

## 52

At noon on Valentine's Day, Brian and Titania came into Eva's room.

She could tell that both of them had been crying. She was not too alarmed — it seemed to her that British people had long ago stopped pulling themselves together, they now cried habitually in public and were *applauded* for it. Those who didn't cry easily were labelled 'anal'.

Brian said, with a sob, 'Mummy's dead.'

Eva said, when she was able to breathe, 'Your mum or mine?'

'Mine,' he wailed.

'Thank God for that,' she thought. She said to Brian, 'Bri, I'm so *sorry*.'

'She was a wonderful mother,' Brian cried.

Titania attempted to take him in her arms, but he pushed her away and went to Eva, who felt obliged to pat his back. She thought, 'This display from a man who "didn't see the point" of buying his mother a birthday present, on the grounds that "she doesn't need anything".'

'She fell off her stepladder trying to reach her emergency cigarettes,' said Titania, her voice breaking and tears welling in her eyes.

Eva was not to know, but the real reason that Titania was crying was because Brian had not given her a Valentine's Day card or a box of Turkish delight, as he had every year since their affair had begun.

Brian said, 'Another casualty of smoking. She's been dead for three days. What kind of society do we live in when an old lady can lie on her kitchen floor dead *for three days* before anybody notices?'

'Who found her?' asked Eva.

'Peter, the window cleaner,' said Brian.

'*Our* Peter, the window cleaner?' said Eva.

'He rang the police and they broke the door down,' explained Titania.

'Yes, and Peter can bloody well pay for a replacement door. He knows very well we keep a spare key here,' said Brian.

Titania said, 'He's in shock.'

Brian shouted, 'He'll be even more shocked when I give him the bloody bill for a new uPVC triple-glazed door with a state-of-the-art mortise lock!'

'No, *you're* in shock,' pressed Titania.

'She was the best mother a man could have,' said Brian, with a quivering lip.

Eva and Titania exchanged a surreptitious smile.

The doorbell rang.

Titania looked at Eva in bed and Brian weeping, and said, 'I suppose I'll have to go.'

When she opened the door, she received her usual reception. Shouts of 'Adulteress!', 'Sinner!', 'Slag!' Try as she might, she could not get used to the abuse she received whenever she was exposed to the crowd.

A woman in a green tabard was holding a huge bouquet of mixed white flowers, wrapped in white tissue and tied with a white satin ribbon. As Titania searched through the flowers, in anticipation of finding a card addressed to herself from Brian, the post van drew up in the middle of the road.

When the florist and the postman passed each other on the path, they exchanged sympathetic small talk.

'Nightmare day!' she said.

He replied, 'Nearly as bad as Christmas!'

She said, 'Still, I'm being took out tonight, for a slap-up meal.'

Titania winced at 'slap-up meal'.

'Does your husband know?' said the postman.

Titania was amazed at the volume and duration of their laughter. They could not have been more amused had Peter Kay himself appeared at the end of the path and launched into a new routine.

Titania found the little card. 'To Eva, my love.'

She yelled at the two delivery people, 'Why do you *do* your fucking jobs, if you hate them so much?'

The postman said, 'What's up . . . nobody love you?' He handed her a large pack of letters and cards bound in an elastic band. 'Just before I left the depot, I seen another big sack for Eva come in. I'll need a trolley tomorrow.'

Titania said, fiercely, 'Valentine's Day is yet another example of how the market commodifies socio-sexual relationships, transforming love from a state of "being" to a representation of "having", and ultimately degrading us all. So, I'm proud that those who love *me* have not fallen into the "card 'n' chocolates" trap.'

She went inside and slammed the door, but she could still hear the postman's mocking laughter. Perhaps she should have used simpler language, but she refused to patronise uneducated people.

Why shouldn't they rise to her level?

When Eva had the white bouquet thrust into her arms, she knew at once who it was from. It was written in Venus's neat handwriting, and she deduced that Thomas had drawn the wobbly kisses on the bottom of the card.

She said, 'If I were in charge of Interflora, I would make it company policy that chrysanthemums were not allowed in bouquets. They smell of death.'

Brian was slumped in the soup chair, talking about identifying his mother. 'She looked as though she was sleeping,' he said. 'But she was wearing those bloody kangaroo slippers that Ruby bought her for Christmas. They're death traps, I did warn her. It's no wonder she fell off that stepladder.' He looked at Eva. 'Your mother is directly responsible for my mother's death.'

Eva kept quiet.

Brian went on, 'Rigor mortis had set in. The doctor had to prise a packet of Silk Cut from out of her dead fingers.' He wiped his eyes with a balled-up tissue. 'She'd made a jelly for herself, in a small pudding basin. It was still on the kitchen table. It was covered in a thin layer of dust. She would have hated that.'

Titania said, 'Tell Eva about the letters.'

'I can't, Tit.' He started to sob, loudly.

Titania said, 'She'd written letters to herself, love letters. Like in the song, she sat right down and wrote herself a letter. And there was an envelope in her handbag, addressed to Alan Titchmarsh.'

Brian wailed, 'Should we put a stamp on it and post it for her? I don't know the etiquette surrounding death and the postal system.'

Eva said, 'Nor do I – and personally, I don't care if the letter to Mr Titchmarsh is posted or not.'

Brian said, sounding a little hysterical, 'Something has to be done with the bloody thing. Do I carry out her wishes or not?'

Titania said, 'Calm yourself, Bri. It's not as though Alan Titchmarsh is expecting a letter from your mother.'

Brian wept. 'She never, ever sent *me* a letter. Not even to congratulate me on my doctorate.'

Eva heard Alexander's voice under the window, and felt huge relief. He would know what to do with the bloody, stupid Titchmarsh letter. After all, he *had* been to public school. She felt herself relax. Then she heard her mother's voice. She looked out and saw Alexander supporting Ruby, who was dressed entirely in black, including a felt hat with black netting halfway down her face.

Titania said, 'I feel we ought to gird our loins.'

They waited – in silence, apart from Brian's sobs – for

Ruby and Alexander to make their way upstairs. They heard Ruby asking him, 'Why has God punished me, by taking Yvonne away?'

He answered, 'Isn't he meant to move in mysterious ways, your God?'

As Ruby came into the room and saw Brian, she said, 'I thought God would take me first. I've got a mystery lump. I could be dead in a week. A gypsy told me in the year 2000 that I wouldn't make eighty. Ever since that day, I've been living on borrowed time.'

As Brian vacated the chair for her he said, furiously, 'Could we concentrate on my mother d'you think? After all, she is, *actually*, dead.'

Ruby said, 'It's made me poorly, Yvonne dying like that with no warning. My lump is throbbing. Yvonne was going to take me to the doctor's. Being as my daughter won't get out of bed.' Ruby touched her breast and grimaced, waiting for someone to question her.

Alexander said, 'Be nice, Ruby,' as though he were talking to a recalcitrant toddler.

Eva said, dutifully, 'Your lump is probably a cyst, Mum. Why didn't you tell me to my face?'

'I hoped it would go away. I told Yvonne, she knew everything about me.' She turned to Brian. 'And she told me everything about *you*.' This was an implicit threat.

Brian said, 'I blame you for my mother's death. If you hadn't bought those ludicrous kangaroo slippers, she'd be alive today.'

Ruby shouted, 'So, you're blaming me for Yvonne's passing?'

Titania said, 'I know I'm not strictly family, but –'

Alexander interrupted her. 'Titania, I think we should keep out of this.'

A gang of teenage girls in school uniform had joined the crowd and were encouraging them to chant, 'Eva! Eva! Eva!' Somebody was keeping their finger on the doorbell. Eva clapped her hands over her ears.

Ruby said, 'And don't expect me to answer that door. That was Yvonne's job. I wondered where she'd been for the last three days. She liked people. Me, I can take them or leave them, but mostly leave them. Yvonne was a big help to me. I can't deal with those people over the road on my own. There's more every day.'

Titania said, hurriedly, 'I have my work. And a life to run.'

Brian stood at the end of Eva's bed and snarled, 'And now, as usual, we're talking about Eva. I should have listened to my dear *dead* mother. She advised me to move out of this house, and reminded me that my marriage is over. So, my contribution to Eva's care ends here. As a bereaved son, and now an orphan, please allow me to mourn for my mother.'

Ruby ploughed on, regardless, 'And there's the funeral to think about. And it's February. I could catch pneumonia. What will happen to Eva, if I'm in hospital, on oxygen?'

Alexander said, 'I'll look after Eva. I'll open the door. I'll decide who comes in. I'll cook, I'll wash her linen.'

'The flowers, Alexander, they are perfect,' said Eva. 'Thank you. But you can't look after me, you have your own work.'

'I've just been paid for a commission. I'll be OK for a few weeks.'

'What about your kiddies?' asked Ruby. 'You can't drag them out of their beds at night.'

Alexander looked into Eva's face. 'No, we would have to live here.'

Brian turned to Alexander. 'My mother is dead, and you take the opportunity to move yourself and your family into my house. Do you think you're going to live here rent free, using my electricity, my hot water, my fibre-optic broadband? Well, sorry, chummy, but there's no room at the inn.'

Titania said, 'Bri, it's awful, ghastly, dreadful beyond words, that Yvonne is dead, but it could be advantageous to all of us if Alexander was on hand.'

Ruby said, 'In Blackpool, that gypsy, she said there'd be a tall dark man.'

Brian finally lost his temper. 'What in God's holy name are you blathering about? My mother is dead! Will you just shut your bloody trap, woman! As to your earlier lamentation, I too wonder why my loving, unselfish mother was taken and you – with your fatuous observations and antediluvian brain – were left behind!'

Ruby cried, 'I didn't murder your mam!' and threw her hands up to cover her face.

Eva shouted, 'Don't call my mother stupid! She can't help how she is!' She felt so enraged that she began to shuffle on her knees towards Brian, who was sitting at the end of the bed.

There was a loud cheer and some screaming when the

crowd saw her pass the window for the first time in several days.

Eva felt a rage build up and then burst out of her body, transforming itself into words of anger and recrimination. 'You lied to me every day for eight years! You told me that you finished work at six thirty every evening because of your passion for your moon project. But your real passion was for Titania Noble-Forester! I always wondered why you were so exhausted and ravenous, and able to eat a three-course meal.'

Titania yelled at Brian, 'So, that's the reason you would never take me for dinner, is it? You couldn't wait to get home to wifey's prawn cocktail, pork chop and plum duff!'

Brian said, quietly, 'I have never stopped loving my wife. I thought it was possible to love two women. Well, three women, including my poor mother.'

'You've never said that you loved me before,' said Titania, her rage dispersed. She spoke into Brian's ear. 'Oh wow! That is such an aphrodisiac. Why don't we have some "us" time, Squirrel? C'mon, we'll go to the shed.'

The doorbell rang as though a mad person were desperate to gain entry to the house.

After a few moments, when nobody moved, Alexander looked at Brian and asked, 'Shall *I* go?'

Brian snapped, 'Please your bloody self.'

Alexander asked, 'Eva, shall I?'

She nodded. He was a good man to have around when there was a maniac at the door.

He gave her an ironic salute and went to answer it.

Titania passed the package of letters she was holding to Eva. 'Half of it's junk, the rest are all for you.' She led Brian by the hand, as if he were a small child.

Eva said, 'Squirrel?'

She looked at the package of letters with dismay. They were mostly addressed to 'The Woman in Bed, Leicester'. A few from the United States said, 'To the Angel in Bed, England'. One from Malaysia said, simply, 'Eva UK'. After the first three, Eva pushed the bundle away.

Each letter contained pain and false expectation.

She could not help people, and the weight of their suffering was too much for her to bear.

She often distracted herself by compiling lists inside her head, and now she stared at the white wall until her eyes were out of focus, and waited for a topic to emerge. Today it was pain.

### Worst pain

1. Giving birth to twins
2. Falling from high branch on to concrete
3. Fingers slammed in car door
4. Ulcerated milk ducts
5. Falling into bonfire
6. Bitten by pig at Farm Park
7. Tooth abscess on Bank Holiday
8. Trapped by wheel – Brian reversing car
9. Drawing pin in knee
10. Sea urchins in feet, Majorca

# 53

There was pain of a different sort the next day, when Brian Junior emailed Eva via Alexander's phone. Alexander printed it out using a complicated chain of Wi-Fi devices, and brought it up to her with a cup of real coffee.

> Mother, I do not find it agreeable to speak on the phone,
> and shall not do so again. In future, I may occasionally
> communicate with you by use of electronic means or even
> risk the vagaries of the postal system.

'Pretentious little shit,' said Eva. 'Who does he think he is – Anthony Trollope?'

She continued to read her son's message.

> I hear from my father that my paternal grandmother is
> dead. It would be hypocritical of me to affect sadness,
> since I feel indifferent to her fate. She was a foolish old
> woman, as was proved by the farcical manner of her dying.
> However, I shall attend her funeral on Thursday. (I cannot
> speak for Brianne, she has a tutorial on that day with
> visiting God-tier professor Shing-Tung Yau. It is rare for a
> first-year undergraduate to be so honoured. Although I
> fear he will be less than ecstatic when he hears what she
> has to say about Calabi-Yau manifolds.)

Eva broke off. 'I pity the poor man. Do you know, Alexander, I don't understand my children at all. I never have.'

Alexander assured her, 'Eva, none of us know our children. Because they are not *us*.'

She turned back to the email with less enthusiasm.

Since we won't be meeting at the graveside, you may be interested to know that my paper proving that the Bohnenblust-Hille inequality for homogeneous polynomials is hyper conductive has been accepted by *Annals of Mathematics* for possible publication in the September issue, and that I have been offered a scholarship to St John's College, Oxford. However, I may turn the latter down. It is hardly Cambridge, and my present location is agreeable to me. There is a café nearby that provides a full English breakfast at a price I can afford. This sustains me throughout the day. Then all I require in the late evening is a little bread and a lump of Edam cheese.

Eva tried to make light of this evidence of Brian Junior's increasing peculiarity. She was alarmed by this email. He had always been the weaker twin – slower to talk and walk – and the one who clung to her skirt when she first took them to nursery school. But she remembered it was also Brian Junior who had charmed passers-by with his smile when she took the twins out in the double buggy. Even then, Brianne had been less attractive. If somebody approached her, she would scowl and hide her face.

Eva continued to read. She felt nothing but a sense of failure, and perhaps, for the first time, had to face the realisation that Brian Junior might have to move to Silicon Valley where he would be able to live and work with his own kind.

> I find it a matter of regret that you will not be attending
> your late mother-in-law's funeral. My father is, and I quote,
> 'Devastated.' I have also spoken to Barbara Lomax, the head of
> the Student Psychology Service, and she assures me that the
> reason you are 'unable' to leave your bed is that you are in the
> grip of agoraphobia, probably as a result of childhood trauma.

Alexander, attempting to lighten the mood, laughed and said, 'Did you see something nasty in the woodshed, Eva?'

She was unable to join in. She read the next few sentences to herself, not wanting Alexander to hear them and judge her.

> Ms Lomax stressed that she has known people to be cured
> within six weeks. However, diet, exercise, self-discipline
> and courage are needed. I informed Barbara that, in my
> opinion, you have no courage, because you knowingly allow
> my father to fornicate under your roof and say nothing.

Eva could no longer control herself, and shouted aloud, 'He's not under my roof! He's in his sodding shed!' Then she continued reading to herself.

> Barbara enquired of me, 'Do you have anger issues with
> your mother?' I told her that I can hardly bear to be in the
> same room as my mother lately.

Eva read the last sentence again. And then again.

What had she done wrong?

She had fed him, kept him clean, bought him decent shoes, taken him to the dentist and the optician, built a rocket out of Lego, taken him on zoo trips and cleaned out his room. He'd been on a steam train, the medical box was always at hand, and she'd hardly raised her voice to him throughout his childhood.

She folded the email printout in half, then into quarters, then into eighths, then into sixteenths, then into thirty-secondths and sixty-fourths. She tried to make it even smaller, gave up and put the wad of paper in her mouth. It was unpleasant, but she could not take it out. Alexander undemonstratively passed her a glass of water and she began to soften the wad of paper like a cow chewing cud, until gradually it turned into a pulp.

With her tongue, she pushed the wad into her cheek and said to Alexander, 'I need a blind at this window. A white blind.'

On the night before his mother's funeral, Brian went to see Eva. He asked her to reconsider her decision to stay away from the church service and the following interment.

Eva assured Brian that she had loved Yvonne, and would think about her while the funeral was in progress, but she could not leave her bed.

Brian said, 'What if it was Ruby, your own mother? Would you leave your bed for her?'

'I need notice on that question,' said Eva.

'I can't bear to think about her lying on those cold kitchen tiles,' Brian said, tearfully.

Eva stroked his hand. 'She was fed up with the modern world anyway, Brian. She couldn't grasp the fact that there was pornography on her Freebox. When she first watched the telly, the newsreader was wearing a dinner jacket.'

'Do you think she had a good life?'

Eva said, carefully, 'As good as she could have, given that she was born into a man's world, and that your dad wouldn't let her wear trousers.'

He said, 'You know those Valentine's Day cards she got every year?'

'An amazing number.'

'She wrote *them* to herself as well.'

'She must have been horribly lonely, Bri. She never got over your dad's death.'

'Were you lonely when I was at work?' Brian asked.

Eva said, 'I was lonelier when you came home, and we were sitting next to each other on the sofa.'

'But we did have some good times, didn't we?'

'We must have, but I can't remember what they were.'

Brian said, sounding slightly annoyed, 'The holidays abroad. Camping in Wales. Florida.'

Eva wanted to concur with Brian, but her memories were a blur of mosquitoes, rain, mud, sunstroke, dehydration, endless driving, bickering and grudging reconciliations.

# 54

The Beaver ancestors had bought a family plot in the shade of a small copse of dense conifers at St Guthlac's. There was no room between the trees to drive a mechanical digger, and roots made digging new graves a trial of strength and stamina.

As the chief mourners were chauffeured up the drive of the forbidding Norman church, to the ringing of a sonorous bell, they saw two young gravediggers throwing small stones at each other. When Brian, Titania and the twins passed the youths, they heard one of them shout, 'You *twat*, you nearly got my eye then!'

Brian ordered the driver of the car to stop. He got out and walked purposefully towards his mother's unfinished grave.

The youths threw down their stones and picked up their spades.

Brian said, 'I know that lessons in inappropriate swearing are on the curriculum at your lame-duck comprehensive, but this *hole* you're meant to be digging will be my mother's final resting place. Do not shout "twat" across her grave.'

He walked back to the limousine.

As soon as the door closed, one of the youths met Brian's eyes, muttered, '*Twat!*' and jumped into the grave.

Brian was about to open the door again, but Brian Junior pulled him away from the handle. 'Leave it, Dad.'

Brian was unnerved. For three miles they had been following the hearse that carried his mother's body. Behind them all the way was Alexander, driving his old van, with Stanley Crossley and Ruby on the bench passenger seat.

Yvonne's sisters, Linda, Suzanne and Jean, were standing around the porch, smoking and tapping the ash into the palms of their hands. Brian thought this, and the fact that they were displaying so much cleavage, was inappropriate. He had not spoken to them for years. There had been an 'incident' at a family christening that had ended badly. His mother had never felt able to tell him the details – all she would say was, 'There was too much drink taken.' But it could explain why they were staring at him with such malevolence.

They stared even harder at Titania, checking her face, hair, black suit, handbag and shoes. She was of great interest to them. How dare Brian flaunt his knock-off in public? His crazy wife had disgraced the family by making a show of herself, and had now insulted them all by not turning up for her mother-in-law's funeral.

They stepped aside to let Alexander, Stanley Crossley and the twins into the church. Ruby had sensed the atmosphere, and scuttled away to find a lavatory.

After everybody was seated, Ruby made a late but dramatic entrance by failing to control the immensely heavy church door. The wind dragged the handle out of her hand and slammed it so loudly that the vicar and the mourners, who were kneeling on cassocks in silent prayer, jumped and turned round, in time to see her rooted to the floor in shock. Stanley Crossley, who was wearing a black armband over his dark suit, was sitting on a back pew. He got up and helped Ruby down the aisle to join her own clan at the front.

She was outraged when she saw what appeared to be a cardboard box up on a trestle near the altar. She whispered to Brian, 'Who left that in the church? Where's Yvonne's coffin?'

'That *is* her coffin,' Brian whispered back. 'It's ecologically sound.'

'What's that when it's at home?'

The vicar began to tell the small congregation that Yvonne had been born into sin and had died in sin.

Ruby whispered to Brian, 'She wanted a walnut coffin with brass handles and a puce satin lining. We looked through a catalogue together.'

Out of the side of his mouth, Brian said, 'Her funeral policy didn't stretch to walnut.'

The vicar looked like a badger in a surplice. He said, in his fruity voice, 'We are gathered here today on this dreadful wet and windy morning to celebrate the life of our sister, Rita Coddington.'

There was angry muttering and stifled laughter as the congregation registered his mistake.

He carried on, 'Rita was born in 1939, the daughter of Edward and Ivy Coddington. It was a difficult forceps birth, which left Rita with an elongated head. She was teased at school but –'

Ruby stood up and interrupted. 'Excuse me, but what you just said is rubbish. The woman in that cardboard box is Yvonne Beaver. Her mam and dad were Arthur and Pearl, and she had a perfectly normal head.'

The vicar sorted through the notes on his lectern, and saw at once that he had mixed up Yvonne Beaver's notes with those of the next service. He readdressed the congregation, saying, 'I can only work with the information I'm given. Before I proceed, could I check a few facts with you? First, hymns. Did you request "All Things Bright And Beautiful"?'

Brian said, 'Yes.'

'And "Onward Christian Soldiers"?'

Brian nodded.

'And now popular music. Did she request "Yellow Submarine" by The Beatles, and "Rawhide", sung by Mr Frankie Laine?'

Brian mumbled, 'Yes.'

'Was she a punch card operator until her marriage?'

Brian nodded again.

Brianne said loudly, 'Look, can you just get on with it?'

The vicar announced, 'The eulogy will be read by Yvonne's grandson, Brian Junior.'

Those acquainted with Brian Junior watched apprehensively as he walked to the lectern.

Alexander groaned, 'Oh, sweet Jesus, no,' and crossed his fingers.

Brian Junior's eulogy was the first time he had spoken in public at a formal occasion. He started well, guided by a website called funeraleulogies.com. When he had used up his conventional script, he improvised.

He spoke of the twins' early memories of Yvonne. 'She was hyper hygienic, and when we stayed with her overnight she would take my teddy and Brianne's monkey and put them in the washing machine so they'd be nice and fresh for us in the morning.'

He looked around the church at the carved pillars and the signs and symbols that he could not decipher. The light outside was low but the stained glass glowed, giving a half-life to the familiar biblical figures in stained glass.

'She took Teddy's smell away,' he said.

Brianne said, from a front pew, 'And Monkey's.'

Brian Junior wiped his eyes using the sleeve of his jacket, and continued, 'I know some of you are worried about the apparent flimsiness of Gran's coffin, so I researched the decomposition cycle of the human body. Given her height and approximate weight, and allowing for the variables of climate and temperature, I reckon that her coffin and corpse will last for –'

Brian called out, 'Thank you, Brian Junior! Step down now, son.'

The vicar hastily took possession of the lectern and, before Brian Junior had reached his place in the pew, had signalled to the organist for the first hymn to be sung: 'We plough the fields and scatter . . .'

Stanley and Ruby sang lustily, neither of them needed a hymn book.

Ruby glanced at Stanley's face and thought, 'It's amazing what you can get used to, given time.'

Eva was luxuriating in the silent house. It had stopped raining and she could tell by the light on the white walls that it was approximately eleven o'clock.

It was quiet outside. The downpour had sent most of the crowd looking for shelter.

She thought about Yvonne, who she had seen at least twice a week for twenty-five years. She dredged out memories.

Yvonne at the seaside, shaking sandy towels into the wind.

Yvonne with a child's fishing net, trying to catch tadpoles with the twins.

Yvonne in bed, crying with arthritic pain.

Yvonne helpless with laughter at Norman Wisdom on television.

Yvonne's teeth clicking as she ate her Sunday dinner.

Yvonne arguing with Brian about creationism.

Yvonne dropping cigarette ash into a casserole she was serving.

Yvonne's horror in a restaurant in France, when her steak tartare turned out to be raw meat.

Eva was surprised to find that she mourned Yvonne's death.


Back in church, the vicar, who was trying to be relevant to the community, led the congregation on the last verse of 'Yellow Submarine'.

When it was finally over, he said, 'You know, life is like a banana. The fruit is inside, but the skin is green, so you leave it to ripen . . .' He paused. 'But sometimes you leave it too long, and when you remember it again, the skin has turned black, and when you finally remove it, what has happened to the good fruit?'

Brian Junior said, from the front pew, 'The banana has produced ethylene, and will eventually oxidize and break down into a new gaseous compound of equivalent mass.'

The vicar said, 'Thank you for your contribution,' and carried on. 'Eventually, Yvonne's body will decompose, but her soul will attain everlasting life in God's Kingdom, and will forever remain in your memory.'

Brian Junior laughed.

The vicar asked the congregation to kneel again while he read them a passage on resurrection from the King James Bible. Only Ruby remained standing. She pointed to her knees, mouthed the word, 'Knees!' to the vicar, and shook her head.

When he'd finished the passage, the vicar looked at the congregation. They were shifting from foot to foot, glancing at their watches and yawning. He thought it was time for the Commendation and Farewell. He cleared his throat, turned to the coffin and said, 'Let us commend Yvonne Primrose Beaver to the mercy of God, our Maker and Redeemer.'

Brian Junior said, very loudly, 'Maker? I think not.' He added, as if he were in an advanced tutorial, 'Variation plus differential reproduction plus heredity equals natural selection. Darwin one, God nil.'

The vicar looked at Brian Junior, and thought, 'Poor chap, Tourette's is a cruel affliction.'

Alexander thought, 'When will this *end*? When will this dreary tight-arsed ceremony be over?'

At the last funeral he'd been to, there was a gospel choir, steel drums and dancing. People had swayed their hips and raised their arms above their heads, as though they were truly joyful that the departed one would soon be in the arms of Jesus.

When the vicar said the words, 'We entrust Yvonne to your mercy, in the name of Jesus our Lord, who died and is alive, and reigns with you, now and for ever,' the congregation said, 'Amen,' as though they were truly thankful that the ceremony had finally ended.

Four undertakers walked solemnly up the aisle, lifted the eco-box coffin on to their shoulders and, to the accompanying sound of 'Rawhide', walked back down the aisle, out of the church and towards the poorly dug fresh grave.

The mourners followed.

Brian sang along quietly with Frankie Laine. He cracked an imaginary whip and envisioned himself herding stampeding cattle across the Texan plains.

When the cardboard coffin was carried to the graveside, some of the angel worshippers from the Bowling Green Road crowd joined the procession. At their head were Sandy Lake and her friend, the anarchist William Wainwright.

Sandy was carrying a single lily she had bought from Mr Barthi's shop. He had not wanted to split a ready-made bouquet of six stems, but she had been so tenacious that he had eventually given up, telling his wife later that he was thinking of retiring and starting a new business where he wouldn't have to interact with people.

His wife had scolded, 'Ha! So, now you are playing with robots? You are going back to university to do a degree in electronics and then a masters in robotics? By then you will be seventy years old, you fat fool! And I will be dead of starvation, and our children will be sweeping the gutters!'

As he stacked the instant rice, Mr Barthi wished fervently that he had not spoken so openly to his wife. It was already a sad day for him. Mrs Yvonne Beaver was a good customer and an interesting conversationalist, unlike her son.

He also missed Mrs Eva Beaver. He used to buy a crate of Heinz tomato soup from the cash and carry especially for her. She ate a bowl for her lunch every day. Nobody else in her family liked it, they had their own favourites.

Back in Bowling Green Road, there were shouts and insults being traded by opposing groups in the crowd. The vampire worshippers were berating the Harry Potter faction.

In an attempt to block out the noise, Eva had set herself the task of remembering all her favourite songs from childhood to the present day. She had started with Max Bygraves, 'I'm A Pink Toothbrush', then moved on to the Walker Brothers, 'The Sun Ain't Gonna Shine (Anymore)', and was presently struggling to remember Amy Winehouse's 'Back To Black'. She knew she had a good voice, with perfect pitch. It offended her when professional singers strayed from a note.

Miss Bailey, her music teacher at school, had entered her into the County Music Festival. Eva was to perform a solo classic, Schubert's 'The Trout', to a panel of weary judges. At the end, she had looked at their smiling faces, automatically assuming they were laughing at her, and had run from the platform, down long corridors and into a garden with benches where the other contestants were eating their packed lunches. They had all stared at her.

At school assembly on Monday morning, the head-mistress, Miss Fosdyke, announced after prayers that Eva Brown-Bird had won the Gold Medal at the County Music Festival. Eva was shocked, and she found the thunderous applause unbearable. She had blushed and lowered her head. When Miss Fosdyke called for her to come up on the stage, she pushed her way along the rows of girls and escaped through the nearest door. As she walked towards the cloakroom, she heard loud laughter from the hall. Finding it impossible to stay in the school, she had collected her coat and satchel and walked in miserable drenching rain around the area where she lived, until it was the legitimate time to go home.

# 55

When the funeral party arrived back at the house, the crowd growled its displeasure at Brian and Titania. Then, after a gesture from Alexander, they grew silent. Photographs of Yvonne's funeral had already been posted on the internet. Some of the regulars had twittered their worries that access to the lavatory would cease with her passing.

As soon as the mourners were gathered inside the hall, they heard Eva singing a familiar tune. 'I stood upon the shore, And watched in sweet peace, The cheery fish's bath, In the clear little brook.'

Titania whispered to Ruby, 'It's Schubert, "The Trout".'

Ruby said, 'Why are people always telling me things I already know?'

When Eva switched to German, Ruby joined in. '*Ich stand an dem Gestade, Und sah in süßer Ruh, Des muntern Fischleins Bade, Im klaren Bächlein zu.*'

The group looked at each other and smiled, and Brianne said, 'Yeah, go G'ma.'

Ruby said, without modifying her voice, 'She practised that bleddy song in English and German for weeks on end. It nearly drove me mad.'

Eva shouted down the stairs, 'Yes, and where's my gold medal now, Mum?'

'Oh, not that bleddy medal again! Get over it, Eva!'

Ruby said to Stanley, 'She knew I hated clutter. She should have put it away somewhere safe.'

Stanley smiled, he was a tidy man himself.

She hobbled to the bottom of the stairs and shouted up, 'It weren't real gold anyway!'

Much later, when Eva asked Brianne how the funeral had gone, she said, 'Brian Junior made a dick of himself giving the eulogy, but it was OK. Nobody cried, except Dad.'

'Couldn't *you* have squeezed a tear out, Brianne? Surely it's only good manners to cry at a funeral.'

Brianne said, 'You're such a hypocrite! I thought you were all for truth and beauty, and all that nineteenth-century shit.'

Brianne was angry and disappointed that Alexander had paid her such little attention. He had spent no more time with her than he had with the rest of the family. OK, so he didn't love her. But he ought to have acknowledged that they had a close bond. She had managed to sit next to him in the church, but she could have been a sack of old potatoes for all he cared.

He had disrespected her. She was upset. She needed to tell her online friends how she felt. She went into Brian Junior's bedroom, and fired up her laptop.

He was already online, posting to Twitter. He typed:

> Gran y = worm bait. She rollin' rollin' rollin' towards nonexist-
> ent Jesus.

He switched tabs to the Facebook group set up in honour of his mother. Using one of his troll accounts, he
began to slag off the crowd outside his house, with particular reference to Sandy Lake. He ended his diatribe by
updating the troll account status to 'Anybody got a spare
grenade?'

Brianne was on the same site, using her own name.
She typed:

> There's a skanky black wasteman outside my front door. He
> thinks he's a doorman, but he should impose a dress code on
> himself cos his locks are rank like dead donkey's tails. Cut 'em
> off, granddad.

Alexander was standing on the doorstep, illuminated by
the porch light. He was wearing his navy-blue Crombie
overcoat and smoking a cigarette.

There were several desperate cries, people begging to
see Eva before the evening deadline. She had started to
give an audience to five people each day. Who she saw
was determined by Alexander, who picked a surprisingly
varied bunch of representatives from the crowd.

This afternoon's consultations had included a 57-year-
old whose mother wanted to marry a man in his
seventies – how could she stop her?

Eva had said, 'You don't stop her, you buy her a bottle
of champagne and give them your blessing.'

The second was a feather enthusiast who believed

366

that Eva was hiding a fine set of wings. Eva had turned round, pulled her T-shirt up to her neck and showed the enthusiast her unadorned back.

There was a teenage girl who told Eva that she wanted to die and join Kurt Cobain in his crib in heaven. And there was a super-obese American man who had flown from New Orleans, having paid for two Business Class seats, to tell Eva that she was a reincarnation of Marilyn Monroe, and he would like to 'conversate' with her.

And, of course, there were the recently bereaved who could not bear the harsh reality that they would never see their loved ones again. They sent notes and photographs, asking Eva to speak to their dead and relay messages from them to the living. Eva worked hard to damp down the emotion in her room. She began to turn away if there were tears.

Alexander ground his cigarette out under his boot and threw it into the gutter. He spoke quietly to Sandy, saying, 'That's it for tonight. Listen to your good side. No shouting to Eva tonight. Have some respect. There's been a funeral here today.'

That night, when Alexander had settled Venus and Thomas in their beds in Brian Junior's old room, he looked out of the window before getting into bed himself. He saw that the only person left on the opposite pavement was Sandy Lake, sitting outside her tent.

She had made herself as comfortable as possible, supplementing her Karrimat with a cardboard and newspaper mattress. With the aid of a head torch, she was reading a magazine dedicated to angel-worshipping celebrities.

Alexander pushed the window sash up a little to let in some air. Sandy looked up immediately, and there was something about her stillness that disturbed him. He closed the window and locked it.

Sandy was down in the dumps tonight. Penelope had abandoned her and gone home to nurse her bronchitis. Sandy had been here for the longest, and still hadn't had a proper audience with Eva. She needed more than a ten-minute session. Eva had been promising her another consultation, but for some reason it kept getting postponed, and Sandy was losing her patience. She needed to tell Eva her life story – how unkind people had been to her throughout her life, and how, when she went to the shops around the corner and talked to Mr Barthi about Eva and the angels, he would refuse to listen.

He had said to her recently, 'Your nonsense is lost to me. I am an agnostic.'

It was Alexander's fault. It was he who was keeping her from Eva. He was jealous, because Sandy had become the world's self-appointed expert on the Eva phenomenon. Her scrapbooks had more press clippings than any of the other Eva fans, and she could recite, by heart, the highlights of Eva's rise to celebritydom. Her iPad had links to every Eva-related site and blog, and she was proud of the efficiency of her news alerts, which constantly searched for Eva updates.

She was the main source for the dissemination of, and

misinformation about, Eva's supposed spiritual powers. Sandy was prone to exaggeration, describing a fictional audience with Eva as being, 'In the presence of an unworldly being. She has an ethereal beauty that cannot be matched in the whole of the world. And every word she speaks is wise and true.'

When pressed by newcomers to the crowd to reveal what Eva had said that was so impressive, Sandy would wipe her eyes and say, 'Sorry, I always mist up when speaking of Eva . . .' Then, after what her audience found to be an infuriatingly extended pause, she would say, 'Eva spake unto me and the words she did say were for my ears alone. But when I was backing out of her room, I saw her rise from the bed and hover there for a few seconds. She was giving me a sign! It was Eva's way of telling me that I have been chosen.'

When cynics questioned Sandy and asked, 'Chosen for what?' the chosen one would reply, in sanctimonious tones, 'I'm waiting for another sign, it will come from the sky.'

Sandy needed Eva to address the world and tell all the countries that were at war to stop. And to help all the kiddies who had no water or food. She was sure that the world would listen to Eva, and then there would be joy in angel heaven, and there would be no more fighting, no floods or famines or earthquakes. There would be peace and joy and love throughout the world, so it was imperative that she talk to Eva.

What could be more important?

She looked up at Eva's lighted window, said a prayer

and climbed inside her tent, where William Wainwright was sleeping like a baby on barbiturates.

It seemed to Eva that every time she looked out of the window, she saw Sandy Lake looking up at her with a beatific smile. The woman had ruined her view of the world outside.

Earlier that evening, Eva had cursed and said to Alexander, 'Does that crazy woman never sleep?'

Alexander said, 'Even when she does sleep, she keeps her eyes open. But don't worry, I'm next door. Just knock on the wall if you need me.'

## 56

In late February, after the twins had returned to Leeds, they settled back into Sentinel Towers with relief – it was impossible to do any serious work in Bowling Green Road. According to Brian Junior, the doorbell rang on a mean average of 9.05 times per hour.

They decided that they would work together from now on. Each would help the other with their essays and assignments, leaving them more time to spend on their Special Projects.

They started with their finances and sold their mother's gift of jewellery in a Cash Generator in the city centre. They agreed that in future they would not allow sentiment to influence their plans.

In the second week of their second term, they had successfully hacked into the university's accommodation records and changed the status of their accounts from 'Rent Arrears' to 'Rent Paid in Full until 2013'. The day after this triumph, which brought each of them an extra £400 a month, they went shopping for clothes.

They sat down on a sofa opposite the changing rooms in Debenhams and talked for a long time about their lives and what they wanted in the future.

Brianne confessed that if she couldn't have Alexander, she wouldn't have any man.

Brian Junior told Brianne that he would never marry. 'I'm not sexually attracted to women or to men,' he said.

Brianne smiled and said, 'So, we stick together for life?'

Brian Junior agreed. 'You're the only person I can stand to be with for more than four minutes.'

When they had tried their new clothes on, they came out of their respective changing rooms and were astonished at how similar they could look. They were both wearing black and, after a few negotiations, and going back and forth to the rails, they ended up with a uniform. It was all black apart from a leopard-skin belt and the silver accessories on their black cowboy boots.

Mindful of their new and certain future wealth, they left their old clothes in the changing room. As they walked arm in arm through the shopping centre, they began to work on synchronising their steps.

A colourist at Toni & Guy obeyed their instructions and dyed their hair magenta red. After a stylist had given them both a severe geometric cut, they left the salon and headed to the best tattoo parlour in South Yorkshire.

When the operative asked them if they were related to the woman in the bed called Beaver, they responded, 'No.'

He was disappointed. 'She's cool,' he said.

They were given a rudimentary test for allergies and, while they waited for the results, they sat outside a coffee bar so they could smoke. Nihilists like them felt it was their *duty* to smoke.

They lit their cigarettes and smoked contentedly

before Brian Junior said, 'Will we ever go back to Bowling Green Road, Brianne?'

'What, and have to interface with those awful people we used to call Mum and Dad? Or, as we now know them, The Great Adulterer and his wife, The False Prophet.'

Brian Junior said, 'I used to love them when I was little – and you did too, Brianne, you can't deny it!'

'Little kids are idiots, they believe in the fucking Tooth Fairy, Santa, God!'

'I believed in them,' lamented Brian Junior. 'I believed they'd always do the right thing. Tell the truth. Control their animal desires.'

Brianne laughed. 'Animal desires? You've either been reading the Old Testament or D. H. Lawrence.'

Brian Junior said, 'Disneyland hurts me. The thought that while we were queuing with Mum for the It's a Small World ride, Dad was back at the hotel paying for a prostitute with his credit card.'

Brianne said, 'We'll say a final farewell to them, shall we?'

Neither of them had a piece of paper. Who used the stuff these days? Together they erased every parental reference from their laptops. Then, Brianne put a virtual fire on screen, and typed in 'Eva Beaver' and 'Brian Beaver'. Brian Junior put his index finger on top of Brianne's, and together they pressed the key that would cause their parents' names to burn, and eradicate their memory for all time.

They discussed the tattoo they would each have.

It would be two halves of an equation that together made one perfect sum.

After they left the tattoo studio, they attracted a great deal of attention – but nobody, not even the lowlife who hung around town in the middle of the day, dared to comment.

Brian Junior drew strength and confidence from his sister. In the past, he had walked down the street with his gaze on the pavement. Now he stared straight ahead and people moved away, out of his path.

# 57

Eva had watched the leaves of the sycamore unfurl. For the first time, it was possible to have the window open. She was on her back doing exercises on her bed, slowly raising two legs until she could feel her abdomen tightening. She could tell that Alexander was on the door from the wisps of cigarette smoke drifting up through the open window.

She had heard him arguing with Venus and Thomas earlier that morning. Neither of them knew where their school shoes were. Eva had laughed when she heard Alexander ask, 'Where did you put them last?'

He was following the unofficial parents' script, she thought.

For how many thousands of years had children been asked the same question? When did children start to wear shoes, and what were they made of? Animal skin, or woven vegetation?

There were so many things she didn't know.

She had also heard Alexander say, 'Finish your food, there are children starving in Africa.'

It had been Chinese children starving when she was a girl, thought Eva.

He had answered Thomas's question, 'Why do

children have to go to school?' with the terse reply, 'Because they do.'

If it hadn't been for the crowd opposite, she would have liked to watch them leaving the house, Alexander dreadlocked and elegant in his navy overcoat, the children in their red and grey uniforms.

Her mother had complained to her that the children's paintings and drawings were 'taking over the bleddy house'. She had added, 'I wouldn't mind, but they're all rubbish.'

Eva could tell that her mother was baking today. The room was full of the sickly sweet smell of the cakes that Ruby would sell later to the crowd.

Eva had asked her not to do this. 'You're encouraging them to hang about, *and* you're exploiting them.'

But Ruby had bought herself a new living-room carpet with the proceeds of her tea and cake sales. She had refused to stop, saying, 'If you don't like it, get out of bed. They'll soon go away when they see that you're just a very ordinary woman.'

Eva turned her head during her neck exercises and saw a pair of magpies fly past with bits of straw clamped in their beaks. They were nesting in a hollow in the sycamore trunk. She had been watching their comings and goings with great interest for a week.

'Two for joy,' she thought.

She wondered if it were possible for a man and a woman to be completely happy together.

When she and Brian had, at his insistence, thrown

dinner parties, the married couples had usually begun the evening with conventional good manners. But, by the time Eva was serving her home-made profiteroles, there was often one couple who were transformed into bickering pedants, questioning the veracity of their partner's anecdotes and contradicting them in tedious detail. 'No, it was Wednesday, not Thursday. And you were wearing your blue suit, not the grey.' They left early with faces as set as Easter Island statues. Or stayed on and on, helping themselves to strong liquor, and falling into a drunken morass of depression.

Eva smiled to herself, and thought, 'I'll never again have to throw another dinner party, or attend one.'

She wondered if the magpies were happy – or was happiness only a human perception?

Who had insisted on including 'the pursuit of happiness' in the American constitution?

She knew that Google could supply the answer within seconds of her asking, but she was in no hurry to find out. Perhaps it would come back to her, if she waited.

Alexander knocked. 'Are you ready for a long-distance lorry driver with two families? One in Edinburgh, one in Bristol.'

Eva groaned.

Alexander said, 'It gets worse. It's his fiftieth birthday next week. Both wives are throwing him a big party.'

They laughed, and Eva said, 'It's my party and I'll cry if I want to . . .'

Alexander said, 'I haven't seen you cry yet. Do you?'

'No, I can't cry.' Then Eva asked, 'What am I doing here, Alexander?'

'You're giving yourself a second chance, aren't you? You're a good woman, Eva.'

'But I'm not!' insisted Eva. 'I resent them disturbing my peace. I can feel their misery clogging up my system. I can hardly breathe. How can I be a good woman? I don't care any more. I'm bored by the people I see. All I want to do is lie here without speaking, without hearing. Without worrying about who's next on your list.'

Alexander said, 'You think my job is any easier? I stand in a cold doorway freezing my balls off, talking to mentalists all day.'

'They're not mentalists,' Eva protested. 'They're just *humans* who've got themselves into a mess.'

'Yeah? Well, you should see the ones I turn away.' Alexander sat down on the bed. 'I don't want to be outside in the cold. I want to be here, with you.'

Eva said, 'I think about you at night. We share a wall.'

'I know. I sleep a foot away from you.'

They both became transfixed by their own fingernails.

Alexander said, 'So, how long are you giving the bigamist?'

'The same as usual, ten minutes is all I can take,' said Eva, irritably.

'Look, if you don't want to see him, don't. I'll get rid of him.'

'I'm a charlatan. They think I'm helping them, but I'm not. Why do they believe everything they read in the newspapers?'

'Forget newspapers. It's the internet. You've no idea, have you? No idea how crazy they are. You lie up here, we provide room service, and you literally crawl under the duvet if you come across something too unpleasant, something that might upset little Eva. Well, just remember that downstairs is where the real work is done, dangerous work. I'm not a trained bodyguard. I read your mail, Eva. I keep some of the letters back. Am I doing any painting? No, I'm not. Because I'm protecting Eva from the maniacs who want to cut her up. Eva the diva.'

Eva sat up straight.

She wanted to get out of bed and put an end to the trouble she was causing. But when it came to swinging her legs round, the floor did not look solid. She felt that if she stood, she would sink through the floorboards as though they were made of jelly.

She was dizzy. 'Give me a minute, please, then send the bigamist up.'

'OK. And start eating again. You're like a bag of bones.' He went out and shut the door firmly behind him.

Eva felt as though she'd been punched in the chest.

She had sensed for some time that she had been behaving badly. She was selfish and demanding and had almost begun to believe that she was at the centre of her small universe. She would tell Alexander he should vacate his room, take his children and go back to his own house.

She wondered if she could manage without Alexander's love and care. She had to protect herself from the awful pain of imagining her life of self-imprisonment without him.

She resumed her exercises, with a series of leg raises. One, two, three, four, five, six, seven . . .

## 58

Ho's parents, Mr and Mrs Lin, were walking along a dusty narrow pavement beside an eight-lane highway.

They were not speaking. The noise of the traffic was too loud.

Two years ago, there had been no highway. This had been a neighbourhood of one-storey houses, shops and workshops, alleys and mysterious pathways, where people made their living in full view of their neighbours. There had been no privacy. If a neighbour coughed, it was heard by many people, and festivals were celebrated communally.

They turned off and walked past a new tower block and a car dealership where shiny new vehicles were for sale. They came to a forecourt where electric scooters were arranged in lines according to colour. Mr Lin had always wanted a scooter. He ran his hand over the handlebars and seat of one in his favourite colour – aquamarine.

As they walked on, Mrs Lin said, 'Look at the old bicycles.'

Inside a mesh fence topped with security lights were hundreds of them.

They laughed together, and Mrs Lin said, 'Who would even think about stealing old bicycles?'

They turned a corner and were on their old street. The rubble had still not been cleared.

They passed the place where they had lived for nineteen years, where Ho had played safely in the traffic-free alleys. Only five of the original houses were still inhabited. One of them belonged to the moneylender, Mr Qu. There were rumours that Mr Qu had contacts within the Beijing Tourist Board, and that he had bribed the bulldozer driver to stop at his house. Mr Qu was afraid of the professional moneylenders who were muscling in on his trade.

Mr Lin called softly at the open door. 'Are you there, Mr Qu? It is Mr Lin, your old neighbour.'

Mr Qu came to the door and greeted them. 'Ha!' he said. 'How do you like living in the sky, with the birds?'

The Lins were proud people.

'It is good,' said Mrs Lin, 'better than living on the ground, with the dogs.'

Mr Qu laughed politely.

Mr Lin had never liked the moneylender. He believed that the interest Mr Qu extracted from his customers was outrageous. But he had visited many banks and had been refused a loan at each of them. He had protested that he would get a second job, and work through the night, helping to build the new Beijing. But he was so frail, and the flesh around his head was so shrunken that he looked as though, at any moment, he would be called to join his ancestors. No bank employee expected him to live long enough to pay off his debt.

Mr Qu asked, 'How is Ho in England?'

Mrs Lin said, 'He is very well. Ahead in his studies and top marks in his exams.'

'Is this a social or a business call?' said Mr Qu.

'Business,' said Mr Lin.

Mr Qu ushered them into the little house and invited them to sit down. He gestured to Mr Lin to carry on speaking.

Mr Lin said, 'We have an unexpected expense. Family. A flood in the countryside.'

'Most unfortunate,' murmured Mr Qu. 'Exactly how much are these expenses?'

Mrs Lin said, 'To replace a floor, mattresses, a cooking stove, clothing for eight people, a television. There is more . . .'

Mr Lin said, 'Better make it fifteen thousand US dollars.'

Mr Qu laughed merrily and said, 'A significant sum! And do you have collateral?'

Mr Lin was prepared. 'Ho himself. He will be a qualified doctor in six more years. From an English university. He will pay you back.'

Mr Qu nodded. 'But for now, he is only a first-year medical student . . . so many drop out, disgrace their parents.'

Mrs Lin said, fiercely, 'Not Ho. He knows the sacrifices we have made.'

Mr Qu said, 'To reflect the length of time before I make a return . . . an interest rate of thirty per cent.'

Mr Lin said, 'You can have a share in Ho's salary for ten years. It will be taken from his bank account, and deposited into yours.' He hoped to appeal to Mr Qu's gambling instinct.

Mr Qu shook his head. 'No,' he said. 'What is the most valuable thing you have in your life, Mr Lin?'

Mr Lin looked to the side and said, 'My wife, she is precious to me.'

When they were walking back, Mrs Lin sat down half-way home on what used to be her doorstep.

Her face was flushed, and she said to her husband, 'The shame, the shame of it.'

Mr Lin pulled the international money order from his pocket and said, 'It was only a business transaction.'

She said, 'But he has humiliated us.'

'How?'

'He did not ask us to take tea with him.'

# 59

Eva's sycamore was in full leaf and provided a fluttering lime-green canopy between the window and the gathering of people on the pavement opposite. Eva could not see Sandy Lake, but she could hear her shouting her disturbing messages throughout the day and night. There was an injunction in place, which was meant to keep Sandy 500 metres away from 15 Bowling Green Road. But she regularly breached the order and, emboldened by the late response of the police, would try to get through the front door and provoke Alexander into losing his temper.

She would push and shove him, shouting, 'Get out of my way, Sambo! I need to speak to senior angel Eva!'

When, at Eva's insistence, Alexander finally made a formal complaint to PC Hawk, the policeman minimised Sandy's 'nuisance value'.

He said, 'Yeah, she is a bit overenthusiastic, but personally I quite like that in a woman. I've been on dates where, after the first few minutes, they've said almost nothing at all.'

Alexander replied, emphatically, 'Ask her out for a pizza then, and I'll guarantee that you wouldn't last beyond a second helping at the salad bar. She's seriously mentally ill. And you should know how inflammatory

"Sambo" is to a black person. It doesn't bother me any more, but add a couple of bored black youths to the mix and you, PC Hawk, have got a riot on your hands.'

PC Hawk said, 'No, I'd take the heat out of the situation immediately. I've been on a racial awareness course. Mr Tate, why not try a bit of banter with her? The next time she calls you "Sambo", why not call her "fatty"? When she gets to know you better, she'll realise that you're a human being, just like her. Tell her you've both got red blood in your veins.'

Alexander looked down at PC Hawk's innocent and ignorant face, and understood that nothing he could say would make any impression on this policeman. He had closed his mind at adolescence and cemented it shut at police training college. He would not be opening it again.

Eva was lying on top of the bed facing the door. It was a hot summer's day and she was irritated by the heat and the buzzing of flies as they hurtled round the ceiling. She was longing for somebody to come in with a tray of food and drink.

Hunger made her panic. She had been left alone several times lately when Alexander had other paid work he had to do.

What would she do if nobody came in for a week? Would she get out of bed and walk downstairs to the kitchen, or would she lie there and allow herself to starve – waiting for her organs to close down, one by one, until the heart sighed and gave up, the brain disconnected its pathways after giving a few exploratory signals, and the tunnel appeared with the bright light beyond?

Eva thought about the inside of her body, the trillions of cells, smaller than the width of a human hair. About the body's immune system which, if threatened by disease, will summon all the good defensive cells to a crisis meeting. About how the cells select a leader who will make the decision to welcome disease or repel it. Like democracy in Ancient Athens, when the citizens met to decide how the city was to be run.

She wondered if we carry our own universe within us, if *we* are the gods.

Alexander knocked and came in. He was holding a piece of A4 paper. He said, seeing how hot and tired she looked, 'Are you up for this today?'

'I don't know. Who's out there?'

'There's the usual swizzle heads. The new ones are on the list.' He looked down at the paper and tried to decipher his own handwriting. 'An agricultural seed merchant who says nobody has ever loved him.'

'Yes, I'll see him,' said Eva.

'Then there's a vegetarian who works in an abattoir. The only work he could find. Should he leave his job? I'll check him for knives.'

Eva raised herself on one elbow and took the list. She said, 'I'm so hungry, Alexander.'

'What do you want?'

'Bring me bread. Cheese. Jam. Anything.'

He stopped at the door and said, 'Would you mind

saying "please"? It would make me feel less like a castrated lackey.'

She said, grudgingly, 'OK. Please.'

'Thank you, madam. Will that be all?'

'Look, if you've got something to say —'

Alexander interrupted. 'I've got plenty to say. I'm sick of seeing you waste yourself, festering in your pit, deciding who is to see the great Eva, and who is to be turned away at Eva's whim? Do you realise I've never seen you on your feet? I don't even know how *tall* you are.'

She gave a deep sigh. The thought of listening to people's misery depressed her. The household she lived with seemed to be permanently miserable, and now even Alexander was showing the strain.

She pleaded, 'Alexander, I can't think straight at the moment. I'm so hungry.'

Alexander put his face close to Eva's and advised, 'Well, get out of bed, and run down to the kitchen yourself.'

'I thought you understood. We have an understanding, don't we?'

'I don't think we do. It feels as though we've got our legs set in concrete. Neither of us can move.'

He went out, leaving the door wide open, as though he couldn't even be bothered to slam it.

Eva picked up the list and read it. She was annoyed to see that Alexander had commented on some of the entries.

Married man – has gay lover. (So what?)

Canteen assistant – showed me bruises. Made by husband.

Detective Sergeant, Drug Squad – addicted to amphetamines. Has frightened himself with crystal meth.

Sheet-metal worker – multiple internet betting accounts. Lost £15,000, plus credit card limit of £5,000. Wife doesn't know. Is still betting, 'chasing losses'.

Full-time mother of six, Ipswich – strongly dislikes her fifth child.

Carpenter – being evicted tomorrow.

Classroom assistant – is frequent successful shoplifter. Wants to stop.

Retired bricklayer – refuses to disclose problem.

Adolescent boy – is cruel to insects, dogs and cats. Is he 'normal'? (For a psychopath, yes.)

Bus driver – drinks at the wheel.

Personal assistant – should she marry man she doesn't love? (No! No! No!)

Baker – spits in dough. (Find out where he works.)

Fourteen-year-old schoolgirl – can she get pregnant if she has a shower after sex? (Yes.)

Married couple – both in late seventies. Wife has cancer of the womb. Will you administer lethal dose of insulin to both? (Dear Eva, please don't agree to murder them, this is going too far, love Alex.)

Schoolgirl aged thirteen – being sexually, physically and emotionally abused by family member.
(ChildLine: 0800 11 11. Police.)

Muslim girl – hates burka. Feels 'suffocated'.

Audio typist – married to A, still in love with B,
but having affair with C.

Failed financier, lapsed Rastafarian, struggling
painter – captivated by bed-bound slightly older
woman. Wants to share bed and take her for a
walk in countryside. (This problem is urgent,
suggest you see this man by appointment
soon.)

She smiled as she read the last item, then stopped as she
heard Sandy Lake shout, 'I'm back! I'm here! I would die
for you, angel Eva! I'll never leave you! They can't separate us! You are my other half!'

Eva wished that Sandy Lake would die. She didn't
want her to feel any pain, only to die in her sleep. She
wanted to tell somebody that Sandy Lake frightened her,
but she did not want to appear weak and needy.

When Alexander returned with a plate of sandwiches,
Eva took one, bit into it, then immediately spat it out.

She shouted, 'I asked for bread and cheese or bread
and jam, not all three! Who eats all three at the same
time?'

Alexander said, quietly, 'Somebody eccentric perhaps? Somebody who can't, or won't, get out of bed?
Somebody who is besieged by her fellow eccentrics?'

Eva pulled the slices of cheese out of the sandwiches and tore at the bread and jam, not stopping until the plate was empty. She licked her jammy fingers clean.

Alexander watched.

He said, 'I'm going to fetch the kids from school, then I'm going home. I'll say goodbye.'

Eva said, 'You make it sound so final.'

'I can't do it, Eva. It's like caring for an ungrateful baby.' He bent down and kissed her on the cheek.

She turned her back on him. She heard the sounds of his departure, his feet on the hall floor, the front door opening and closing, the shouts and whistles from the crowd as he passed them, the sound of his engine, the gear change as he turned the corner, then nothing.

She was alone.

She missed him immediately.

# 60

Brian's sheds were still filled almost to overflowing with Titania's possessions. He had forbidden her to bring anything else from the house she had once shared with her husband, but there were certain things she could not do without: her autumn and winter wardrobe, the Welsh spinning wheel she had picked up in Florida, the post-modern cuckoo clock from Habitat, the Victorian chaise longue she had bought for £50 from a stallholder who she thought of as gullible (only to find it was riddled with woodworm and cost her £500 plus VAT to be restored and recovered).

Brian was manoeuvring his bulk around Titania's stuff in the extension shed they called the 'kitchenette'. Titania looked up irritably from the book she was reading, *Hadrons and Quark-Gluon Plasma*. She had just noted in the margin, 'Not according to Prof Yagi. See his paper ref: JCAP Vol. 865, 2 (2010).'

She said, 'Brian, you're tutting like a village gossip. I know it's inconvenient to have my things here, but I can't store them at the old house, can I? Not now he's renting it.'

Brian said, forcing himself to sound reasonable, 'Tit, I admit I'm a little annoyed that I'm sharing my space with the culmination of the junk you've collected over the years, but have I once complained? No. Will I be pleased when it's gone? Yes.'

Titania said, 'Please! If you ask a question and answer it *yourself* again, will I go mad and do you serious harm? Yes, yes I will!'

They lapsed into sullen silence, each knowing that, if certain words were said, it would be like leaving the comparative safety of a muddy trench at Ypres and going over the top to the carnage of the battlefield.

In the long, tense silence, Titania reassessed their affair. It had been quite exciting, at times, and what other man would understand and sympathise when the particles were not behaving themselves and refused to correspond to her theories?

Brian knocked his ankle bone on the Welsh spinning wheel. He shouted, 'The fucking thing!' and kicked out at it, hard.

He was not to know that the spinning wheel represented Titania's bucolic retirement – she and Brian would keep hens, and there would be a good-natured dog with a black patch over one eye. They would take Patch to the village shop to pick up *Nature* and *Sky & Telescope*. She would buy bags of wool from the cooperative sheep farm, spin it and knit Brian a sweater in a pattern of his choice. She couldn't knit or sew, but there were classes she could take. It wasn't rocket science. The seeing would be good in the Welsh hills. There was a tiny Spaceguard outpost at the 24-inch reflector observatory in Powys. They would link up with the scientists there, and Brian would advise them and carry out consultancy work. He was a well-known and highly respected astronomer. They could easily avoid the peak hours for school tour groups.

Titania saw the spinning wheel rolling towards her, the wooden spokes clattering as it turned. She screamed, as though the wheel were an errant heat-seeking missile. She shouted, 'Go on! Why not kick all my lovely things to pieces! You're nothing but a bully!'

Brian shouted back, 'You can't bully furniture, woman!'

Titania yelled, 'It's no wonder Eva's mad and lives in a room with no furniture at all! You drove her to it!'

To her amazement, Brian wove through her possessions, took a couple of boxes off the chaise longue, lay down and started to sob.

She was bewildered by the drama of it all, and said, 'I'm sorry, Brian, but I cannot live like this. I want to settle down in a house with proper designated rooms. Henry Thoreau may have been happy living in a shed, and three cheers and multiple gold stars for him, but I want to live in a house. I want to live in *your* house.'

She was pleading now. Their honeymoon period of living together in the sheds was long over. She was looking forward to being a seasoned and contented couple.

Brian whined, 'You know we can't live in my house. Eva wouldn't like it.'

Titania felt a switch click inside her head. It was raging jealousy kicking in. 'I'm sick of hearing about Eva and I hate the sheds! I can't stand to live in them for a minute longer!'

Brian shouted, 'Good, go home to Guy the fucking Gorilla!'

She screamed, 'You know I can't go home! Guy has rented it out to the Vietnamese cannabis farmers!'

She ran out of the shed complex, across the lawn and into the main house.

Brian had a fantasy that Titania would run through the middle of the house, out through the open front door, and then down the street and round the corner. She would carry on running: through back gardens, on to minor roads, on cart tracks, on a winding path up the hills, down the hills and far away.

Brian wished that Titania would vanish, just vanish.

# 61

Alexander carefully let himself out of his mother's small terraced house in Jane Street. He did not want to wake her, she would ask him where he was going and he didn't want to tell her.

He was nervous about leaving the kids in her sole care – she was too frail now to pick them up and, being an old-school disciplinarian, she was not sympathetic when Thomas screamed with the night terrors or Venus cried for her mother.

He crept along the pavement until he was out of ear-shot of the house, then he quickened his pace. He could tell from the cool night air and the faint smell of decay that autumn was waiting to take its place. The streets were quiet. Cars were sleeping next to the pavements.

He had three miles in which to rehearse what he was going to say to Eva about their relationship. Although perhaps he should first establish whether or not they *had* a relationship?

Back in the day, after Alexander had returned from Charterhouse with an alien upper-class accent that even his mother had laughed at, he had spent many hours in his room with an old-fashioned tape recorder, trying to minimise his vowels and slacken his jaw. He kept well away from the local gangs, the Northanger Abbey Crew and the Mansfield Park Boyz. Alexander wondered if Miss Bennet would have liked Mr Darcy more, or less, had he strolled through the Pump Room with his arse hanging out of his baggy jeans, showing the label of his Calvin Klein underwear?

Now all Alexander could hear were his own footsteps echoing in the moonlit streets.

Then he heard a car approaching, its sound system booming out gangster rap. He turned to look as the old BMW passed him. Four white men, short hair, over-muscled. A tin of gym supplements on the back window. The car stopped just ahead of him.

He braced himself and, hoping to appear friendly, said, 'Evening, guys.'

The driver of the car said to his front-seat passenger, 'Do me a favour, Robbo, get the toolbox out the back, will you?'

Alexander didn't like the sound of the toolbox. All he had to defend himself with was his Swiss Army knife, and by the time he'd found a suitable blade . . .

He said, 'Well, I'll wish you goodnight then.' Fear had forced him to drop his street accent, and revert back to Charterhouse.

The four men laughed, but without humour. At a gesture from the driver, the three remaining men got out of the car.

'Lovely plaits,' said the driver. 'How long you had them then?'

'Seventeen years,' said Alexander. He was wondering if he could outrun them, though his legs had turned to mush.

'Be a relief to get rid of 'em, won't it? Nasty, dirty, filthy things hanging down your back.'

Suddenly, as if they'd rehearsed it, the three men pushed him to the ground. One sat on his chest, the other two held down his legs.

Alexander allowed his body to go limp. He knew from experience that any show of defiance now would bring a beating.

He let himself into Eva's house with the key she had given him. He took his shoes off and carried them upstairs, together with his shorn dreadlocks.

When he got to the landing, Eva called, 'Who's there?'

He walked softly to her doorway, and said, 'It's me.'

She said, 'Can you put the light on?'

He said, 'No, I want to lie down next to you in the dark. Like we did before.'

Eva looked up at the moon. 'The man in the moon has had work done on his face.'

Alexander said, 'Botox.'

She laughed, but he didn't.

She turned to look at him, and saw that his dreadlocks were gone. 'Why have you done that?'

He said, 'I didn't.'

She put her arms around him.

He was rigid with an old rage. He asked, 'What's the most important quality a person could have, something that would benefit us all? Even the bastards who cut off my hair.'

Eva stroked his hair while she thought about his question.

Eventually, she said, 'Kindness. Or is that too simple?'

'No, simple kindness, I'd vote for that.'

In the early hours, he allowed Eva to level his remaining locks.

When she was finished, he said, 'Now I know how Samson felt. I'm not the same man, Eva.'

Alexander had been thinking for some time about what was important.

He said, 'We all of us – the fools, the geniuses, the beggars, the A-listers – we all need to be loved, and we all need to love. And if they're the same person, halleluyah! And if you can live your life and avoid humiliation, you're blessed. I didn't manage to do that, people I didn't even know humiliated me. My dreads *were* me. I could face anything with them. They were a visible symbol of my pride in our history. And, you know, my kids would hang on to them when they were babies. My wife was the only person I allowed to wash and retwist my dreads. But I would have let you. Whenever I thought about my old age, I pictured myself with white dreads, *long* white dreads. I'm on the beach, in Tobago. There's a travel brochure sunset. You're back at the hotel, washing sand and confetti out of your hair. Eva, please get out of bed, I need you.'

Out of all his seductive words – Tobago, beach, sunset, confetti – the only word Eva heard clearly was 'need'.

She said, 'I can't be needed, Alex. I would let you down, so it's better if I stay out of your life.'

Alexander was angry. 'What *would* you get out of bed for? The twins in danger? Your mother's funeral? A fucking Chanel handbag?'

He didn't wait around for her to see him cry. He knew her attitude to tears. He went downstairs and sat in the back garden until dawn.

When he left for the long walk home, Ruby was out early cleaning the front porch and doorstep with disinfectant and a soapy mop. When she saw Alexander, she gave a delighted little scream and said, 'A new hairdo. It really, really suits you, Alexander.'

He said quietly, 'It's my late summer cut.'

Ruby watched him walk down the road.

He had lost his easy movements. From the back he looked like a stooped, middle-aged man.

She wanted to call him back, she would make him a cup of that bitter coffee he liked. But when it came to it, she tried and tried but she couldn't remember his name.

At daybreak, Eva watched the sky change from sludgy grey to opalescent blue. The birdsong was heartbreakingly optimistic and cheerful.

'I should follow their example,' she thought.

But she was still angry at Alexander. *He* couldn't be needy. *She* was the one who needed support, food and water. Sometimes she had to drink out of the tap in the en suite. Her care rota had almost broken down since Ruby's memory lapses had intensified.

But how could she complain? All she had to do was get out of bed.

## 62

Eva was lying flat on the bed, staring up at a crack that meandered across the ceiling like a black river running through a white wilderness.

Eva knew every millimetre of the crack – the backwaters, the moorings. She was at the helm of a boat as it journeyed, seeking peace and pleasure for those on board. Eva could see Brian Junior, motionless, staring into the deep water. Next she saw Brianne, trying to light a cigarette against the wind. Alexander was standing at the wheel with his arm around the shoulder of the helmswoman, and Venus was there, attempting to draw what was undrawable – the speed of the boat, the sound it makes as it pushes through the water. And look at Thomas, trying to wrest the wheel from Eva's hands.

She didn't know where they were going. The crack disappeared under the plaster cornice. Eva had to turn the boat and journey against the wind and the flow of the river. Sometimes it was moored against the bank, and the passengers disembarked and trekked in the wilderness, on soft white sand.

But there was nothing for them there.

When they walked back to the boat, Eva gave the

wheel to Brianne, saying, 'Care about something, Brianne. Take us home and keep us safe.'

The clouds rolled across the ceiling, the wind blew in their faces. Brianne held firm and took them home.

# 63

At eight o' clock precisely, Eva was shocked awake by an atrocious noise from outside. She sat up and knelt at the window. Her heart was beating so rapidly she found it a struggle to breathe.

There was a man standing on a branch of the sycamore wearing a safety harness and a hard hat and goggles. He was cutting at an adjacent branch with an electric saw. She watched in horror as the branch broke and was lowered to the ground by a rope. Other workmen were waiting to free the branch from the rope, to remove smaller branches and twigs and feed them into a racketing shredder.

Eva banged on the window and screamed, 'Stop! That's my tree!'

But such was the din outside that her voice could not be heard. She opened the sash window and was immediately hit in the face by a spray of splintered bark. She closed the window quickly. Her face was stinging, and when she touched her cheek she had blood on her fingers. She continued to shout and gesticulate at the workman in the tree. She caught his eye once, but he turned his back on her.

She was horrified at how quickly the tree was disassembled. Soon there was only the trunk left. She had a small hope that her tree had only been drastically pollarded and would sprout new growth in the spring of next year.

The noise stopped. The machines had been turned off. She could see into the front garden now that the branches had gone. The workmen were drinking tea.

She knocked on the window and shouted, 'Leave the trunk, please leave the trunk!'

The men looked up at her window and laughed. What did they think she was doing? Inviting them upstairs?

The machines started up again and in a short while her tree trunk had been turned into logs. The light in the room was harsh after the dappled green glow she had been used to.

She felt cold, though she was covered in sweat. She climbed under the duvet and pulled it over her head.


In the early afternoon, Eva heard a ragged cheer from the crowd and Peter's ladder appeared level with the lower window frame. She straightened her camisole, put on the shrunken cashmere cardigan she was using as a bed jacket and automatically ran her fingers through her hair.

Peter shouted through the glass, 'Still here then?'

'Yes!' she shouted back, with forced good humour. 'Still here.'

Eva wondered how anybody could be so heartless. Didn't he care that her magnificent tree was gone?

'Magnificent?' he laughed, when she said this to him. 'It was a sycamore, they're the weeds of the tree world.' He added, 'I don't want to be cheeky, Eva, but what's happened to your face?'

Eva was not listening. 'It was Brian,' she said. 'He hated that tree. He said the roots were coming up through the pavement.'

'They were,' Peter confirmed. He wanted to move the topic on from that bloody tree. 'Only a hundred and twelve shopping days till Christmas,' he said, climbing into the room.

Eva could hear Sandy Lake screaming, 'Eva, I'm getting cross with you now! Why won't you *see* me?'

Peter laughed. 'We're getting Abigail a motorised wheelchair. Well, us and Social Services.'

Eva asked, 'Peter, would you do me a favour? Would you help me to board the window up from the inside?'

In his opinion, she had gone downhill fast – in the old days, they would have had a cup of tea and smoked a fag together. 'Sure,' he said.

Peter had learned, in his twenty years of window cleaning, that the customers on his round were a bit eccentric, not one of them was normal. The clothes people wore in bed! The unexpected squalor of their houses! The weird stuff they ate! Mr Crossley – who had so many books he could hardly walk between the rooms for them!

Barricading a window from the inside was no big deal to Peter. He had suitable materials in the back of his van. He was often asked to board up a window after a domestic or a football had shattered the peace. He went back down the ladder to an ironic cheer from the crowd.

When Peter went to his van, Sandy Lake hovered around the tailgate and interrogated him about Eva.

'Can she hear me in her bedroom?'

Peter said, 'She can hear you all right.'

Sandy thumped the side of his van and yelled, 'I have this very important message! It's appertaining to the future of our earth!'

He turned his back to assemble the chipboard and tools he would need. Sandy Lake saw her opportunity. She dashed across the road and climbed up the ladder like a fifteen-stone mountain goat.

When Eva saw Sandy's weather-beaten face in the window, she pulled a pillow towards her as though it were a shield.

Sandy stared at Eva and said, 'Well, now I'm really cross! What happened to you? You're just an ordinary woman! You're not special at all! You shouldn't have any grey in your hair or crow's feet around your eyes – and they're not laughter lines!'

She tried to clamber over the sill, but the ladder moved slightly. Sandy looked down, and further down, and then further down still. Some say that Sandy swooned and fell, others that she caught the hem of her maxi skirt under the heel of her ankle boot. Peter thought he had seen a pale hand push the ladder away from the sill.

Eva imagined she felt the house move slightly when Sandy fell into the overgrown lavender bush that Eva had planted years before. There were screams of horror and of excitement. Sandy had landed in an ungainly position, and the anarchist hurried to pull the maxi skirt down from around her waist, where it had bunched. William sort of loved Sandy, but he had to, obviously, kind of, be honest and tell it like it is and admit that the sight of Sandy's naked lower regions was totally inappropriate.

Sandy wasn't dead. As soon as she recovered consciousness, she rolled away from the spiky lavender and lay flat on her back. The anarchist took off his leather flying jacket and put it under her head.

When the ambulance arrived, the female paramedic chided her for climbing a ladder in a maxi skirt and high heels. 'That's an accident *whimpering* to happen,' she said, in disgust.

Eva and Peter started to board up the window, to the sound of the crowd's cheers and shrieks of excitement and dismay. Now they could see Eva in her nondescript clothes, with her unbrushed hair and bare face, they could not hold on to their previous belief in her.

PC Hawk shouted, 'If she was a true saint, she'd be *perfect* in every way!'

A man with binoculars shouted, 'She's got sweat patches under her arms!'

A woman wearing a man's suit and a dog collar said, 'Female saints do *not* sweat, I think that Mrs Beaver has been posturing.'

PC Hawk had been ordered to get rid of the crowd. He shouted, 'She's been taken over by an evil spirit, and the spirit is in the holy chapatti!'

Some followed him to view the chapatti, which had been painted with preservative, varnished and was being exhibited in the local library. Others started to pack their belongings. There were emotional leave-takings, taxis came and went, until there was only William Wainwright sitting inside Sandy Lake's tent. He might try to visit her in hospital tomorrow – but then again, he might not.

He was an anarchist, wasn't he? And nobody could pin him down.

# 64

The twins were working on Brianne's newly acquired desktop computer. They were exploring the labyrinthine corridors of the Ministry of Defence, after a failed attempt to destroy their father's credit rating. It was hot in Brianne's room and they were sitting in their vests and pants. Flies buzzed over half-eaten sandwiches.

From the open window they could hear students calling to each other, enjoying the Indian summer. A group of them were sitting on the grass outside Sentinel Towers, laughing and drinking from cans of cider.

A girl's fragile voice sang 'Summer Is Icumen In'.

Brianne muttered, 'Fucking Performing Arts, don't they ever stop performing?'

The girl's voice was joined by others until each voice was weaving an intricate vocal pattern.

From a room where politics students had gathered to drink Polish vodka and condemn every known political system came the sound of bombs falling and machine-gun fire. They were remarkably good impressions – evidence of long hours of practice and, conversely, of the few hours spent in lectures or writing essays.

Brianne said, looking at the screen, 'How many years, Bri?'

It was their private joke, short for, 'How many years in prison?'

Their hacking was motivated as much by curiosity as it was by the accumulation of money.

Before Brian Junior could reply, there was a shocking crash and the door to the room fell in on them, followed seconds later by the sound of Brian Junior's door collapsing. He tried to reach the computer to wipe the hard drive, but his wrist was chopped by a black-gloved hand. There was roaring shouting confusion.

Brianne was handcuffed, then Brian Junior. They were told to step over the splintered door, sit on the bed and keep quiet. Brian Junior could not work out who the people in the black overalls and smoked-glass helmets were.

It pained them both to see their computer, laptops, smartphones, cameras, notebooks and MP3 players packed carefully into evidence bags and cardboard boxes.

Brianne said, 'You must know that we're only eighteen.'

A woman's voice said, 'Yes, and playtime's over, children. You work for us now. So, if you wouldn't mind removing your underwear and spreading your legs.'

When the twins' orifices had been thoroughly examined, and they had been put into white forensic suits, they were led away. The other students in the block had been told to stay in their rooms and keep the main entrance clear.

Two people carriers with blacked-out windows waited for them at the kerb, their engines running. They were not allowed to speak before they got into separate cars, but Brianne communicated to Brian Junior that all would be well, eventually. And as Brian Junior was turned away from her, she shouted, 'I love you, bro!'

Ho was lying in his own bed, kissing Poppy's pregnant belly. He spoke to the baby, asking if it was a boy or a girl.

He should have been dissecting the cadaver he had been allocated, a Mrs Iris Bristol. She had donated her body to medical science because she'd spent her funeral money on a 46-inch 3D television. Ho was thinking that he ought to go back to Mrs Bristol and replace her intestines, which were strewn across the dissecting table.

Poppy had sent him a text:

Come at once

He had removed his gown, mask and boots and hurried to Poppy's side.

She needed money again. She explained why to him, but it was a complicated story and Ho's English was not top notch. Sometimes he thought the English textbooks he had used in China were a little out of date.

Since he had been in England, he had not heard a single person say, 'Top hole!'

Poppy smirked at the memory of Brianne and Brian Junior being led away, in silly white suits and handcuffs. She was glad she had made the phone call. The person on the other end had asked her to keep an eye on the rest of Professor Nikitanova's students, and she'd said delightedly, 'It would be a pleasure.'

## 65

Brian was watching the repeat of *Loose Women* in room twelve of a Travelodge in a suburb near Leeds. He didn't know what the Loose Women were talking about. And he had never heard of the orange man with the grotesquely white teeth and sticky black hair. The man was being interviewed about the county where he lived, Essex, but all he could say about this location was, 'It's *reem*.'

Brian tried to apply formal logic to the problem. Could he decode it given the paucity of the information?

Earlier, he had stopped off at a retail park and bought a blue paisley one hundred per cent acetate dressing gown. He had debated with himself whether or not to buy some matching slippers. He looked around for some assistance. He needed a woman's point of view. He had approached a young woman in Marks & Spencer's uniform who was newly returned after five weeks of sick leave due to stress.

He said, 'I'm a mere man . . .'

What Kerry, in her nervous state, heard was, 'I'm a merman.' She tried to remember what a merman *was*, then it came to her – a merman was a mermaid's partner.

Brian continued, 'And as a hapless male, I'd like some

advice. I have a lady friend who's more or less your age. Can you tell me what's cool on the street regarding dressing gowns and slippers?'

When Kerry didn't answer, he prompted, 'Would a dressing gown and slippers be considered sophisticated bedroom wear or, as the kids say, "a turn-off"?'

Kerry, who was only passing through men's shoes on her way to her tea break, hesitated. Her inability to make a decision had been a large part of her problem. She stammered, 'I don't know. I can't help you.' Then she fled, knocking into a male mannequin dressed in discounted Late Sun pastel beachwear.

Brian was disgusted. M&S were fêted for the quality of their shop assistants.

He had taken his dressing gown and slippers to the Food Hall where he bought a large baguette, French butter, cheese and a bottle of cava. Champagne was wasted on a young girl, he thought. On an impulse, he had grabbed a bag of multicoloured lollipops. As he stood in the queue he was in a state of mild sexual arousal. He was looking forward to his early evening assignation.

He had been careful over the summer – each time they had met in a different hotel. Brian hadn't seen Poppy since their last meeting, at the Palace Hotel in Leeds.

She had said then, 'My love for you is infinite, Brian.'

Brian had been tempted to correct her use of 'infinite', but instead had said, 'I love you more than there are stars in the sky.'

They had been lying together, looking up at a Victorian brass light fitting which Poppy was afraid might fall from its mountings and kill them both. She wouldn't want to be found all mashed up with an old fat bloke who was nearly a pensioner.

She had placed his free hand on her belly and said, 'Bri, we're going to have a baby.'

Brian was not keen on babies. After the twins were born, he had volunteered to work in Australia but had been turned down on the grounds that he was now 'a family man'.

After a tiny pause, he had said, 'How marvellous.'

She could tell he didn't want the baby. She didn't want Brian either. But whoever had said life was just a bowl of cherries had forgotten that inside each cherry was a hard stone, waiting to catch the unwary, resulting in a chipped tooth, a choking fit, slipping and falling.

All caused by those innocuous little cherry stones.

Now there was a gentle knock at the door. Brian leapt to his feet, pulled Eva's comb through his beard and opened the door.

Poppy said, 'What took you so long?' She was wearing an orange poppy in her hair, and a flower-sprigged prom dress with Mary Jane shoes. She was not wearing her new piercings, and she had washed her face clean of make-up.

When Brian opened the door she was dismayed to see that he was in an old git's dressing gown and the type of slippers that cartoonists draw. He was also carrying a mug of Horlicks, the smell of which made Poppy heave. What Poppy saw when the door opened was the grandfather illustration in her *Heidi* book. Brian's beard hadn't turned white yet, but it would not be long. His ankles looked so frail and pasty in the big slippers that she was surprised they could hold him up without snapping. He pulled her inside as though he were taking delivery of Semtex.

Brian said, 'Darling, you look so sweet, so charming, so young.'

Poppy sat on the end of the bed with her little finger crooked in the side of her mouth.

'In other circumstances she would have looked gormless,' thought Brian. But this was his Poppy, the mercurial child/woman whose presence he craved. He turned on the MP3 player that he had dug out of a drawer at home for the occasion. He searched the short playlist, found *Songs for Swingin' Lovers*, selected 'You Make Me Feel So Young' and pressed play.

'Ugh!' thought Poppy. 'More of that dead bloke, Frank Sinatra.'

When Poppy went into the bathroom, Brian lay on the bed and arranged the dressing gown so that his pale upper thighs were exposed. Because his feet had hard skin and corns, he kept his slippers on.

When she came out of the bathroom, she was naked apart from the flower in her hair. Before she turned the light off, her slightly swollen belly was in profile.

Brian thought, 'I wonder if it has been scientifically proven that Homo sapiens can actually expire from a surfeit of love? If so, I'm a dying man.'

Poppy gritted her teeth, and thought, 'C'mon, Poppy, come on, girl, it'll all be over in five minutes. Close your eyes and think of Brian Junior.'

After the little struggle on the bed was over, and Brian lay on his back gasping for air, Poppy looked down at him and thought, 'He looks like an overfed, dying goldfish.' She said, 'Wow! That was awesome! Wow! Wow! Amazing!'

Brian thought, 'Eva never once responded to my lovemaking like Poppy does.'

Poppy climbed off him and went back into the bathroom. He heard the shower over the bath running, and for a moment he thought about joining her. But his knees had been giving him gip lately and he wasn't sure if he could lift his legs over the side of the bath. He suspected arthritis, it was in the Beaver family genes.

Poppy stayed in the shower for a long time. She spent most of it sitting in the bath and watching the hot water spiralling down the plughole.

When she got out, Brian was in a deep sleep. She found £250 in his wallet and, on the 'personal details' page of his Letts Diary, the code to his debit card. After checking his trouser and jacket pockets, she found £7.39 in small change and his phone. She scrolled through some of his photographs, they were mostly boring stars and planets. However, there was one of Brian with his wife and kids, taken in front of a gigantic rocket.

Brian and the twins looked like dorks, but Eva was beautiful. Poppy's throat tightened. She knew she wasn't beautiful or nice or famous like Eva, but she had something that Eva would never have again, her youth. Her own flesh was smooth and tight, and men like Brian would pay heavily to touch it.

As she dressed, she composed a plan. She grabbed the little pencil and pad that the hotel provided and sat down at the desk to write.

Start going to lectures.

Prostitute self with more old men.

Seduce married lecturer, tell him after one month
  I'm pregnant.

Accept payments towards cost of baby.

Go on holiday to Thailand when baby nearly due
  (disguise bump from airline).

Have baby.

Sell baby.

Return from holiday in mourning.

Show photo of pretty deceased baby to all three
  lovers.

When she was dressed, and the flower had been put back behind her ear, Poppy took Brian's phone and texted:

> dear Brian I taken ur £ to buy baby
> clothes and equipment. got to rush.
> essay to write on Leonard Cohen.
> his part in America's post vietnam
> melancholia. let's meet again sooner
> than soonest. as the yanks say, missing
> you already! love, your little Poppy. p.s.
> taken ur card for taxi.

## 66

Alexander heard a police siren, but he carried on painting.

He had waited for the sun to rise over the far corner of the cornfield. He had almost given up before he had properly begun. The loveliness of the corn as it responded to the breeze was, given his limited skills, too fine to capture with a brush and watercolours.

Almost an hour passed before he stopped. He unwrapped the tinfoil from his cheese sandwiches, and unscrewed the lid of his Thermos flask. Why did coffee always smell better than it tasted?

As he ate and drank, he was conscious that he was happy. His children were well, he had no serious debts, his paintings were beginning to sell – slowly. And now that his locks were gone, he could go into a shop without the shopkeeper hovering over the panic button.

He forced himself not to think about Eva, who he had not seen for what seemed like an eternity.

He and Eva had never sat at a table together and shared a meal. They had not danced together. He didn't know her favourite song, and now he never would.

Ruby was glad she had Stanley to talk to. She told him about Eva's increasingly erratic recent behaviour, singing and reciting poems and making lists. She also confided that Eva wanted her door to be boarded up, apart from an aperture that would enable food and drink to be passed through.

Stanley said, 'I don't want to alarm you, Ruby, but that does sound fairly *mad*.'

Peter had boarded the door up, with Eva passing him the nails. By the time Ruby came back from tea at Stanley's house, the job was done.

There is nothing Eva can do now but sort out her memories, and wait to see who will keep her alive.

There is a chink of light in Eva's room. It comes from the badly boarded-up window. It shines on to the wall opposite. Eva lies in bed and watches the intensity of the light. Just before the sun goes down, the light puts on a show of orange, pink and yellow. The colours of confectionery. The chink of light is vital to her. She has put it there herself and now she is terrified that somebody will take it away.

She wants to be a baby and start again. From the stories Ruby tells about Eva's infancy, she has concluded that it was grim: she was pushed to the bottom of the garden to scream. Ruby's voice came to her when the twins were babies. 'Don't pick them up when they cry, you'll mollycoddle them. They need to know who's boss from the start.'

Whenever Eva tried to cuddle the twins, their little bodies would go rigid and two sets of eyes would stare into her own without even the ghost of a smile.

# 67

In the world outside, the *Sun* headline blared, 'Eva Starves!' And there was a quote within the front-page story:

> Mrs Julie Eppingham, 39, said, 'The last time I saw her, I was horrified. She is obviously anorexic. But she won't talk to me or look at my new baby. She obviously needs medical attention.'

Nurse Spears was walking through the surgery waiting room when she saw a copy of *The Sun* that had been discarded by a patient. She picked it up and read the front page. Her first thought was for her career. She should have visited Mrs Beaver more often to check for bedsores and muscle atrophy – and her mental health.

She drove round to Bowling Green Road and sat outside in her car, reading Eva's full notes.

Sandy Lake knocked on the driver's window with her good hand. The other was encased in plaster. As yet nobody had written on it. William didn't do writing on plaster.

She asked, 'Is Eva poorly?'

Nurse Spears wound the window down and said, 'I can't disclose information about my patients.'

She wound the window up, but Sandy Lake was beyond shame and continued to ask questions. Nurse Spears felt intimidated by the woman in a silly knitted hat. She was relieved when she saw a policeman. She parped the horn and PC Hawk walked towards the car.

He didn't believe in hurrying, he was always solemn and purposeful. He bent down at the driver's window, and Nurse Spears asked if he would escort her to number 15.

Sandy Lake demanded to accompany Nurse Spears.

PC Hawk said to her, 'You're supposed to be five hundred metres away.'

Sandy said, 'I'm going further than that soon. William and I are going to live in a squat.'

Nurse Spears said, 'That's shocking.'

'Why? It's my own house.'

PC Hawk looked at Nurse Spears, and waggled his forefinger at his temple.

Nurse Spears snapped, 'I'd already worked that out.'


Upstairs, in the pitch dark of her bedroom, Eva was nearly through the gentle exercise regime she'd copied from PE lessons at school over thirty-five years ago. Eva hated any lesson that involved communal showers. She was amazed that some girls stood around naked, talking to the PE teacher, Miss Brawn. Eva was ashamed of her towel, which was not big enough to wrap around her body, and was grey and musty because she repeatedly forgot to take the thing home to wash.

Over breakfast in the 1970s it had been Ruby's pleasure to teach her daughter good manners. On one such occasion Ruby had taught her that, should there be a conversational lull, it was Eva's duty to fill it.

Eva was an earnest girl at twelve and anxious to do the right thing. Once, when walking back from the athletics track in the extensive school grounds, she had caught up with Miss Brawn as their steps became synchronised. Eva had not known whether it was right to stay synchronised, fall back or run ahead. She snatched a quick glance at Miss Brawn's face. She looked unbearably sad.

Eva blurted out, 'What are you cooking for Sunday dinner?'

Miss Brawn looked startled, but said, 'I thought a leg of lamb –'

'And will you make a mint sauce?' asked Eva, politely.

'Not make, *buy*!' said Miss Brawn.

There was a long silence, which Eva filled with, 'Do you have roast potatoes or mash?'

Miss Brawn sighed and said, 'Both!' Then she continued, 'Didn't your parents teach you that it is bad manners to ask so many personal questions?'

'No,' said Eva, 'they didn't.'

Miss Brawn looked Eva full in the face and said, 'You should only speak when you have something worth saying. Idiotic questions about my plans for Sunday lunch are not appropriate.'

Eva had thought to herself, 'I'll keep my mouth shut, and I'll think my own thoughts.'

And after all those years the grown-up Eva could still

smell the cut grass, see the sunlight on the old red brick of the school building, and feel the thud of humiliation in her heart as she ran from Miss Brawn's side, to find somewhere to hide until her cheeks had stopped burning.

Eva finished her exercises and lay on the bed on top of the duvet. She could not stop thinking about food. Her principal feeder, Ruby, had a very lackadaisical attitude towards time, and the rota kept getting messed up because Ruby was increasingly forgetful, and sometimes forgot Eva's name.

Stanley opened the front door of Eva's house, saying, 'How do you do?' to the nurse and the constable. He shook their hands, led them into the kitchen, and said, 'I need to call on your expertise.'

As he wandered around the kitchen making tea, he said, 'I'm afraid Eva's condition has deteriorated. She managed to use her considerable charm on Peter, our mutual window cleaner, and subsequently she has been barricaded into her bedroom, with only a slit in the door that we on the other side can peer through and, in theory, pass her a plate of food.'

As soon as Stanley said the word 'barricaded', PC Hawk saw the scene in his head. He would provide the intelligence, call for a Special Support Unit, and would be present when Eva's door was shattered with a metal battering ram.

Nurse Spears saw herself at a medical tribunal, trying

to justify her neglect of a bedridden patient. She would plead overwork, of course. And it was true – there were only so many diabetic foot ulcers, injections and wound dressings she could fit into one day. She said, 'When I get back to the surgery, I will inform her doctors. We may be talking a mental health intervention and admission to a unit.'

Stanley lied, quickly, 'No, she isn't *insane*. She's entirely rational. I spoke to her this morning and made her a boiled egg with white bread soldiers. She looked very happy, I thought.'

Nurse Spears and PC Hawk exchanged a look which said, 'Who cares what civilians think? It's we professionals who make the decisions.'

Leaving their tea on the table, the three of them went up to Eva's barricaded room.

Stanley went up to the door and said, 'You've got visitors, Eva. Nurse Spears and Constable Hawk.'

There was no reply.

'Perhaps she's sleeping,' he suggested.

'Look here,' asserted Nurse Spears, 'my time is precious.' She shouted, 'Mrs Beaver, I want to talk to you!'

Eva was working through songs from the musicals in her head. She sang 'Being Alive' from *Company* throughout Nurse Spears' monologue about insane people she had cured.

Titania put her lips to the slot in the barricaded door and said, 'Eva, I need to talk to you.'

Eva groaned, 'Please, Titania, I'm not having an in-depth conversation about your relationship with my ex-husband.'

'It's about Brian,' said Titania.

'It's always about Brian.'

'Look, can you come to the door?'

'No. I can't get out of bed.'

Titania pleaded, 'Please, Eva, use the White Pathway.'

'I can only use it for one purpose.'

Eva had no strength left. She had felt it leaking from her for some days. She could hardly lift her arms and legs, and when she attempted to move her head off the pillows she could only manage a few seconds before dropping it back with relief.

Titania said, 'We could have been good friends.'

'I'm not good at friendship.'

Titania peered through the slot and thought she could see a small shining light and, below it, a prone white figure. She said, 'I came to say how sorry I am for those eight years of lies. I'm here to ask your forgiveness.'

Eva said, 'Of course I forgive you. I forgive everybody everything. I even forgive myself.'

Titania had been surprised at the awful state of the house. It appeared that most of the machines had broken down. Ominous cracks had appeared in the kitchen walls. The drains were stinking.

Titania said, 'Look, let me take this door down, Eva. I want to talk to you face to face.'

'I'm sorry, Titania, but I'm going to sleep now.'

Eva could tell from the lack of light on the wall that it

was dark outside. She was hungry, but it was her own rule now that she would not ask for food. If people wanted to feed her, they would come.

When Titania went downstairs, she found Ruby making a pile of sandwiches. Titania was shocked at how much Ruby had aged.

## 68

Ruby apologised to the two doctors and the nurse for the unswept dead leaves in the front porch. 'As soon as I sweep 'em up, others blow in.'

'It is the nature of things,' said Dr Lumbogo.

When they had congregated at the bottom of the stairs, Ruby said, 'I can't remember the last time she ate anything hot. I chuck food in to her.'

Nurse Spears said, 'You make it sound like the lion house at the zoo.'

Ruby said, 'My memory lets me down now and again. And anyway, I can't get up the stairs easy now. I'm still waiting for that new hip!'

She looked at Dr Lumbogo, who said, 'You are on the list, Mrs Brown-Bird.'

Dr Bridges asked, 'Do we know if she's likely to harm herself or others?'

Ruby said, 'I've only seen her violent once, and that was at a woman dragging a kiddy along on its knees.'

Nurse Spears said, 'There has been an aggressive undercurrent in all my dealings with Mrs Beaver.'

'But no overt aggression?' queried Dr Bridges.

Nurse Spears said, 'I wouldn't turn my back if I was alone with her.'

They climbed the stairs and stood around outside

Eva's door. Eva was huddled in a corner of the room against the bedhead and the outside wall. She hadn't washed for days and she could smell an earthy pungent odour that was not unpleasant to her.

She was so hungry that it felt as if her flesh were melting away. She lifted her white nightgown and felt her ribs – she could have played a melancholy tune on them. There was food next to the door. Local people had posted sandwiches, fruit, biscuits and cakes, but she wouldn't get out of bed to pick them up. In desperation, Ruby had thrown apples, oranges, plums and pears, hoping to hit the bed.

When Eva was asked who the Prime Minister was, she replied, 'Does it really matter?'

Dr Lumbogo laughed. 'No, they are all blockheads.'

Dr Bridges asked, 'Have you ever harmed yourself?'

Eva said, 'Only when I have a bikini wax.'

When asked if she had thoughts about harming others, she replied, 'Nothing really matters, does it? Not compared to infinity. Look at you, Dr Bridges, you're composed of a mass of particles. You could be in Leicester one second and an eighth of a second later be on the far side of the universe.'

The two doctors exchanged a complicit glance.

Dr Lumbogo whispered to Dr Bridges, 'Perhaps a rest in the Brandon Unit?'

Nurse Spears said, 'You'll need an approved mental health professional, and may I suggest a Section Four?'

*

Later, when the doctors had gone, Ruby put her hat and coat on and went to Stanley Crossley's house.

When he opened the door, she said, 'They're taking Eva away.' She couldn't bring herself to say Mental Health Unit. There was something about the word 'unit' that chilled her.

He steered her through the books in the hallway and sat her down in the neat sitting room, where the books were in stacks against the walls.

Stanley said, 'She isn't mad, I've known mad people. I've been mad myself.' He laughed, quietly. Then he asked, 'Does Alexander know about this?'

Ruby said, 'I've not seen hide nor hair of him. Brian's never in, now that Tit woman has gone. Yvonne's in a better place, and we haven't heard from the twins in months. I feel as if I'm on my own.'

Stanley put his arms around Ruby and felt her yield against him. She was gloriously soft and squashy, he thought.

He asked, 'Doesn't my face bother you, Ruby?'

Ruby said, 'When I look at you, I can see the face you used to have. And anyway, by the time you get to our age everybody's face is buggered up, i'n't it?'

Now that there was no chance of an audience with Eva, her acolytes drifted away until only Sandy Lake and William Wainwright remained.

The two of them had many long conversations. They kept their voices low out of consideration for the neighbours. They both agreed that Prince Philip had murdered

Princess Diana, that the first moon landing had been filmed in a studio lot in Hollywood, and that George Bush had ordered the Twin Towers to be destroyed.

Sandy had made cocoa for them on her Primus stove. While they were sipping the hot liquid, William told Sandy about the slaves who processed the cocoa beans.

Sandy said, 'I can't sleep without my cocoa!'

William said, 'We'll nick the next tin, right?'

He put his arm around her broad shoulders. She pressed her cheek against his prickly five o'clock shadow. An owl screeched behind them. Sandy jumped in alarm and William tightened his grip, pulling her towards him.

He said, 'It's only a owl.'

'*An* owl,' she corrected him.

'Yeah,' he said, 'a owl.' They sat together and talked until the moon bathed them in a milky warm light.

# 69

In the early hours of the 19th of September, Eva woke to darkness. She immediately broke into a cold sweat. She was afraid of the dark. The house was quiet, other than the small noises that all houses make when their occupants are out.

She tried to control her rising panic by talking to herself, asking why she feared the dark. She said aloud, 'There was an army greatcoat on a coat hanger on the back of my bedroom door. It looked like a man. I lay awake all night, staring at the coat. I thought I'd seen it move – imperceptibly, perhaps, but it definitely moved. I felt the same terror when I walked by Leslie Wilkinson's house. When he saw me coming, he would stand in my path and demand money or sweets before he let me go. I would look towards his house for help, and saw and heard Mrs Wilkinson singing as she washed up at the sink. Sometimes she would look up and wave while I was being tormented.'

Eva told herself the story of how she had fallen into a deep ditch lined with ice and snow and couldn't escape. How her friend had gone home and left her there most of the night, still trying to find a foothold that would enable her to clamber out. It had taken three blankets and two counterpanes before she stopped shivering.

The day a man, a stranger, had called her 'a big ox' when she trod on his toes in the scrum of Christmas shoppers outside Woolworths. She had taken his voice with her into every changing room since.

Once, she had found a decomposing human hand in the reeds of the canal bank. The school had not believed her and had punished her for being late and, again, for lying about the hand.

She didn't want to think about the baby she had miscarried in Paris, to whom she had given the name Babette, and how she had returned from the hospital to the spacious apartment to find him gone, taking his elegant possessions and her young heart with him.

She wanted to cry, but the tears were stopped somewhere in her throat. Her eyes were desert dry, and there was a ring of ice around her heart, which she feared would never melt.

She spoke to herself again, harshly this time. 'Eva! Far worse things have happened to other people. You have been happy in your life. Remember the snowdrops in the birch wood, drinking from the brook on your way back from school, running downhill into sweet velvety grass with the edible stalks. The smell of baking potatoes as they cooked in the embers of the bonfire. Your earliest memory – opening a horse chestnut with help from Dad and finding a shiny brown conker inside. A miraculous surprise. Defying the "No Trespassing" signs and dancing in the ballroom of an abandoned mansion. And the books! Laughing in the middle of the night reading P. G. Wodehouse. And in summer, lying on a cool bedcover reading, with a bag of sherbet lemons by my side. Yes, I have been happy. Listening to my first Elvis LP with my first boyfriend, Gregory Davis – both equally beautiful.'

She remembered watching surreptitiously as Brian tenderly fed the twins, in the middle of the night. It was a lovely sight.

When she was half asleep she surveyed her happy memories and found that cruel reality kept crowding in on them. The birch wood had been replaced by an estate of tiny houses, the brook was full of tipping waste. The hill had been flattened, there was a One Stop Centre in its place, and Brian had never again fed the twins in the middle of the night.

Alexander was in a late-sown barley field with the permission of the farmer. They had exchanged emails, and the farmer had waved from his tractor when they saw each other in the middle distance.

He was using oil paints now, and was trying to convey the importance of every blade of barley, the feeling that without one there would not be a hundred or a thousand or however many millions of barley stalks there are in a seven-acre field.

He felt his phone vibrate against his heart. He answered it reluctantly. He had just reached a place where his brush had become an extension of his body. He didn't recognise the number but answered anyway.

'Hello.'

'Is that Alexander Tate?'

'It is, and you are?'

'It's Ruby! Eva's mother.'

'How is she?'

'That's why I'm ringing. She's gone downhill, Alex. They're sending a –' Ruby glanced down at a scrap of paper and read '– a "mental health professional" with a "Section Four". He's bringing the police with a battering ram.'

Alexander quickly packed his painting equipment and ran with it to where his van was parked on a grass verge. He drove along the country roads at speed, recklessly cutting corners and impatiently overtaking slow-moving vehicles. He used the horn so many times that he reminded himself of Mr Toad.

Parp! Parp! Parp!

He pulled up outside Eva's house and was dismayed to see that the tree she was so fond of had gone. He ran to the front door, and realised that the crowd had gone, leaving nothing but a few stains on the pavement.

Stanley and Ruby came to the front door together. Alexander could tell from Ruby's face that there was something very wrong. The three of them went into the kitchen and Ruby recounted what had happened since Alexander had last seen Eva.

'That tree coming down was the last straw,' she said.

Alexander looked around the kitchen. There was a patina of grease and dust on the surfaces, upturned cups were stuck to the draining board. He declined Ruby's offer of tea, and ran upstairs.

He saw Eva's door and, through the slot, the darkness

within. He called to her. 'Eva! Listen, my love, I'm going to my van. I'll be less than two minutes.'

Inside her room, Eva nodded.

Life was too difficult to travel alone.

He returned with his toolbox. He said, through the slot, 'Don't be scared, I'm here.'

He began to kick at the door to the sound of splintering wood. He used a crowbar to remove the remaining nailed-in pieces. When the door was fully open, he saw her on the bed hunched against the boarded-up window.

She had set herself the task of facing up to all the unhappiness and disappointments in her life.

Ruby and Stanley hovered behind him.

He asked Ruby to run a bath for Eva and find her a fresh nightgown. To Stanley he said, 'Turn all the lights off, will you, Stan? I don't want her to be dazzled.'

He stepped over the decaying food and splintered wood and went to Eva. He took her hand and held it tight.

Neither of them spoke.

At first Eva allowed herself a few polite tears, but within seconds she was crying open-mouthed and without restraint for all three of her children and her seventeen-year-old self.

When Ruby shouted, 'Bath's ready!' Alexander scooped Eva up, carried her into the bathroom and lowered her into the warm water.

Her nightgown floated to the top.

Ruby said, 'Let's take it off. Put your arms up, there's a good girl.'

Alexander said, 'I can take over now, Ruby.'

Eva said, 'No, let Mum.'

Eva slid down and allowed herself to dip her head under the water.

Downstairs, in the sitting room, Stanley was building a log fire.

It wasn't a cold day, but he thought Eva would like it after being shut in for so long.

He was right.

When Alexander carried her in and put her on the sofa in front of the fire, she said, 'It's kindness, isn't it? Simple kindness.'

# Acknowledgements

I send my thanks to Sean, Colin, Bailey, Louise and everyone at Michael Joseph who helped me with this book.

# Acknowledgements

I am indebted to several people from across the country and beyond for their help in putting this book together.

# CELEBRATING 30 YEARS
## OF SUE TOWNSEND

Turn the page to find out more about
Sue Townsend, read a Q&A on her writing process
and the much-loved Adrian Mole series, and to read
more about the other books Sue has written

**To find out even more about Sue don't forget to visit**
## www.suetownsend.co.uk

# Sue Townsend

# Sue Townsend

Sue Townsend was born in Leicester in 1946 and left school at 15 years of age. She married at 18, and by 23 was a single parent with three children. She worked in a variety of jobs including factory worker, shop assistant, and as a youth worker on adventure playgrounds. She wrote in secret for twenty years, eventually joining a writers' group at the Phoenix Theatre, Leicester, in her thirties.

At the age of 35, she won the Thames Television Playwright Award for her first play, *Womberang* and started her writing career. Other plays followed including *The Great Celestial Cow* (1984), *Ten Tiny Fingers, Nine Tiny Toes* (1990), and most recently *You, me and Wii* (2010), but she has become most well-known for her series of books about Adrian Mole, which she originally began writing in 1975.

The first of these, *The Secret Diary of Adrian Mole aged 13¾* was published in 1982 and was followed by *The Growing Pains of Adrian Mole* (1984). These two books made her the best-selling novelist of the 1980s. They have been followed by several more in the same series including *Adrian Mole: The Wilderness Years* (1993); *Adrian Mole and the Weapons of Mass Destruction* (2004); and most recently *Adrian Mole: The Prostrate Years* (2009). The books have been adapted for radio, television and theatre; the first being broadcast on radio in 1982. Townsend also wrote the screenplays for television adaptations of the first and second books, and *Adrian Mole: The Cappuccino Years* (published 1993, BBC television adaptation 2001).

Several of her books have been adapted for the stage, including *The Secret Diary of Adrian Mole aged 13¾: the Play* (1985), and *The Queen and I: a Play with Songs*(1994) which was performed by the Out of Joint Touring Company at the Vaudeville Theatre and toured Australia. The latter is based on another of her books, in which the Royal Family become deposed and take up residence on a council estate in Leicester. Other books include *Rebuilding Coventry* (1988) and *Ghost Children* (1997).

She is an honorary MA of Leicester University, and in 2008 she was made a Distinguished Honorary Fellow, the highest award the University can give. She is an Honorary Doctor of Letters at Loughborough University, and a Fellow of the Royal Society of Literature. Her other awards include the James Joyce Award of the Literary and Historical Society of University College Dublin, and the Frink Award at the Women of the Year Awards. In 2009 she was given the Honorary Freedom of Leicester, where she still lives and works.

Sue Townsend was registered blind in 2001, and had a kidney transplant in 2009. She writes using a mixture of longhand and dictation.

# Sue Townsend

**Does the thirtieth anniversary of the first publication of the Secret Diary feel like a milestone or a millstone?**

A milestone. He's certainly not a millstone. I think that authors who complain about the success of their most well-known characters are fools; although they mostly do this in private.

**How did you spend your thirtieth birthday?**

Nursing a month-old baby called Elizabeth; she was the last of my four children.

**How has Adrian changed over the last 30 years?**

In *The Prostrate Years* Mole has become more physically attractive, and is a much more sympathetic character.

**Which is your favourite Adrian Mole book?**

*The Prostrate Years*. I've had a lot of health problems and wanted to write about serious illness, yet still write in a comic form.

**Do you have a favourite diary entry from the last thirty years?**

Saturday April 3 1982 – The last line in the last entry of *The Secret Diary of Adrian Mole, aged 13¾*. Written after he had tried glue sniffing and accidentally stuck a model aeroplane to his nose: '*I rang Pandora, she is coming round after her viola lesson. Love is the only thing that keeps me sane...*'

I also like the sequence of entries in the same book made when Mole

s trying to paint his bedroom black to cover the Noddy wallpaper; only to be
repeatedly thwarted by the bell on Noddy's hat.

### What has been Adrian's biggest mistake?

ɔ ignore the many persons who have told him that his serial killer comedy,
'The White Van', and his memoir 'Lo, the Flat Hills of my Homeland',
are unpublishable. Mole does not suffer from a lack of self-belief in this
egard. Also at the Dept of the Environment when he misplaced a decimal
point, and erroneously stated that the projection of live newt births for
Newport Pagnall was 120,000.

### And his greatest triumph?

He still believes his awful novels will be published one day.
That he is still a decent, kind person.

### If Adrian Mole was a teenager today, what would he be doing and writing about?

would be exactly the same, but he wouldn't be using Twitter to memorialize
his life. He would keep a secret diary. Mole's privacy is still intact.
He would not use social networking.
There are still Mole types everywhere, watching the absurdities of
the world from the sidelines.

### Are there any plot decisions that you made that you subsequently regretted?

I should not have made Bert Baxter so old. I hated it when
I had to kill him off at the age of 105.

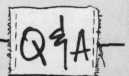

# Sue Townsend

I regret Mole's marriage to Jo Jo, and the subsequent birth of William. It
tiresome (as it is in life) to have the child constantly there, or having to ac
for his whereabouts. It restricted Adrian's movements. He always had to
at the nursery at 3.15 p.m. every weekday. I solved this for myself by sen
William to live with his mother in Nigeria, and then forgot about him

*Are any of the characters in the books, such as Adrian,
Pandora or Pauline, based on anyone in particular?*

All those characters have elements of the author within them.

*Before you put pen to paper, was there any point where Adr
might have been a girl? If so, did she have a name?*

No, girls are more sociable, they talk to each other about
their emotional lives; boys don't.

I once wrote a column for the *London Evening Standard*, which took the
of a diary written by a teenage girl called Christabel Fox. It didn't work fo
and after eighteen months it didn't work for the *Evening Standard* eith

*What does the future hold for Adrian?*

I don't know, but hopefully he will go onward, ever onward.

*What limitations/opportunities are there to writing in diary for*

There are no limitations. The diary is one voice talking to you about peo
places, events, high emotion, low spirits and the minutiae of everyday l
Diaries have a simple structure. You just plod on, day by day, week by w
month by month, until you've written a book.

### What do you enjoy/dislike about the process of writing?

With each writing project I have a different type of nervous breakdown. I am convinced that I have chosen wrong words and placed them in the wrong order. Once published, I never read my own work.
There are sometimes a few exhilarating moments when the words come easily, when the tone and rhythm feel right.
It's great that writers don't have to leave the house and struggle through the rain to their place of work. They can lie in bed all day with a pen and notebook, which are the minimum requirements. Unfortunately I cannot allow myself to loll about in bed for longer than about six hours, as I am still brainwashed by the Calvinist work ethic.

### Which authors have most influenced you as a writer?

In rough chronological order:
Richmal Crompton, Charlotte Brontë, Alfred E. Nuemann (*Mad* comic), Harriet Beecher Stowe, Mark Twain, Dickens, George Elliot, Oscar Wilde, Chekov, Dostoevsky, Tolstoy, Kingsley Amis, Evelyn Waugh, George Orwell, Stella Gibbons, Iris Murdoch, Flaubert, John Updike, Richard North.

### Do you get much opportunity to meet or interact with your readers?

I've become a recluse lately as a result of ill health and late-onset shyness, but on rare outings I like to meet readers.

### Is there any truth to the rumour put about by one A. Mole that you stole and profited from his life?

Yes. I ruthlessly exploited him. But he can't afford to sue me due to the new legislation on legal aid. Mole no longer qualifies. He should have taken me to court years ago.

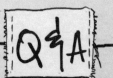

# THE MOLE BOOKS

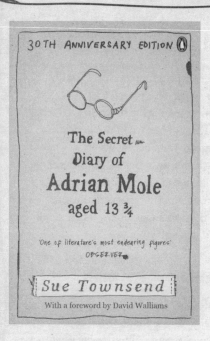

30TH ANNIVERSARY EDITION

The Secret *in* Diary of **Adrian Mole** aged 13 ¾

'One of literature's most endearing figures'
OBSERVER

**Sue Townsend**

With a foreword by David Walliams

**FRIDAY JANUARY 2ND**
I felt rotten today. It's my mother's
for singing 'My Way' at two o'clock in
morning at the top of the stairs.
my luck to have a mother like her.
is a chance my parents could be alco
Next year I could be in a children's

Meet Adrian Mole, a hapless teena
providing an unabashed, pimples-a
all glimpse into adolescent life.

'Townsend has held a mirror up
the nation and made us happy t
laugh at what we see in it'
*Sunday Telegraph*

**SUNDAY JULY 18TH**
My father announced at breakfast that
he is going to have a vasectomy. I
pushed my sausages away untouched.

In this second instalment of teenager
Adrian Mole's diaries, the Mole family
is in crisis and the country is beating
the drum of war. While his parents
have reconciled after both embarked on
disastrous affairs, Adrian is shocked to
learn of his mother's pregnancy.

'The funniest, most bitter-sweet book
you're likely to read this year'
*Daily Mirror*

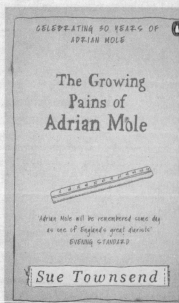

CELEBRATING 30 YEARS OF
ADRIAN MOLE

The Growing
Pains of
**Adrian Mole**

'Adrian Mole will be remembered some day
as one of England's great diarists'
EVENING STANDARD

**Sue Townsend**

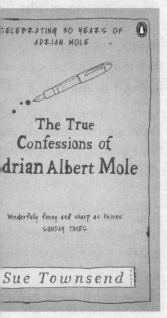

## The True Confessions of Adrian Albert Mole

'Wonderfully funny and sharp as knives'
SUNDAY TIMES

Sue Townsend

### MONDAY JUNE 13TH

I had a good, proper look at myself in the mirror tonight. I've always wanted to look clever, but at the age of twenty years and three months I have to admit that I look like a person who has never even *heard* of Jung or Updike.

Adrian Mole is an adult. At least that's what it says on his passport. But living at home, clinging to his threadbare cuddly rabbit 'Pinky', working as a paper pusher for the DoE and pining for the love of his life, Pandora, has proved to him that adulthood isn't quite what he expected. Still, without the slings and arrows of modern life what else would an intellectual poet have to write about . . .

'Essential reading for Mole followers' *Times Educational Supplement*

### THURSDAY JANUARY 3RD

...ve the most terrible problems with ...y sex life. It all boils down to the fact that I *have* no sex life. At least not with another person

...ally given the heave-ho by Pandora, ...n Mole finds himself in the unenviable ...ion of living with the love-of-his-life as ...es about shacking up with other men. ...se, as he slides down the employment ...der, from deskbound civil servant in ...rd to part-time washer-upper in Soho, ...nds that critical reception for his epic ...*Lo! The Flat Hills of My Homeland*, is ...not quite as he might have hoped.

...very, very funny book' *Sunday Times*

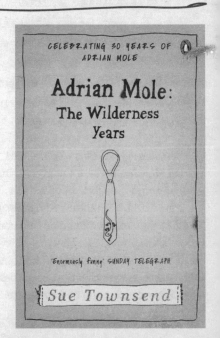

## Adrian Mole: The Wilderness Years

'Enormously funny' SUNDAY TELEGRAPH

Sue Townsend

## Adrian Mole:
### The Cappuccino Years

'Quite possibly a classic' *DAILY MIRROR*

### Sue Townsend

**WEDNESDAY AUGUST 13TH**

Here I am again – in my old bedroom.
wiser, but with less hair, unfortunatel
atmosphere in this house is very bad
dog looks permanently exhausted. Ever
the phone rings my mother snatches
as though a kidnapper were on the

Adrian Mole is thirty, single and a fat
His cooking at a top London restaura
has been equally mocked ('the sausag
my plate could have been a turd' – AA
and celebrated (will he be the nation's
celebrity offal chef?). And the love of hi
Pandora Braithwaite, is the newly electe
for Ashby-de-la-Zouch – one of 'Blair's
He is frustrated, disappointed and under

'Three cheers for Mole's chaotic, non-achieving, dysfunctional family. We need
*Evening Standard*

**MONDAY JANUARY 3, 2000**

So how do I greet the New Millennium?
In despair. I'm a single parent, I live with
my mother . . . I have a bald spot the size
of a jaffa cake on the back of my head . . .
I can't go on like this, drifting into early
middle-age. I need a Life Plan . . .

The 'same age as Jesus when he died',
Adrian Mole has become a martyr: a single
father bringing up two young boys in an
uncaring world. With the ever-unattainable
Pandora pursuing her ambition to become
Labour's first female PM, his over-achieving
half-brother Brett sponging off him, and
literary success ever-elusive, Adrian tries to
make ends meet and find a purpose.

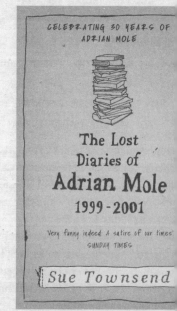

### The Lost Diaries of
## Adrian Mole
### 1999-2001

'Very funny indeed. A satire of our times'
*SUNDAY TIMES*

### Sue Townsend

'One of the great comic creations of our time.' *Scotsman*

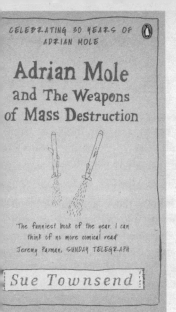

**WEDNESDAY APRIL 2ND**

My birthday.

I am thirty-five today. I am officially middle-aged. It is all downhill from now. A pathetic slide towards gum disease, wheelchair ramps and death.

Adrian Mole is middle-aged but still scribbling. Working as a bookseller and living in Leicester's Rat Wharf; finding time to write letters of advice to Tim Henman and Tony Blair; locked in mortal combat with a vicious swan called Gielgud; measuring his expanding bald spot; and trying to win-over the voluptuous Daisy . . .

'Completely hilarious, laugh-out-loud, a joy' *Daily Mirror*

**SUNDAY 1ST JULY**
**NO SMOKING DAY**

momentous day! Smoking in a public ce or place of work is forbidden in ngland. Though if you're a lunatic, a isoner, an MP or a member of the Royal Family you are exempt.

lrian Mole is thirty-nine and a quarter. lives in the country in a semi-detached erted pigsty with his wife Daisy and their hter. His parents George and Pauline live the adjoining pigsty. But all is not well.

e secondhand bookshop in which Adrian rks is threatened with closure. The spark fizzled out of his marriage. His mother is tening to write her autobiography (*A Girl ed Shit*). And Adrian's nightly trips to the tory have become alarmingly frequent . . .

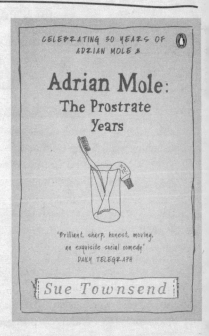

'Unflinchingly funny' *Sunday Times*

# THE MONARCHY HAS BEEN DISMANTLED

When a republican party wins the General Election their first act in power is to strip the Royal Family of their assets and titles and send them to live on a housing estate in the Midlands.

Exchanging Buckingham Palace for a two-bedroom semi in Hell Close (as the locals dub it), caviar for boiled eggs, servants for a social worker named Trish, the Queen and her family learn what it means to be poor among the great unwashed. But is their breeding sufficient to allow them to rise above their changed circumstance or deep down are they really just like everyone else?

'Kept me rolling about until the last page' *Daily Mail*

## OUT JANUARY 2013

'There are two things that you should know about me immediately: the first is that I am beautiful, the second is that yesterday I killed a man. Both things were accidents . . .'

When Midlands housewife Coventry Dakin kills her neighbour in a wild bid to prevent him from strangling his wife, she goes on the run. Finding herself alone and friendless in London she tries to lose herself in the city's maze of streets.

There, she meets a bewildering cast of eccentric characters. From Professor Willoughby D'Eresby and his perpetually naked wife Letitia to Dodo, a care-in the-community inhabitant of Cardboard City, all of whom contrive to change Coventry in ways she could never have foreseen . . .

'Splendidly witty . . . the social observations sharp and imaginative' *Sunday Express*

# What if being Royal was a crime?

The UK has come over all republican. The Royal Family has been exiled to an Exclusion Zone with the other villains and spongers. And to cap it all, the Queen has threatened to abdicate.

Yet Prince Charles is more interested in root vegetables than reigning . . . unless his wife Camilla can be Queen in a newly restored monarchy. But when a scoundrel who claims to be the couple's secret lovechild offers to take the crown off their hands, the stage is set for a right Royal showdown.

'Wickedly satirical, mad, ferociously farcical, subversive. Great stuff'
*Daily Mail*

# Behind the doors of the most famous address in the country, all is not well.

Edward Clare was voted into Number Ten after a landslide election victory. But a few years later and it is all going wrong.
The love of the people is gone.
The nation is turning against him.

Panicking, Prime Minister Clare enlists the help of Jack Sprat, the policeman on the door of No 10, and sets out to discover what the country really thinks of him. In disguise, they venture into the great unknown:
the mean streets of Great Britain . . .

'A delight. Genuinely funny . . . compassion shines through the unashamedly ironic social commentary' *Guardian*

# Enter the world
## of Sue Townsend . . .

This sparkling collection of Sue Townsend's hilarious non-fiction covers everything from hosepipe bans to Spanish restaurants, from writer's block to slug warfare, from slob holidays to the banning of beige.

These funny, perceptive and touching pieces reveal Sue, ourselves and the nation in an extraordinary new light. Sit back and chortle away as one of Britain's most popular and acclaimed writers takes a feather to your funny bone.

'Full of homely, hilarious asides on the absurdities of domestic existence . . .
What a fantastic advertisement for middle-age –
it can't be bad if it's this funny' *Heat*

'Gripping and disturbing.
Utterly absorbing'
*Independent*

Seventeen years ago Angela Carr aborted an unwanted child. The child's father, Christopher Moore, was devastated by the loss and he retreated from the world. Unable to accept what had happened between them, both went their separate ways.

However, when Christopher makes a horrifying discovery whilst out walking his dog on the heath he finds that he is compelled to confront Angela about the past. As they start seeing each other again can they avoid the mistakes of the past? And will their future together be eclipsed by those mistakes of yesterday?